Praise for *The Theoretics of Love*

"What to say about Joe Taylor's brilliant, ambitious new novel? That it's a mystery story wrapped in a literary romp? That its chorus of voices are all convincing, beautifully realized, and full of energetic duende? That its sentences are often Nabokovian and its characters straight out of CSI-Wonderland? That I am in awe of it? All I can say is read it. This is a big-hearted, generous novel—a storyteller's wet dream—that keeps opening out into fresh marvels. It might knock your socks off. This novel should make him a belletristic star."

— Corey Mesler, author of *Memphis Movie* and *Robert Walker*

"Why isn't Joe Taylor famous? I laughed out loud three times in the first chapter of *The Theoretics of Love*. A few chapters later, I felt my heart would break. There's nothing theoretical about Taylor's talent. You'll love this love story."

— Charles McNair, author of *Pickett's Charge, Land O' Goshen, The Epicureans,* and *Play It Again, Sam*

"Joe Taylor is a quirky genius of a storyteller. In vivid, beautiful language—sometimes erudite, sometimes edgy—he tells of eccentric characters who are in search of the genuine. *The Theoretics of Love* is emotionally profound, a great joy to read."

— Anthony Grooms, author of *Bombingham* and *The Vain Conversation*

"Joe Taylor is a wonder and a gift to us all, and especially to Southern letters. I'm grateful for his generous spirit, for his big-hearted writing, and, of course, for his astoundingly beautiful beard."

— Brad Watson, author of *Miss Jane*

Also by Joe Taylor

STORY COLLECTIONS

Some Heroes, Some Heroines, Some Others

The World's Thinnest Fat Man

Masques for the Fields of Time

Ghostly Demarcations

NOVELS

Oldcat & Ms. Puss: A Book of Days for You and Me

Let There Be Lite, OR, How I Came To Know and Love Gödel's Incompleteness Proof

Pineapple: A Comic Novel in Verse

THE THEORETICS OF LOVE

A Novel

Joe Taylor

NewSouth Books
Montgomery

NewSouth Books
105 S. Court Street
Montgomery, AL 36104

Published in the United States by NewSouth Books, a division of NewSouth, Inc.,
Montgomery, Alabama.

Library of Congress Cataloging-in-Publication Data

Names: Taylor, Joe, 1949– author.
Title: The theoretics of love : a novel / Joe Taylor.
Description: Montgomery, AL : NewSouth Books, [2017].
Identifiers: LCCN 2018052613 (print) | LCCN 2018055344 (ebook) | ISBN 9781603064262 (Ebook) | ISBN 9781588383303 (hardcover)
Subjects: | GSAFD: Mystery fiction.
Classification: LCC PS3570.A9395 (ebook) | LCC PS3570.A9395 T48 2017 (print) | DDC 813/.54—dc23
LC record available at https://lccn.loc.gov/2018052613

First Printing

Design by Randall Williams

Printed in the United States of America by Sheridan Books

The Black Belt, defined by its dark, rich soil, stretches across central Alabama. It was the heart of the cotton belt. It was and is a place of great beauty, of extreme wealth and grinding poverty, of pain and joy. Here we take our stand, listening to the past, looking to the future.

To Tricia

"As long as the firmament of You is spread over me,
the tempests of causality cower at my heels,
and the whirlwind of doom congeals."

MARTIN BUBER, *I AND THOU*

"I have killed them, to be sure, but I have not eaten them. I killed them because of war, God, chance—forces outside myself; but it was assuredly because of my own will that I did not eat them. This is why in their company I can now gaze at that dark sun in this country of the dead."

SHOHEI OOKA, *FIRES ON THE PLAIN*
TRANSLATED BY IVAN MORRIS

Contents

Acknowledgments

"The Lover's Paradox" APPEARED in slightly different form in *Quarterly West.* "Dumb Show" appeared in slightly different form in *Bayou.* "Tilting the Blame R" appeared in a slightly different form in *Trajectory.*

In the late 60s when I attended the University of Kentucky, a wonderful professor of physical anthropology taught there. On occasion the Lexington police would consult her about a body. Though her real personal life was quite orderly, she serves as the inspiration for Professor Clarissa Circle. Also, I've compacted several of my philosophy professors from that period into Professor John Hart. Those professors influenced me far more than they would have thought possible. As far as I know, no ritual murders took place in the 1960s or any time at the University. In art, truth travels a different highway. The Afleet Alex incident at the Preakness took place two years later than in this novel. In art, truth travels a different racetrack, also.

I want to thank the following people for their insights concerning this novel: Grace Bauer, Jerome Goddard, L. A. Heberlein, Kat Meads, Corey Mesler, Stephen Slimp, and Tricia Taylor.

The Theoretics of Love

1.

Monkey Meat

Years 1999–2000

(Clarissa, Willy, Methuselah, Pebble)

It wasn't Knoxville's infamous bone farm that pushed me into forensic anthropology, but books: *Keep the River on Your Right* and *Fires on the Plain. Keep the River* poses as cultural anthropology. I found it in a used bookstore, and since its cover depicted a goldenly flowing Amazon where my boyfriend and I might someday canoe, I hugged it to my post-teenage bosom and scooted money across a glass counter—carefully, because the storeowner was a moist-handed pervert. Once home, I found *River* to be a New York Jew's South American field diary of becoming . . . not a hip New Ager, but a cannibal. Jane Austen and her wannabe nymphs paled, they fainted. Two weeks later I blundered back to the store, where the wet owner puffed wet lips: "Didya enjoy Schneebaum?" I blinked at his jism-caked black hair. "*Keep the River on Your Right,*" his voice wheezed. "You bought it two Saturdays back. Didya enjoy it?" He leaned backward for another book, creaking his stool and giving me an eyeful of belly button. He licked two fingers before handing over the last of my life-changing duo: *Fires on the Plain.* "This one's just as good. I've been saving it just for you." *This one* was also about cannibalism. "Ee-e! Monkey meat, monkey meat," its Japanese narrator keeps giggling as he eats dying comrades on some Pacific World War II island.

Thus were delivered the cultural shards that broke my literary spine (to tangle a cliché). To the horror of friends and professors, I moved from English to anthropology, reading Levi-Strauss so thickly that my roommate began sneaking out with my boyfriend. Drunk, they wrecked his car. He died; she went into physical rehab, never to be heard from again. "Monkey meat, monkey meat," I chanted to my empty apartment. "Ee-e!"

But to claim those books pushed me into forensic anthropology isn't quite true. At a lunch hour on anthropology's second floor I spied two female graduate students reassembling a skeleton. They hovered like miniature goddesses, and I gawped until they motioned me in—on the sly since I hadn't had a hepatitis shot. Becoming as wired and glued as those skeletal bones, I pursued a PhD in forensic anthropology, so engrossed that upon finishing my dissertation the only political news I could envision was the Gulf War at one end, which frolicked like an endless fireworks display, and Monica Lewinsky at the other end, which frolicked like an endless Altoids commercial. Monkey meat, monkey meat framed my life. If we humans don't eat one another literally, we do so figuratively. Only short mandibles keep us from gnawing one another's raw hams. I even theorized that we'd live better as honest cannibals, for we'd undergo some meaningful human contact, if only gustatory. (As you can see, whatever culture three years as an idealistic English major *in*stilled, my ex-roommate, my dead boyfriend, and forensic science *dis*tilled.)

Still, compromise asserted itself, and my monkey meat mantra publicly fluffed into, "No one ever touches anyone."

No
One
Ever
Touches
Any
One.

Ever, never, ever.

I remained near my alma mater's Knoxville campus to complete a year of post-doctoral consultation at the sly instigation of my committee chair, who hinted that a university "northward" would soon announce a lucrative opening. So I farmed my dissertation into three reputable papers. More importantly, I solved a grisly double murder as county consultant. Flesh had been boiled off the bones of twin murders that surfaced on a Native American mound after a buckling freeze. The local sheriff, a drunken weekend country guitar player like my runaway dad, assumed they belonged to long-dead Injuns—his term—but grudgingly called me in since the county was already wasting—his term again—a consultation fee. After a rudimentary inspection, any first-year doctoral student could have ticked off suspicions: Don't these bones emit a smell of rotting meat? Don't they give a greasy feel? Aren't they fresh-dead white instead of gray-brown from absorbing the surrounding earth's chemicals? The list theoretically could have meandered to carbon-14, though save for the Kennewick Man that method rarely plays in North America.

Voila! Murders recognized (and soon prosecuted) and my watered-down, popularized dissertation picked up by a university press whose publicity manager hyped a photo-op of me atop that burial mound balancing two skulls in my two manicured hands.

In truth, what tipped me off wasn't the age of the bones but the fact that the skeletons weren't buried east-west as the surrounding Native Americans were. Instead, one lay at a forty-degree variance, the other twenty degrees off true east. Then my olfactory did come into play, for a good deal of marrow—albeit cooked—remained in the larger bones. Half-frozen, they emitted no smell, but the lab reeked ten hours later as pelvises, femora, humeri, and tibias thawed, belonging to one male and one female, Caucasian brand.

So I performed the dating jazz that helped convict the murderer, a disgruntled lover. Not long after, my dissertation director delivered the promised hot tip about a northward academic/forensic post. So in 1999, at just two days over thirty-two, I found myself moving over the Smoky Mountains like Daniella Boone to teach at the University of Kentucky.

Eventually I'm going to describe the house I rented in Lexington and its owner, because like the forty- and twenty-degrees off kilter, both house and its owner would simplify the puzzling glut of ritual murders that surfaced during my first spring semester in Kentucky. But let me start where the house and owner started: with the department of anthropology.

When I reported to the university in late July, the only person of consequence present in the department was its secretary, a fifty-nine-year-old matriarch who sat as erect as a Marine and who immediately adopted me as a beloved daughter. "A bright young woman with a doctorate like you," she commented as I filled out my federal tax withholding form, "and with a charming name like Clarissa Circle, won't be keeping that single deduction for long." I made a face at the form and bore down on the pen. After filling out nineteen more forms—from three key authorizations to sick leave checklists—I said, "You mentioned a rental house over the phone . . ." The secretary, Mildred, absolutely beamed from behind a pair of glasses thick enough to raise home fire insurance. Thin purple lips parted and she handed me a name and a phone number on the proverbial three-by-five filing card.

"Dr. Kiefer? Who's he?" I asked, reading the card.

"*She* is a psychiatrist. She occasionally offers select faculty members houses for rent."

"Select?"

Mildred the secretary smiled, and perfume wafted thickly enough to be reminiscent of the Red Sea parting algae and fish for Moses. She said: "We may have thirty-some thousand students enrolled on campus, but we're still Southern and small. Dr. Kiefer knows two vice presidents and several deans; whenever she has an opening in one of the three houses she bought for her daughters, who've moved away, she asks for a list of incoming candidates and makes her choice. You're the lucky one."

"Am I?"

"Oh yes, dear. Her houses rent for a song and they're all near the university. And she's a model landlord." Giving another file card a secretarial fold that amazed me with its two-fingered deftness, she said, "Here's the address. And here's a key, too, if you want to go see." She fingered a pink notepad and a set of office keys. "I could drive over with you."

So we drove over, since Momma obviously wanted to get out of the lonely building. Even walking through the rising heat off a hot parking lot toward my Jeep, her carriage still resembled that of a Marine, not a sixtyish woman lumbering toward retirement. Fascinated, I commented on how well she carried herself.

"My husband's a chiropractor," she said. "Bones, just like you."

Well yes, I thought, bones, just like me.

It turned out that the rental house was within walking distance of the anthropology department—for me anyway, since I love to walk. As Mildred and I rounded the street's corner, we spotted a woman smack between our ages—my older sister, Mom's first daughter?—staring at the house and taking notes. Despite chiropractic, Dad and Mom hadn't accomplished much with this older daughter's carriage, for she curved over her notebook like a squiggled ancient Greek letter: chi, theta, take your pick. Her stance was corrupted further by the purple bag dress she wore. Athenian purple? Crucifixion purple?

"Someone else is looking to rent," I commented, blinking at the bag dress and matching purple slippers as I pulled to the curb.

"Oh, no," my new secretary cum momma replied. "Dr. Kiefer doesn't advertise her houses."

When I stopped, I could see that the woman wasn't taking notes, but sketching—presumably the house. With a scared bunny hop, she twisted to glance at my Jeep, giving an unnatural grin that showed entirely too many teeth. She then skittered toward the end of the block. Getting out of my Jeep, I watched her realize that the street dead-ended, which warped her forty-year-old pace.

"Odd, isn't she?" my adopted mom commented, stepping onto the lawn.

The woman twitched her shoulders. She faced a steep embankment and the exposed roots of two maples. Apparently she was contemplating scrambling over the entangled roots just to escape us.

"Lord, let's give that poor neurotic mess a break and go on inside," I whispered.

"You're a sweet girl," Mom the secretary replied.

Unlocking the door we found the house completely suitable for a single woman, weirdly compact despite having an upstairs and basement. This was because an enclosed garage, probably an oddity for the fifties when the house was built, took up a third of the first floor. After striding across the living room and taking in the bonus fireplace, I stared out the dining room's back window to see a bulbous white rose bush, the size of a honeysuckle vine, nearly filling a compact backyard sloped fifteen feet below the window. I don't particularly care for plant life and ditto, I presume, would be plant life's concerns for me. The less I had to do with this rose bush, the better off we'd both be. If I never attempted fertilization or watering, it might even fill the entire back yard and eliminate mowing. Grudgingly, I admitted its blooms were "gorgeous," echoing Mildred's comment. Pressing my nose against the window I estimated the slope the house was built on: about thirty degrees. How many bodies could be bulldozed under that slope, I thought. Then I walked into a kitchen just large enough to store pastries and make coffee. What more could a modern professor want? So the huge rosebush, the weird neurotic female artist, the fireplace, the tiny kitchen, the strange tilt of the land from front to back, and the cheap rent decided me in an inexplicable combination.

"You're right, this is a bargain," I said, turning to not find Mildred.

"I'm upstairs, dear," she called.

Climbing, I encountered a musty odor and more weird architecture: a bathroom at the top of the steps, a bedroom on either side, and a walk-in closet across from the bathroom that hid a four-foot ivory Christmas tree actually—actually!—made of overgrown test-tube-cleaning brushes. Had one of the good doctor's three weird daughters combined a science project with the holiday season?

On the drive back to the anthropology department, I spotted the purple neurotic woman leaning her forehead against a bookstore's plate glass window. She must have recognized my Jeep in the window's reflection since she moved out to the curb to follow us with her gaze as we continued down the street. She again started sketching—drawing the rear end of my Jeep Cherokee?

"Odd doesn't touch her," I told Mildred. "Maybe psychotic."

Mildred hummed in answer and tilted the passenger side mirror to keep an eye on the woman in case she retrieved an assault rifle from the bookstore's yellow garbage can.

Back at the department, I called this model landlord. Could I meet her at her office, she wondered. I asked directions, had them confirmed by Mildred cum secretary cum mom, then wended my way.

DR. KIEFER'S OFFICE NESTLED in a dell (note how quickly I was picking up Kentucky phrasing) which itself nestled beside a children's hospital. In a two-story cut-stone house that would be impossible to build these days, the office's three or so thousand square feet held *Kiefer, Thompson, and Associates, Psychiatry & Counseling.*

After talking with the secretary, this one young and chipper, I entered the waiting room where a woman's gaunt, sun-wearied face jerked so quickly that a vacuum was formed. Her eyes twitched cataract pale, though she wasn't all that old, and hair closed around her skull in the most non-descript cut and color I'd ever encountered, like a spider web whose wisps embedded in her sun-cracked face. Her upper body pulsed, emitting an ultrasound hum. As her shoulders began to jerk arhythmically and her right foot began to stomp alternating gold and ivory tiles, I sat far away and blinked my best professorial blink. I turned toward the plaques on the walls of Dr. Kiefer's forest green waiting room. From them I learned that Dr. Kiefer was a true psychoanalyst; that is, she'd obtained her M.D. from the University of Pennsylvania then continued a routine of Freudian-based counseling in New York City. Doing arithmetic with the graduation dates, I let out a boy-whistle, something men find offensive and alluring at one and the same time.

"Are you happy then?" the pulsating woman asked, knitting her brows. Her thinning hair held just enough red to accent the forest green walls.

"I'm all right," I answered, squeezing my knees together. Looking into her milky gray-blue eyes, I stopped short of announcing I'd gotten a new job, for having encountered enough resentful hill folk in Tennessee I knew this Kentucky one would take bitter, inconsolable umbrage at any creature other than herself landing a new job.

"She's . . . *all right*," she snorted. Then she resumed pulsating.

What I'd whistled about was that my math indicated that Dr. Kiefer had begun—begun!—her practice in 1955. Dwight D. Eisenhower was president, Jack Kerouac released *On the Road*, and a woman's place—thank you—was beside the oven, and if she didn't want to wind up *inside* that same oven she better not sweat when she shifted her cute little round buns to pull out a roast, just in case Daddy wanted a hunk of post-dinner pleasuring. So . . . to achieve a medical degree Dr. Kiefer must have attended the University of Pennsylvania during or directly after World War II—

"Professor Circle?" Dr. Kiefer herself, I presumed, stood in her oak doorway, as impressive as her stone office building. Imagine Oprah Winfrey at 80, make her complexion white, her hair silver-gray, and give her back all of that glorious weight she once carried. That was the presence Dr. Kiefer commanded. As I nodded, her eyes shifted toward the pulsating woman. "Sally Anne, your son left through the back way again. He's waiting for you in the parking lot."

The woman absolutely hissed in reptilian syntax, stomped a gold tile, and stood to depart without a word. Wordless also, Dr. Kiefer and I waited until we heard the outer door open, then close. It dawned on me that the pulsating woman also walked younger than she looked, like Mildred and unlike the petite purple artiste who'd stood sketching the house I was about to rent.

"I thought she was a patient," I said.

Dr. Kiefer raised an eyebrow and replied in a brash singsong, "Wai-ull, she should be. She's mostly what's wrong with her son." When I showed surprise she continued, "I'm entirely too old to worry over medical etiquette and the betraying of minuscule patient confidentialities. I call a spade a spade. That woman's a walking vial of poison. From the hills and angry that anyone ever got her pregnant in them, then carried her out of them."

I'd hit that one on the head, anyway—from the hills and pissed. Just moved a zip code up, from TN to KY. Dr. Kiefer nodded toward her office, so we walked in. No proverbial couch, but a brown leather love seat that must have cost a pretty penny. Two windows, one looking out at summer-shade trees glowing emerald in the afternoon sun, the other at the hot parking lot. Framed in the latter window was a skinny teenager in jeans and a yellow t-shirt leaning against a green station wagon, his brow on the hot metal window chrome and his arms dangling loosely at his side. He twisted grotesquely, using his skull as a pivot and ending with the back of his head against the chrome, his arms once again dangling. His t-shirt pictured a pathetic-looking Jesus crowned by thorns. Crossing his arms over Jesus' face he began rocking his head side-to-side. His hair was as black as the coal filling the mountains his momma hailed from. A cardinal flitted by, surprising me. Then the pulsating mother came into view.

From behind a large desk that looked like cherry, Dr. Kiefer cleared her throat and held up my recent book to draw my attention from the window. I must have shown surprise, for she smiled grandly. "If this field had been available back when I went to college, I might have entered it. Lurid enough to satisfy anyone's eccentric taste, I'd imagine. Do you expect many dealings with the Lexington police?"

"They've already contacted me. Not about any particular case, just to offer a modest retainer. I'm replacing a man whom I gather they weren't particularly happy with."

"That would be Professor Ty-ler, the col-lect-or." She chortled under heavy blue glasses, frowned and took them off to give them a wipe with a Kleenex. To complete this she had to fight huge breasts barely restrained by a navy blue blouse with a sailor boy white lapel. Here stood an earth mother to succor the lamest of lame; step aside, Oprah. Dr. Kiefer continued, "The Fayette municipal government joined with the university to get a grant for forensic equipment, but rumor goes that Professor Ty-ler sequestered himself to polish arrowheads after the first bloated corpse drifted into the lab." Dr. Kiefer gave her bra strap a tug. "Young dear, maybe you could spend some of that modest retainer to consult with me about this theory of yours that keeps beating through the lines."

"Theory?"

"No one ever touches anyone."

"I . . ." I glanced at my book where she'd placed it on her desk—had I actually written those words in it? Yes, I suppose I had in the afterword, though couching it in a language that was acceptable to my publisher: *Working in forensic anthropology, one is tempted often to think that, no one or no thing ever touches anyone, but . . . blah blah blah.*

"I can buy that coming from an English major," she continued, sitting down to groans, one emanating from her and the other from her exquisite maroon leather chair. "Either that or its equal but opposite commonplace, that everyone touches everyone. From an English major, yes, but from a physical anthropologist specializing in forensics?"

I heard a shrill scream in the parking lot and glanced to see the green station wagon launching out, backwards. It lurched to a stop then squealed taking off. Dr. Kiefer didn't budge.

"It's my defense mechanism," I mumbled, still staring out the window.

"See? We're making progress already. By the time I die, which is when I expect to retire, you'll face the world as a re-ha-bil-itated human." Dr. Kiefer followed my gaze out the window. Tires again squealed, from braking this time. Then the station wagon launched onto the road to the blaring of horns. "I wish I could say the same for those two."

"How'd you get my book?" I asked stupidly after losing sight of the station wagon.

"Mildred's been pushing you ever since you accepted the job. I sure didn't pick it up in a used bookstore. The one near the house you're renting is good, by the way. The two out in the shopping centers sell romance and porn. For new, you can't beat Joseph-Beth's. You and Mildred went by and saw the house, yes?" When I nodded, she smiled grandly and pulled out the rental agreement, which I read quickly, as it was brief and clear of the typical jargon. I looked up at a red Mexican clay figure sticking its tongue out from a shelf. That was likely what the second and third bookstore owners would do if they heard Dr. Kiefer's comments about their stores. The hill woman and her son . . . well, those two might do a bit more than stick out their tongues upon hearing her appraisal of them. A crown of thorns? Carving knives?

"Why so cheap?" I asked as I signed. "And why to hand-picked UK faculty?"

"Every landlord I've met complains about bad experiences with students. Let's just say those landlords don't know the half of it. In the early seventies I unwittingly rented to three male students straight from the jaws of Bosch's hell . . . At least there were supposed to be only three. I think over a half a dozen males and females wound up living there." She gazed over my head to the ceiling. "Yes . . . Bosch. Dante's inferno would have been much too elegant."

DR. KIEFER'S RENTAL HOUSE was lovely—deceptively so, it would prove some time later. But for then it was truly lovely and truly a bargain, despite its odd layout, what with a dining room/living room combination hogging 80 percent of the first floor's livable space, while a kitchen and utility room claimed what wasn't already taken by that indoor garage. The front of the house was built into a sharply sloped rise, so the dining room looked down onto the backyard as I already said. The upstairs held the only bathroom, at the head of the steps. Two large bedrooms lay on either side, a hall separating them. I couldn't imagine half a dozen people living in the house—even if they were acid-dropping hippies willing to orgy every night.

In the basement, which had rough-hewn stones painted green for walls and its own entrance and its own windows viewing the backyard from ground level, I placed a weight set and stationary bike. For the first year, I grunted or pedaled while concentrating on a huge furnace or on the beautiful and sprawling Van Fleet rosebush outside the windows. Over the second year I slipped in a dresser, bookcase, and sleeping couch so that an occasional graduate student could stay there on the QT—no rent, with the stipulation that evacuation might be immediate, should Dr. Kiefer find out.

Willy was the one who told me the name of the rosebush. We met in November, when heavy rains exposed a skeleton lying beside a stone fence built by slave labor a century and a half before, and I was called for my first consultation with the Metro police. After being escorted to the site by a polite young policeman with a pink complexion, and after marveling at the interlaced stone fence and assessing the land's layout, the first thing I did was to kneel and feel the half-exposed skull. Then I gave it a long sniff.

To my left I heard a hiccup-laugh and turned to see the most beautiful black man I'd ever laid eyes on. Lanky and mellow yellow, but bouncy enough to hold twice the caffeine of Mello Yello. I smiled, he smiled. Dr. Clarissa Circle, meet Sergeant Willy Cox. In an hour we ascertained that the skeleton was over seventy years old and likely belonged to someone who died by the fence during the Great Depression, also likely struck by lightning since charred wood and other indications of a large oak mixed themselves around the bones, and since two vertebrae had fairly exploded, probably where the gentleman was leaning against the tree and the lightning had exited. Willy Cox and I then got down to business and went out that night for martinis at a bar skirting the university.

I was carrying on a family tradition, for the reason my mother had to move to Knoxville when I was finishing my PhD was that she started dating a black man and the hometown folk couldn't stand that. Nuh-unh, as Southern blacks say-sing. Banning interracial dating was evidently one thing the blacks and whites agreed on. Nuh-unh, the white folks hollered back in a counterpoint-jazz-sizzle. But Mom and this man rattled their own tambourine. Mom once confided that everything I'd ever heard about black male physiology was true, at least as far as he was concerned. I can still hear her giggling as she clinked ice in her tumbler to let me know that she'd run out of Crown Royal. Well, they were disappointed with Knoxville, since it was barely ready for miscegenation in the late 80s, but the two of them stuck around campus and everyone pretended to be liberal. Long story short? I was primed for Willy. Anyway, his smile warranted exploration.

AIDS was easing off everyone's mind when we met, Americans owning a notoriously brief attention span—over a decade had passed since AIDS came around, right? Speaking of the 80s, I mean. So we wound up at my house that first night. I awoke next morning to see Willy staring out my back window, spraddle-legged and holding a cup of coffee. Any man who can brew his own coffee would strike most women as a catch, especially atop the two rounds of mating ritual we danced during the night, but I was holding out. Willy must have heard my breathing change when I awoke, because without turning around he said,

"That Van fleet rosebush must be thirty, forty years old. I bet it's gorgeous in early and mid-summer."

"Flowers?" I asked.

"Yeah, my momma loves roses. I hated the hell out of them until a couple of years ago, when I grew enough sense to wear gardening gloves."

"The thorns, you mean."

He turned around. "Yeah sure, thorns. Sounds like you need some coffee to give Dr. Clarissa some clarity."

What I needed was his tan ass back in bed, so I whistled my best Lauren Bacall. It worked.

That began a relationship that's proved to almost—and *only* almost, I insist—disprove my theory of no one ever touching anyone. By spring of my first academic year at UK, Willy had gotten a promotion to lieutenant and we had broken up and molded back together three times as I dated or he dated someone else. And it wasn't like either of us expected three to be the magical number. Still, that spring of 2000 brought a bizarre case that would bind us, regardless of our waxing and waning emotions.

IT WAS MORNING ON the last Saturday in April, which meant that the next Saturday would be Derby Day, 2000. Even working in an ivory tower can't completely exclude one from the surrounding *zeitgeist*, in Kentucky that translating as Derby Day and college basketball. I prefer lanky boys to lanky horses, but horses were the *soup du jour*, or should I say *entrée du season* since March Madness had passed. I was lying in bed reading a particularly vexing article correlating bone-knitting and diet when the phone rang. I let the answering machine screen it for me:

"Dr. Circle, it's Detective Cox."

It was Willy. He always prefaces professional calls with the "Dr. Circle, Detective Cox" bit so that even if we've been arguing like alley cats, I'll pick up. I did, though manufacturing a groan to let him know that it was before rise and sunshine on a Saturday.

"A surveyor found a skull," he said.

"A skull . . . This can't wait until Monday?"

"A weird skull, it's been dyed or painted black. And that's not all. It looks like this skull may be surrounded by several more graves. I'm guessing up to ten, and I'm guessing about twenty-eight years ago."

I sat up. "God, Willy, can you keep everyone away until I get there?"

"I've got them all taking photos and combing the perimeter. This one may be big enough that I get bumped off though, so you need to hurry before Jackson gets wind."

"I'm dressing right now."

Captain Jackson was to a forensic anthropologist what grave robbers were to Schliemann, the discoverer of Trojan War's Troy. Dogs were *el Capitan's* latest innovation. He'd let loose a kennel of beagles he and a friend were training to get at the bones or flesh. Do I need to go into arf-arf details as to why that's a bad forensic move?

I followed Willy's directions, playing a good dose of Gregorian chant to prepare myself for the worst. Gregorian chant, by the way, must stand to my atheism like Willy stands to my No One Ever Touches Anyone theorem: hope springing eternal.

"God, what is that crap?" Willy asked as I buttoned down the electric window to my Jeep.

"Exactly," I answered.

"Huh?" He held a cup of coffee to his nose—there'd been a cold snap with threats of a late snow that managed not to show up.

"It's Gregorian chant, songs praising God and his choirs of angels."

"Sound like dat-dere God fella need to gets hisself a new choir." Willy occasionally slipped into fake black dialect just to give people a spasm. Or maybe it was to remind himself of his roots, though his dad was a physician who remained eternally pissed off at Willy for becoming a lowly cop.

I reached out the window to grab Willy's coffee, then nearly spit it out. I'd forgotten that he took it with enough sugar to supersaturate Styrofoam. He laughed his burp-chuckle and led me to a Thermos before we went on scene.

Willy was right: there was a circle of graves, seven for sure, maybe eight, though that eighth looked more like a natural depression. Willy held up his hand just as a police photographer was about to step on one of the graves, after already having stepped over the perimeter tape.

"Back, back, the Goddess of Bones is here."

I squinted at him over the steam of my coffee. That name—Goddess of Bones—has stuck with the police force ever since. It's better than what my students call me.

Something must have caught my eye, because I asked Willy to back everyone off even more. Humming Gregorian chant as best I could, I stood with my coffee, staring for maybe five minutes until I saw it: another likely grave, this one outside the circle—outside the police tape even, which we then had to expand.

"I'm afraid to ask, Willy," I said once he'd finished expanding the tape. "Where's this lacquered skull? In some bloodhound's jaws?"

He pointed to a group of police cars and I tried not to groan. The skull was propped on a hood like an ornament. Even as I watched, a plump cop cozied his ugly plump mug next to the skull and placed two fingers behind it in the child's version of devil-horns to pose for his picture. Cop humor: nearly as infantile as forensic anthropologist humor.

"Is that a barn over there?" We were standing in a woods looking out at what was once pasture, but now was covered with scrubby trees.

"What's left of one. Used to be a tobacco and cattle farm. Now all due for Sweet Sarah Subdivisionland."

"Just like the rest of Fayette County," I replied.

"Already spoken like a true native. Like I said, a surveyor came on the skull early this morning."

I appraised the sun, which was lower than I'd ever seen, except when it was descending toward the opposite side of the globe to bring on nightfall. Really? I never would have guessed it did that both coming and going. A miracle. Shivering and sipping the coffee, I thanked my genes I hadn't gone into surveying. What if the pervert-o bookstore owner had licked his fingers and handed me a book about landscaping techniques prevalent in Jane Austen's city of Bath instead of *Fires on the Plain*? Maybe I should send the guy a Donald Duck pacifier, with my thanks.

Staring back to the site, I mentally listed the three graduate students available. Saturday, so all three would be hung over, and the two undergraduates worth anything would be too. Five stumbling, headachy helpers, at least eight graves. Excavation was going to take all weekend and then some. When I told Willy, his only comment was that Captain Jackson would be champing at the bit once he got back to work Monday. I immediately recalled two more undergraduates and started making phone calls over my new-fangled (then) cellular while I walked to the police car and stared at the blackened skull and mandible. Whatever paint or dye had been used, it had thinned enough in places that I could make out a couple of important identifying factors.

Skulls do stare back, don't let anyone kid you. And they talk, given enough time and measurements. This one looked like a late teen's since the bone hadn't quite knitted into unity, a late Caucasian teen by the cheekbones and brows. M or F, I couldn't be certain because of the mud and dye, though I guessed female. The left canine or eyetooth was missing; the left front incisor was broken. At least a dozen fillings showed where the dye hadn't taken to silver, so the owner either loved sugar or had some dirt-poor dental genes.

The owner'd also had a dirt-poor run of luck, it appeared.

"Willy!" I exclaimed, motioning him away from the newest cop to join the party. This one had brought a dozen donuts for the picnic, speaking of sugar.

Willy edged over, glancing back to his two friends who were snickering and gyrating their hips. One grabbed his crotch, so I closed my eyes. I didn't even want to imagine what tales Willy spread about me at the macho cop station.

"Willy, what made you say this site was twenty-eight years old? Are you holding out on me?"

He gave a grin and pulled a plastic bag from his pocket. From where I stood, what looked like two coins, quarters, were in it.

"1972 quarters," he confirmed. "Both of them. The surveyor said that one was wedged in the skull's eye socket. He's the guy who pulled the skull from the ground. Over there."

I glanced 'over there' and bit my lip, nodding like the crazy woman in Dr. Kiefer's waiting room. "Where's the dirt that was inside the skull?"

Willy shrugged.

"Damn it, Willy!" I thought about his wiry arms wrapping around my back. The next time they did I'd give his bony shoulder a good bite, turn him on to the finer pains in life. That would give him something to shrug over.

"Um, he said it was full of sand, not dirt."

"He? Sand?"

"The surveyor. Yeah, sand. One of the guys said it was like someone was trying to shrink the skull."

I rolled my eyes, but later found out that was pretty much right.

It took us until Wednesday to excavate the graves, eight in all. Fortunately there was a juicy double murder Monday morning that caught Jackson's attention, and then the upcoming Derby Day riveted him even more. All eight bodies had quarters in or around their skulls, presumably placed on their eyes, two pairs from 1972, counting the two quarters in the lacquered skull, six pairs from 1973. The other odd thing about the seven bodies in the circle was that only one of them showed any physical harm as the cause of death, though perimortem sawing of the ribs indicated a possible ritual removal of the heart for all seven. At least this is what we first thought. The one that had a skull fracture and a cracked scapula represented the largest of the bodies. It's hard to crack a scapula: we're talking tire iron or breakdown bar. I'm not sure a typical pine two-by-four would do it, at least if its flat side was used. Willy, the students, and I conjectured that the remaining people had been drugged then smothered while unconscious. Maybe the big guy came out of the drugs sooner than expected and started fighting.

The skeleton outside the circle, the burial that made me extend the nice yellow tapes, had been decapitated. The lacquered skull presumably belonging to it had been found roughly in the center of the circle of seven. A good deal of the headless skeleton had been lacquered, too.

"Sweet," was Willy's comment.

As I said, on Wednesday afternoon we finished bagging the bones. The graduate students were busy fitting the last skeleton into the university's van, the cops were busy gossiping and drinking coffee. Willy gave my crotch a brush with his fingertips. "Still think that no one ever touches anyone?" he asked.

"We'll see."

He frowned and insisted that he was going to hang around, give the area a last sweep.

"If you find something you'll tell me, right?" I asked.

"Sure," he answered, not looking at me. I thought of the quarters. The damned guy was like some amateur gourmet chef who promises to share his secret recipe, then when you step out of the kitchen to refresh your drink or powder your nose he throws in four spices and a wine sauce he hasn't shown you and never will.

The graduate students and I toted the skeletons back and laid them out on tables for cleaning and reconstruction. As next morning's sun streamed in the windows, a graduate student noticed a crack in the C-4 neck vertebra of one skeleton. We immediately found that three others revealed similar indications of a perimortem wound.

"Whoever did it must have been trying to puncture the larynx," I conjectured. "Maybe with an ice pick." At this, two students present left the lab. Half an hour later I found them sitting by Mildred's desk, drinking a concoction that smelled remarkably like whiskey and Coke. A good momma, all right. She shook her head and offered me a "Coke" too. I refused, but on remembering the pale faces, I carried two cups down to the lab. Funny, those students had all made it past the ritual removal of eight hearts, but the ice pick discombobulated them. And so the skulls, which had already been staring back at us, began to talk. But their speech came slowly, slowly.

By the time Derby Day was over and July was sweltering upon us, we had sexed and aged all the Does into Johns and Janes. Three Johns, five Janes; ages varying from fifteen or so to forty or so; height varying from five foot even to six-three, the latter being the one with the cracked scapula and skull. All Caucasian. By late July I wound up sleeping a one-nighter with the solitary male graduate student. This meant that Willy and I were in for argument number four. I certainly hadn't meant to sleep with Thomas—not that he was unpleasant looking or anything, but I don't make students a habit. He was an inch shorter than I am, had a Latino look about him, despite his hazel eyes and a moustache that never would quite fill in. Here's what happened: Thomas and I had sexed and aged the last skeleton together, which roughly fit Thomas's own description. He made it through that. But damned if we didn't get a positive dental I.D. on our first skeleton the next day, a Friday, and damned if it didn't turn out to be a friend of Thomas's father, a male friend who had disappeared twenty-seven years before, just as he was beginning his second year of law school. This spooked the boy, so I took him home for a drink and . . . and guess who spent the night . . . and guess who then showed up in the morning.

"There's a black guy in your back yard, doing something to that big bush," Thomas said, coming from the bathroom.

I groaned, knowing it was Willy fertilizing or pruning or pissing on the damned rosebush. And I groaned doubly because I knew he'd want to grill Thomas and his dad about the single identified corpse. And then maybe he'd want to kill Thomas when he figured out he'd spent the night with me. Extenuating matronly circumstances be damned.

"Hell," I said. "Do you know how to make coffee?"

"Um, do you have a kettle?"

"Never mind."

Walking downstairs, I started a pot and directed Thomas to carry three full mugs down to the patio by the outside back steps when the gurgling stopped. "Completely S-T-O-P-P-E-D. Otherwise, scalding water will spill all over the counter." Thomas blinked his hazel yes. I pointed at the Mr. Coffee machine, as much to inform Thomas as to clarify in my own mind where the gurgles would come from—hopefully not from Willy's contorted male envy. Then I gathered milk, sugar, spoons, and pointed out a tray to Thomas. "And for god's sake go back upstairs and get dressed," I added, remembering Willy's new Glock he was so proud of. Twelve rounds, plus one in the chamber, hollow points, etc., etc.

"Well sure," Thomas said.

"Shoes too."

"Of course."

I did just the opposite. I paraded down the steep back steps, and under my virgin white robe lay a red nightgown flimsy enough to give Willy the heebie-jeebies. My thought was to allay arguments over Thomas. When the robe's terrycloth belt fell loose, Willy gawked and he didn't bat an eye as I informed him that Thomas was in the house, about to bring us coffee. I congratulated myself on a fine tactic and pressed my left hip against Willy as we gathered chairs around a glass table under the patio's aluminum roof. But when I told Willy about Thomas's father, about how he knew the dead man we'd identified, that begat a volcanic tremor, and out spewed Willy's obsession with proving that everyone touches everyone. His bulldog intent to connect Thomas's father and his dead law school friend and thus make them two such everyones became apparent as Thomas carried the tray down the steps, for Willy took the tray from Thomas and simply said, "Tell me about your dad."

So. So even before the coffee was poured and the sugar spooned, I reappraised my nightgown: I could have been wearing cleats and a football helmet for all Willy cared. Arnold Schwarzenegger, Clint Eastwood, Madonna, and Ronald McDonald could have all spent the night, for all he cared. He continued haranguing Thomas until I finally walked up to the kitchen on the pretense of making more coffee. Staring at the Mr. Coffee, I wondered what life would have been like if I'd remained an English major. How many more *Fires on the Plains* and *Keep the Rivers* would I have found? Would imagined terrors have been more disconcerting than the actualities I encountered as a forensic anthropologist? About that time a fraternity brother from the house behind mine gave a war whoop. I pictured Dr. Kiefer wagging a thick finger to say, "Romanticism, my dear. Your novels would have been about as har-ro-wing as that child's war whoop." And she would have been right.

I carried more coffee down the steps, along with six stale donuts. Willy and Thomas gobbled the donuts, one having the excuse of being a cop, the other of being a student. I literally wiped sugar flakes from both their lips. By this time Thomas had been infected with Willy's web of mystical intrigue, so he paid as scant attention to my finger wiping his lip as Willy did. The only thing that kept me from baring a tit was the humbling likelihood that neither would notice it.

With one last sip of coffee, Willy insisted Thomas drive him to his dad's place in the next county so he could interview him. They looked to me with the obvious insinuation that I should go with. I ground my teeth to keep from laughing. Imagine moi straddling the front console between them, and guess what lying under my delicate hands and between my delicate knees: their libidinal idea of sugar-flakes. Back roads to the next county sounded like a three-way—I mean three-*hour*—trip. Or maybe that was my wishful thinking. At any rate, I said, "No way. You two fellas ride and talk boy talk. I'm going to shop at the new mall." What I really wanted to do was check out all eight skeletons, especially the one that came so close to Thomas's age and build. Willy rolled his eyes, knowing how I hate malls. The original mail order queen I am, just like I'm the original bone goddess.

So as they walked to Willy's car I ascertained visually what I already knew tactilely: Willy's ass was a lot tauter and cuter, despite his age. But Thomas's wasn't so bad, either. Probably the skeleton we ID'ed once carried a nice one about, too. Forgive the graveyard humor, but it comes with the field.

I WAS DRESSING FOR the lab when the phone rang.

"Professor Circle?" I barely had time to say yes, when the male voice continued, "I'm sort of a, uh, local historian. I have information that might be of use on the eight skeletons you found."

Alarm bells clanged, so I cradled the phone between shoulder and cheek and opened the bedside table to retrieve a snub-nose .38 that Willy'd been teaching me how to shoot—when we were getting along, of course. Neither of us trusted ourselves on the range otherwise. I felt its heft and did a few curls with it, listening to the bullet casings softly click in the chamber while the phone guy continued his spiel.

"—Look," I interrupted. "Surely you realize that I don't officially work as a policeman. Why don't you contact Detective Cox? He just left, or I'd let you talk to him. Hold on, I can give you his direct office number." I figured this info-bit might cool the guy's tool.

"Don't bother, I know it. Detective Cox and I are presently on the outs. I hear that you and he are, uh, presently on the ins. Unlike how he treats you, he won't talk with me when we're on the outs."

I momentarily envisioned Willy and this man with his slight hill twang groping on blue satin sheets as lovers, then found myself ridiculously peeking at the receiver as if a hi-tech Japanese TV screen might reveal the two sweet buttocks of Mr. Telephone Man's ass. But no way on either, for Willy was plenty straight and my phone was GE. Even a womanizer type of straight, and even a dirty ivory GE.

"I'd be happy to meet you somewhere public—a coffee shop maybe?" the ass-less voice offered.

I walked to my bedroom window, the front one that looked down on my street, and I asked, "You know where The Demitasse is, on Woodland Avenue?"

"Sure . . ."

I didn't pick up the conversation's thread for a moment, because the neurotic woman who'd been sketching the house the day I drove by with Mildred was once again holding a sketch pad and appraising my other bedroom window. And once again she was dressed in solid purple, with the addition of a scarlet and white neck scarf. I stepped back from where she might see me. Her sandy hair was so curly and windswept that I wouldn't have been surprised to see a squirrel pop out to twitch its cute nose, or a baby robin stretching out its wide-open beak.

". . . Professor Circle?" It was the ass-less voice on the dirty ivory phone.

"I'm here. Look, there's someone standing out front on my lawn who I need to see. What say we meet there in an hour?"

"That's fine. I have a long beard."

"I don't. See you at The Demitasse." I hung up and ran downstairs, pulling on a blue blouse along the way to go with my white jeans. The moment I snatched open the door, the woman dropped her sketch pad. By the time I sprinted halfway to her, she fumbled picking it up then started to run without it.

"Wait! I just want to talk!"

I detected a hesitation, but it didn't last. And she didn't make the mistake of running toward the dead end this time. Well, I wasn't about to chase her. Giving one last look as she disappeared around the corner, I picked up the pad.

"Oh no," I said aloud to whatever plant and animal life might be listening in the mid-morning mist.

The top sketch depicted the left upper corner of my rental house. Perched on the dormer of the second room's front window sat a young girl's head, on guard like a gargoyle. Her thick black hair wandered down over the shingles and gutter, subtly turning into a viscous vine that reached the ground. I supposed that all that luxurious, tendriled hair was eventually going to lead somewhere: to my front door, to the small flower bed that Willy'd planted with marigolds, to the oak mostly on the neighbor's property, I couldn't tell. There was a small tear in the paper; it must have happened when I interrupted the artist.

How could she have drawn all this from the time that Willy and Thomas left, not twenty minutes ago? I realized that of course she hadn't. It was sketched in pencil, something she could take up and leave at whim. I flipped through: two more penciled sketches of the house, sans heads or anything weird that I could immediately spot; one chalk pastel of a lovely young girl in her late teens standing in a forest, palms outward in a stylized Thai goddess pose, raven hair pulled neatly back; and the last one, another pastel of a heavy, tall, malevolent looking man in his mid to late twenties. Though he was white, his black hair splayed in an unkempt Afro, several strands ending in snakeheads. A male Medusa? His blackened brows arched, and his goatee ended in a dagger's point. There may have even been a ruby on its tip, or was it blood? Blackened lumps for eyes, saucy cheeks to match the ruby. Surrounding his whole body like an inverted halo were talismans and hex signs. Pentagrams and crosses lay around his feet, ensorcelling him. Dr. Kieffer would find this a telling drawing.

Beneath those four pieces lay a canvas-board acrylic of my house.

I carried the sketchpad inside to my dining room table, where I Magic-Markered a black note on a sheet of yellow legal paper:

Tomorrow,
I'll leave your art pad
inside this storm door.

For then, though, I carried the pad with me for a jaunt to the coffee shop.

. . . And did he ever have a beard. Salt and cinnamon—not pepper—his beard was so long that it forked in the middle, giving him two beards. A little shampoo, conditioner, and brushing would go a long way, pal, I thought, closing one eye to see if the perspective improved. It didn't; instead I spotted a ponytail, too. My, my, a time-warped hippie. He was sitting, so I couldn't tell about his ass, though he did have a nicely mesomorphic build with just enough paunch to show maturity. A regular adipo-weightlifter.

I passed the patio's low iron fencing and walked up to him. "I'm Professor Circle."

He stood up to bow slightly in Southern Gentleman fashion; then he offered a handshake in post-Southern liberation fashion. "I'm Methuselah," he said.

I blurted out a laugh.

"That's okay," he said, no doubt thinking that I'd apologize for my sudden laughter. "Everyone laughs. It's a nickname I picked up some time back."

"In your antediluvian past?"

He smiled, and though I couldn't locate any teeth under his floundering burnished red and gray beard, his eyes danced at my joke, so I felt comfortable enough to sit down and order an espresso.

"Did you catch the person out front?"

My pulse stumbled; then I remembered that before I hung up the phone I'd told him about someone being out front. "No," I said, "but I brought something of hers along."

He glanced at the sketchbook and his brows shifted. Our waitress brought my espresso with a double side of cream. The waitress looked familiar, the way all college students sooner or later do to a professor. Meanwhile back in the Old Testament, Methuselah began tugging at his beard in masturbatory delight as he glanced at her legs and her hips. No doubt which camp this boy made his bed in—not that I'd taken my vision of him and Willy sliding over silken sheets seriously. When the waitress roamed out of sniffing range he glanced at the sketchpad in my lap.

Look, maybe it would have saved some time if I'd just showed him what the woman out front of my house had done. Maybe a year's worth of time. But I didn't show him because he said,

"Was she in her early fifties, the woman with that sketchpad? Honey-colored hair with gray streaks, either in a, uh, long ponytail or scraggly? Thin?"

"Yeah, that pretty much fits her picture. Scraggly and thin. Do you know her?"

"I know of her. She's a fixture in the, uh, leprechaun community."

"Leprechaun?"

"Lesbian. Though she's pretty much a-sexual."

I considered how she'd skittered away both times, more like a frightened mouse than even a rabbit. And I'd caught sight of her eyes, wild amber yellow. She must have been reasonably attractive once. Still could be, given enough sedation—say fifteen Librium capsules—so she could sit and run a hairbrush though her hair without sailing it through a window at an imagined peeping tom. As it was, though, her entire frame had vibrated, even when I spied down from my window upon her sketching and she had no reason to think anyone was peeping. And that frame of hers had absolutely quaked when I opened the door.

A car drove by, horn blaring. I jumped, just like she had. Gripping the table I took a breath. What would it be like to live your entire life as a mouse? No patio cafés, for sure. I realized that the hippie-hermit-historian was talking:

". . . Seems she went to the police about her suspicions before the fall semester finished, but the Metro police weren't taking kindly to lesbians in those days—"

"Do they now?"

"You're new to Lexington. A lot of chic horsy people profess that religion, and horsy people have pull and money, so the police are at least polite about matters. The times, they are a-changin'."

Fearing he was going to pull incense from under his beard and sing Bob Dylan, I downed a shot of espresso, followed it with cream, and asked why he wanted to meet me.

"There were rumors in the early 70s about a blood cult. Most people blew them off, thinking that could only happen with Charlie Manson and, uh, California. Anyway, plenty of other things were keeping Lexington busy, what with a couple of students being questioned by the FBI for uttering threats against Nixon, the burning of the ROTC building, protest marches, drugs and all. By the time anyone got around to the cult, it had disappeared, if it ever existed."

"So you think this blood cult might be linked to the skeletons?"

He shrugged. I had an urge to reach and tug his beard for good luck, but I restrained myself. He wasn't my type. "The rumor was that this cult was killing people who resembled its members so that they would have a, uh, bodyguard in the next life. Another version of the rumor had it that the cult killed people so that the members would be guaranteed eternal life, never die or need a bodyguard."

"Lovely," I replied. "And this blood cult was comprised of university students?"

"College students mostly, yes."

"Well, they haven't got much more sense these days. The times, they aren't a-changin' all that much."

"Othingnay ewnay derunay ehtay unsay."

"Beg pardon?"

"Nothing new under the sun. Didn't you speak pig Latin as a child?"

"I never was a child," I replied, thinking my remark seemed more appropriate to the bearded one facing me—ripped untimely from his mother's womb, but twenty years late instead of a month early. Actually, I had a reasonable enough childhood, considering my dad was a drunk—a vegetative, guitar-playing one, not an abusive one.

The bearded one grunted.

We spent a quarter hour more talking about this cult and the skeletons. There really wasn't much to go on, but Methuselah remained adamant that I tell the story to Willy, saying that he would form some type of connection. *Of course he will*, I almost blurted. You could provide him the vital measurements of Secretariat's wondrous, proud stallion dong and gonads ,and he'd form a connection.

But I didn't say that, I just grunted in tit-for-tat. Then damned if my foot didn't edge toward the bearded one's four or five times, as if it had a mind of its own. I kept telling it that No One Ever Touches Anyone, but it kept wanting to play footsie anyhow. Finally my mouth got in on the game. This I can blame on the second espresso the waitress brought, supposedly from a student of mine inside the café, though I suspected old long beard of a ploy to keep me around. Anyway, my mouth said,

"I'll tell Willy. You have my phone number. What's yours?"

He obliged me by writing it down on a napkin, just as if we were at a pick-up bar. Under it he wrote the name, "Gina."

"Gina?" I asked, reading it.

"The name of your artist friend's young girlfriend, the college student who disappeared. The one I told you about."

Told me about? Crap. Not only does No One Ever Touch Anyone, but they rarely listen to anyone either. Double crap. I tucked the napkin in my purse. "That's right," I said. "Gina. What was her last name?"

"Mason. Gina Mason." He repeated that and what I'd missed and ended by saying, "I wouldn't tell Willy where you got that information—at least not until he and I are on better terms."

"By that time, he and I will be on the quits."

"It all goes to prove my point: the steady state theory."

"You mean like the beginning and ending of the universe repeating itself over and over?"

"Exactly," he answered. "Except with people instead of stars."

A cop drove by, a friend of Willy's. He slowed, giving Methuselah and me the twice over. It's hard to cheat on a cop, even when you're not cheating, just laying provisional groundwork for doing so. Methuselah and I nodded at the cop before he drove off; then we parted ways.

Steady state. Gaseous mixtures expanding and heating, cooling and shriveling. Just one more variation of No One Ever Touches Anyone, as far as I was concerned.

Gina, Gina, Gina, I thought on walking into the lab. We'd tucked Mr. Reggie T. Gibson away after positively identifying him. That left nine deep-dish stainless steel tables, two holding skeletons that had nothing to do with the eight we found. One had been discovered in a cave outside Winchester, and we were reasonably sure it was a Native American well over two centuries old, though I held off confirming that to give our students a chance for study and measurement. The other skeleton was that of a young woman in her late twenties who, since we estimated her death to have occurred only about a year prior, would have demanded our undivided attention were it not for the eight corpses of the spectacular mass murder.

I walked along the five tables holding females, my tennis shoes squeaking on the shiny black tile, until I came to the table holding the decapitated skeleton whose bones and skull had been shellacked with a mix of resin, paint, charcoal, and glitter. The glitter hadn't been visible until we began our preliminary removal of dirt. We'd halted and took a hundred and five photos before steaming glitter, paint and shellac off.

It was eerie how we'd had so few leads, considering that the murderers had been polite enough to stick quarters from 1972 and 1973 in all the victims' eyes. Doing this had narrowed the missing persons search considerably, but still no workable in-state matches. Mr. Reggie T. Gibson had thrown in a new geography since he'd disappeared in Cincinnati, his hometown. Murderers—we had begun to think of them in the plural not because of the ritual heart removal (which typically would indicate a single male), but because of the logistics of the burial ground itself, which indicated a religious rite as opposed to a psychotic one. Well, I suppose I should conjoin: a psychotic religious rite. But, not even Gregorian chant could drive believers to this level of psychosis. Supporting this conjecture was the fact that seven of the surrounding trees held scars of carved runes, hieroglyphics, and even Sanskrit—all having to do with life after death according to the four language experts consulted, and all about thirty years old according to the forester Willy consulted. We also thought of "murderers" in the plural because it was hard to imagine one person possessing enough charm to cross the sexual and age barriers represented by the eight corpses, the oldest being young forties and the youngest being mid-teens, although all eight were Caucasian.

Then came Reggie from Cincinnati. It was conceivable that the murderers didn't waylay hobos or waifs in Fayette County but traveled to other cities to find victims and brought them back to the farm for the ritual burial.

The farm itself was a dead end. In the early seventies it had covered six hundred acres. The barn had already been abandoned at that time. The owners had died childless, passing the land to the wife's younger sister, who promptly sold it.

I surveyed the five females whose skeletons were spread out on the five tables. One of our office clocks had an annoying fault of clicking when its minute hand touched the hour. It did this and I turned to see that, sure enough, it was exactly noon. Feeling something touch my wrist I jumped. The skull that had been shellacked was staring at me.

"Gina?" I imagined flowing hair draping the skull, a silly freshwoman giggle crossing those oddly spaced and enamel-poor teeth. Leaning to study the vertebrae, I remembered that this one had no ice pick puncture. Two of the others didn't either, though one showed an abnormality that might indicate the nick of such a wound—or it might indicate some scavenger's gnaw mark. All the corpses except this one with the shellacked skull had been buried bodily intact, though minus their hearts. This corpse—Jane Doe 11-2000—had been dismembered and—I only told Willy and one graduate student this—partly defleshed before death, as indicated by myriad carving hash marks on the bones. And the left front incisor had been cracked during the perimortem stage, since the crushed enamel showed no signs of replenishment. That led to the possibility that this incisor had been extracted after death for a second choice souvenir. A *memento mori*, that phrase ringing back from my sophomore English literature course.

"Gina? Gina, how'd you do in English lit?"

"   "

Corpses and skeletons do talk, but not that way. I shook my head and carried Jane Doe 11-2000's chart to my office, where I ran through students named Gina for the academic year 1972-1973. Two Ginas showed up. One must have had an Amazon for a mother, for this Gina was listed as five-foot-eleven, huge for back then, large enough for now. Her Amazon mother obviously hadn't smoked or drunk during pregnancy, and maybe even discovered prenatal vitamins before they became standard. Goodbye, Gina Louise Morgan. I hope you're having a good life raising basketball players. The other Gina was the right size, give or take two inches, which I was willing to do. But this Gina had graduated in nursing and was even on the alumni list, though with a marital name change. Goodbye Gina Jackson-Tyler. Hope you're representing the university with fine bedside manner.

I went back a year, forward a year. All dead ends, just like the street I lived on with its tumbling embankment.

An outside door was unlocked and the fire safety bar clanked open, echoing through the hall. Crap. I'd forgotten to phone security and they were rushing to check. I jumped to start the coffee pot—any little thing to keep them on my side. A requisition had been placed for alarm locks and cameras but a requisition in a university setting is a requisition is a requisition is a requi . . .

"Sorry guys," I said opening my door and glancing down the hall.

But it was a guy and a gal. The guy I recognized. Hedging for retirement, he didn't need to be involved in some break-in by a criminal looking to destroy evidence, or by a creep looking to horde it. Hell, neither did I. I'd been stupid not to call them and check in, but being rebuffed by both Willy and the grad student this morning, and then the Methuselah fellow with his news at the coffee shop, had thrown me.

"Sorry," I said again. "I meant to call but someone gave me a name that might fit one of the corpses and—"

Bill Reynolds—Officer Reynolds to you peons—held up his hand. He sported a most lovely silver goatee, which earned him the nickname of Officer Elf-King with my graduate students.

"Is that coffee I smell brewing?"

What a nose. I nodded. Bill introduced me to his partner, a new female campus cop shadowing the old guy for training. I'm sure this tickled him pink, since he was a widower and this woman wasn't bad-looking as far as women cops go, though typically stout for the breed. Bill and his goatee looked like they could still manage a tumble in the bed. Not my type, I kept telling myself whenever we wound up alone. Lord, that might be my codicil mantra to my already codiciled mantra. Monkey meat, monkey, er, No One Ever Touches Anyone—ever—er, Not my type, not my type, not my type.

We poured coffee, and the new woman cop wanted to see the lab, so I obliged her. I wound up pulling out pictures of the skull when it was painted and glittered.

"This is Gina when she—" I caught myself and looked to Jane Doe 11-2000. The female cop, whose name I'd already forgotten, took the photos of the glittered skull and sorted through them while sipping her coffee with slurps. A cool one.

"Gina?" Bill asked.

I looked at his rheumy gray eyes, then focused on his silvery goatee. "I don't know why I keep calling Eleven-Two-Thousand that. I was given a name by this character named Methuselah . . ."

Bill chuckled.

"He the lech who was trying to put the moves on me the other day?" the female cop asked.

"The same one," Bill said, stooping to look into Gina's eye sockets. I've often thought you could see the world through eye sockets, a reverse globe spinning inside every skull. Steam from Bill's coffee created a mist that added to that *myst*icism—a terrible pun worthy of an ex-English major. Bill must have meandered along the same mystical lines, for he stared so long that when he straightened his knee joints popped.

"Why Gina?" He gave his trousers a tug. With only a tiny peep I could see that he dressed on the right, and sizably so.

"Methuselah—"

"He put the moves on you too?" the female cop asked.

Well no, my dear, it was *I* who was playing footsie with him. "Uh, I don't think so," I said. "Not yet. But he got my phone number."

"There you have it." She turned back to the photos.

"Why Gina?" Bill persisted in good pit bull fashion.

"Methuselah said that this woman who keeps stopping by to sketch my house had a lesbian lover named Gina, and that she reported her missing to the police."

"A student named Gina?"

"I think so."

"From fall of 1972?"

I shrugged. "Yeah, probably."

The damned clock did its hourly click thing—could it be one already? I looked over Bill's sizable shoulders to see that it was.

"I remember her," he said. "Regina was her name."

"What?"

"Sure. I remember her. A sophomore who supposedly disappeared over Halloween. She made a big splash for about a week and a half, until she stayed in the news long enough for the Catholic orphanage in Covington to inform the police that she'd revisited them the previous day, making their life miserable, so no one needed to worry about her being dead. The nun who called intimated that most of her co-workers wished she *were* dead since she'd broken out windows and used a good deal of profanity."

"Did she come back to school here?"

"Kids were dropping out right and left then. But if I remember correctly, a dungeons and dragons group—a class that was part of the so-called 'free university'—that group told the student newspaper that she showed up to one of their excursions and told them she was hitchhiking to San Francisco."

The woman cop gave a snort, so she was listening.

"Five-foot-two, eyes of . . . brown," Bill chanted over his coffee.

"Yeah?" I said.

"Yeah," he said. "Her picture and a biographical description ran in *The Kernel* and *The Lexington Herald* both. You know, back then our physical anthropologist spent his time classifying Indian bones and arrowheads, especially arrowheads."

I nodded.

"Not like it's your fault, of course." He glanced around at the array of skeletons. "I like you a lot better anyway."

I nodded again.

The two of them left after I promised to be a good girl and check in and out with the police office until we installed the automatic alarm system and security cameras. I typed *Regina* into a computer search and came up with two, one who graduated seven years later, and one who received all F's for her fall sophomore semester and never returned. Bill's Gina, no doubt. The little orphan girl who raised a stink then ran off to sing Hare Krishna or sell drugs or her body—or do all three.

I started a national search for Gina and its variations, coming up with six possibilities. One I could rule out right away: she'd broken her left forearm as a ten-year old. Eleven Two Thousand had a broken ankle and plenty of lousy teeth, but her arms had been just fine. Another had broken ribs. Somewhere, I realized, there was one set of parents waiting for someone like me to send them news of their lost Regina with her broken left fore-arm, and another set waiting for news of the Regina with her busted ribs. Just like someday I'd no doubt receive news of my alcoholic father and his prominent scoliosis found whiskey-drowned behind a pawnshop, broken guitar in hands. The remaining four Reginas didn't mention any broken bones, but to be safe I sent for their dental records.

When August came and the dental records arrived, they revealed one missing girl with miraculously carrie-free teeth, the other with a calcified break in her mandible from abuse as an infant. The mandible shows why I never quite trust the preliminary records, since these four were supposedly clean of any bone breaks or fractures. The other two were Native American and African American. Either rest or walk in peace, my dears. There *is* always that latter faint hope for missing persons: that against all odds they've succeeded in disappearing to create a new abuse-free life and are walking in daily freedom. For a handful, that may be the case. But they hardly rule out the predominant pattern of drugs and death: Willie Nelson, for example, isn't some plastic surgeon's remake of my dad, Lonnie Circle.

The bottom line was that not a single Gina, Regina, not even Jeanette or Jennifer, matched the Jane Doe skeletons we held at that point.

2.

Dumb Show

Year 2001

(Gray)

rhyme-time-mime: I remember how the outside of the campus building was fairy-tale glowing with safety lights showing hot moths chasing one another. Glowing, showing, but it wasn't snowing. Even more, I remember the high-low chatter of beautiful women and handsome men who were going to be engineers and lawyers and doctors. And too much snore more, I remember the smell of perfume that caught in my nose and my lungs, knitting my chest like my grandmother's red and black afghan. Afghan is a hard word to rhyme. You try it.

I stood on the sidewalk, in the shadows that led to the building. Then I saw this beautiful girl who was thin and short with honey hair that I could see moths through. She was talking with another girl with black hair that frizzed and curled all up. Someone lit a cigarette by them, and they moved away. My mother smokes, so I thought it was good that they moved away. The girl with the lots of black hair that curled coughed once, loud, at the guy who lit a cigarette; then she and her honey-haired friend walked inside the building. I could see them walk inside, I mean I could see their beautiful backsides besides. The thin girl's shoulder blades protruded like two tiny reverse breasts.

Feeling in my front left pocket I felt some bills, dollars and five-dollar bills, so I moved to the left across the grass, nearing the man who was smoking, until I could see through the glass doors. I saw the beautiful girl with the honey hair and her friend standing before a display case. *Hamlet,* the sign outside the glass doors said. It showed a picture of a man dressed in black holding a skull. Ever since I'd been going to college I'd been dressing in black. My mother said that black was the Devil's color and that people who wore too much of it were opening theirselves to Him. But that's just not true.

"Can I help you?"

I looked through this new glass, and then where the sound of her voice had come through a round hole in the new glass, surprised that I'd already walked through the doors by the smoking man. On the other side of the new glass stood a beautiful girl with a beautiful smile. Or maybe she was sitting on a stool; I was afraid to look because I might see knees. I think she was in a class I was taking, a math class, where the teacher wrote on the board and spread chalk dust in the air. Everywhere.

Some people stood in behind me. I could smell that they smoked. And I could smell whiskey, too.

"Can I buy a ticket?"

"Do you have a student I.D.?"

I showed her the I.D., but she said that she needed to scan it. Already, after only two weeks, so many people had to touch my I.D. The rays from scanning made it soft, the leftover scaly skin made it hard. This time it felt both soft and warm when she handed it back. A lot of times it felt that way, though four times it felt cold and hard.

"Four dollars," she said.

I pulled the bills from my pocket, dropping some, and when I bent down I saw a woman's feet and toes in golden high heels with lots of straps so I had trouble standing up, wobble trouble, I mean.

I handed the girl from my math class four dollar bills that I hoped weren't too crumpled or wet, since I'd been sweating, since it was late summer, early fall and all. She gave me a ticket and the person who smoked and drank whiskey behind me pushed against my right arm, so I couldn't say anything about math class, so I just walked toward a door, where someone nodded at me, wanting to touch my ticket.

The beautiful girl with honey hair and her friend with black hair still stood by the display case. The girl with the honey hair looked like she had on maroon pajamas. I didn't know you could go to plays in pajamas. But maybe they weren't pajamas, maybe they were pants. *Slacks*, my mother calls them. The girl's friend with the curly black hair had on blue jeans, but they weren't blue, they were black. And you know what my mother says about that. I turned and went to the water fountain, since they hadn't gone in. There was a piece of chewed green gum stuck on the wall next to the water fountain, so I didn't drink anything, just started the water and bent to pretend, so that the person who'd walked behind me for a drink wouldn't think I was crazy or anything.

I saw that they were going in, so I hurried and let the man rip my ticket. I sat three rows behind them in the play. Before the lights went out, I saw that the honey-haired girl had a beautiful long neck. Even three rows back I could see her vertebrae and how her neck was so long that it curved in, then came back out. When Hamlet hit his mother and threw her on the bed with the red satin sheets, I started to get sick and had to hold onto my knees, and then onto the armrests. I could hear the woman next to me breathing. She was older than my mother even, but she wasn't as old as my grandmother.

I saw my English teacher when a bunch of lights glittered in the play. She was a student too. She told us that she was working on her PhD in Shakespeare. That was why she was here. She told us about this play yesterday. She said we were lucky to have this professional group here so early in the semester and that she'd seen it in Boston and that it was very innovative. She likes to use words like *innovative*. All I'd like to do is work at the Toyota place in Georgetown. But sometimes I think that I'd like to be a psychiatrist like Dr. Kiefer, who is even older than my grandmother. One time I was staring at her breasts so that I didn't have to look at her mouth or eyes, and I thought that they were so huge that a catfish could swim in them. Not my grandmother's breasts. I wouldn't do that, stare at them. My grandmother is 62. I always forget how old my mother is, but I think that she's 42. I'm not 22, or things would be easy.

Dr. Kiefer might be 82. Really.

I see a man that looks like the man that's been lugging around my mother lately. Lugging, slugging, fugging. She's smoking and stinking up the house with perfume, and he's smoking and stinking up the house with whiskey and cum. I want to move out and I've looked at the want ads for maybe some kind of pizza cook, though I'd really like to work in a clothing store or maybe a shoe store. But not really a shoe store, though it would be nice if all the customers were as beautiful as the girl with the honey hair, or even her friend with the curly black hair. I'd touch their instep in just the right way. I was a pizza cook in high school. That way I didn't have to play sports.

Lights flash and loud music starts, so something's changing. This *Hamlet* is set in Las Vegas, my English teacher told us yesterday. There's a ghost, and Hamlet is snorting cocaine with his friend, but what I remember most, like I said, is Hamlet slapping his mother with a loud crack and throwing her on the bed with the red satin. I had to hold my knees then, and all I saw was the honey-haired girl whose neck looked like my mother's neck. I saw her and her beautiful friend turn to one another and smile. I couldn't see how they could smile about Hamlet hitting his mother. Then he kissed her on the head and rubbed her hair back from her cheek from where he'd hit her. I did that with my hand—next to my knees, I mean. Rubbed, I mean.

I went back in after half time but mostly I just slunk down and watched her honey hair silhouette off the stage lights. And her friend's black hair, too. I pretended that a moth was still flitting behind the honey hair, or maybe in front of it—that is, between it and the stage. The old woman next to me didn't come back and neither did her male friend, whose eyes looked like he wore mascara. I saw them padding on one another's feet before the play started, they were both wearing sandals like they were old hippies or something, so I guess that's what they went off to do, pray for peace. Of course, of course, of course I know what they really went to do. I'm not stupid. I remember once putting on my mother's mascara. It scared me because it wouldn't come off, and she was at work and coming home. I couldn't fit into a pair of satin white high heels she had, no matter how hard I pushed. I had to take a bath and use dish soap and Pine-Sol to get the mascara off. I'm glad my little toe didn't break in the high heels.

The dumb show came, and it creeped me out, since the fake uncle and the fake queen descended on maroon silk cords to twist about one another over the fake king they were going to kill. There was music from an acoustic guitar and a saxophone, but they didn't talk. Life's like that. I think that's why people invented saxophones and guitars. So that people wouldn't have to talk. It all goes back to the Tower of Babel.

So that was the first time I saw her. After the play had its say, I followed her and her friend inside to a pizza place that was two blocks away. I was glad that they didn't have a car, because I didn't have a car neither. My mother's boyfriend said I shouldn't be driving her car, cause it would be a temptation to me to park and do things.

"Jan! Ashley!" some asshole jock-looking guy said as he walked inside to her from the pizza door. But he lit a cigarette and she blinked and coughed at him, so he went to talk with his two jock friends, though I guess they couldn't be jocks and smoke, though maybe they took a lot of steroids and cocaine so that it didn't matter, with their big lungs and all.

"I've got a killer psych test at eight on Monday," I heard Ashley say to her friend, the black-haired girl, Jan. "But you go ahead." Ashley's nice and polite, isn't she? I knew which was which because I watched the jock's eyes when he called out their names.

I think that Jan wanted to go back and sit with the three jocks, but she said that she probably should call it an early night too. I was glad that I sat real near them, even though it made me nervous, because Ashley had the softest, politest voice. And I couldn't believe that she was taking psychology. Maybe I would do that instead of Toyota.

+ = -

Eight o'clock Monday isn't hard to find, because I keep a schedule book from before when classes started. There are two eight o'clock psychology classes on Monday, Wednesday, and Friday. I like those classes best because they're shorter than the Tuesday and Thursday classes.

In books I read, there are astersicks. That's what I call them. I know what they are.

But how about plus equals minus instead of an astersick? Weird, huh?

Astersicks look like stars, and no one living in a city ever sees stars. Soon the world won't know there are stars. When you repeat the same word, that's called identity rhyme. There'll be kids who will never see a star and think that people are kidding about them or maybe that we blew them up with nukes. Rebuked by nukes.

I get to the first eight o'clock psychology class at twenty till. The janitor has just unlocked the building and is going through it unlocking rooms. It would be nice to have his keys. It would be nice to go around campus unlocking rooms for professors and pretty girls.

Twenty-two people walk into the classroom. I tap my foot on the old green and ivory tiles and pretend that I'm a big shot gambler working a blackjack table. Twenty-two. Bust. One guy walks in at seven minutes after. Twenty-three. Double bust. The teacher came at one minute after. This is a junior level class. I didn't think she was that old, not with her soft, pretty voice. Ashley, I mean. But she isn't here, so maybe she isn't that old.

Old and mold. But Ashley is gold. I bet she could even make my name sound soft. "Eye-sach." And she would lean to kiss me with her lips all puffed just like they were Saturday night when she ate bits of her pepperoni and muchroom pizza. I know how to spell mushroom. But muchroom is funny.

"What is abnormal?" the professor is saying. He is sort of screaming, I guess since it's so early he's afraid students will fall asleep. He had thick glasses and a thicker forehead. His glasses were greasy and filmy. When he walked in, I mean. He closed the door and crinkled his stupid brow and dirty glasses at me. "A thin line, a thin line," he now says. I could stay out here and listen to his whole stupid lecture through the stupid closed door. I think that Dr. Kiefer told me something like that thin-line stuff, too. Dr. Kiefer agrees with me—that I should move out and live away from my mother, that is. But she thinks I should get a roommate or even live in a dormitory. Dormitories are for cretins. So are roommates, unless they're beautiful with honey, satin, chestnut, almond, creamy mead hair. Grendel tore up a mead hall. She was the mother, not the monster. It's just like Frankenstein. He was the father, not the monster. She was there too much, he wasn't there enough. The mother, the father, I mean.

It's sixteen minutes after, so I leave for the other class. Stupid, stupid, stupid. She said she was having a test, and this guy's screaming about thin lines, so I could have left nine minutes ago when twenty-three double bust walked in late.

The other eight o'clock psychology class is in another old building on campus. I like the old buildings because they have cubbyholes and corners and doors leading to little rooms and thin halls. Some have marble that I can lean my cheek against. And some have colored granite tiles like the last one did. It takes me a minute to find the room and I start to worry that he'll let the class out early, but no, she's taking a test, so that won't happen. But what if she's really smart and finishes early? She looked really smart. Her eyes were dark blue, and her skin was like soymilk. And she laughed a lot during *Hamlet*. There must have been funny things that I missed. Or maybe she was talking with her friend about something womany.

The room is quiet. This professor's left the door open and he stares at me like I'm doing something bad. I check my pockets, though I really want to check my zipper and see if my fly's open. I think that this has something to do with psychology people. Staring I mean. Dr. Kiefer does that sometimes. Maybe staring rings their things.

There are two stairwells. That could be a pun, you know. If I wanted it to be one, I mean. I walk to the nearest stare well and sit at a desk that's in the hall. I have a math book, so I open it. I like the signs. They look like Arabic. If we ever go to war with Arabia, the signs would look like this. I know there's no such country as Arabia anymore. I just mean in general. When we go to war we'll be helping the Jews, even though they killed Christ. But I think the Moslems would have too, if they'd been around. I think a lot of these professors and students would have too, if they'd been around.

What I like about math, besides all the neat signs, is that it's like a tee-tiny puzzle when you solve a problem. It's like Moses or Aaron tapping the rock, and water gushing forth.

Shit. She goes to the elevator. She hugs her books close to her breasts. She's thin, but she still has nice breasts. I look to see it's going down. There's only one damned floor below. Doesn't she want to conserve energy?

I run down the steps and am almost beside a stone lion when she walks out. I follow her to the cafeteria. She sits down with her black-hair friend and a guy who's fat and has a head of poofy black hair like a black guy. Black, black, black. His shirt's out of his pants. I check my zipper as I carry a Coke to a table.

But there's cracker crumbs and mustard on this table, so I have to move closer. The girl with the black hair looks at me. I think her hair's really raven. I think I'm going to stop wearing black. Maybe my mother's right.

= + & -

She really is a psychology major, and I know where she lives!

That is the plus side. The minus side is that the raven-Satan haired girl lives with her. Maybe I won't have to rent an apartment, maybe I can rent a room. That way it wouldn't cost as much. My mother's boyfriend says I got to work. I don't think he does. I think that's called projection protection. I read up about being a psychology major. She goes to two other classes on Monday, Wednesday, and Friday. One's another psychology class, and one's an English class just like I'm taking, with another graduate student teaching it who's probably getting her PhD in Grendel from the way she looks.

I got to touch her this morning. We were on the elevator and some guy pushed in and she backed into me. She hit my hand, which was covering a book, which was covering my embarrassment that I got from looking at her beautiful neck and smelling her priceless proud perfume. Yes, I mean what you think I mean. I had an erection projection and the book was in front of it for protection.

"Sorry," she said in her whispery way, looking back and blinking. I think she recognized me. That's good, because we can talk soon. I'll tell her I saw *Hamlet* and that as a psychology major I think that Freud was exactly right. About Oedipus. She'll know what I mean.

I got off the elevator too and walked behind her toward her class, which was the same math class that I take. I don't mean exactly the same like identity rhyme, but the same course and the same subject, like regular rhyme. Same name but twain. That's odd—that she's taking the same course, I mean—because I'm a freshman and this is my first semester here. I cooked pizzas all last summer. Maybe I shouldn't have quit that job. I almost followed her into the class, but the teacher was there, and it was the same chalk dust teacher that I have for my real identity rhyme math class. He looked at me strange and I turned around, pretending I made a mistake thinking this was my real class because I saw him in there. That's what I'll tell him if he asks. But this is a Tuesday/Thursday class, and I hate them. It's too long to sit, the room always begins to smell like people grease.

!² = Δ + ה א ق څ

That first thing might look like an exclamation point to you, but it's a sign used in probability. I'm not sure that the squared sign after could really work, like would it make things squared probable? Life is cubed probable, I think. A dumb show. And then the next sign, after the equals, is from calculus. It means change. A tee-tiny change. And then the plus is plus, and then the screwed-up looking E means Sum. It's from calculus too. The rest is Hebrew and Arabic horseshit.

And today is Tuesday, September 11.

I saw her crying in the cafeteria when they showed for the life-cubed time the second plane crashing into the twin Manhattan towers. I had to walk up behind her when she was crying, even though her Satan-haired roommate was standing with her. Raven-Satan.

"Terrible, horrible, audible," I said, standing behind her.

She turned. Her soymilk face was red under her blue eyes, and so was her nose. I was going to give her something from my pocket to wipe away her tears, but her Satan-haired roommate stared at me.

"Audible?" Raven-Satan said, and before I could answer, she said, "Why have I seen you so much lately?"

"My father works in the Tower A," I said.

Several people turned to look at me.

"He and my mother are divorced. He doesn't work on Tuesdays."

Ashley was blinking at me, and a tear ran down her cheek like a leak on an old sink. The porcelain and all, I mean. But there wasn't any rust on her face, because her face was like soymilk and maybe cherries. Because it was so red, I mean.

"That's good," Ash said.

"Let's go home," Raven-Satan the roommate said, giving me a bare-bear-glare. I know her roommatey name, but I don't want to use it.

It's Jan, okay?

When they were at the steps, I started to follow them, but the Satan-haired girl looked back, so I turned around and said, "Terrible, horrible, audible," to some guy whose mouth was open. He just nodded like a Venus flytrap plant, so I guessed that they were showing the plane crashing into the building again.

I walked by an old house that had a rooms-for-rent sign. I stared at the sign and wondered what it would be like to crash a plane into a building. Would your head burst first, or would your chest? Could maybe your whole body shove through the cockpit glass and scoot across the building's shiny waxed white floor, by a row of twenty computers and knock over a rolling swivel chair because it's going so fast that it doesn't know what it's doing, and then maybe blast through a window on the other side of the building to sail over New York City skyscrapers and people before the burning jet fuel caught up with it?

"The room costs ninety dollars a month."

I was staring at a bedroom that was next to the communal bathroom. It smelled musty, but for once that was nice because it was better than cigarette smoke and cum. There were both males and females living in the house. I knew that because I could smell perfume from the first two doors I passed. One was watermelon and one was hippie patchouli. There was a sink in the room, and I wondered if I'd be able to hear the bathroom, since the room she showed me was next to it.

"Isn't it horrible, terrible, and abominable what happened this morning?" I asked.

"What happened?" the woman said. "I've been upstairs reading my mysteries."

I liked her, and I told her that I was going to take the room, but that I had to get my checkbook. She said she'd hold the room for two hours.

"No smoking in the rooms!" my happy sappy future landlady called out when I was on the sidewalk.

"I'm a Christian," I answered.

"They smoke just like the rest of 'em."

Horrible, terrible, audible, I thought.

+ = -

That's still the best one. Plus equals minus, I mean.

My mother's stupid boyfriend broke my CD player, he was so happy hurry hasty to get me moved. He passed me his stupid orange-labeled half pint of Early Times in his stupid green pick-up and I shook my head. "Suit yourself," he said. I thought how stupid that saying was: are you supposed to dress yourself? Is that what it means? Everyone but Prince Charles does that.

Every time I pass a TV at the university I see towers burning and black smoke. I hate TV because it reminds me of flies and mosquitoes and gnats. There's a space in the communal kitchen, which is across from the communal bathroom and the steps leading upstairs, a place that has a TV, but it's broken. That's good.

The boarding house is three-and-a-half blocks from her house. I walked by it five times the first night. Her house, I mean. Wednesday, I mean. She and Raven-Satan rent the top floor, and I can look into two of the windows just walking down the street. I saw her twice. Once she was carrying a book, and once she was talking on a phone. I wish I could see her feet from the street. I saw her feet when we went to eat pizza, and then once when she walked out of the psychology class and I was sitting beside the lion. It started to rain, or maybe I would have talked to her that day.

- = +

In some ways that works as well. Putting minus first, I mean. It's like physical anthropology and Darwin. Growing from a mistake. Survival of the furriest. I know what he said. What he wrote. Fittest. I know.

I'm supposed to see Dr. Kiefer every Friday. This is the first time my mother won't be coming with me, even though she never comes in to talk. She takes off for a long lunch. Sometimes she stops at a bar and doesn't go back to work. I think that's where she met her smoking boyfriend, who pours concrete for a living. He smells like a.) cigarette smoke, b.) Early Times whiskey, c.) limestone from concrete, d.) cum.

"Wai-ellll," Dr. Kiefer says when I sit down and stare at a bright red cardinal in the window behind her. "Some big news, I understand."

It figures that my stupid mother would tell Dr. Kiefer. I don't see why my stupid mother doesn't come and talk to her instead of me.

"It's terrible . . . and awful." I don't rhyme anymore when I talk to Dr. Kiefer, because last June I noticed that she always put a checkmark in her notes whenever I rhymed. She tried to do it so that I wouldn't see it, but I did. "It's cowardly and dastardly." I felt okay with that, since everybody else in the damned country was saying it. Me, I couldn't see how flying a plane full of jet fuel into the side of a skyscraper was cowardly. Dastardly, yeah, but that's only half the rhyme that isn't really a rhyme.

"You mean what happened Tuesday?"

"Yeah, sure."

"What's your reaction?"

"It's cowardly and dastardly," I repeated, looking at the cardinal behind in the window again. Its female mate had flown nearby, so it hopped off. They do that, you know. Cardinals, I mean. They look out for one another. One will eat and the other will keep watch. I've seen them do it.

"Is that why you moved out of the house? What happened Tuesday in Manhattan?"

"It was on all the TVs everywhere. I can't help but see it. It's like the Tower of Babel."

"How so?"

"All those people in two tall buildings . . ." I stopped to think of two hard-on dicks standing next to one another instead of tall buildings. I think I thought this because I was talking to a psychiatrist. I mean, I don't think it's my fault that I thought this. "All those people talking and then gone. In the university cafeteria I stood behind a girl—" I could feel my heart beat here when I thought of Ash's neck "—who was crying when the second plane crashed into the second tower.

"I . . . no, her friend took her down the stairs, away from the TV."

"What were you going to say?"

Both cardinals had flown away, so I stared at the bit of blue sky I could see through the trees, whose leaves were already turning a pale yellow.

"I was going to say that I wanted to touch her neck and tell her it would be okay."

"Her neck?"

"She had a long neck. But then her friend took her away."

"Gray, what do you think she would have done if you had touched her on the neck?"

"I really wouldn't have touched her there. I meant maybe on her shoulder."

"What do you think she would have done if you had touched her on her shoulder?"

"I don't know. She was sad and crying and all."

I know you don't touch people on the neck. It was horrible, abominable, and audible. I would have said this, too, because it was, except that I didn't want to watch Dr. Kiefer write checkmarks down.

"Have you seen her anymore?"

"Around," I said.

"How many times?"

I had to stare at Dr. Kiefer's boobs so that I wouldn't have to look at her eyes that are so gray and straight.

"Just twice," I said. "She gets out of psychology class the same time that I get out of math."

- = +

Dr. Kiefer never got me to say that I had moved out. I know she wanted me to tell her that, but since my stupid mother had already told her, I didn't want to Tower of Babel. I already Tower of Babelled about how many times I'd seen Ash. It's been 47 times.

Just before I finished up business on Friday, Dr. Kiefer told me that I should make some friends. Maybe join a campus group.

"There's a Baptist group," I said, thinking that I could get her to move her bra strap that supports the two guppy tanks she carries around. She's an atheist, I can tell. Even if she doesn't wear black. There's a foot-tall Mexican statue of a blood god behind her. It's made of red clay that probably has twelve dead virgins' blood in it. I know it doesn't have dead virgins in it. I don't think those guys that flew that plane into the building are going to have ten virgins waiting on them in heaven, either. And if they did, they wouldn't be virgins long, would they? That was a joke. The clay's probably from Georgia. There's probably some goon hillbilly from the Tennessee mountains making those foot-tall statues. He probably thinks ten virgins are going to play his fiddle for him in heaven.

"That'd be fine," Dr. Kiefer had said about the Baptist group.

Which scared me. Because she didn't even pause and because she meant it, I mean. Maybe I'll go to the Catholic group. My mother would hate that.

Ashley sometimes goes to the cafeteria after her two o'clock Monday, Wednesday, Friday anthropology class. But she wasn't there by the time I got back. I went to my room and smelled it. I could hear girls flushing the toilet, which was all right.

+ = -

Outside her English class on Monday made 48 times. That's 11 more than our ages added, because Ash is a year older than me. I planned to talk to her at time number 37, but I was on a bus and she was walking down the street. I pulled the cord three times, but the stop was a block away and when I went back I couldn't find her. A fate date that didn't mate.

"My dad's ok," I said, looking up when she walked out of the class.

She stopped, then started backing away.

"We met on September 11," I said. "I was watching the—" she was a psychology major, so maybe I shouldn't rhyme, I realized— "the airplane flame." I bit my tongue.

"I remember," she said, sort of coldlike. "I'm glad that your dad's okay."

"Would you like to—"

"I've got to meet my boyfriend for lunch," she said.

It was just 9 o'clock and she didn't have a boyfriend. Don't you think I'd know that after 48 times?

"That's okay. I just wanted you to know that my dad's all right."

"That's good. I'm glad." And she walked away. I didn't follow her because I knew she'd look back. And she did. I pretended to be reading my math book against the lion. She almost bumped into someone because she was looking back. It was a male, and she jumped.

+ = -

Halloween was coming. 134 times. I decided that whenever glass was between us it only counted half. I decided that I was a like a cardinal, watching out for his mate whenever I walked by her second-story apartment. We're hunting Bin Laden down. I think of him running from cave to cave at night when the sky spies can't see him all that well. He wears black, I bet. When he's not talking on TV, I mean.

135 times, and I couldn't believe my luck. It was just like the bus time, but better because I didn't have to pull a cord. She finished one line in the cafeteria just when I finished another. I couldn't believe that I hadn't seen her across from me. And she hadn't seen me, either. Fate never abates.

"Hello, hello," I said. That's a rhyme I sometime sneak in on Dr. Kiefer. It's called identity rhyme. Did I tell you that already?

"Hello," she returned in that quiet voice of hers and then began looking for a table. There was only one anywhere near, because the place was packed because of a sudden rain. I took a deep breath and heard a bolt of thunder. I know thunder doesn't bolt, but it really does, if you think about it. Lightning is frightening, thunder is a wonder.

"There aren't any seats," I said, following her. "Can I sit with you?"

"My boyfriend is meeting me here."

I had seen two different guys inside her apartment. And neither of them had come back. "Tower of Babel," I said.

"What?"

"The Tower of Babel. From the Old Testament. You're a psychology major, so you should know about that."

I was still standing, waiting for her to invite me to sit.

"How did you know that I was a psychology major?"

"You told me when we first met, watching the World Trade Center."

"Tower of Babel," she said, looking at me accusingly. "I never told you that." Do you see what I mean? I could tell just from her neck and her blue eyes that she was very intelligent. And then she said, "I'd rather eat alone, okay?"

"Okay," I answered. Two people were getting up four tables away. Only one of them took her tray. French fries and bloody ketchup were left on the other tray, with a piece of lettuce that looked like it had cum on it. The cretin guy was probably a bastard son of my mother's boyfriend. I forced myself to sit in the empty spot and not look back at Ash. She needed space.

When I turned around, she was gone.

+ = 1

I thought that I would try that, something different. I skipped all three of Ash's Thursday and Friday classes. But I had an obligation as her cardinal to walk by her apartment each night, though she left on Friday night, and I think that Raven-Satan saw me walking by. They do have a car, a red one that Raven-Satan drives. That fits.

Saturday was a football day. Go Big Blue.

Her house was on the way to the library. I got a job cooking at the pizza place where we met for the second time. I like to look from the oven to the table where she sat. Her house was on the way to that too, if I walked catty-wampus just a bit. So I was walking back after working there during the day. If I went home and took a shower in the same stall that three girls took a shower, I wouldn't smell like onions and mozzarella, and maybe we'd meet on a high rate fate date.

I tripped a bit on the sidewalk when her house was coming near, just like I always do. It was nearly dark, but not as dark as in a cave with Bin Laden.

"I want to talk to you!"

An old guy who had a beer tummy and a guy in his twenties who probably still played on some high school football team stood in front of me.

"I don't know anyone about anything," I said.

"What the fuck does that suppose' to mean?" the semi-high schooler said.

But the beer gut man just raised his palm. "I want you to stay away from my daughter. Do you understand?" He punched me hard with two fingers, just like a coach did on the only team I was ever on.

"I don't know you! Keep your creep hands off!" I was carrying a sack with two pieces of pizza, and I threw it at him. The semi-high schooler hit me on the cheek good and hard and I fell back, then started swinging and kicking, but they grabbed me and the gut rut began hitting me in the stomach and face and I felt snot come from my nose, so I kicked him and then I was on the ground where my head hit a tree root.

"Stop it! Stop it! You said you were just going to talk to him!"

It was Ashley. Even though I'd never heard her scream I knew it was her. She was acting just like a cardinal and watching out for her mate. I looked up and could see her standing in yellow jeans and a dark shirt. I could see the veins on her feet, too, because she was wearing white-strapped sandals.

"You goddamned pervert!" the fat gut yelled and he kicked me.

"Stop it, Daddy, stop it!"

"I'll stop when he stops looking at you that way!" And he kicked me again, and then the semi-high schooler kicked me again.

"Tell them that you'll stop. Tell them you'll never follow me again," Ashley said. Raven-Satan was standing beside her. Even in the near dark I could see her eyes glaring staring at me. But I really only saw Ashley, and I thought that maybe she was crying for me like she'd cried for the World

Trade Center people. I blinked and then someone kicked me again.

"Stop it, or I'll call the police, Daddy. He won't follow me anymore. Ever. Tell them!" she said, chirping like a cardinal and squeezing her wings together.

"Mom," I said, looking at Ashley's bright cardinal sigh-eyes. "Mom."

3.

Lap Dancer

Years 2002–2003

(Clarissa, Willy, Lauren, Methuselah, Callie)

Because I was late for mid-morning class, I caught the "Wanderin' Wildcat," UK's campus trolley. After fumbling two full minutes for my faculty I.D. and showing it to an importantly impatient graduate student moonlighting as a bus driver, I huffed into a seat. "*Seig Heil*," I grumbled to no one in particular, since I recognized this student from the German department, which was located across from anthropology. Hearing me, a garishly made-up, though attractive, black-haired woman in her mid-fifties spoke:

"When this trolley first started, no one had to show an I.D. That was the deal student government cut: free transportation for everyone, student, staff, faculty, or street bum."

"Really," I replied as flatly as I could, wanting to focus on my upcoming lecture. But instead of the class or the woman facing me or even the idiot graduate student cum bus driver, I kept thinking of Willy, who was PO'ed at Methuselah and me for sleeping together. Well, Willy'd been sleeping with a damned bottle-blondie student of mine from a year before who was now working as a police clerk at the courthouse. So there I sat, twenty-three angry minutes from delivering a lecture on the physiological differences between Caucasians, Asians, Hispanics, and Blacks. *Black males are huge assholes, that's one major difference*, I was likely to say if I didn't get Willy off my mind. Either that or I'd shove the lectern over and strut from the auditorium biting my lips and clacking my yellow high heels to find Willy's hand-me-down nine-millimeter automatic and target practice on his high-yellow AfricanAmerican ass, dimpled or not.

Suddenly, the damned woman who'd been sitting across from me was sitting next to me, a knight jumping in a human chess game, skittering over the aisle while the bus moved. Lord, did she ever lean on perfume to top her make-up. But that didn't change my first impression: she was damned good-looking with gray-blue eyes that drilled on forever, dimples Barbie would kill Ken for, and an upturned nose that surely had flattened any number of men during her life.

"I've heard that you have a really strange double suicide case you're working on."

"It seems," I replied after recoiling from her voice, which reverberated banjo loud in close proximity, "that I'm always working on strange cases. They come with the forensic territory."

"Sorry: I didn't introduce myself. I'm Lauren Bates. I write the *Riding the Rothschild* column. It went into syndication twenty-nine years ago, so I've been writing it for thirty-five years and I'm damned near ready to throw in the old computer. In fact, every night I envision the screen imploding to suck both my Siamese cat and me into cyberspace. Hell, if I was a whore working that long, my pussy'd be as dry as a piece of beef jerky—and I don't mean my Siamese cat."

Lovely. A fifty-something woman pretending to be Ernest Hemingway or Jack Kerouac. Maybe that came with the journalism territory. Would she pull out a silver flask and offer me a shot of Maker's Mark as wampum for the inside scoop on the double lover's suicide? To waylay the possibility I said, "I've read your column. I like its curmudgeonly slant."

"I hear from students that your lectures deal out their own curdmudgeonry."

The trolley stopped and her shoulder bumped mine. Though it was mid-May, the weather was coming on June bug hot, so most of the trolley's windows were down and I could hear a sorority singing, their voices chirruping. I double-checked my watch: 9:39 a.m. What could they sing about at this hour, especially one week into summer session? Twenty-one minutes until class. Two jocks got on the bus. They gave Ms. Bates and me the once-over then moved to younger territory with the two bleached-blondies sitting five rows back. They're everywhere, I told myself—jocks and bleached-blondies. Upon inhaling the jock-o aftermath, I concluded that the two males needed to get their act together, because their colognes clashed.

"Well," Ms. Lauren Bates said, scooting her hips. "Are you going to tell me about the double suicide?" I could still feel warmth from her shoulder.

"I'm not free to talk about pending cases. I'm especially not free to talk about them with a reporter. I'm a police consultant, not a member of their staff, much less a spokesperson."

"Spokeswoman." Her eyes, now a bright and wired blue as if the jock cologne had irradiated her irises and hormones, looked both at and through me. "Spokeswoman. I know you're not. Methusy told me that."

"Methusy?"

"Methuselah. We dated in the '70s when he was whacked out on reefer and Boone's Farm wine. We still keep in touch."

Methuselah was the one who'd found the decomposed bodies. He discovered them in a cabin that perched on some mountainside property. Mountainside land was about the only land in Fayette County that hadn't become subdivision, and flat, bluegrass Fayette didn't boast of much mountainside except near the Kentucky River—cliffside, really. The cabin had belonged to another curmudgeon, this one a World War I veteran who'd holed up there after escaping the trenches, machine guns, and mustard gas. Methuselah—Methusy—had heard a rumor that the guy'd kept a fifteen-volume diary about the Great War and the Great Depression: that was why M went searching. But his search for a diary was stopped cold by two decomposed corpses inside a cabin. No relation to the doughboy, and a good thirty years after his death date, they were double-handcuffed to a thick-legged Empire Era chair that was bolted to the floor. (That Empire Era designation courtesy of Methuselah's font of historical information.) Both chair and bolts had been sturdy enough to remain intact for the almost two years they'd gone undiscovered. Not that anyone knew the exact amount of time, since the double suicide note wasn't dated. Still, it didn't take a PhD in forensic anthropology to tell that they hadn't been dead since the Great Depression, for instance. All it took was a nose or eyes.

Alive, they'd been nude, and their heads had been Duct Taped tightly facing one another in a last lover's kiss. Those heads—or the remaining skulls—had fallen into their two ilia, which lay cupped in one another on the seat of the chair, while the remainder of their skeletons had fallen to the hardwood floor. The typewritten lovers' suicide note read, "In Death We

Find Eternal Freedom—Love, Denny & Alicia." The female's left hand was handcuffed to the chair; her right hand remained loose. To caress? To rip off the duct tape if the romantic notion wore thin and they changed their minds? The tape *had* been partly ripped at, after all. But then the keys to both sets of handcuffs had been tossed across the room and the chair was bolted down, so that wasn't the answer. Well, romance and romantic notions, no doubt, lie in the eyes of the beholder and beholden. It did make for a kinky but final lap dance.

Despite the suicide note and the free hand, Methuselah, Willy, and I remained incredulous. It certainly was *physically* possible, the double suicide and the duct-taping and the handcuffing, what with her one hand staying free. The tape pattern, according to some body mechanics genius who no longer worked for the department, fit what she might accomplish with that free right hand. She could even have tossed the keys over her back to land them against the wall. But standing in that cabin and listening to birds singing outside, I had pointed out that one would expect the male to tie the final knot, so to speak. Willy immediately countered that if he'd said that, I would have accused him of sexism. Methuselah had chuckled in agreement. Across the room, a beautiful rosewood guitar propped against a wall resonated his chuckle. This traceable expensive musical instrument and the typewritten note, created from an antiquated manual typewriter since filled with mud dauber nests, made my forensic lab work a matter of confirmation. The female had been a UK music major in performance guitar. The male had worked at a used record/CD/tape store.

"I knew the girl—woman," Ms. Bates said, looking away from the two jock-boys who were chatting up the blondies near the back of the bus. "She was twenty-four and working on her master's in music performance."

I nodded.

"Methusy knew the male. He sold CDs at a chain store and was thirty-one going on seventeen," Ms. Bates added.

Methusy, I thought. *Well, speaking of thirty-one going on seventeen, how about fifty going on fourteen, dearest? Isn't it time you retire the Rothschild column for a shopping mall column?* I once more insisted that I wasn't free to comment on the case. We rode in silence for the next few moments until my stop came up. When I stood and exited the trolley, she followed.

"It won't do any good," I said, barely turning as she caught up with my hurried strides.

"What if I just tag along and use you as one of my feature stories? You know, 'Bounding About with Dr. Bones while Bumping on the Rothschild—I mean the Wanderin' Wildcat." She sighed. "Alliteration, it's the bane of journalists."

Too miffed by her persistence to chuckle, I continued walking and shrugged. Methuselah had informed me that The Wanderin' Wildcat was called The Rothschild during the first four years of its existence in some perverted hippie, free-the-rich-from-their-money attempt at irony. "All right. Come along. I've got to teach class in eleven minutes. You can sit in, just don't fall asleep or use your cell phone or leave abruptly."

"I'll be a model student," she promised.

AND SHE WAS, SITTING in the back of the classroom, taking notes as I told the class they needed to separate political correctness and facts, because discernable and verifiable physical differences existed among the skeletal structures of Caucasians, Asians, Hispanics, and Blacks. "And males and females have the same number of ribs, so you can put the Bible aside for a bit, too," I added.

Every time that I went through this spiel, I expected some English major to accuse me of racism, or some wisenheimer jock to ask about the relative size of penises between black and white males. I always figured I'd quip, "I'm not sure, I'll have to do more personal research." But damned if a male student didn't finally ask that in this very class, the one, naturally, with a reporter sitting in the back, and damned if I didn't simply refer to my seating chart and reply, "There's no research backing that claim, Mr. Hardaway, but you're welcome to apply for a grant if the subject interests you personally."

Half the co-eds in the class gave me a grin and a close-chested thumbs-up.

"Nicely done, the penis bit," Ms. Bates beamed after class.

We were heading toward my office after I'd fended off the usual student questions about an upcoming test. Our secretary Mildred coughed as we walked by, so I stopped. Straight-backed as always, she gave Lauren Bates the eye and whispered that I had a visitor, "the double ponytail guy," as she called him. *Methusy*, as Ms. Bates called him.

Sure enough, when we entered the corridor to my office I saw him move from a display case of Dr. Tyler's arrowheads to do a double-take at Lauren and me strutting together. No doubt male fantasies of us both laying him in a tumbling lap dance atop my desk were forming in his mind, say, with Lauren tugging his long beard and me tugging his hippie days ponytail while he tugged his . . .

"Men," Lauren sighed, evidently also catching his look as we walked. "We really ought to do it to him. Put him through the ringer, the two of us. I've got half a roll of Scotch tape in my handbag, and surely you have paper clips and a stapler in your office. We could think of something kinky to do with the combination and that damned ponytail beard of his. Accessorize it."

I chortled, my mood having lifted after the penis question. But the moment was fleeting, for Methuselah evidently had beans to spill about the lap dance case, as Willy called our double-suicide. "I just got back from talking with Detective Cox," he said even as I was reaching for the keys to my office.

His statement threatened to reinstate my funk. One week, and the two of them were already speaking. I doubted it would be so easy for Willy and me. It typically took us at least a month to get over an attitude.

"I found the remains of a ropewalk on the land."

"A what?"

"Ropewalk," Lauren interrupted. "You're obviously new to Kentucky and our marijuana controversy. Ropewalks were long, skinny sheds where lengths of hemp were wound into rope to save our fighting boys in all kinds of wars."

"Fine." I unlocked my office and headed for the coffee pot. Caffeine was a habit I'd picked up from Willy, detective extraordinaire, playboy ordinaire. Before him, I'd stuck with sugar-free hot chocolate on late night- and early morning digs. Fortunately, so far at least, I'd been able to avoid a donut addiction.

"What land?" I asked Methuselah while starting the coffee and watching Lauren make herself at home in a green velvet chair I'd picked up at a garage sale.

"The lap dance land."

To keep Methuselah quiet, I moved my eyes heavily toward Ms. Bates, but he just gave his beard a thrice-through with his hands and continued blithely:

"And that's not all. On the ropewalk's floor I found a Kentucky agate in the form of a cabochon, and guess what it fit?"

"A what in the form of a what?" I asked.

"Kentucky agates are prehistoric stones, minerals. A cabochon is a cut, something like a knight's shield."

This from Ms. Bates. I really wished that she and Methuselah would swap encyclopedic knowledge somewhere more fitting, say, over at the library.

"A knight's shield. Well, that's great," I said. The coffee began to perk. "Did you find any suits of armor or broken lances, Methus . . . y?" I couldn't resist. Giving a quick glance to Ms. Bates, he blushed straight through his fifty-five-year-old wrinkles. This is what I get for sleeping with someone almost old enough to be my father: scarlet crevasses. Just then, a bug-eyed student peeked in and wanted to know if he'd missed anything in class.

"We had a pop quiz," I replied.

When his eyes bugged even more Ms. Bates suppressed a giggle, knowing damned well we'd had no such thing, that it had been straight lecture, excepting the question about penis length.

"Was it worth much?"

"A quarter of your grade."

"Really?!" His larynx started bobbing.

"Not. We went over what we were supposed to go over on the syllabus: race identity and bone structure. You can get notes from someone." Undergraduates typically represent a slower sub-species of human, and sure enough the kid didn't take the get-notes-from-someone hint, but stood unmoved, as if maybe I'd Xerox my lecture for him, or maybe loan him both my textbook and PowerPoint for a week or so. Or maybe just drop everything, chase my visitors out, and re-deliver the entire lecture while he sat on my lap and drank a Budweiser and played air guitar. But bless Methuselah, he leaned toward the pale lad in his most creepy Methuselah fashion and tugged his two-foot long beard to intone,

"Young man, we're discussing a recent double murder. On the cliffs, along the Kentucky river. A male, just your age. And his girlfriend. College students. From this very University. Mangled. Rats and blowflies fed on them for months. Half his jaw was missing."

The kid skittered away.

"Good job, Methuselah," I chortled. "You get a buss on the cheek." I gave him one.

"Murder? I thought it was a suicide," Ms. Bates said.

"Well yeah, I—"

"Look, you two, I started this morning out late, so murder or suicide, cabochon or no cabochon, I've got another class in an hour and a half, plus paper work for the lab. Can't this all wait until tomorrow, for instance?"

"That's when Detective Cox wants to go out there."

"And *I'm* invited?" I asked, flabbergasted.

"He told me to come ask you. That's really why I'm here." Methuselah shrugged and poured himself a cup of coffee from the pot that wasn't finished brewing. It's my pet peeve when people do that to give themselves a cup strong as a bull, leaving everyone else three cups of hot semi-tea after brewing. Willy does the same thing. Maybe it's a male trait.

"What about me?" Ms. Bates asked, her voice husky again.

"You mean coffee?" Methuselah lifted his cup in a mock toast.

"You know damned well what I mean, Methusy."

"Take it up with the lieutenant."

"I'll do just that." And she got up and left, her heels clicking purposefully down the hall.

"Do you want another buss on the cheek, Methuselah?"

"I'd rather have one on the lips."

"That's gotten us in enough hot water already."

But he'd already closed my office door and was leaning against it tugging at his beard and smiling, so I thought, *What the hell. It's summer semester, my class notes are already written, and Willy can't get any madder.*

"What did the damned carbuncle you found fit, by the way?" I asked as Methuselah's beard tickled my cheek.

"The toe ring that the dead woman was wearing."

"Um," I replied, giving his beard a tug.

ON THE NEXT DAY after a brief lunchtime faculty meeting—something the cultural side of the department enjoyed in a ghoulish way, always wanting to hear what morbid messes the other physical anthropologist and I had gotten into lately—I was free. That meant that the four of us were heading to the river by 1:30, with Lauren and me sitting in the back, the boys up front. Cuban style, as a Tennessee friend always commented.

Oh yes, Lauren had gotten *her* way with Willy of the Wandering Ways. As soon as I spotted her waiting by his car I didn't feel so guilty about Methuselah in my office. But that was just rationalization, for on the ride over she emitted more of a mother/big sister attitude toward Willy than anything romantic or sexual. And he, no doubt, was pumping the journalist for puzzle pieces to this and every other case he was working on, most notably the eight ritually murdered bodies we'd found over a year ago.

If the drive over was hot because of four passengers in a compact car with a bum air-conditioner, the stroll down the hill toward the river made for a steam bath. We didn't go to the cabin; instead, we walked down a winding and steep slope to the bare remains of a shed the three of them kept calling a "ropewalk." Just last week after Methuselah found the two skeletons, the cops cut short their reconnaissance after one got bitten by a copperhead. So Methuselah bought some fancy thick boots, intent on finding the diary. What he'd found was the mysterious ropewalk. Now on the way there, we passed a dozen marijuana plants; I was certain it was marijuana because I'm a big girl with a PhD in forensic anthropology, but I would've suspected something even if my degree'd been in philosophy or math just from the way Methuselah's and Lauren's noses kept sniffing in tandem.

"I'm pretending I don't see all this shit," Willy said at last. "I mean, you're talking about buying this property because of the ropewalk, right, Methuselah?"

"Well, this shit's part of the point, isn't it?" Methuselah countered.

"There's not enough here for a commercial crop—unless there's more elsewhere," Lauren offered.

"Right. But how much was here two years ago if this much is still growing volunteer? I mean, could that be the reason behind those two bodies?"

We all four stopped as Willy surveyed the land leading down to the river. Like I said, it turned awfully steep, but also awfully dense, hence the copperhead. The previous afternoon I'd done some research about rope and hemp, which means that I asked a graduate student. One reason that Kentucky raised and produced so much hemp for our sailors was its muggy summers. Another was its abundant river bottom. And if you can grow hemp for rope, you can grow marijuana for dope. That rhyme courtesy of my three years as an English major, thank you.

The three of us joined Willy in studying the steep slope. I freely admit that I couldn't see a thing except sunshine harshly reflecting off the river. I put on my sunglasses, expecting maybe one of the Presidential Bushes to flash by in a thundering cigar boat, followed by an entourage of Secret Servicemen. Please, please tell me that this family isn't in line to replace the Kennedy clan as our faux royal family.

I watched Willy's shoulders: he was rolling them to work out a kink in his neck. I reached to offer a massage but stopped short, remembering we were on the outs. Besides, his shoulder dance might have been an "I'm thinking" movement, not an un-kinking movement. Ow, more rhyme, sorry. Anyway, when Willy thinks, it's metaphorically possible to hear wheels ticking and it's literally possible to hear muscles tightening bones. He spent a minute or so staring until an orange and black Monarch butterfly weaved through the damp air. Then he grunted, looking at me to make sure I saw it. Since he'd momentarily forgotten he was mad at me, I touched his wrist and pointed out two more marijuana plants. He grunted again, which I took to mean that he remembered he was mad at me.

"Drug assassinations are usually pretty efficient affairs," I said to no one in general. This was true: a bullet to the back of the skull and either a shallow grave or chopped body parts spread along interstate highways. That M. O. fits the murder of any drug dealer who's slipped up. So the lap dance deaths didn't fit. Too complicated. And as I looked around I really couldn't imagine more than three or four dozen plants surviving willy-nilly harvesters, being so close to a river where boaters and skiers were constantly traveling. It was miracle enough that the bodies in the cabin hadn't been discovered, despite that the cabin was covered up to its roof with vines, despite copperheads, rattlers, and moccasins. So I became convinced that drugs didn't play a part at all, that it was a bizarre lovers' suicide. Hell, all lover's suicides are bizarre. Hell, all lovers are bizarre. Willy's shoulders kept rolling, his wheels kept whirring, speaking of bizarre.

Now, spring and early summer can push a forensic anthropologist into the weeds quicker than a New York minute for two reasons: the ground is thawing from buckling winter freezes, and people are anxious to get out into the warm weather. The year before this one we'd had sixteen cases by this month. Admittedly, that number had swollen when a surveyor found a skull and the skull subsequently exposed a mass burial site containing eight skeletons, six of which we still kept stored for identification. So far this spring, my lab held only the lap dance couple, a college coed who'd been found inside an abandoned freezer, and a backwoods, shallow grave drug assassination carried out just as I said: a single bullet to the back of the skull. In other words, we were running light. I kept waiting for another shoe to fall.

So my mind forebode when Willy gave up searching for whatever slinky link or inspiration he was searching for and we fought our way through weeds and briars to the "ropewalk," which consisted of four rough-hewn log walls leaning into one another just waiting for time to be done with them. Supposedly, Methuselah had cleared this all with a machete three days before. Tell that to the scratches on my face and arms.

"That cabochon thing, Methuselah," I said. I'd been getting into the "Methusy" nickname all day in my office the day before, but here in front of Willy, using it wouldn't come off too jolly.

"Yeah?" he asked. "There it is, see?" He meant the ropewalk.

"You said it fit something, but you never said what." As soon as I spoke, I remembered what he'd said. At the same moment I remembered why I'd forgotten, that is, our being amorous in my office.

"Her toe ring."

We reached what was left of the structure. Methuselah poked at two logs with his walking stick. A red wasp flew out at him and he swatted at it and backed off.

"Leave them alone, Methuselah. They're part of God's plan: you leave them alone and they leave you alone. Do unto others, et cetera. Didn't your son Noah and his Ark teach you that?" Willy commented.

"Noah wasn't his son," I said. "Was his five times great grandson."

"In your dreams, both of you," Methuselah replied nastily.

This ropewalk was about thirty meters long. A straight shot; we could see the back entrance and the front. The roof had all but fallen. My understanding of these structures via my graduate student was that workers would entwine eight- to twelve-foot strands of hemp to form them into a rope. Pre-machinery, of course, which meant that this building was over a hundred-fifty years old, even given poor Southern standards of industrialization. Methuselah conjectured that a flood had covered it with mud, which preserved what was left, if I could use that term, since it was less than what had been left of the two lap dance skeletons. We stepped inside and could hear the hum of mud daubers on the timbers. Methuselah bent to the dirt floor and picked up what looked like another piece of jewelry, but it was just a striped river pebble, which nonetheless launched a speech as he rolled it importantly between his thumb and fingers:

"After the Civil War there was these fellers from Kentucky—"

"Fellers?" Willy groaned.

"Oh, give him his melodrama." Lauren walked over and tugged Methuselah's beard. Since I'd met him last year it had grown several inches and he now kept three yellow hair bands binding it into a ponytail. I found myself hoping that Lauren and her perfume and mascara would re-entangle with Methuselah and his beard. Get me off the hook for my grievous mistake. Mistakes, plural, counting yesterday. Methusy wasn't my type. Willy, oh yes, Willy was.

"Thank you, Lauren," he said, touching her cheek. "At least someone respects dignity."

Even as Methuselah gave us a hurt sniffle, Willy and I simultaneously rolled our eyes at one another. So we were on our way to making up. Maybe everything, including the Lap Dance Case, was resolving.

"Fellers," I said prompting Methuselah to continue. He blinked and smiled wickedly.

"There were these two fellers from Kentucky named Slack and Arnold who deposited a sack of precious gems in a San Francisco assay office after one of the gold rushes. Then they just vanished like the smart country cousins they were. The bank president tracked them down, planning to work a con on the Kentucky bumpkins to swindle them out of their claim." Methuselah gave us all a grin. "But the real con came from the bumpkins. They took a blindfolded scout sent from this bank president out and showed him anthills filled with precious stones. The scout reported back to the president and a syndicate—you'll like this, Lauren—a syndicate who represented folks such as the Union Army's General McLellan and Europe's Rothschild family. All of them were taken for the tune of over half a million in post-Civil War money. About twenty million today. You see, the anthills were filled with precious stones because the cousins, Slack and Arnold, had seeded them."

"Rothschild, just like we used to call the Wanderin' Wildcat," Lauren commented. "That's a funny story, Methusy; what made you think of it?"

Methuselah tugged his beard. I watched for strands of hair breaking or entwining like rope but was distracted by a boat approaching on the river below us. I could, however, smell rotting wood from a nearby fallen tree. Yep. Yep, I thought, just as surely as there are larvae in that tree trunk, some rotting but connecting strand of beard—like DNA gone berserk—was about to insert its terwilliping self into Methuselah's terwilliping tale. Willy, he was leaning forward in expectation, almost heaving. I closed my eyes and inhaled the smell of rotting wood. These strands of entwining evidence, they're better than sex, aren't they Willy, I wanted to comment. Instead I spied a three-foot section of the skinny table they once used to form the rope still standing because of its thick ironwork support, and I walked toward it. Behind me, I heard,

"Slack. The guitar player, that murdered girl; her middle name was Slack. A family name."

I touched the table and it fell, leaving me holding a sliver of dry, useless wood.

"I'm walking around in a large circle before I scream," I announced.

"It could happen," Willy almost shouted. "There could be a connection!" His yelp sent a rat scurrying. No doubt it was toting a mouthful of Slack family semi-precious stones from under the ropewalk's foundation.

I stepped over a breech in the wall. Could Willy really think that there might be a connection between two Kentucky con artist cousins from a hundred and thirty years ago and the murder of the Kentucky guitar performance major and her dwork CD-selling lover from two years ago? Could he? Do rivers flow? Do Kentucky basketball fans always think that next year will be the championship year? Are pickles sour? The ones that aren't sweet, that is? Of course, of course. So let me guess. What was the other cousin's name . . . Rothschild? No that was the name of the trolley and an ultra-rich European family of arms manufacturers and wine makers. McLellan? No, he was a Civil War general. Well, whatever the second cousin's name, it would likely be the name of the CD store where the dwork worked. Or at the very least that store would have sold a CD by a band named after the cousin. The Slackards. The Slackerds. The Slackurds. Didn't matter how it was spelled; it would be an indispensable clue.

I looked at the sky through the trees. Sweat was sheeting off my neck and arms. A fly landed for a taste and I swatted it. Behind, I heard Lauren's sharp laugh. She must have found Willy's and Methuselah's ever-growing lame connections amusing. I usually did too, but there'd been some odd thing haunting the air since last month when I'd gone with the police and Methuselah to a room rented by a woman I'd dubbed *Petite Artiste*. We'd sifted through her paintings and sketches, but came up with no clue to her whereabouts. She'd been on and off sketching and painting my rental house since I moved in well over a year ago, and she'd evidently been a lesbian lover to one of the women whose bodies had lain in that mass gravesite. When I confronted her with a reconstructed death mask of the girl she'd flipped out. I guess you could say I had a connection to the Petite Artiste just like Slack had a connection to the dead guitarist. Connections, spidering through the hot and humid Ohio Valley air to render it evermore repressive.

With that thought and Lauren's laughter still ringing, I trudged up the hill, picking up a stick to whack the bushes and scare off the snakes. I'd been at it about ten minutes when I caught a blur to my left: two hummingbirds circling erratically. They were feeding off a wild honeysuckle vine. Then I spotted three gravestones.

Family plots are common in Kentucky just as they are in Tennessee and all the rural North and South, though they're usually not situated on the side of a river since the EPA would no doubt frown on the possible water contamination. When I closed in, I could count five headstones altogether. Rubbing my hands over one I saw they were old enough for their contents not to concern me professionally. I bent to read the one my fingers ran along: *Arnold.*

Crap. *That* was the second cousin's name in Methusy's goofball story. I read three more. *Arnold, Arnold, Arnold.* I just knew that the fifth headstone closest to the fragrant honeysuckle would read *Slack*, as in Give me some, Lord.

THOUGH I WAS WRONG about the fifth tombstone—it read Arnold too—I was correct about the oppressive feeling and the other shoe falling. About a month later, in mid-June, a woman's corpse was discovered under a ledge by church picnickers. It was the Petite Artiste. And when the July Fourth holiday was just starting, the lap dance case took a huge back seat, for her murderer wound up at my house, and I wound up pumping eight of thirteen nine-millimeter rounds into him as he tried to rape me in my bedroom. Dr. Keifer, the psychiatrist I rented from, was sweet as sweet could be, not only understanding my need to move but helping me financially with relocation, then offering counseling under the guise of friendship. Or friendship under the guise of counseling. She suggested that I attend a victim support group because of the rape attempt, but in my cynicism I judged that my No One Ever Touches Anyone theorem would play too prominent a role in any group, especially one named "support." So I declined. Besides, Willy and Methuselah dropped their jealousy acts and became ultra-supportive. And Mildred, my faux mother, was supportive. My real mother had gotten herself a real job in Knoxville and a boyfriend to boot, but still, she was supportive. My department chairman was supportive, my students were supportive, my neighbors, old and new, were supportive. Hell, even Dr. Bug, my friendly campus entomologist who had troubles of his own, was supportive.

But there remained the matter of my dad, whom I'd flashed on when the creep was trying to rape me. Why should I remember Dad at a point like that? So all summer long I walked the streets of Lexington like a bag lady on amphetamines and let memories of Dad worry me while I let my friends support me.

Now, months later, in October, supportive Willy suggested getting out of the city and visiting the spectacular autumn leaves. So we returned to the river, driving to the land Methuselah indeed had wound up buying, wanting to restore the ropewalk, supposedly the only one left in Kentucky. Methuselah had found evidence in the form of tax records and bills to indicate that the ropewalk had been used the first year of the Civil War until Northern machinery completely superseded it.

"Bless his historical bones, he's actually done manual labor on this, hasn't he, Willy?" I said when we reached the structure, which could cast true shadows now.

"Manual labor meets Methuselah. Wonders never cease."

We stared at the newly hand-hewn logs that formed the walls. Methuselah had gotten volunteers from Eastern Kentucky University to help with the restoration. All that remained was to finish the low roof and to restore the actual table, the last scrap of which I'd sent to its maker in May. The original table would have been only a bit over a foot wide and would have wound through the room in the shape of a squished S. Methuselah assured us that this design was unusual for a ropewalk: most tables were made in a concentric circle or were simply straight in hugely long buildings without walls. Willy and I walked around, admiring the restoration. The smell of lumber filled my lungs and I felt better than I had since . . . since the jackass tried to rape me over three months back.

During May, Methuselah and Willy had—of course—discovered the Arnold family graves up the hill where I'd stumbled on them before that hell at my house broke loose. Though there hadn't been a Slack grave in the plot, Willy and Methuselah kept scouring for one all summer, Methuselah getting himself stung by a slew of hornets in the process. What Willy and Methuselah missed with the Slack name on a tombstone they made up elsewhere, for Methuselah not only discovered the old coot's World War I diaries buried in a metal box near the ropewalk, but learned from them that the old coot had trained at Fort McClellan in Louisville. Wait. Hold on. Are you getting lost in all this magnificent information? Well. Remember how General McClellan of the Grand Union Army invested money in Mssrs. Arnold's and Slack's precious stone scam out in far western anthills? Well,

Fort *McClellan* in Louisville is where this World War I vet trained, get it? And there's more, oh yes: a cave on this property held a lode of Kentucky agates. Semi-precious stones, like Messrs. Arnold and Slack used in their scam, get it? How all this semi-ancient history would fit with the double-suicide of a classical guitarist and her dud music shop boyfriend, how it would fit with seventeen dilapidated acres containing twenty-three hemp plants that might indicate a marijuana crop, and how it would fit with a collapsing ropewalk, a teetering cabin, and a toe ring made of . . . carbuncle? . . . no, of cabochon—well, Willy and Methuselah had yet to figure *that* out. But they would. Ariadne with her golden thread had nothing on them.

"Let's go up to the cabin," I said, glancing back at the river and grabbing Willy's elbow. Some leaves were turning deep purple and orange and red already. Because of the river? That didn't make sense.

"Do you think you . . . we should? The chair's still there, Clarity."

I shrugged. After all, throughout the summer I'd steamed off and identified eleven corpses from the surrounding counties, not counting the poor woman whom I called the Petite Artiste, the one who led her murderer to my house. So what problem would a flimsy chair present?

I arrived steps ahead of Willy—no surprise, because I'd turned into a walking fool the entire summer, cramping my friends' calves and tendons just like I was Plato running a peripatetic philosophy camp. It had only been three weeks into the fall semester that I'd . . . ahem . . . slacked up.

Willy stopped below and stared up at me as I urged him on. Wiping sweat from his brow he laughed. The river wasn't visible from the cabin, but a breeze shifted and yellow autumn leaves cascaded. Willy sneezed with fall hay fever. I, on the other hand, inhaled, thinking myself cured. Trauma over, done, forgotten, let's trot on through life's peripatetic path, right? Right. No problem, lady bean.

Willy struggled up the last few steps, slipping a bit, and the heroine named *I* hurried down to steady him. "This excursion has really worked, Willy. I mean bringing me out here to see the leaves and the river and Methuselah's ropewalk and all. Maybe we should volunteer to help him."

Willy grunted.

Under a bush by the cabin's door lay a scrap of yellow police tape that

Methuselah had overlooked. Willy picked it up and pocketed it.

"A guy killed himself out in New Mexico," he said, fist still bulging in his pocket. Speaking of bulging, can you believe that Willy and I had not done the beast with two backs all summer? I knew this was killing him, and I kept apologizing, apologizing, apologizing. But I just couldn't get past putting my head on Willy's bony shoulder or lightly kissing his sweet thin lips without envisioning and feeling that damned asshole murderer trying to poke his prick into me goat-style. And I couldn't get past flashing on my father, either. So my rushing to grab Willy's elbow and tug him up, that boded well, didn't it?

"Hear me, Clarity? A guy killed himself in New Mexico, south of Santa Fe and the university there."

"Yeah?"

"Broke into a bar at three a.m., wrapped a blue bra around his neck, propped a crucifix on the table in front of him, leaned it against a big hornet's nest, then stuck a colt revolver in his mouth and pulled the trigger. Wham. He'd had lunch with his boss that day—jalapeño sardines. He seemed fine, his boss said."

Willy had stepped into the cabin after his news info bit and stooped to look at the chair where the couple had committed suicide. Hearing him scratch his fingernail along the white paint, I was afraid he was going to scrape off a layer and discover a new color and somehow connect that New Mexico story with this Kentucky one, maybe the blue bra. Robin's egg blue? I tiptoed to see, but there was only white. At least the bra hadn't been Kentucky cardinal red. At least the jalapeño sardines hadn't been freshwater carp from Lake Herrington. Giving up on the paint, Willy bent on impulse to look under the chair. No, it wasn't impulse: it was pure Willy: check out everything 'cause everything's connected to everything, everywhere and everyhow. By the way, Willy wasn't assigned as star investigator in this still open case. For some reason—Willy claimed it was because the crime scene lay by the river—Captain, oh excuse me, Major Jackson bumped Willy so Captain—excuse me, Major Jackson could personally investigate this case, bringing out his pack of hounds, which tore up vegetation and small trees along the hillside. The uptake is that one dog drowned in the river, though none had been bitten by snakes. One down, eleven to go. You think that's crude? Are you thinking of anonymously calling the SPCA on me? Then you haven't worked with Jackson and his corpse-mutilating hounds.

Anyway, we couldn't pick up the chair, because it had been bolted to the floor, which is why the couple didn't tilt it over in their death throes, which was why their kooky suicide plan worked.

Now Willy moved from his knees to his belly. When he yanked a small wasp nest from under the chair, I thought of the New Mexico hornet's nest the guy'd propped in front of him before blowing out his brains. Lord. Blue paint would have been better.

"Willy, please . . . you're not going to make a connection—"

"Relax, Clarity. My point is that all that stuff meant something to the New Mexico guy. He was a draftsman for an architecture firm. He didn't leave a note, but the right person could fit it all together, I bet, just like a blueprint. Hey, wait." Willy's legs kicked out, raising dust. "Come here, Clarity, and look at this."

I did as he asked, bending down on the opposite side of the chair, but he directed me to come to his side and look with the light striking against the chair's underside. I did, feeling his warmth next to me, feeling the cool wood floor underneath. Soon, I told myself, soon it will be like it used to be: Willy's wonderful tan butt next to mine, his wonderful muscles enveloping me . . . and no intruding memories. I blinked and smelled dust on the floor before speaking:

"Is it writing?" Whatever was under the chair looked the dirty brown of long-dried blood, and it looked to be outlining what appeared to be "Nt Dny," with what could have been other letters or hieroglyphics surrounding those jumbled letters. I flipped on my back. Well, maybe an *e*, or maybe an *o*. Maybe another *e*, about an inch above. Maybe a second *n*? Or an incomplete *o*?

"*Not . . . not Denny*, do you think?"

The guy who'd killed himself along with the classical guitar player—Alicia was her name—was named Denny. Willy crowded next to me, scooting me out of the way to let in more light. I scooted him back. And with my new angle and the light, I could see it for sure:

"*Not Denny.* That's it. *Not Denny.* Willy, I have an idea. Come on. Get up and sit on the chair." I twisted about and shook his shoulder. Our noses were nearly touching as we lay on the floor. I could smell coffee on his breath, warm coffee, warm breath, and the cool floor.

"Why?" he said, stifling a sneeze.

"Because I'm going to sit in your lap and see whether I could reach down and scratch this in. What fingernails we found from her right hand were broken, remember? We just assumed that came from belatedly trying to free herself and lover boy. Maybe it was from scratching in this message." I looked to where the guitar had stood, propped in a corner. "She was a classical guitarist, wasn't she? They grow their nails long on their right hand, don't they?"

His cheek moved along the floor in a nod. I loved those caramel eyes of his.

The guitar had been a deep maroon; it had somehow weathered most of the two years' worth of seasons and stayed beautiful, even with four of its six strings popped from temperature changes inside the cabin. The keys to the handcuffs had bounced off it, leaving two dents, which I'd thought odd—for someone who loved guitar music, I mean, to throw metal at an expensive guitar. We'd been told it was a Hill Guitar worth several thousand. Next to the guitar had lain what was left of their clothes. Mice had used them for nest-making.

"Come on," I said, standing and looking down at Willy. "Let's see if she could possibly have reached down and dug this message in with her nails."

He stood but balked. "Clarity, this isn't a good idea."

"Come on, Willy. It's sunny outside. I can hear bees and birds. I'm okay; I'm over it. Just don't sneeze on me, all right?" I tried to giggle like a sorority girl, but it came out a squeak.

With a grimace and a shrug Willy glanced into my eyes. I nodded abruptly, urging him on, so he sat in the chair.

"Hold both of your hands against the supports." I reminded him how the guy's hands had been cuffed to the chair.

He did, and I started to sit down.

"Clarity. Whoa, whoa. You really think this is a good idea? You sitting on me like this, in here?"

Let me confess: I hate it when a man is smarter than I am. It wasn't a good idea. It was a rotten idea. It was a suck idea. It was a bozo idea. It was a trainwreck idea.

Nonetheless, in my surety and wisdom I sat and pushed my face into Willy's because the two lovers had been duct-taped together nose to nose, mouth to mouth in some exasperating comment on eternal love in the face of death. Moving my right hand under the chair I shuffled my nails—sure, I decided, if I had real nails I could scratch in all that stuff—given time. And Alicia had plenty of time, for it likely took her seven days or so to die of dehydration.

Scritch, scratch, scritch, I pretended, feeling the grooves that I was suddenly sure that Alicia had dug with her nails. Meanwhile, Willy, God bless his deprived male hormones, got a hard-on with us so nose-to-nose and lap-to-lap, and his hard-on poked me.

I screamed.

I screamed.

I screamed.

NEXT EVENING, I WAS in the victim support group.

It went like I expected: for the most part group members were either into the voyeuristic aspects of my ordeal or looking for some way to twist matters back to themselves. With hindsight, I suppose that's the whole point. I mean the victim babbling details and the group comparing and commiserating. But babbling didn't work for me, not then. So, after three weeks I just sat on a stuffed chair and listened at each meeting, thinking that listening might do me some good for once in my life. Shut up, Professor; you lecture enough as it is.

In mid-December, something pertinent to the Lap Dance suicides happened. A new victim—she was mugged and robbed outside a bar—started attending group and she mentioned during our second meeting that one of her ex-lovers had wanted to commit a double suicide by tying her and him to one another in the sex act and starving while they humped and listened to an endless loop of jazz. I pointed out that they would have died of thirst, not starvation. My "mundane" observation was not particularly welcomed, since everyone wanted lurid details from this new victim—ropes? Handcuffs?

Air-conditioning? Wearing make-up and perfume? No cigarettes? No coffee?

"Dehydration wouldn't have been mundane when she was dying," I pointed out. Then someone got on the subject of autoeroticism and hanging, ignoring the girl's need to clear the air. (See my above comment about a lack of support versus a wealth of self-interest.) Autoerotic suicides, I fear, are also rather mundane when you're the investigator. Kentucky and Tennessee each average about three cases per year; Florida hauls in over thirty. No other comment on the land of Mickey Mouse is needed. Hollywood probably has a thousand.

The woman, in her late twenties, approached me after the meeting:

"You teach at UK, don't you?"

She was tall, nearly six feet, and had a hound-dog face with lazy brown eyes, and some of the longest fingers and legs I'd ever seen. Her skeleton would be a snap to identify. If you think that's a weird observation, I know an oncology nurse who's always appraising the veins on people's arms and hands, gauging how easy a needle stick they'd be. Try that on for weird.

"Yes," I answered. "I teach forensic and physical anthropology there. That's how I know about the timing of death by dehydration."

"I'm a music major. Classical guitar."

You can bet this made bat wings flap in my belfry. And my name isn't even Willy.

Since a light snow had fallen, it was bright in the parking lot under all the safety lights. We were standing by the church building that the support group met in, and heat from an opening door suddenly pushed on my back. I turned and a woman whom I took to be an assistant preacher nodded at us, then re-closed the door and locked it. The young woman I'd been talking with lit a cigarette and apologized, saying that she'd started smoking the day after her ex asked her to commit to the suicidal lap dance.

"You know, really, that was more traumatizing than the mugging. The kid just grabbed my purse and spun me around and I fell on gravel. Technically, he never laid a hand on me."

"You're a music major," I said after getting upwind of the smoke. I wanted to move her back on track. She looked at her cigarette, mistaking my intent for an accusation.

"Yeah, but it's not like I need my voice in classical guitar. My teacher claims the smoke's going to ingrain into my guitar, but he's making that up. Django Reinhart smoked like a gypsy campfire and played like a gypsy fiend. Smoking never hurt his guitar."

"Does your—did your ex-lover play guitar, too?"

The parking lot was emptying. One guy who'd especially been interested in the mechanics of the double-suicide drove by with his window rolled down and pointedly waved at the student. She vaguely waved back and moved closer to me.

"Don't start dating him," I suggested.

"Yeah," she said. "No kidding."

We watched the cars trail out of the parking lot, both of us hanging around one another for some real conversation after the support group fiasco.

"My old boyfriend was—still is, I guess—a supervisor in the financial department of LexMax. He told me it was the most boring job he'd ever had, that he'd rather manage a record shop. He could have, too, because he knew more about music than most music majors. That's what attracted us. We met at a concert. I play classical guitar but I'm nuts over jazz, too."

"What was his name?" I asked.

"Paul Truelove."

She inhaled her cigarette and it glowed. I inhaled icy air and I glowed. Denny Truelove was the one who'd killed himself with the lap dance. Paul Truelove, I'm pretty sure, was his twin brother. I didn't tell her this, figuring she had enough problems already.

Her name was Callie. We drove to a coffee shop, where we stared at snowflakes, hoping they were a passing fancy, and chatted and promised to sit next to one another for the next support session, though I told her I was likely going to slack off once spring classes started. She was, too, she said.

"How long ago did Paul—your ex-boyfriend—suggest all this suicide business?" I asked as I paid our bill, insisting on picking up the tab since she was a student.

"It was the fifth of June, a Saturday. I was robbed three weeks ago, right after Thanksgiving."

"How long did you two date?"

"Well, not at all after that, even though he told me that it just jumped into his mind because of his brother who'd disappeared two years before, which didn't make any sense at all to me. He tried to call me all summer, and sent flowers by a florist and CDs by mail. One of them was the song he'd said we should listen to when we committed suicide." She laughed quietly and shook her head, indicating her disbelief of it all.

"And the song was?"

"'Asturias de Leyenda.' Not jazz at all like I said back in the support group, but a classical guitar piece, the version played by Segovia. Paul heard me practicing it, I guess. My dad told me I should refuse everything from the creep—my dad's word, though I didn't disagree after consideration. I started sending everything back and Paul finally stopped."

"So, how long had you two dated, before he talked about the suicide deal, I mean."

"Not that long. We met in January at a jazz concert. So just about half a year."

"Did you know a student guitarist named Alice?"

She shook her head.

"Alicia, I mean."

"Oh, yeah, she was the one they found dead with some guy, isn't she? I didn't know her; I just got accepted into the program last year. Why?" Her brown eyes widened. "Is that how—"

"No," I lied.

I lied because the police had never given out any information beyond the double suicide. Methuselah had discovered the lap dance couple in early May. Was Paul Truelove—I was now pretty sure he was the twin brother—was he sharing empathy genes over his twin brother's death? Or was it something else? What else *could* it be? And then I wondered if the police ever released the circumstances of his brother's death even to him, to Paul, that is.

The next evening I dutifully reported what Callie said to Willy and Methuselah. They usually came to my office together the day after my support group in case I needed support, but this time we met at a private Christmas party for cops and their ilk. The weather had turned nasty icy on top of the previous night's snow.

"Weird," they both responded. "Who knows what lurks in the human mind," Willy added nonchalantly, for it turned out that Paul Truelove had been inadvertently told how his brother died by the notorious keeper of the hounds, Major Jackson.

"That's it? *Weird*? You two with your carbuncles and General McClellans and Slacks and Arnolds and toe rings and New Mexico suicides can only come up with *weird*?"

"Well?" they asked, ganging up on me.

"We'll see," I said.

The party was being held at a fairly new place called Adam's Ribs out on Nicholasville Road. About an hour later I caught wind that there was a pot starting on which one I'd go home with, Willy or Methuselah. I spotted—well I heard—Lauren Bates give a throaty laugh by one of the fireplaces, and right away I knew she was behind the pot. I'd fix that little game. Screw her.

"You both want to go to my house? I'm getting tipsy and it's a long drive back to town with the roads as lousy as they are. I've got some Maker's Mark."

MY MOTHER CALLED TWO days before New Year's. Knoxville had gotten a blanket of snow; we'd gotten sleet and rain.

"Your father wrote," she said.

That left me staring out the window at barren winter trees.

"He said he found my name in one of those computer searches. He said he'd read about you solving that murder mystery up in Simms County. On that Indian mound."

"That was three years ago, Mom." It was nearly four, actually.

"I know, hon. He sent a CD. He's in a country band, playing guitar and fiddle in Texas honky-tonks."

"Is the CD any good?"

"Well, he's not Willie Nelson." She sighed. "He said to 'tell his Larissa that he's sorry.' He wrote some other morbid stuff about how if you ever found his body you could identify it through the calluses on his left hand's fingertips from playing the guitar and fiddle."

"That's it?"

"It's more than I expected. He didn't give any return address. You want the CD?"

"Use it for a Frisbee. Dwayne's got a retriever, doesn't he?" Dwayne was her new boyfriend. "What's he sorry for?" I asked on impulse, immediately regretting my mouth.

There was silence. "Well, you know . . . leaving."

"That's it?" I said again.

"It's more than I expected. We're having a repeat conversation, Clare." Clare, Larissa, Clarity, See-See Bones, the Goddess of Bones. Sometimes I felt like a heroine in a Russian novel with my multiplicity of names.

The support group met that night. I drank coffee and stared at everyone. Callie and I walked out together again, and she lit up another cigarette. I'd carried my own Thermos of coffee with me this time, since whoever brewed the church's coffee was thinking in terms of Betty Crocker and tea. Willy's influence again.

"He called me," Callie said, blowing out a mixture of smoke and vapor.

"The creep in the green shirt?" That was the guy who'd rolled down his window and eyeballed her for the past three group meetings. Even as we spoke he was standing beside his car in the cold, hitting on some other woman in the group. The trouble was with that word "hitting." It seemed likely to turn literal.

"No, Paul. He said he was sorry about all the stuff he said. Said it was because they'd found the body of his twin brother who'd been missing for two years. That I shouldn't tell anyone about it, that I should forget it all."

I held up my coffee, and made up my mind. Callie was older than I first thought: in her late twenties, not that much younger than I was. So I figured we could bond, in support group parlance. "I got a phone call from my mother today. My father, who left us when I was eleven, wrote." I looked to the creep and the woman. She'd brushed him off and was starting her car. Good move, sister. I turned back to Callie. "You want to go for a drink?"

We went for more than one.

And I found out something even stranger than what I'd bargained for. Callie told me that Paul had never mentioned his twin brother until they were in the mall last spring at a CD shop and someone called him *Denny*.

Even to the point of insisting, calling him that. So Callie had learned that his twin brother had disappeared. And it soon came out that he and his brother used to play games like switching jobs for a couple of days. And they'd switched girls in high school and college. When Callie asked if they'd done it after college Paul said no, but he blushed and his answer caught in his throat, so she figured he was lying.

"I almost stopped dating him then," she said. "I mean, even if his brother had disappeared, any guy who'd do that on a regular basis, well, what could he think of the women he was dating?" She looked around the bar we were in, The Office Lounge, a skinny shotgun style affair with a single sick Christmas tree, one of those frosted snow affairs, glowing under a broken TV. We'd been getting some once-overs, but it was too early for anyone to make bolder moves and both of us planned to leave before that warlock hour arrived.

"Do you think that your dad . . ."

"My dad," I filled in after her pause continued for too long.

"Do you think he did something sexual to you?"

I must have looked angry or shocked, because she added, "I mean you said that you called out 'Daddy' when the guy was raping you."

"I said that?"

She nodded. She had such a hangdog face—pretty at times, especially when she smiled—that I could never suspect her of any dissimulation. And anyway, I probably *had* said that, since I'd done it. I took a drink of whiskey and grimaced.

"What I think, what I've concluded, is that he must have come home one night and put his hands all over me and scared himself to death, which is one reason why he left Mom and me." I bit my lip and looked back to the twinky white X-mas tree. "The other reason being that he was a worthless alcoholic." In memories I'd been getting whiffs of not so sweet whiskey breath in my face and rough hands on my tiny breasts, but were they real memories? I read all the time about psychologists implanting memories, so could a walking human trauma like the murderer who tried to rape me, implant them too?

After more talk about fathers and men in general, we eased back to

Paul and his dead twin brother. Something kept ringing odder and odder about their role-switching. Before we said so long to the Christmas tree, I arranged for Callie to meet Willy.

WILLY'D BEEN BUMPED OFF the case by the Captain become Major. The Major who'd not even bothered to look under the chair where the two lovers were handcuffed because he was so busy sunbathing by the river. The Major who was happy with my DNA results and the dental identification—well, I was too, I must admit—the only glitch being that the lower mandible had been likely carried off by a scavenger, and the last dental record we found for Denny came when he was eleven. Both twins had gone in for the appointment together. Their uppers matched perfectly, though Denny had two fillings in his lower. And the lower was precisely what was missing. But the Major didn't care about the case now that winter had arrived—there was no reason to visit a cold river with clouds hanging over it, right?

But Willy of the Wandering Ways was always interested in Capital T Truth, served cold or hot, cloudy or fair. So I asked him to ferret other details. Still, no later dental records for either twin were to be found, for Capital T Truth, ready money, hot summer showers or cold wintry storms.

"And we can't just ask Paul to pose for a dental X-ray. We still have habeas corpus and the fifth amendment."

"Unless you're Muslim," I commented, thinking of the detainees in Cuba and the United States during the September 11th aftermath. "You don't suppose that Paul converted—"

"Can it, Clarity." Willy, being a policeman, remained much more understanding of George Bush's civil un-liberties than I did. And maybe they were both right. Who knows? Detaining in the defense of freedom is no vice?

The two sets of fingerprints on the typewriter, a keepsake that once belonged to the twins' father, had matched the two latent sets in the used CD shop and in the apartment where the typewriter came from, Paul had informed the police. I reminded Willy that the brothers shared not only their apartment, but as Callie said, their jobs, on the sly. And sometimes their women too, I added, to raise Willy's eyebrows and get his gears moving. *Not*

Denny, I reminded him. *Murder,* I thought. *Murder*, I said. Late February and I was converted to that outlook.

Fingerprints had never been taken off the chair. Not, Willy insisted, terribly odd, since the chair was a mass of bones, dried skin, blood, and mouse scat. But he would have checked, I know. If both sets showed up there, we might have a case for murder and not suicide. You see, one of the twins had a half-centimeter longitudinal nick on his left index finger—which twin was the question, for the corpse's fingerprints were long gone. When Willy did check, only one set showed up—other than the murdered girl's of course. So which set was on the chair was the question that still remained the question.

I asked Callie to bring me something that might still have her ex-boyfriend's fingerprints on it. "That's easy," she said. "All the Jimmy Smith CDs he brought over and left. I haven't played them since we broke up. The jewel cases would still have his fingerprints, wouldn't they?"

They did. And they did. That is, they held both sets of prints, one with the nick and one without. But the twins couldn't have been having Callie on, because one of them had been dead for nearly two years. And the lab didn't feel confident enough to differentiate between the ages of the latent prints since the CDs had been in Callie's apartment for nearly half a year. Still, what was a supervisor in finance at a computer peripherals manufacturer doing with the collection Callie described of over one thousand CDs and about as many tapes and records?

I have to tell you that this all was very odd. I mean my wandering through this case in a whodunit way. It's always Willy doing that, or if not Willy, then Methuselah. Never me. "Never say never," a fifth grade teacher once told me. Just to contradict her, I'll never reveal her name, though she taught me right when I was undergoing puberty and menstruation—being the first in my class, for I'd started in the summer and was a pro at inserting tampons by September of that year. Fifth grade was when I turned eleven, was, in fact, when Daddy left Mom and me.

Back to my whodunit theory: Callie said that the surviving twin admitted he and his defunct brother used to surreptitiously swap girlfriends. What if swapping got out of hand? What if both brothers fell in love, but the girlfriend had no idea? Or maybe she did have an idea and left one for the other? And on top of that, what if the opportunity for a triple-fold raise presented itself at the same instant as revenge for faithless or unrequited love? Bottom feeders in retail don't bring in much money, after all. But a twin could never murder his twin in such a grisly manner—death by dehydration. Never say never. Consider: a man of the cloth preaching love of Christ could never murder upwards of twenty-four people, could he? That same man of the cloth could never murder a neurasthenic artist who whimpered every time she inadvertently stepped on an ant, could he? Never say never.

A father could never attempt sexual congress with his eleven-year-old blooded child, could he? Never say never.

No One Ever, Never, Ever Touches Any One.

I went into a two-day tailspin.

"Jesus, Clarity," was Willy's response.

And then both he and Methuselah went into tail-spins, Methuselah fine-combing the shack and the land around it and the ropewalk for evidence, Willy interviewing the surviving twin, people who'd known the dead MFA guitar candidate, and poor Callie, the living MFA guitar candidate. Interviewing, interviewing, interviewing. I finally interceded for her because her face was showing strain: "Willy, all that she's in the victim group for is a simple purse-snatching. She's starting to act as nuts as I was last summer. Lay off the questioning, would you?"

He sighed.

Spring started. Robins chirp-chirped, and trees burst into greenery. Willy and I were braving the outside after a rain, posing in front of the library as the model interracial couple for a campus and a country bogging into Christianity as a cover for hatred under the leadership of an oily Texan. Christ, as in the Jesus one, that same Christ unless I'm sorely mistaken, preached, "Love thy neighbor," not "Shun thy neighbor."

While Willy and I were on the ins, Methuselah and Lauren, modeling after the general climate, were on the outs. Callie, God forbid, had taken a romantic interest in Methuselah. But hey, even the winter/spring, old guy/young gal variety of love had to be better than sliding cruise missiles into people's high-rise windows.

"He did it," Willy said, flipping an acorn off the library steps we sat on.

I was going to make a quip about President Bush or Jesus Christ, even though I knew Willy was talking about Paul Truelove. All I did, though, was shift my chilled butt and say, "We all think he did it, Willy, but we can't find that lower mandible and the hen-scratching underneath that chair isn't going to prove anything beyond a reasonable doubt. If that."

"She's right. It really wouldn't do much even in civil court," our resident wannabe lawyer Methuselah said. We were supposed to meet him and Callie and he'd just walked out of the library. He was smart enough to remain standing and keep his butt off wet, cold concrete. He suddenly pointed,

"Look! A raccoon!"

It was. A raccoon in the middle of UK's campus, carrying something red. For a moment I imagined that red would be the clue we needed to convict Paul, aka Denny, Truelove of murder. Raccoons are known for hording, right? Maybe it was the lower mandible wrapped in a red bow as a belated Christmas present.

A shrill whistle sounded and the raccoon stopped and looked over its shoulder. A lank squire straight from the eastern hills strutted onto the scene and the raccoon clambered up his jeans to perch around his neck. The red was a rabies tag. The guy spotted us staring at him and waved.

"That's what I should do," Willy said. "Keep a kennel of ferrets and raccoons and set them loose on every crime scene before Jackson sets loose his damned dogs."

"He's surely not still doing that, is he?" Methuselah asked, eyeing a tall blonde coed carrying a guitar case. Callie, I realized.

"Not as much since the Goddess of Bones here had a talk with him." Willy rubbed my knee and two male students looked askance, their scowls disappearing when they saw it was me. Or did they spot the Glock under Willy's sport coat? Or did they think that Methuselah was an avatar of God the Father come down to preach interracial, interdenominational love? So many options, so little time.

I sighed. "You're never going to get an answer about Paul/Denny Truelove, are you, Willy?"

"I will. One way or the other, I will."

Callie spotted us and waved. A bounce lilted her step, and Methuselah shifted from foot to foot. Willy and I rolled our eyes in unison. Jealousy? Cynicism? So many springtime options, so little time.

Mom called on May 5th, the Monday after Derby Day, around lunch. I was dancing my professor act from stainless steel table to stainless steel table, testing students on bone identification. Mildred opened the lab door and interrupted, telling me to pick up in my office.

"Your father's dead," my mom said when I did. "I found out an hour ago. In Texas. A town called Lubbock."

"How?"

"Just how we always expected, Clarissa." And she broke down crying. Of course he'd been killed in a car wreck after wedding himself to a dried-out river gulley.

"I'm shipping the body home."

"Mom!"

"His mother's still alive. She'd want that."

My coffee pot let out a belch though I had to admire Mom's reasoning. After hanging up, I walked back to the lab and finished testing my students.

Willy drove me down to Tennessee for the funeral, his snotty macho boss saying they'd have to be giving family leave time to queers soon, so they might as well give it to girlfriends. The world can always hope Jackson's pack of dogs will get the wrong scent someday and head for his testicles.

The funeral was a non-event, though I did wind up with Dad's guitar, since one of the band members sent it, saying that Dad wanted me to have it. I didn't even want to travel the Freudian route on that one. Damn you, Lonnie Tom Circle. Damn you and your whiskey breath and your guitar-picking fingers.

"Whoa!" Callie commented when I showed her the guitar at my house. "A Gibson Hummingbird."

I looked at the plastic plate on the guitar and saw that, indeed, there was a hummingbird on it, the outline of one. "Is that good?"

"About five thousand dollars' worth. Or more."

She lifted it out of the case, tightened two strings and played a soft tune I recognized: "Blue Bayou." Dad had sung it on the CD Mom sent me, wisely ignoring my request to turn it into a Frisbee.

I shrugged. "You wanna buy it cheap? My dad's friend sent it collect, $275, saying Dad owed him some money."

Callie laughed, though I hadn't. "Not my style of guitar. Country twang. I could likely sell it for you, but don't you think that you . . ."

She stopped. From the look on my face it must have been clear that half of me wanted to bash the guitar with a hammer, half of me wanted to give it to the Salvation Army, and half of me wanted to take lessons until I could play "Blue Bayou" and every other Roy Orbison and Johnny Cash song there was. She handed me the guitar, showing me how to hold it.

"Why don't I give you some lessons? I actually started out playing rockabilly, you know. My granddad's influence."

So we sat for an hour at my kitchen table and I chased away the birds outside in the feeder with my playing. If I were ever going to write a self-help book, I'd title it, *One Step Forward, One Hop Back.* Or maybe, *Start Fretting and Stop Fretting.*

A few days later Callie led Willy and me to a guy who was sure that Paul Truelove was really Denny Truelove. Turns out that the guy worked at the CD shop and had been wise to the fact that Denny and Paul switched up, though he never let on. He said his mom had died of skin cancer so he always checked out people's moles. Denny, the supposedly dead twin, had a purple one on the back left side of his neck.

"Right here." He pointed to a place just behind and below his earlobe.

Callie blanched.

"That's why I was sure it was Denny, not his brother Paul."

I was fingering a Bjork CD. Willy claimed she missed a good chance of being Black, with a sultry voice like she's got. It was beginning to appear that Callie missed a good chance of being dead. What chance had I missed with my dad, Lonnie Tom Circle, the Tennessee Troubadour turned Texan?

Keep The River On Your Right stands as an important book in my life. A narrative anthropological study, its narrator was a homosexual Jew run off to Peru.—Look! Jew/Peru. Chance rhyme! So lean life takes on lean meaning.—Anyway, this gay Jew claimed, after eating the heart of a human enemy in Peru, "I am a cannibal, yes, but I am no savage."

"A cannibal, yes, but no savage." I never quite bought into that. Stepping from New York Hassidic to Peruvian cannibal to regain innocence? Lo, the noble cannibal? Is this what Denny Truelove believed, that he could duct tape himself to Callie in a morbid lap dance and thus regain innocence after he'd murdered his twin brother Paul and his ex-lover in the same fashion?

But that's conjecture, your honor. In the Daubert Case, handwriting experts were challenged in court. The challenge was overruled. In the Mitchell Case, fingerprint experts were similarly challenged. That challenge was also overruled. There'd been no Truelove Duct Tape Case, and we didn't come across any handwriting other than what had been scratched by a bloody fingernail underneath a bolted chair. And we had too many fingerprints—or not enough, depending on your view. We did have a small purple neck mole and a witness. We did have, somewhere I suppose, two lower teeth with fillings. But we also had a missing lower mandible, the Fifth Amendment, and habeas corpus, so those identifying fillings, presuming they did reside inside the living twin's mouth, were of no use. And that small purple mole? Geesh, even Hang 'em High Clint Eastwood wouldn't send someone to the chair with that as the only proof.

"He'll slip up," Willy said one evening. We were sitting on my porch staring at traffic, my new house's one drawback. I thought of the guy who'd murdered the Petite Artiste, who'd only slipped up by returning to my rental house, his ex-rental house. So I worried about Callie and the Truelove creep. But Callie took care of matters in her own fashion: she fell in love with Methuselah and moved into his three-story Victorian brick house on High Street, where she played guitar while he sorted through scraps of Lexington's history and two attack Dobermans paced the bottom floor.

It was Willy who slipped up, by dating another secretary. In recompense, I walked into a bookstore and seduced its owner, a guy who'd never acknowledged me on any previous visit. I even drove said owner out to a murder site right under Willy's nose, pretending he was a new graduate student. Then I concocted a very elaborate and unprofessional joke to play on both men involving a human molar, of all things. So Willy and I kept mimicking the steady-state theory of an expanding and shrinking, but not very wise, universe. Lauren, too, fell into her old ways, at least according to Methuselah, by going after graduate students. Denny/Paul Truelove did try to date another guitar performance major, but Callie had spread the word. Soon he quit his (his brother's?) Lex-Max job and left to work at a CD/DVD chain in Cincinnati. Willy notified the police there and shrugged. He was batting .750, since he'd solved three of four recent murder cases, including the unlikely solving of the drug assassination. "Some things, we just aren't meant to know," was his comment about the Denny/Paul Truelove conundrum.

Thank you, Werner Heisenberg. Your uncertainty principle certainly comes in handy.

Then one Wednesday evening in August when Methuselah's air conditioner had broken down and I was learning a four-chord "Blue Bayou" from Callie, sweat ran down my cheek and I experienced a sudden smell of whiskey, a sudden sure feel of my father's hand cupping my right breast. "Jesus, Larissa, what'm I doing?" I heard his voice saying as clearly as a ringing church bell, as clearly as I saw a bird fly outside the kitchen window in the evening air. I stopped playing mid-chord and more sweat fell, just as I remembered a tear falling off Daddy's face onto my hand, which had grabbed his the moment it touched my breast. Or had warm whiskey drooled from his lip? Or had . . . thank you, thank you, Werner Heisenberg, but enough possibilities are enough. It didn't matter, anyway, for that hot drunken night was the last time I ever saw my father alive.

"Are you okay, Clarissa?" Callie asked.

I wiped sweat—a tear disguised as sweat?—with the back of my hand and proclaimed stupidly, "I am no savage."

"You wanna quit and talk, maybe over some iced tea?" Callie asked, her brows furrowing.

"How about over a gin and tonic and lime?"

Soon I confessed what I'd just remembered about Dad. Then I told Callie about my boyfriend getting killed in my roommate's car while they were running around on me. Then I told her about my ups and downs with Willy, which she'd already witnessed. "And thereby stand," I intoned, an importantly foolish professor, "the sources of my No One Ever Touches Anyone Theorem."

But the case is closed on my dead college boyfriend, and I guess I hope the case never will be closed on Willy. In kindness I want to think that Daddy drunkenly envisioned his caressing my tiny left breast as the ultimate love between father and daughter, then sobered and caught himself. In kindness, I want to think that Denny Truelove projected his brother's and that young woman's suicidal lap dance—not murder!—into his own misguided fantasy of undying yet dying devotion. Insistent lovers clasping forever unto dust here on lovely terra firma. The ultimate physical and spiritual bond. And get this: in kindness, I even want to conjecture that a handful—two hands full—of warped but ultimately gentle spiritual constructs worried the man who ritually killed the Petite Artiste. Oh, how I want to think that about him as he lies in a coffin seeping formaldehyde through the eight bullet holes in his torso.

So maybe, maybe, maybe I too harbor fantasies of an eternal lap dance. Maybe we all do. *I am a lap dancer, yes, but I am no savage.*

4.

The Case of the Missing Sandwich

Year 2002

(Willy)

The triple clues in the New Mexico Case pushed heavy on me even when I read them as they played out over what my good friend Methuselah calls the "cop wire." Everyone else in the station was listening to a meth head hooker scream about how someone stole all her Derby winnings. Derby been run and done four long months back, sweets.

But set to a screaming meth head in the station or to Miles Davis here in my apartment, the triple clues in the New Mexico Case wouldn't balance; they just kept dealing sad-dad blues. Listen to 'em wail: a loser named Robert DuFresne breaks into a bar at three a.m. to place three things before him, a blue brassiere, a crucifix, and a nearly three-foot hornet's nest. He wraps the brassiere around his neck; he leans the crucifix against the hornet's nest, which he's propped on a table. Neat and clean. Triumvirate. Like the Romans: *Veni, vidi, vici.* But instead of conquering, he totes in items four and five, a Colt revolver and a .357 slug to blow out his brains. He totes in chaos and imbalance to spatter blood, bone, and flesh on the ceiling, the bar mirror, and the floor in a pattern some cop like me keeps trying to render into sense.

I close my eyes and listen to Brother Miles. Here in my apartment's sanctuary, he sets all matters right with *Bitches Brew.* His trumpet warbles to convince me I could dance a spiritual Conga line circling the nation's borders, to convince me I could astral-stroll backward in time two evenings back to that New Mexico bar where Robert DuFresne reportedly drank every night. There and then I'd set matters right, despite my kinky Negroid (as Professor Tyler, the ex-UK physical anthropologist used to say) hair; despite my thin, non-Negroid lips. Yep pardner, Brother Miles blows so wild that my high yellow skin and I could astral-project and pass as Tex-Mex in that Albuquerque bar's dim light. So we do:

"Hola, Pablo." A nod. "Hola, Miguel." Another nod, though Pablo and Miguel both excuse themselves and walk out the front door. So maybe the high yellow isn't going over too well tonight? With a shrug I look to the bartender. "Hay-Zeus, how's it hanging with the señoritas?" Jesús simply waves his white bar rag, so I turn toward this Robert DuFresne character. He's what I'm here for anyway. And just what does he have wadded in his right pants pocket but a blue brassiere? I sit on the stool next to him and order *tres cervezas,* one for me, one for Robert, and one for the bartender, Jesús. Yep, pardner, with the help of brother Miles it appears that I've leaped, leapt, and lopped both space and time to arrive in New Mexico two yesterday evenings ago to cure this impending little visitation of chaos—and, pardner, I'm going to cure it *before* it happens for once, not screw up like with Clarity and that damned asshole who busted into her house. Because *after*, well after arrives way damned late, *comprende*?

"Robert, Robert, Robert," I chant, scootching on the stool and preparing my spiritual Conga line. "You looking . . . not well, *amigo*." In false Tex-Mex, non-Afro, non-Kentuckian speech must I speak, to gain Robert's confidence. I grip the bar's wood and lean back to examine the silky blue strap still sticking from his pants pocket. I know it's a blue brassiere, he knows it's a blue brassiere, but to everyone else it must be some exotic measuring device he employs in his blueprinting work at the architecture firm down the street. So I proceed carefully. I lean forward and repeat:

"Not looking too well a-tall. Woman problems?"

Giving a start, Robert pushes the blue strap deep into his pocket and obstinately remains stoic and silent, so I gallantly continue:

"My bitchin' bitch . . ." (No, no, no: hip-hop and rap are o-u-t, out.) "*Mi carmecita*" (that had better mean "my little sweetheart"; my Tex-Mex flounders near non-existent), "not one month ago she slept with my good friend, a man with a ridiculous ponytail beard that almost turns his face into a donkey's ass." I mimic my good friend Methuselah stroking his three-foot long beard with its three hair bands, in his preposterous phallic manner.

"No kidding," I add, "why would any woman sleep with something like that? Curiosity? Kink? Practice her hair-stylin' technique?"

Robert laughs. *That's good, Robert,* I think. Push out the pain.

"Women," I add, prodding.

"Women," he agrees.

Hay-Zeus the bartender, he's grown a thick black moustache since walking away, or maybe I didn't notice it, which indicates that I'm slipping—for a big time observant homicide detective, I mean. Anyway, Jesús faces us and sips the beer I bought him, then carefully wipes foam from this new thick black moustache. I can't help but picture Methuselah running his cupped hands down his sandy-colored ponytail beard in what I used to think was public masturbation but have since learned is a not so secret come-on to women. A stupid come-on, which stupidly works. My right leg begins to twitch.

"His girl," Jesús stops preening facial hair to gesture with tremolo fingers and indicate that this girl of Robert's was some slender and lovely lady, "his girl left him three weeks ago."

Three, I think. *Does that recurring number indicate a missing link?*

"Three and a half," Robert says to correct the bartender. "She had the biggest hazel eyes—"

"It's a medical condition," Hay-Zeus interrupts. Robert waves him off, but Jesús insists, saying he knew her mom and dad. "It's called Graves' disease."

Two college student types open the front door amid a blast of New Mexico evening sunlight and I notice Robert's back straightening, his hand gripping his beer bottle. From the cop wire, I know that Robert's supposed to be 33—again that whammy double-3—but he looks more like 63 with his worry over his so-slender lady. Jesus leaves us to take the collegiate drink order, Budweiser, no doubt. Or maybe a frozen mint julep daiquiri dotted with M&Ms. He doesn't card the students, so I guess he either knows them or the law around here's lax. It's out of my jurisdiction, being New Mexico, but I never bother with underage drinking anyway. The Puritanical bug that's bitten America hasn't bitten me. Maybe alcohol will distill a little tolerance into the younger set.

"*That's* why she left." Robert, he's glaring at the two male students as he speaks. "To go to college." He spits out *college* as if it's a raw cruciferous vegetable. Cauliflower.

"Your girl?"

"Regina was no one's girl but her own. That's what Tomas and Hay-Zeus keep telling me."

It's my turn to tense. Regina, the name of the coed who got herself murdered in some cult twenty some years back, the one who pushed Clarity and me along. And it was our pushing that drew her murderer back to Lexington and to the house he used to rent when he attended college, the house Clarity rented as a physical anthropology professor who contracted with the Tomas police—that's me in the picture there—to identify molding or desiccated corpses. Yes, wail on, brother Miles; let your trumpet shriek all the globe's proba- and improbabilities, all its coincidences, all its syncopated synchronicities. Doo-wop-doo.

"One night, three and a half weeks ago, she asked me to marry her." Robert points with his beer, a Dos Equis, to the front door, working out his own synchronicities and improbabilities. "Right out there."

"Why didn't you say yes?" I try to ignore the two in *Dos Equis* as a non-coincidence.

"My stomach was sick." He shakes his head. "I swear by the blood glowing on the *Sangre de Cristos* mountains I can't think of one damned other reason. I loved her. I love her. Puppy-sick loved her. Puppy-sick love her. She was always coming up with off-the-wall stuff. Once she threw a rattlesnake party. Talked me into driving into the desert with her and shooting the damned things, bringing them home and frying them, serving them with tortillas and hot sauce. I loved her. She was beautiful, with big hazel eyes."

"The medical condition," I prompt.

"Hay-Zeus doesn't know what he's talking about with that."

The college boys have settled down, after a whoop at something or other. "What's all this about your stomach being sick? Were you nervous?"

Robert peels at his beer label and snorts. His hands are shaking like a long-time alky's. The boy's got it bad—and as the blues folks say, that ain't good. "No. Well, yes, nervous, but it was because I ate three tins of jalapeno sardines and half a box of crackers with my boss and the crew for lunch. We were at a site, in the hot sun."

I nod. The college boys want Jesús to turn on the TV. He shakes his head. Good man, give 'em a life lesson. You go to a bar to talk; you stay at home to drool.

"So you didn't eat anything else but—"

"jalapeños and sardines. And crackers. And Coke."

You should have eaten a sandwich, I think.

"I should've eaten a damned sandwich," he says.

"This was three and a half weeks ago?"

He shrugs and succeeds in peeling off half the label with those trembling hands. I hear an involuntary sniffle escape. And that ain't good . . .

Just as I start to down my beer, I spot the crucifix on the dark Tex-Mex wall, Jesus's namesake hanging in burnished bronze to overlook matters. This reminds me that I need to verify some clues, so I make a wild guess.

"There used to be a big hornet's nest in here, wasn't there?"

Robert's finished the beer I bought him and signals Jesús for another. I tell Hay-Zeus that I'll get this one, too, and I put down a ten. "I'm celebrating," I add when both Jesús and Robert give me a look like they're wondering if I'm a fag on the make, a Black fag on the make in a brown and white town. "I'm getting my lady back." Just a cop, fellas, doing his job—that's what I am.

"Thought you said she slept with your best ponytail friend."

My leg lurches again, and I grit my teeth. "She did, but there were pressures I have to make allowance for. She got raped by a creep who'd already killed a dozen people." *Almost raped*, I think in deference to Clarity, but then Clarity's not here.

"Holy sheet," Hay-Zeus says.

Sheet? Damn, Jesús, my Tex-Mex sounds better than that and I'm a Black boy from Kentucky. "You got it right, Jesús, but she blew his brains out with a Glock nine-millimeter before he got too far. Eight bullets in, five exited right on through him. Spent bullets, bone fragments, pink brain bits, and blood spattered over her bedroom floor and wall." I aim this description at Robert DuFresne, knowing just what he's planning later this very night. I'm trying to instill reality therapy about what he'll be leaving behind for his friend, this mustachioed bartender, to clean up. But Robert's Adam's apple just bobs and gulps beer. Jesús, though, makes a sour face, says something about the times, and heads for the register.

"Wait until he brings back your change and goes on up front," Robert says. "Then I'll tell you about the hornet's nest."

In a minute or two Jesús delivers my change and walks to wait on two older señoritas who just strolled in. They're dressed in jeans and matching yellow blouses, and they're eyeing the college boys. Robert begins:

"Women." He clunks his bottle on the bar. "Hay-Zeus is a lot older than he looks." Robert stares into the bar mirror to say, "And maybe I'm a lot younger than I look. Thirty-three, same age as the real Jesus when he took a trip up the Mount of Skulls and hung on the cross."

"Golgotha," I say. That factoid courtesy of Methuselah, my Roman Catholic good friend who crucified me on little Golgotha by sleeping with Clarity. So there's one damned three that didn't turn out so damned hot. Three friends, I mean. Menagerie a trio.

"Yeah. Golgary. So Hay-Zeus fought in World War II. He enlisted in the Navy after Pearl Harbor. His señora, she cleans out the hacienda the secundo he leaves, takes a ride to a pawnshop and disappears. The hornet's nest she leaves behind." Robert shakes his head as if to slosh out bad memories. "Or maybe she gave it to a neighbor. Anyway, that's all that's left for Hay-Zeus when he comes back a year and a half later: a hornet's nest he one time found up in the mountains. Women."

Robert's eyes clear as he looks at me. They're a bright sky-blue. Maybe he and the señorita with the hazel-eyed medical condition were never meant to get together. Genetic and evolutionary mismatches.

"So what'd you eat today?" I ask.

"Sardines."

"And jalapeños?"

Another snort. The younger of the older señoritas—I give a detective glance to her ring finger to see it's barren—walks by on her way to the ladies' room.

"Slow learner."

Maybe Robert said that, maybe I did, or maybe even she did: I'm not sure. Hay-Zeus stands up front catching the last sunlight, so it couldn't have been him. Anyway, the slow learner bit has gotten me re-evaluating matters. Would a mayonnaise and Velveeta sandwich pack enough culinary oomph to turn Robert's funk? Velveeta? Understand that I've already checked Hay-Zeus's menu, and that's one of five items this joint serves, warmed Velveeta on two warmed flour tortillas. There must be a Mexican Elvisito living in town.

Funny, I've untangled all the clues now—the hornet's nest, the blue bra, and the crucifix—and they make complete sense. The hornet's nest represents angry unrequited love, the blue bra represents obsession with Regina, and the crucifix, well Robert's already said how he identifies himself with Jesus at 33 ascending the cross. The fourth and fifth matter intruding on that triumvirate, the two that need to be balanced, are the jalapeños and the sardines, not the Colt and the .357 slug, which will never show tonight, given the right balance, inserted by the right person—that's me in the picture there. So all I need to do is toss in a missing sandwich. I've nearly amassed all the clues, just like I nearly had all the clues to convict a deep-creep creep of murdering a dozen people. But the sandwich, it remains missing. I pick up the single-sheet menu this joint offers. The nicotine and grease coating the plastic ooze into my fingertips. *After*, it always arrives too damned late, I tell myself for encouragement. *Now* is what you want.

"That night she asked, that night outside the front door . . . I tried to touch her . . . Regina. A large white car . . . a limo parked across the street . . . started up, and I looked at it. So when my fingers reached, Regina was already five steps off the porch." Robert pauses like he's just deciphered a stain on the bar that's been nagging him forever. "No one ever touches."

He chugs his beer, and I choke on his words, which come so close to what my darling girl Clarity always says, her little mantra that keeps her sane, I guess. *No One Ever Touches Anyone.* Hell, she even said this after that deep-creep creep raped her—or tried to rape her. Even after she spattered him across her bedroom with my Glock machine pistol. That counts as a touch, a palpable touch, does it not, m'lord?

But Clarity, Clarity, you might be right. Missing or not, a sandwich won't balance any damned thing; it's just a hunk of salami keeping two well-meaning bread slices from touching. Or a hunk of Velveeta in this case. But then, there's nothing to keep us humans from at least trying to touch, is there? Just like Methuselah and me joining forces to pull you from your rape trauma—even though neither of us could prevent that very trauma. So now I'm time-traveled here with Robert DuFresne and his missing sandwich. Even though it may be too late, don't I have to try? What's the option, Clarity? Your No One Ever Touches Anyone?

I overcome grease and nicotine and wave the plastic menu at Jesús. Maybe now he doesn't have a moustache, or maybe it's turned non-Mexican blonde. It doesn't matter, just like it doesn't matter that I'll never really astral-time-travel here, no matter how hard I concentrate on *Bitches Brew*. Still, Brother Miles' trumpet rings as bright as Joshua bringing down Jericho and making the sun stand still. So, closing my eyes to the maybe blonde, maybe coal black, maybe non-existent moustache, I call out, "A couple of Velveeta with mayo on tortillas, one for me and one for him, would you, Hay-Zeus?" I nod toward Robert, who's bouncing his head to some non-jazz, sad cowboy lope-along on the jukebox. "He needs something."

"We all do, honey," the younger but still aging señorita adds, emerging from the ladies room to waft her perfume at us.

"Isabel, she is right, *señor*," Jesús replies. "We all need just one tiny, friendly touch to make the single a duel." Tugging his moustache—yes, it's black—he winks at Isabel, who sways off toward the front.

Did Jesús's English slip with the word *duel?* Maybe, maybe not. Maybe a duo duel is all we can ever get. Despite the communion of union we think that we want to get, what arrives is the permanently missing link, the permanently missing sandwich. Not survival of the fittest, just survival. Exhaling, I turn to search Robert's sky blue eyes. What I find instead is my stereo's green and red LED lights. What I hear instead is a trumpet's echo. Giving a blink, I separate my vestigial tailbone from my couch to phone Clarity, leaving Robert, Hay-Zeus, Isabel, and the beautiful vixen with Graves' disease to their own worlds—Clarity and me to our own duo duel. After all, we all need something, don't we?

5.

Critical Mass

Years 2002–2004

(Methuselah, Willy, Callie, Clarissa)

"The shining sky provides."

Since the sitting gent with gracious aplenty white and flowing hair spoke more to the air than to any bystander, I deduced he was enunciating a stoic acceptance of our late June Ohio Valley heat. But then as he rubbed his rump on the concrete bench and wiped sweat from his equally plentiful and white eyebrows, he elucidated other items that did the job of providing, barely pausing for breath. I had considered approaching him and conducting my usual reconnoiter of old-timers, sifting for Kentucky folk wisdom and stories, but his crazed mantra hustled that notion away. His persistent mantra, however, did engross a young dishwater blonde methhead, who shifted into a straddle-legged pose while twitching her facial muscles, likely wondering whether the old guy could come up with five bucks for a blowjob.

Then she noticed me, a wannabe Kentucky Colonel local historian with a foot-long beard and matching ponytail, and gave a twist of her hips. I shifted so she could see how my sun-bleached ponytail nearly matched her hair. *Good Lord*, I thought, turning toward a grassy space where once stood a bronze stallion and rider commemorating General John Hunt-Morgan, irregular of the Confederate Army. *Good Lord*, I iterated, *look at yourself*, meaning me, not her, though she could use a mirror-check, too.

What's his problem? the meth head no doubt wondered. Out of five-dollar bills? His problem—that is, my problem—lay in the fermenting connection among a renegade Confederate general, his stallion, a methhead, and a hoary-haired gent babbling unrelated babbles. Obviously, my friend Willy the dashing detective was getting to me with his Jungian synchronicities. The methhead rubbed her hip and slapped sweat off her upper lip, no doubt realizing that the two characters before her indicated a bad start for the morning.

"The earth provides . . . the street provides . . . the moon provides . . ."

As the white-haired oldster jabbered, a stray phrase bounced along the hot air to hit a nerve in the methhead's right leg. A stick-thin leg, since she was young and on meth, like half of rural Kentucky. If she were mentally rehearsing her business proposition about orally collecting seed, her timing proved off, for a motorcycle cop turned onto Main Street and she had to scurry away.

I remained, remembering how fraternity kids used to paint the nuts of General Hunt-Morgan's bronze stallion red once a year, in the fall, as part of their hazing process. Was that why the city fa/mothers finally carted the metal hulk away? Or was their decision a bow to northern industrial influence? Or pressure from African Americans? Lo, Kentucky, which tried to secede from the Union *after* the Civil War; lo, that Commonwealth, once more juggling, jaggling, jiggling to please all.

"I had a dream," the oldster intoned, changing pitch and format.

The motorcycle cop was riding a sedate Japanese make with real mufflers, so he actually heard this. Being assigned to traffic, he just shook his head at the loony case, nodded at me, then sped off. I, however, flushed with embarrassment upon realizing that I was clutching a five-dollar bill near my belly button. Had part of me wondered whether the thin young girl and I could mosey into a deserted alley? Was part of me wondering where she had carried her thin legs off to? But why flush and embarrass over those thoughts? Wouldn't I be providing not only charity—since I surely would have tipped her another five—but also a lesson in work ethic? In from the Appalachian foothills, didn't she clearly stand in need of employment? My wavering conscience was trying my case in a moot court, however, for she was gone, gone, gone, like some half-ass rock and roll song.

The oldster turned to stare at a row of pigeons on a building's lowest ledge and consequently cooed in singsong: "I had a dream, I had a dream that I was talking with my brother, who's been dead for twenty-one years. My brother told me I should come again over to Lexington. My brother said people here need me."

An approaching young couple gawked so hard that I wondered whether the statue of General Hunt-Morgan and his horse's ochre balls had reappeared in some David Copperfield magical illusion. But no.

"'Cry out,' my dead brother told me. 'What shall I cry out?' I asked."

I tossed my five bucks in the old guy's lap. The couple nervously clasped hands. Ah, of course. Youthful embarrassment upon hearing the word *dead*. And dead for twenty-one years, no less—just about the number of years they'd populated the globe. And the methhead? Sixteen years of splaying her legs on this earth? Seventeen? Callie, who'd moved in with me several months back, was twenty-nine. Was I regressing? Would I start haunting elementary schools, offering local history lessons about Lexington? Was I trying to re-enter the womb? An odor of urine-soaked clothes interrupted my speculation.

"My brotha!" a voice yelled from the curb. "What he say I gotta do?"

This aged black oldster who'd hobbled onto the scene with an ebony cane glared at me, his eyes pasted with the filmy luster of a long-standing drunk. Satisfied that I was sufficiently unnerved, he turned to glare at the young couple, who also backed off. Then he approached the seated, white oldster.

"My brotha, Sanna Claus . . . he been dead twenty-one year. What my brother tell you?"

The white oldster continued his chanting, which I couldn't make out. Had the black wino's stench affected my hearing? It was certainly strong enough to do so. The wino leaned until I thought he was going to snatch the five-dollar bill I'd tossed to the white oldster. But no, he was intent upon the old man's singsong as it filtered through that snow-white beard.

"Pu-raise Jesus," the wino said, suddenly straightening. His cane clattered to the sidewalk and he lightly walked away.

Thus—and this brings about my entire point—thus Honest Paul Thomas, as the oldster would soon be labeled, recruited his first disciple. And thus began Honest Paul's journey as Lexington's street-corner prophet, something one wouldn't particularly expect to find in a mid-sized city. But then, Lexington had housed one of America's two heroin addiction centers in the 1950s and 60s, and Lord knows what other oddities central Kentucky's swank horse people imported for the remainder of last century. So this street prophet was starting Lexington's millennium out just fine, though—to be sure—nearly three years of it had already slipped by unnoticed after the Y2K computer boondoggle and the Satanic armageddon that wasn't. Even the fall of the twin towers and the second Gulf War had left Lexington unscathed, causing less harm than a February ice storm that shut the city's power for nine days. Lexington: a mid-sized burg in Kentucky that John Hunt-Morgan and his horse had deserted. Lexington: a mid-sized burg holding no towers spectacular enough to attract Al Qaeda.

But now a prophet had arrived.

That same afternoon, Clarissa Circle sat in the front parlor taking guitar lessons from my girlfriend Callie. After they finished I carried them iced tea , then sat on the rose loveseat, thinking of this new prophet. "What if, you two, a person could piece the future together just like we piece the past?"

Callie banged out an incoherent chord on her guitar and rolled her eyes.

"I'm serious. What if a person could somehow do that?"

Clarissa laughed and petted our male Doberman. Right now our female was too young to carry, but Callie and I were planning on giving Clarissa a pup soon to ease her anxiety about living alone. We weren't sure what her two cats would think, though. "Would this person," Clarissa asked, "piece the future together as effectively as you and Captain Willy Cox piece the past?"

"Doubting Thomas." I stood to walk upstairs and look down on Limestone Street. I could hear them laughing, and then Callie played part of Vivaldi's *Four Seasons* on her guitar. Callie was good for Clarissa, who was still getting over a terrible scene in her old rental house with a murder suspect. Terrible as in she wound up shooting and killing the idiot in self-defense. Terrible as in he'd been trying to rape her. *Trying* was at least how we all phrased it.

Mid-morning of the next day I walked down to the courthouse to find that Honest Paul Thomas—though that moniker had yet to make its appearance—had again claimed the concrete bench that sat before the space that once showcased General John Hunt-Morgan's stallion's balls. Do you think I have a fixation on this long dead General, his stallion, and his stallion's balls? Well I do. I have a fixation on anything that represents the past and gets shuffled aside in some puritanical cleansing. What did the communists call it? Historic purging? We Americans surely wouldn't do anything those red commies would do. Would we? Would we?

There he sat—Honest Paul, I mean—before that empty space, where once stood . . . well, a statue of you-know-who-with-his-you-know-whats. Within weeks, Honest Paul would be viewed as sitting in front of the Fayette County Courthouse as nobly—more nobly, some would argue—than any circuit court judge or Confederate horse with red balls.

"I thirst!" the wizened oldster shouted, making me jump. Three alcoholics, including a nearby psychology master's candidate from the university, hopped on the wagon. People tell me, though I have no proof other than hearsay, that the young methhead who first spotted Honest Paul Thomas also heard this very shout as she was finishing a five-dollar blowjob, and that she stared up to a cloud scudding over a low building as her john zipped up and handed her a twenty-dollar tip and a registration sheet for the local G.E.D, and that she subsequently entered our junior college system and wound up working as an L.P.N. Beware, though! History's paths strain, filled as they are with glorified data, falsified conclusions, mistaken motives, and hubris. In short, you can never be sure.

So too, the path of a true prophet always drops crags and precipices right alongside peaks. Thus, not two days after Independence Day, when a long-bearded, pony-tailed stranger carried him an iced tea, Honest Paul Thomas loudly groaned: "All shall perish in fire. All." That night at four in the morning, a swank bar not one block away was torched. This calamity presented a nadir to Honest Paul's prophetic internship, for the arsonist, who remained to admire his work, received burns over much of his body when a CO2 cylinder inside the bar exploded, and consequently under guard at Central Baptist Hospital he babbled how "the old snowball by the court house" had inspired him to torch the bar. The bar's owners, ex-basketball players from the university, suggested in a TV interview that "Honest Paul's" public predictions should henceforth be banned. The prophet now had a moniker—and two enemies. But despite any "henceforths" and despite Homeland Security, we do basically honor a national constitution, and what law was Honest Paul breaking? He wasn't begging, for other than an occasional chili dog or chicken wing forced upon him, he took no money. He placed no tin cup at his feet, kept no upturned bowler hat in his lap to collect coins.

And so Honest Paul remained, though rumors of a sanity hearing now and then trickled over the grass where the red-balled stallion once stood. That stallion and its red balls . . . yes, they still weigh on my mind. If the past can be flushed so easily, what of the future? In minor example, will a veterinarian declare that our female Doberman can't conceive or that our male is sterile? In major example, right now Callie claims that when she finishes her degree in performance guitar she'll start taking gigs but mostly remain here in Lexington with me and compose. *Mostly:* an interesting adverb. In time will she move to Oregon to perform outdoors? And in weightiest and greatest example, George W. claims he'll bring the troops home by X-mas. Both the North and the South thought the same, during the American Civil War. And they did! After all, no one ever said on just *which* future X-mas that homecoming might take place. And no doubt some President beyond George W. indeed will manage to extricate us from Iraq and Afghanistan . . . by some gloriously distant Christmas.

Oddly enough, the public fury of those two bar owners instigated a new phase for Honest Paul. Within a week, lunchtime guaranteed a crowd of two or three dozen around him. People would shuffle up, ask a question, and garner whatever fragment of his singsong fluttered by. A young woman, for instance, wondered if her fiancée were right for her, since he was a law school candidate and she was in cultural anthropology:

"Chew slowly," Honest Paul replied.

She nodded, took one step away, and spun about to gush, "Thank you! Oh thank you! You've made up my mind!" Tears filled her eyes as she ran off.

A certain gent with a ponytail and a foot-long grizzled beard couldn't hide his smile.

"What if," I asked Callie and Clarissa again after their weekly guitar lesson, "someone recorded the questions and answers of the old guy down at the courthouse? And what if a pattern emerged?"

"Someone?" Callie asked.

"Lord, Methuselah, you sound like my ex-friend whose name I'm not saying."

Clarissa was talking about Captain Detective Willy Cox, whom she'd spotted rubbing hips with "a red-headed bimbo." I *did* sound like him, for he was always connecting more dots in his murder cases than contained in a three-foot by two-foot paint-by-number set of *The Last Supper*.

By the time mid-August heat hit Lexington, a quasi-formal line was demanded by simple crowd behavior. At times this line stretched around the corner to the fifth parking meter. Once more I should clarify that Honest Paul didn't really reply to anyone's individual question; rather, he rolled out a monologue with a pace akin to a stand-up comedian or a preacher, incorporating breath pauses into his singsong. And the line moved accordingly — if not accordianly. During one breath pause I noticed an oddly familiar woman in a teasing yellow skirt displaying her still handsome knees and legs. I even caught the slightest hint of a curtsy as she squared her hips before Honest Paul.

"My husband wants to invest our portfolio in tech and oil because he swears this Afghanistan/Iraq war is going to spread. Should we?"

"The poor are always with us," Honest Paul said.

"I knew it!" The woman skipped away, though stopping before me to glare at my beard and ponytail. "Hippie days are long gone. Guess you never got the word."

A whiff of familiar cologne prevented my replying to the woman, whom I recognized as a failed lover from decades past.

"He's part of the act, ma'am," a voice attached to the cologne said.

The woman looked at Detective William Willy Cox, whose African-American complexion had been paling lately. This was because lately Detective Cox lived a driven life, currently pushed by a double murder of two UK students who were making out along railroad tracks during a party. Since examining their corpses during Derby Week three months back, he had grown pale. To top that, a fella labeled as Red Jack had escalated just as Willy had predicted. This turned Willy even paler, for he was just waiting to be called in for a Red Jack robbery gone haywire to end with murder. Maybe Willy'd been growing pale since birth. It wouldn't surprise me to find his grade school picture revealing a youthful face as dark as ebony.

"Part of the act, huh?" The woman tugged her skirt like a flitting yellow butterfly, teasing me with what was no longer available and tossing one last glare my way while addressing Willy. "Well, that figures. He fits right in."

Detective Cox and I watched her walk off.

"A sway like that, if a man could freeze-dry it, would earn him a fortune," the good detective said.

"Or give him a heart attack."

"She acted like she knew you."

"From college. We dated."

"College. So you admit you did go to college here?"

I didn't answer right away, because behind us, Honest Paul was raising his voice in a chant. We turned to see a man heaving in the heat at whatever Honest Paul was sing-saying. Detective Cox gave a non-believer's snort.

"I didn't say I was in college," I replied at last. "She was. Transylvania."

"Right." Detective Cox looked me in the eye. His brow paled, and I feared that I'd have to perform mouth-to-mouth. With a backward jerk he said, "Just keep your act back there under control. He's already made some powerful enemies."

"He's not—"

"Don't even bother denying that the two of you are in cahoots. I've seen you buying his lunch." He gave a last glance to the woman who'd been talking to me, focusing on her hips as their sway forced a twelve-year old boy to sidestep.

"Look, Willy, you believe that everything can be connected; it's part of your job. What if—" and I showed him a pocket tape recorder and gave a nod toward Honest Paul— "what if someone fielded all these questions and his answers and—"

Detective Cox just walked off.

I felt the tape recorder's vibration in my palm, and I looked to the woman's hips, still visible a block away, outlined in yellow. Part of me tripped after them, my ponytail and beard bouncing to catch up, and part of me raised my hand, thinking to yell out her name. But that notion made me flick off the tape recorder. Instead of glaring, she should have yanked my beard off: we'd slept together four or five times and precisely what I couldn't remember was . . . her name.

Is that any way for a local historian to act? Any way for a human to act?

THE WOMAN WHOSE NAME I couldn't remember reflected the mix of followers that Honest Paul was acquiring. Whatever her name, she had acquired money—that cold question about war and portfolio investment indicated as much. Other questions from other believers poured in with the same mix: "Should I send my son out of state to Duke, or should he stay here and attend UK?" / "Should my wife and I build an addition to our house or move?" / "My girlfriend says she's pregnant. Should we get married?" / "My husband might be laid off by Toyota over in Georgetown. Should we still buy my brother-in-law's mobile home?" / "My sister's hounding me to go to the Baptist church with her. Should I go?"

When football season rolled around in August, Honest Paul even fielded questions about point spreads: "Tennessee is favored by thrteen and a half in its opener. I want to bet five hundred against them. What do you think?"

"The sound of children was heard at the gate."

"I knew it. It's going to be an upset. Thanks, man! Thanks!"

I'd held off asking Lauren Bates about Honest Paul. Lauren was a one-time lover and a full-time local historian like I was. I'd held off partly from fearing she'd steal my idea for her column—or even worse, for her projected book. Finally, I broke down when we accidentally met in the library: "Lauren, what if—"

"No, Methuselah. Detective Cox and his professor girlfriend have already told me your hare-brained theory. The old guy's nuts. Maybe as nuts as that creep Red Jack robbing stores and plaguing young female clerks. Maybe as nuts as you and Detective Cox, though I doubt it. Let's talk about something sane: did you know that some horsy people are quietly rumbling about funding an endowed chair in physical anthropology, speaking of our mutual professor friend?"

"That's sane? Why would horsy people care—"

"There's outward sane and there's inward sane. Any good reporter can tell you that . . ." With those ellipses bouncing off shelved books, she walked off to leave me staring at the library's microfiche screen.

Along with those ellipses stretching from that late summer until Christmas, daily lines stretched almost around the block, like a snake coiling on itself, readying to bite its own tail. Everyone remained orderly, though, and

Honest Paul kept refusing money, despite that a good many bills and coins were tossed on the ground—once as much as one hundred and thirty-three dollars and twenty-nine cents.

After Christmas, suicide bombings and fears of further domestic terrorism kept the winter lines lively. And the creep Red Jack that Lauren had mentioned was escalating his game plan: he originally targeted young female clerks to rob, giving them a kiss and leaving a red jack playing card. Then he began exposing himself and pissing on their legs. The cops were keeping this quiet, but rumors spread. And now he was cutting. Willy thought even more violence was right around the corner. As it was, Red Jack had become violent enough that people stopped joking around and asking Honest Paul for his identity, like he might be a game show celebrity.

But their other questions remained steady. Paul would even hold court when there was up to five inches of snow. Someone donated a Sterno heater, which radiated a halo of warmth and left the snow at bay in a semi-circle about Paul. By mid-April tax time, Paul had been holding court for over nine months. And with Keeneland racetrack's Spring Meets, a new phenomenon started: tourists.

Lexington had adopted a trolley tour whose opening coincided with the Keeneland Meets. As one of Lexington's unofficial historians, I rode on its opening day and listened to a fat, six-jowled man giving a speech about this and that historical fact when he should have been handing out pork barbecue recipes. He never mentioned any historical atrocity Lexington had committed, including destroying the state's most beautiful train station with its multitudinous cathedral windows and then, shortly afterwards, leveling a movie theater with separate balconies for coloreds and whites, plus a built-in stately pipe organ. For what? For two parking garages. The Ben Ali, the theater's strange moniker, was taken from an early Kentucky Derby winner, who was named after his owner, a Kentuckian who did well enough in the California Gold Rush to become a sketchy thoroughbred horse breeder who alienated East Coast breeders for decades. So if those two edifices were passed over, it goes without saying that the demise of the red nuts on John Hunt-Morgan's stallion was passed over. I turned to Lauren Bates, who of course was sitting across from me taking notes as the trolley bumped along.

We both rolled our eyes at the man's sappy spiel. I showed her my pocket tape recorder and mouthed, "What if—" She groaned. At least she didn't yank my beard, like the woman in yellow might have rightly done.

"I'm surprised you could abandon your idol long enough to take this ride," she chided, leaning toward me. "Aren't you afraid you'll miss some rolling wisdom, speaking of *what if*?"

It was a warm spring day and the trolley's windows were down, so as we passed Honest Paul—my "idol," Lauren insisted—the passengers could not only see the line of homage before the old man, but also hear him speak:

"Fish are meant to swim in schools, humans are meant to walk in pairs."

"Oh-h, sweet," a lady seated in front of me lilted upon hearing his words. Her voice echoed the sentiment of the crowd on the sidewalk, especially that of a young blonde woman who went dancing off, just glad to have received a bona fide Honest Paul prediction. If Detective Cox had sat on the trolley with us, he would have grabbed his thin gut in disgust with an onset of disbeliever's diarrhea.

But my real surprise came when the fat man with the microphone at the head of the trolley commented: "Honest Paul has quickly turned into Lexington's most revered sage. Like the Sphinx of old, Honest Paul offers advice to weary citizens. And like that ancient Sphinx, Honest Paul neither expects nor accepts any pay other than a thank-you for his answers."

It really was a good thing that Detective Cox wasn't sitting next to me, for I would have wrestled for his pistol and shot the fat blabbing idiot, who knew as little of Egyptology as he did of local history. The Sphinx didn't give answers, it asked questions. And it exacted a terrible, mortal payment for all wrong answers.

Here I should confess the reason why I stationed myself near Honest Paul. No Sphinx am I, but I do resemble those internet scientists who maintain a 24/7 site to constantly forcefeed their supercomputer factoids in hopes that it will sparkle with intelligence upon attaining a mystical critical mass of wisdom and self-awareness. Like that computer, I was gathering critical mass with my mini tape recorder. For when all of Fayette County came to Honest Paul, it also came to me. At what point might my tapes achieve local critical mass?

So again, I must ask, "What if?"

It was the end of another June, making one year in Lexington for Honest Paul. As a kid I'd catch a huge green June bug and tie a string to its leg and watch it fly in a helpless circle, trying to expand its bounds. If Hinduism ever proves true, my accrued bad karma from those suffering June bugs will cost me a dozen lifetimes as a grub worm. Or ten years recording cricket sounds in hopes of learning their secret language and the Rosetta Stone to nature's webbing ways. So far, this summer was too cool for June bugs, much cooler than last year's, when Honest Paul first appeared.

"Excuse me. Didn't I graduate from UK with you in '77?"

"No, Detective Cox. I never attended the University." Having smelled his cologne, I answered him first, and then turned around, reeling when I did, for his pale had extended to nearly white. "Uh . . . are you . . ." but I held back from inquiring after his health.

Willy nodded at Honest Paul. "I learned that he really did have an older brother who died twenty-two years ago in July. This brother lived in Lawrenceburg and looked just like Honest Paul. Local kids used to call him Santa Claus, because he'd travel to Lexington and walk around with a huge white beard and bare feet in any weather—snow or sleet or ice. Since I was black, he of course didn't travel to my part of town."

This was the first time I'd ever heard Detective Cox make a bitter reference to his race. Our fifteen-year-old relationship had endured plenty of ups and downs: with him coming to me for some bit of local research and how it might impact a crime, with me worming specifics out of a case to pad away in my reservoir of local history. "Willy," I said, reaching to touch him. Then I pulled away, for the coldness of his skin gave me shivers.

"The red planet is war, the blue planet is love," Honest Paul proclaimed.

"Listen to that horseshit. How can you stand here with a straight face? And tape-record it, to boot?"

I shrugged. "We all collect data however we can. Myself, I couldn't sort through murdered people's clothes and study powder burns and blood spray patterns."

"At least I get results."

"So does he."

Detective Willy Cox snorted. Two people were approaching Honest Paul for advice. Willy commented snidely, "He's developed a twitch in his beard."

I looked to see that however improbable, this was true. Honest Paul's cheek was jerking, which in turn was twitching his white beard. All of a sudden, Willy grabbed my elbow. I'm constantly surprised by the strength in his wiry hands.

"Look! It's true! I can't believe she's coming here—here, to see him. Him."

I followed Willy's gaze and spotted Clarissa Circle. Professor Clarissa Circle. Willy pulled me behind a lamppost and series of newspaper stands, as if they would hide us. Clarissa was tallish for a woman, with eagle gray eyes, so she'd spot us. But Willy was right about one thing: what could possibly bring her here?

"One of her damned male university hanger-on students told me she was coming. I had to bite both my damned semi-African, non-Negroid thin lips to keep from laughing." Willy grabbed me again with his talons. "*You* don't have any idea why, do you?"

Menace vibrated in his voice, but I've been clean with Clarissa ever since lovely Callie moved in with me. Still, I sputtered, sputtering being my only defense.

"I . . . uh . . . no . . . uh . . . I uh—"

"For god sakes, shut up. No, you don't have any idea. For all you know, she's going to ask about the Piltdown Man."

I sniggered, but then added, "You don't suppose it's about . . . about that guy who . . . do you?" 'That guy who.' That would be the murderer Clarissa shot in her bedroom as he tried to rape her.

"That's been over a year done and gone," Willy said.

We both let it go. Clarissa had been hard candy on and off ever since that night—worse than her previous marshmallow on and off. Sometimes she was okay and going out with Willy, Callie and me, sometimes she "acted out" in social work jargon, dating men she'd pick up from who knows where or how.

Willy bent for a newspaper and the heavy butt of his pistol bumped me. Remaining bent behind the rack, he handed me the sports section—no doubt as a joke since I'd made my disdain of sportball clear. I followed his lead, though, and placed the newspaper before my face so that we could hide and listen to Professor Clarissa.

The sports section backfired. Out of sheer boredom, I read the page. The discovery of a possible Indian burial mound near a prominent horse farm's studding stalls was causing a controversy, since Amerindians wanted the surrounding acreage declared sacred. The horsy owners claimed that disgruntled farm labor had planted the bones, like a William Faulkner character might have burned down the barn. If true, this was savvy sabotage, since insurance would more than cover a barn burning, while unearthed Indian bones would be considered an act of God, shoving insurance out of the payment loop. The article stated that a physical anthropology professor from the University was being asked to pass judgment. Well, well, well. I recalled Lauren's telling me about the endowed chair. Just how greased could horsy palms be? I thought to show the article to Willy, who would appreciate its wandering ways, but Clarissa reached Honest Paul and burst forth with her question:

"What," she said, giving a heavy inhalation. I peeked over my sports section to see her nervously glancing about—quite out of character. "What is truth?" she blurted.

I'll be damned. Just like she was jesting Pilate pulled from the New Testament and plopped into bluegrass horse country.

Honest Paul didn't hesitate, but of course he never hesitated, for he was never really answering anyone's question: "I make the rivers a wilderness: the fish stinketh because there is no water, and dieth for thirst."

The Bible, I supposed. I'd have to look it up. Detective Cox dropped his section of newspaper and stood with his mouth open. Professor Circle turned to see him.

"Willy," she called. "Willy, walk me somewhere, anywhere. Please."

Could it be? Could Clarissa Circle, the queen of No One Touches Anyone, could she be beginning to wonder, "What if?"

"Go," I whispered to Willy.

BY SUMMER'S END, DELEGATIONS from both Covington and Louisville had visited Honest Paul. The Louisville delegation tried to bribe him into coming to Churchill Downs; the Covington delegation, true to its gangster roots, was actually planning on kidnapping the man, it seemed.

This had two results. Firstly, a policeman was assigned to Honest Paul whenever he was holding court before the courthouse. Secondly, two billboards were erected off the northern and southern approaches of I-75, the southern one hanging off a cliff's side like a bizarre religious admonition:

Lexington: the Athens of America

Honest Paul: the Seated Sage

Some bearded, pony-tailed personage had evidently mentioned to the city fa/mothers that Lexington used to take as its nickname "Athens of the West," since Transylvania was the first college west of the Appalachian Mountains. Soon after these billboards went up, the snake actually did wind around the block and bite itself daily as travelers from nearby states stopped to pay homage to Honest Paul.

In a way, Clarissa Circle had a bigger fight than she suspected, even though she was honest, even though she did land an endowed chair for the physical anthropology department. You see, it turned out that the supposed Indian bones were just three dead pre-Civil War slaves. —Oh, you can be sure that the horsy PR and news releases weren't phrased that way, with the loaded word "just." But no matter how the news was phrased, the message got across to Lexington's African American population. Dead Amerindians = sacred ground. Dead niggers = horse stalls. And among that population, while his skin color still held, anyway, was Detective Cox, who was having his own problems:

"The bitch is dating some vice president from Lex-Mart."

His cinnamon cologne drifted as sharply as his voice.

I turned to see a man whose face could have passed for a Ku Klux Klan sheet hung out during an overnight storm. "Willy. I'm sorry, man. You know that ever since . . . you've just got to give Clarissa time."

"'Nothing Ever Touches Anything,' he replied, ignoring my case-worker plea for patience with Clarissa. "If I've heard her yap that spiel once, I've heard it a hundred and fifty thousand times—almost as many times as you have stray hairs, Methuselah. And seated over there we have Mr. Everything Touches Everything." Willy meant Honest Paul, who'd been expounding on birds for the last half hour. From the crowd reactions I'd seen so far that morning, blackbirds and crows were interpreted as a "No," robins and sparrows as a "Yes." Blue jays seemed to indicate caution, say in taking a new job, or changing mates. Willy snorted as Honest Paul called out, "The jay is a jangler squawking against the wind."

I didn't dare remind Willy that he himself was a prime exponent of the everything-touches-everything philosophy in his own detective work. Just as I didn't dare remind him of the portable recorder in my pocket that was busily gathering data for . . . The Big Shabang?

"I heard about the murder trial," I offered. It was a case that should have been open and shut, but just went haywire.

"Damned lawyers. As if life isn't fucked up enough already." Willy gave a bullfrog croak, as if life had spasmed his epiglottis. He recovered to look at me: "Give her time, huh? Hell, what's your latest take on the game of life, Methuselah? Still with steady-state?"

"No. Critical mass."

His nose twitched, and hints of brown returned to his skin color, in patches about his eyes.

"Like a computer, or like brain weight," I explained. "Accrue the right amount of input and—"

Willy laughed sharply and popped the recorder in my pocket with his trigger finger. "Yeah, sure; it could happen. Maybe in the year forty-eight thousand Anno Dominoes. Meanwhile, what about us poor slobs? Do we just keep playing checkers without a board?"

I felt the recorder's slow tickling whir and thought of Callie, who'd been searching for an academic post teaching guitar and who had, against all odds, landed one in Cincinnati. It's just one hour away, I kept telling myself. Things will hold. Our female Doberman was expecting in four weeks. Things will hold. Clarissa had already told Callie about the LexMark VP. I overheard them talking downstairs as I was reading a Lexington woman's diary from World War II. When Callie'd asked about Willy, Clarissa had started sobbing, her sobs creeping up the banister and bouncing off the turn-of-the-century plaster walls. Things will hold. Things will hold. Things will hold.

"Diamonds were once soft leaves and bark." That came from Honest Paul, who'd evidently tired of the bird motif.

"How can I ever thank you enough," an octogenarian—if she was a day—replied, her voice creaking like a rusty screen door to a histoplasmotic chicken coop. Straightening her back as well as she could, she walked away, leaving room for the next supplicant.

"Bullshit," Willy hissed at both the woman and Honest Paul. "Hey, let's change the subject. You remember the guy who screwed around with Clarissa and owned that bookstore? You surely remember the little piece of underage slink he wound up marrying, don't you?"

Underage slink. Before I mounted my high horse I thought of Callie, since I was twenty-seven years older than she was. There's no explaining love. That's all there is to it, folks. A Daffy Duck cartoon makes more sense. Even our female Doberman was giving our male hell lately, though she'd nuzzled him to prime the pump a couple of months ago. So I nodded at Willy's question. I did remember the girl's big green eyes and her lithe frame, whose every move amid the books fascinated me.

"Yeah, well did you see where they found those damned paired stamps we spent all night looking for in his shop? Their picture was in the paper a couple of weeks back holding those stamps between their cute little Cupid noses. Yeah, not only found that damned pair still together in a book, but sold them for a cool nineteen grand through some cornball coin and stamp dealer who's been dating the ex-sheriff's widow. I know the guy. And you know what the two of them are gonna do with the money he gave them?" Willy's shoulders began shaking. He was so tickled that he couldn't wait for my reply. "'They're going to start a publishing house here in sweet ol' Lexington that specializes in soft porn poetry."

"Soft porn poetry?" I grinned insanely. Inwardly, I wondered if I could get some of my own soft porn poems published.

There was a lovely woman with a guitar
Who promised she would never stray far.

LEXINGTON'S NEWSPAPER, the *Herald-Leader,* had been running Honest Paul's opening and closing lines daily. Even the ministers at Good Calvary Baptist Church occasionally gleaned his lines for sermon topics. And, as if in honor of his second Christmas season in sweet ol' Lexington, Meaty Meters, the nation's premiere and only soft porn poetry publishing house, published its first three books. One was written by the "Underage Slink," one was co-authored by that stamp dealer and the widow of Fayette County's last sheriff, and the other, ahem, was peppered with verses stolen from Honest Paul and suitably altered. I wonder who could have written it, to the accompaniment of a classical/jazz guitar?

One winter afternoon before Christmas, a snowstorm blew in and Clarissa called. She wanted me to drive over and try some wine a friend had given her. Callie had taken the Cincinnati job and was away for three days, so if I went, I'd have to go alone. Driving on black ice would be safer, since Willy had just started back in to dating Clarissa and was having her house watched 24/7. You see, she'd dumped the Lex-Mart vice president for Willy, but he remained wary, fearing she'd start acting out once more, start re-testing her theorem that Nothing Ever Touched Anything. Over the phone, I told her the Doberman pups would be eight weeks old soon and that Callie would be back in a day, to hold the wine until then.

Then, with the start of the spring semester, students from KA, the Old South Fraternity, had visited Honest Paul *en masse* after finding a cache of photos of John Hunt-Morgan's stallion's red nuts and some cans of still viable paint.

"Shouldn't Lexington reinstall the Confederate General's stallion?" the fraternity's spokesman asked, his chest stuck out.

"When dinosaurs walked, the earth thundered with farts," Honest Paul replied.

A cheer went up from the fraternity, and another cheer went up from some young blacks standing by, both evidently interpreting Honest Paul's answer favorably. Had the blacks learned of the encounter through a bearded local historian and a black homicide detective anxious to prove that Everything Touches Everything? Maybe. Whatever, the police were on the spot before you could say "red stallion balls."

Reporters for grocery store tabloids, swarming the city before Christmas for the birth of the nation's first soft-porn-poetry industry, caught sight of Honest Paul and had been regularly running articles on him, too. Then a dozen or so religious magazines and papers picked up the game. And here came both *Southern Living* and *The New York Times*.

"Horse damn shit," Detective Cox said. He'd taken to chewing cigars, and he spit part of one out. I watched it spin on the sidewalk to land lopsided.

I wasn't about to argue. Callie was renting a day room in Cincinnati. Professor Clarissa was seeing a bartender after a New Year's Eve argument with Willy. The January cold snap had caused a dearth of murders, so Willy's pacing had grown frantic. Everything seemed like horse-damned shit, except the soft-porn-poetry business: I'd made three hundred bucks in royalties.

"Willy, what brings you—" But I stopped, for I saw Clarissa standing in line again. Willy pulled his quivering hand from beneath his winter coat and the butt of his pistol remained prominently outlined. We both awaited Clarissa's approach.

"What is truth?" Clarissa asked when she finally wound her way to Honest Paul.

"The same damned question she asked before!" Willy hissed. "What? She gone pre-dementia from all that fucking? Her damn bartender using lead-coated rubbers?"

A week later, and the morning was icy, though the radio claimed it was warmer than it had been for weeks. A white car skidded by as I walked toward the spot where John Hunt-Morgan's stallion used to eject ethereal sperm from his cardinal-red, cast-iron balls and penis. Like a stoned ballerina, the white car performed two complete circles on an errant patch of ice. Willy got out and began to run. I ran after him.

We reached the empty bench at the same time, Willy shouting an incoherent question. As he did, I smelled Lawrenceburg whiskey, not cinnamon cologne.

We both stooped and squinted at a small card with minuscule blue lettering:

Honest Paul has moved to Chicago.

"To Carthage?" Willy said dully.

"To Cincinnati," I countered dully.

We continued to squint, trying to make out the ridiculously small print.

"Horse damned shit!" Willy shouted. "He's just like a goddamned anthropologist or lawyer. Can't ever give no straight answer!" Willy pulled out his pistol and emptied the clip, sending the card sailing and cracking the cold concrete bench.

My eyes widened as the shots echoed off the cold buildings surrounding us. "God. Come on, Willy, let me drive you home."

"I'm in a damned unmarked car."

"That's great. No one will suspect I've stolen it. Anyway, I know every cop in town; they'll let it pass. Let's go get drunk."

"I already am."

"No shit, Sherlock."

Miraculously, we got in the car and drove away before anyone showed up to investigate the gunfire. I pumped Willy to discover that he wasn't on duty. He blubbered out some question he'd been meaning to ask Honest Paul. I couldn't make any more sense of it than I had of the tiny calling card on the concrete bench. I thought about Honest Paul, about the silent tape recorder in my pocket, about the soft porn poems, and, of course, about Callie, wondering if someday she'd leave an unreadable calling card that was really a departing card. Was it true? Do connections trickle through every possible thing, great and small? Could one person eventually accumulate enough facts to make sublime sense, to reach a critical mass of knowledge, to answer any Sphinx's questions? Or . . . or was Clarissa's No One Touches Anyone the real take?

"Willy, listen up. What if . . ."

But he'd passed out, his thin frame one more fact pressing my shoulder and dislodging my neck. Driving onward in the unmarked car, I kept resolute watch to gather more facts, certain that unmarked ice stretched out everywhere, touching everything.

6.

Live, Evil

Years 2001–2002

(Clarissa, Gray, Willy, Pebble, Methuselah)

By Derby Day in May of 2001, a bit over a year after discovering the eight bodies in the mass grave, we'd ID'd only two, one being a coed from my alma mater in Knoxville who disappeared as a freshman, the other being a guy from Ohio who was last seen in Nashville. So one man, two women had been identified, if you count Gina, who I alone was counting. Her identity was a voice in my head I couldn't deny. Willy drove me nuts on the Knoxville coincidence: "Everything and everyone do touch, Clarity, can't you see?" Clarity was the nickname he'd given me because I needed so much caffeine in the morning. I liked the nickname fine, though no one but him used it. What I didn't like was *him* that summer. So I reverted to playing tennis, forsaking men forever. They're just not my type.

While I pounded tennis balls, I sent the six unidentified skulls off for facial reconstruction. I even got Mildred to put a racket in her hand three different times. That was twice more than I got any of the professors, except a guy in the philosophy department who really gave me a run on the court. But not elsewhere, for I was off my feed, as my guitar-playing, whiskey-drinking daddy used to say.

Then in August, just a week before UK started back, a restaurant called Adam's Rib opened. It had a pick-me-up-will-you-please-before-I-go-hormonally-insane patio bar, so I went, before I did.

"Clarity?"

"Hell," I muttered on hearing that voice behind me. I'd been peeping under the bartender's armpit to watch him mix a pitcher of margaritas, but on hearing that voice I glanced at the garnet pinkie ring my dad had given me and wished that it had been handed down from an Uncle Merlin instead, so I could twist it and disappear. I could even smell Willy's damned cologne, so I didn't bother turning around. "No UT-Knoxville stuff, Willy, promise?"

"Promise."

He took the barstool next to me, and we eventually moved to sit by a creek and drink and watch people circle about one another in a beehive dance to match the honeybees circling the remaining late marigolds in boxes on the patio's railing.

Now take a breath, because akin to old Albert Einstein, I want to break time up here, so let's slip the Milky Way back a billionth of a spiral, back nearly a year: After talking with Methuselah and Bill the Elf-King cop, after ordering the two dental records that would prove valuable only in canceling out possibilities for the decapitated female corpse, I returned home one Friday in late summer to once more find no response to the placard left on my front door for the Petite Artiste. Come the next day, a drizzly Saturday, I dutifully placed the sketchpad behind my screen door as I'd been doing, as I'd promised in my handy yellow placard. The pad stayed there for two more weeks, along with another yellow note saying, "Your sketch pad is inside the door." I replaced the note. I replaced it again, with a pink one. This went on for a good half of that fall semester, and then one day both note and pad were gone. I put up another note:

"You could at least have written Thank You."

One of my neighbors confirmed that the skittish, mousy woman had walked off with the artist's pad—not before sketching the house, though. A week later the same neighbor told me that the mousy woman was at it again with the sketching, so I rewrote the same accusatory sign, this time with purple ink and pink paper, just to irritate her.

Approaching Halloween, I came home to find a florid charcoal note on the pink paper: "Thank you. Your house is haunted. Don't you hear her crying?" *Haunted* was underlined three times, as if in a charm. And that was it for communication between us.

Now exhale, and let's spin time and the Milky Way forward one billionth of a spiral, back to Adam's Rib again, back to mid-August 2001 again, just before the fall semester came upon us. As I said, Willy and I were sitting by a creek, drinking a nice Medoc and waiting for steaks. "You know what I'm going to do, Willy?"

He edged his knee against mine and started rubbing, but I shifted away. "Nu-unh, buster, not so fast."

"Okay, Clarissa, what are you going to do?"

Willy has thin lips, and an on-and-off moustache. This summer was one of the offs, so I could see his lips pursing almost purple against that gorgeous butterscotch skin of his as he straightened up. Good, I thought, I've backed him away from the nickname Clarity. Like I said, it wasn't that I minded his using Clarity, it's just that I was glad I'd backed him off in general.

"Halloween seems to be her season."

"Her?" he asked.

"The roaming artiste who may have been Gina's salty dog lover. So. To start her season Wal-Mart early I'm going to take a picture of that reconstruction as soon as it comes in from . . ."

Willy smiled sardonically, and I realized that I was broaching the subject of the University of Tennessee without his help, for that was where the nearest reconstruction studio was, housed in forensic anthropology and occasionally stealing a sculpture student away from UT's art department.

"When it comes in," I continued while watching a yellow jacket catch a last minute whiff of marigold, "I'm going to take a photo of it, blow that up to poster size, and place it on my front door for my strange artist friend."

"Not even considering that you're being awfully sure that the skeleton you keep calling Gina is the Gina Mason who was reported alive by at least two dozen witnesses, you're getting a tad gruesome, aren't you?"

"No one has to know that it's a reconstruction of a murder victim."

"Come on, Clarity, you can't look at those things without—"

Our waitress approached, cocking her hips to balance our steaks when a customer drunkenly lurched in front of her. She didn't spill one drop of oozing blood. I bet myself that in time I would deal with killers just as careful; like whoever did in the eight corpses, especially considering the punctures to the larynx, presumably to prevent their screams. When the waitress set my steak down, blood pooled around the mushrooms and I started to laugh, realizing what I'd just been imagining before fine-dining. I also realized that what Willy had burst out about the facial reconstructions was true. Modeled from skeletal remains, they were always so generically creepy that they conveyed death's icy hand as surely as if the Grim Reaper were hoisting the original bloodied head atop a cold steel scythe.

We bit into our steaks with zeal.

Some things are predictable: Willy and I did wind up sleeping together. But others aren't so predictable: I didn't put a photo on my front door screen because,

"Oh no," I whispered, uncrating the boxes from the reconstruction team in Knoxville in the beginning of the fall semester. All I had to do was fetch a long dark wig from our storeroom and place it on the next to last head I'd just pulled out, Jane Doe 11-2000, the decapitated one that originally had the glitter on it, to see a three-dimensional image of the young girl my peripatetic artist friend had drawn perched atop my second bedroom dormer, images that I'd photographed, of course.

"Gina."

"Gina, Gina, Gina."

The generic chocolate brown eyes that the expert had chosen stared mutely. Sometimes, even graveyard humor won't save the day. I called Bill, who was almost always on day shift because of the seniority he'd attained with campus security.

Two other cops came with him. Curiosity killed the cop, I supposed.

"Shit," he said, on seeing the reconstruction sitting on the stainless steel table.

The young cop with him shrugged. The slightly older cop shrugged.

"Has Mildred seen this?"

I shook my head.

"Why don't you call her?" He didn't take his eyes off the reconstruction, and I could see his head shaking back and forth the slightest bit.

I phoned Mildred, asking her to come down, adding that maybe she should sneak some medicine with her. When she insisted that the department chair was still in the office, I insisted louder. She'd become attuned to gruesome and could tell from my voice that "medicine" would likely prove necessary.

"All right, dear. Give me a minute, will you?"

I was holding the receiver away from my ear so that Bill could hear. He took the phone.

"Mildred. This is Bill Jackson, security. Bring enough for me, too, would you?"

Minutes later, she entered the lab carrying her large green purse, which she set by the phone when she saw that we were staring at five reconstructions. She swayed and looked at Bill, who'd regained his color. The reconstructions were facing away from her.

"I'm not going to like this, am I?"

"Both of us are too close to retirement to like it," was his reply. "Bring your purse over here."

She did as Bill suggested and walked around to stare at the five heads, focusing on Gina's. She looked from me to Bill, to the other two campus cops. I could see her larynx working. "Oh," she said finally, her fingers skittering as if they wanted to comfort the head. "Oh, oh, oh. It's that poor girl from . . . the one who disappeared in the 70s, but then supposedly reappeared. It's her, isn't it?"

"Gina?"

They both looked at me.

"Regina. I think that was her name," Mildred said.

"Mason," Bill added, covering his face. When he pulled his hands away, he hit himself in the forehead so hard that I thought he'd fall over. Shaking off his blow he spoke: "Her two ex-roommates talked to me." His eyes went to the ceiling as if a movie screen were playing memories. "I can still see them, both squinky little bleach-blondes, both with screechy hill accents. Their daddies were likely miners or farmers who ate cornbread and beans for ten years so they could afford to send their daughters to UK. Both girls swore that Gina would never do anything like what was reported by the orphanage in the newspaper, that she just wasn't the violent type." He almost put his hand on the reconstruction, but pulled back. "They told me that she'd gotten drunk one night and admitted that she fell in love with one of the nuns, and had even come on to her, but the nun had simply brushed it aside, when she could have made big trouble. It was that same nun who'd somehow gotten her a huge scholarship to attend college, the roommates told me. They said that this nun still wrote Regina from somewhere out west where she'd been transferred. They said Gina—" he finally placed his hand on the wig covering Gina's bald cast pate— "Gina, yeah, that's what they called her—that Gina planned to give money regularly to the orphanage once she graduated and got a job. A female teaching assistant from English said pretty much the same thing later that same afternoon. Not to me, but to another officer." He looked toward Mildred's purse and she compliantly pulled out her medicine. "But then we got that report from the Free University group and let matters slide. I mean, their report capped the orphanage's report about the girl named Gina supposedly going wild. Drugs and all, you know, we figured, could really flip a kid around, especially a kid who was an orphan and a wannabe lesbian to boot. So we let everything drop."

Mildred unscrewed her medicine and offered the bottle to Bill. Sometimes Old Forester can do more for a heart than a nitroglycerine pill.

I called *The Kernel*, the campus newspaper, and since I was teaching a couple of journalism students who badly needing a presentable grade, Xeroxes of pertinent issues were delivered the next day. It had already been a daily paper in the seventies, so there were a dozen articles about Gina, and four different photos. Out of professional courtesy I forwarded a Xerox to the Knoxville wonder magician who'd reconstructed Gina's face, so he could be proud. I also called Willy and then the Methuselah fellow, whom I'd all but forgotten. It turns out that he and Willy were back on good terms, so all three of us wound up staring at the reconstruction, the newspaper articles, and photos.

"Gina," I said, trying not to look too hard at the Methuselah guy, who'd taken to wearing his beard in a ponytail like a mare ambling backwards, "was evidently the name of my weirdo artist's girlfriend. The weirdo artist who draws my house, I mean. The one whose drawing matches both the newspaper photo and the reconstruction."

Of course Methuselah had been the one to tell me this, but I figured our meeting at The Demitasse should be laid to rest. And I'd told Willy about the mousy artist stumbling in front of my house plenty of times already, so he knew that much and more. As the clock on the wall did its click-thing, he shook his head and said that pulling her in officially for questioning would be counter-productive, telling me that five years back when someone complained about her walking the streets she'd gone catatonic when a female officer picked her up on a vagrancy charge even though she was carrying 110 dollars in her four pockets, in two-dollar bills, plus quarters in change.

"Two-dollar bills? Quarters?" I said.

Willy shrugged. It was sunshiny bright outside, and something glistening caught my eye from the roof of a nearby building. "Enough that everyone in booking was laughing, enough that the clerk weighed them rather than counted them. I think six pounds was the number."

Methuselah pointed out that quarters had been found in the eyes sockets of all eight corpses. This was privileged information not made public, and I could see that Willy was angry. It wasn't because Methuselah had ferreted anything out by bribery, since the guy was on good terms with nearly everyone in the police department. It was because he, Detective Willy Cox, hadn't made the connection between the artist's obsession with quarters and the eight corpses first. Willy of the tangling webs.

"Boys, boys," I finally had to intercede as they shuffled around the lab, as if sparring for a first kiss from Gina's facial reconstruct, or a final dance with her skeleton.

"What if you put up another sign? What if you talked with her?" Methuselah offered, while staring at, of course, me.

"Alone?"

"She doesn't do well with males," Willy said.

Neither do I, I thought. But I gave in, went home and taped another yellow placard on my screen door, just like I had a year previously, though this note read,

I need to
Talk with you
About Gina

This time, four neighbors joined in on watching for the mousy artist.

What they weren't on the lookout for—any more than all of America—was two airliners crashing into Manhattan's twin towers. I usually start my days listening to the local AM, then switching to Kentucky Public and NPR. That morning, though, I started off with a CD of Vivaldi's *Four Seasons*, a guitar version by Christopher Parkening. And that morning I brewed China black tea instead of coffee. And on that so beautiful morning I dressed in walking shoes, gave the Gina placard a pat, noting that I'd need to replace it since the weather had taken its toll, and glibly started out for a two-mile jaunt I'd outlined. I got as far as the used bookstore and through its windows saw half a dozen people watching TV. As many times as the TV stations showed the second plane crashing into the tower, it could hardly be called coincidence that I stopped by when that was airing. It was, I suppose, a mild coincidence that a student I'd had in my second semester was dabbing tears from her eyes when I peeked through the window. So I walked in to see what was going on.

And I found out.

I went straight to work, dressed rather shabbily and not caring. Mildred had hooked up a TV near her desk that faculty and students were watching. I saw the plane crash into the tower several more times, but when I saw those people leaping out of windows I'd had enough and walked quietly to my lab . . .

Where a graduate student had secreted in a TV from her office, and once more over half a dozen students were watching. The odor hood was roiling, since we'd been told that another body was coming. "The plane from Blue Grass Field reported in," a student walked in and announced. There'd been a rumor that a fifth plane, other than the three that hit the towers and the Pentagon and the one that had crashed in Pennsylvania, had broken contact after leaving Lexington's airport. As students sighed in relief, something caught my eye and I saw that the cabinet holding the reconstructions from UT was open. A girl I didn't recognize stood near it, and she shoved a silver object into her purse then turned to stare at the TV. One tower collapsed, then the second, and I was mesmerized until there was a muffled sob and an announcer started talking. Meanwhile, the girl walked out the door, taking her nondescript blue jeans and mousy brown hair and blouse with her.

"Who is that?" I asked my graduate student, pointing to the departing student's back. She didn't know. None of them knew. They supposed that she'd come in to watch the TV.

I tried to picture what she'd stuffed into her purse. It had been compact and silver. A camera? When I rushed into the hall it was empty.

That afternoon, directly after lunch and the dismissal of the TV from the lab, I went out to buy a lock for the cabinet.

"The sons of bitches," the guy selling the lock commented. I nodded and tried not to see the TV behind him.

With all the national hullabaloo, my Gina sign didn't get a re-do until Saturday. Then it went through several more re-dos, through the bombing of Afghanistan, and the Sunday before Halloween.

HALLOWEEN WAS GOING TO be a bust for kids. Rumors of anthrax candy were already spreading. We'd just shifted off daylight savings time, so it became dark at five. Even Bin Laden couldn't change that.

Knock, knock.

Onomatopoeias are stupid if you think about them. We'd had rain for two days, so those two knocks at my door sounded coffin-heavy, especially with the time change, the premature dark, and the generally panicked September 11th atmosphere. What to do but flip on the porch light and open the door?

There she stood, sketchpad protectively covering her chest, and a huge grimace curling her lips down.

"What about Gina?" she demanded, punching at the poster then glancing as if someone might round the corner of the house or emerge from the attached garage.

"Do you want to come in?" I asked.

She clutched the pad closer, if that was possible. I guess it was, since a top corner bent. She stood shivering, and I looked down at her purple house slippers. It was definitely jacket weather, and it had quit raining. Her slippers were soaked and muddy; she looked as if she'd been walking outside for hours.

"You sure?" I asked. "It's chilly."

Still grimacing, she nodded, glancing again at the garage door, then peeking over my shoulders to the staircase.

"Well then, what if we go to The Demitasse? I can drive us there."

A violent shake of the head, and her chin rubbed the sketchpad, giving off a faint scratch as if she might have menopausal whiskers. Just as I was on the verge of throwing my hands up in a Willy gesture of frustration, she spoke:

"Used bookstore. Walk."

"Okay," I said. "Let me get my bag and jacket." I went to get my coat, but hearing her movement, I called out, "Will you wait?"

"Meet you."

"No, it'll just—" But when I turned to finish my sentence, she was gone, her purple raincoat blending with the onset of night. "Neanderthal conversation. A good god-damned thing I'm an anthropologist," I announced to my house. "You walk. Me walk. Go separate. It no rain. See tooth-tiger gump-gumping in garage? Carry big gun."

On that note I changed out a blue purse for my new orange Halloween one, putting in the two snapshots of Gina's reconstruction, one with the black wig dangling in early 70s hippie fashion, the other bald. Alongside, I snuggled my gift from Willy, his old snub-nose .38. Trick or treat for Neanderthals. Walking out, I slammed the front door loudly enough that I figured the mousy artist would hear it a block away and hop over a couple of sidewalk cracks at one leap.

When I arrived at the bookstore, I noticed that its "New Proprietor" sign was still up, though barely visible in the dark. The guy had bought the store in mid-July, and here it was Halloween. Through the window of the brightly lit store, I could see this new owner, a relatively young guy as used bookstore owners go, crooning solicitously over the mousy artiste, who'd actually calmed enough to sit at his round reading table. I could only hope that the cup he was handing her held herbal tea, not coffee. But on recalling her monosyllabic conversation, I figured caffeine might just do the trick and force her to toss in a few verbs, adjectives, and pronouns, complete a few sentences. Whatever, I felt certain the next hour was sure to be trick or treat, in the Halloween spirit.

I walked in.

"Is this the friend you were telling me about?" the owner asked the mousy artist, who sat sipping from her cup like a little girl, using both hands. When she shook her head the cup and saucer rattled. The owner looked at me and smiled, saying, "Welcome!"

Then she blurted, "Not friend, but the one."

Oh darling boy, I wanted to tell this handsome owner, *you just aren't accustomed to her kidding, cosmopolitan ways. She picked them up in gay Paree. She's only slumming now, pretending toward Neanderthal. In truth she's a multilingual attaché.*

But maybe he *was* used to her ways, because he shrugged and indicated a chair where I could sit across from The Loquacious One. I smelled hot chocolate as I walked to the hot tea and coffee service he kept for customers.

"I didn't know you had hot chocolate," I said, hesitating before pouring coffee.

He glanced at The Loquacious One, whose honey hair wisped. "I don't usually," he answered. "She—"

"Coffee's better anyway. Good, strong, and very black." God, I sounded like my mother. She and Willy would be so proud.

When I sat, the owner stood awkwardly nearby, and I thought he was actually going to recognize me from the times I'd been in or from when I stood watching the TV on September 11th. Of course he didn't—why break a track record? But his presence did cause The Loquacious One to bury her snout in her mug as if she were dipping for a Halloween marshmallow. With her third snort, he got the hint and carried his own snout—considerable enough to put me in mind of other, lower, pubescent matters—away.

"Gee. Nuh." This soughed from The Loquacious One like wind from an Afghan cave.

I waited, but nothing else emerged from the cave's mouth. "What do I know about her," I prompted.

She nodded. Outside, two students walked by. Don't they ever do anything but giggle or laugh, even at night? Well yeah, they whine when they fail my exams.

"When was the last time you saw her?" I asked, turning again to my table partner, who likely hadn't laughed or giggled—discounting hysterics—for a quarter century.

"Too long." The Loquacious One studied the back of her hand, making me imagine age spots. But she wasn't that damned old.

"You taught her?"

"Loved her, taught her." Gripping the cup she glared at me as if she were going to throw it at my lovely gray eyes, so I leaned backward, pushing the chair. When her breathing hit a rhythm close to rap music she wheezed, "He . . . did *he* send you?"

I raised my hands in surrender. "I don't know who *he* is. I teach at the university, just like you used to. I have a PhD in physical anthropology." I waited, but no light clicked. Her whole frame shook and she was still gripping the cup with deathly intent. Hell, I decided, might as well go for it. "My specialty is forensics. I examine corpses and skeletons for the police."

She let go the coffee cup, and with both hands she yanked her hair hard enough that several thin strands floated onto the table.

"Gina," she said.

"I think so. But the orphanage has lost all her medical records." This was true. The minute Bill and Mildred identified the reconstruct as Gina, I'd contacted the orphanage. The nun who answered promised to get the records to me the next day, but an hour later she called to say the records were missing. "Do you want to help us—the police, I mean?" I now asked the Loquacious One.

"*He* . . ." she stutter-started and stopped abruptly.

"Who is this *he*?"

"He."

Neanderthal again. A college student walked in, not laughing, amazingly. Even more amazing was the fact that she walked into a bookstore. Oddly enough, she vaguely resembled Gina. I mean the thin body and the coal black hair, nothing else. The resemblance must have been strong, for The Loquacious One stared until I could see that she wanted to jump up and run her hands over the girl's skin in affirmation. The girl crinkled her brows—at me! Why me? Did she think I was cutting in on her turf? I blinked in girl-code: *Baby doll, if you want the mess sitting here drinking hot cocoa, you're more than welcome. She's not my type—in spades.* Then I turned back to the Petite Artiste.

"Did Gina have any odd identifying marks? Had she ever fallen and broken a bone?" I figured I better leave the dental fillings out for the moment. Matters were gruesome enough. The skeleton that we tentatively identified as Gina had broken her ankle when she was very young.

"Ankle," The Loquacious One said, just as if I'd prompted her. "Limp. Right leg."

I bit my lip and looked to the student, who now stood heaving her shoulders in the English literature section. Oh dear heart, I wish you well, I thought, not wanting to turn back to my solitary tablemate, wanting instead for this student heaving out sighs in English Lit to suddenly age twenty years and be named Gina and walk over and say, "Hi, Mary" or "Hi, Tamara. Can we motivate to your apartment, can I study your sketches? Can we read some Sylvia Plath? Can we cuddle? Can we make desperate and happy lesbian love?"

But the girl simply skimmed a blue paperback while the Loquacious One spoke,

"Gina," she said, actually prompting me for once. "Tell."

A gust of wind banged the door, and a sheet of rain pelted the display windows. They say—*they* meaning forensic anthropologists and police in general, that families receive peace from knowing that their loved one is dead, from knowing that they can stop wondering. It may be so. But I've personally never heard anything other than wails or cold choking sobs at the positive identification of a corpse. Damn you, Willy Cox. Damn you, Methuselah whatever-your-last-name-is, for leaving me to confront this poor sad woman alone.

"Some skeletons were found on a farm," I said.

"*He.*"

I ignored that pronoun-al exhalation for the moment.

"Eight. You may have read about them last year."

The hot chocolate mug was skittering in a small circle on the table and she kicked me accidentally. Another gust of wind blew against the window. She kicked the table.

"One of the skeletons had indications that she'd broken her right ankle as a child." The bookstore owner had started talking to the student, putting the moves on her, for all I knew—no, he was simply trying to make a sale. I looked at the woman across from me: staring at her hot chocolate mug, wrinkling her brows and waiting for the hammer to fall. "She also had a good many dental fillings, fifteen." I paused, wishing that it would start raining for real, so that I could think of grander, more metaphysical things, such as fungal growth patterns. But the weather stayed dark and cold and windy, and the bookstore owner and the young student began comparing notes on *Wuthering Heights*. Lord yes, wouldn't it be wonderful if ghosts did return? If kismet unfulfilled on earth could become fulfilled in the howling winds of a cold Halloween heath on a deserted winter farm? But nothing ever touches anything, no one ever touches anyone. They massacre, they kill, they vaporize, but they never, ever touch.

"I have a picture," I blurted. "A post-mortem reconstruction. It's something that can be done from—"

"Skeletons. I know."

"Yes."

"Show."

I pulled out both photos and placed them on the table.

The mug fell to the floor and broke. A great, dark wail arose in pulses, gaining in pitch until I reached for my ears. She pushed from the table, only to collapse onto the floor. Before anyone could help her, she was up and out the door, crawling halfway there before lunging to stand and open it. And then the rain did start, in great, cold bucketloads.

I TOOK A CAB home, staring at the greasy black hair of the driver. It was thick and curly, and if you drizzled enough gasoline over it to strain out the grease, it would likely hang past his shoulders. He was about forty-five but looked sixty, and he left the damned interior light on while driving all six blocks to my home, staring at me in the rear view mirror, grinning now and then—I guess in hopes that I'd invite him in to see *my* sketches. Is this *he*? I wondered, being accidentally correct in a grammar that had fallen aside with the times and my anthropology PhD. Is this *he*? Has *he* figured out that his petite artiste friend was about to spill the bones about Gina? Despite the rain, I had him stop four houses away from mine, at a two-story rental filled with muscle-builder students. I handed him a ten, the smallest I had. Anxious not to touch his hand, I told him to keep the change. A five-dollar tip for a five-dollar ride. Not bad. Another grin. One tooth was missing, another ready to fall out.

After he drove off I ran to my house and unlocked its door, then climbed the steps to towel off in the bathroom. Through the upstairs window, I could see the fraternity on the block behind gearing up for tomorrow's Halloween party. Rain sheeted in one angry blast, then another. The boys were drinking and hanging jack-o-lanterns on their covered patio, listening to their ever-present music. This was one of the fraternities that kept a clean reputation as far as the date-rape drug, so I was always friendly to them. God knows that male egos are fragile enough during extended puberty and need all the adult female encouragement they can get.

The fellas let out a fraternity cheer and raised their beers in a toast. Forsaking that window, I walked downstairs to sit at the dining room table, from where I kept watching the frat boys while reading a forensic journal that had arrived in the day's mail. It rained hard for another hour then slackened. I began to hear sounds—from the attic, from the basement, from the second floor, and from my bedroom. Grabbing my Halloween purse that lay glowing on a nearby chair and pulling out the .38, I called Willy. He answered his cell phone with his cute little hiccough-laugh.

"She knows something, Willy," I whispered without even giving him a *Howdy pardner*.

"What? I can't hear you."

I had to repeat myself, my shoulders shivering from noises I kept hearing, from dark corners I kept seeing.

"She identified Gina?" he asked when he finally understood me.

"Did she ever. The broken right ankle was from before the orphanage. When she saw photos of the reconstruction, she went berserk and ran out of the bookshop."

"Bookshop?"

"She wouldn't come in—" I heard another noise upstairs, maybe a rotten branch falling on the roof. "Willy, I'm a nervous wreck and I'm scared. She kept talking about some *he*. She knows something. Can you come over?"

Silence. Crap, he's with a damned bitch, I figured. But that wasn't it. He was out drinking with his erstwhile pal Methuselah. Twenty minutes later, the two of them were de-spooking the whole house with me. Otherwise I would never have had any rest. They left out the attic because the thick turquoise paint to the cubbyhole door obviously hadn't been disturbed for years. For twenty-eight years, as it turned out. And the thick, obstructive paint job was purposeful, as it turned out. But that's later.

Of course Willy wanted to know what The Loquacious Petite Artiste had said, but I begged off. "Tomorrow, please, Willy. In the daylight. It'll keep."

So the three of us sat in the dining room and listened to Methuselah gab about Lexington's history: a flu epidemic directly after World War I took several thousand lives; a Main Street lynching in 1919 took one. A dugout in an America Legion Field, now covered by blacktop from Man o' War Drive, used to fill with the blood of a murdered baseball fan every time it rained. When Methuselah offered that bucketloads were probably bleeding onto the right-of-way even now, all three of us looked out the window to see blinking jack-o-lanterns from the frat house. By ten-thirty, we were past one fifth of Old Forester, opening a second. The frat boys had stopped decorating, though they left their electric jack-o-lanterns on. Methuselah dug out a Leonard Cohen CD I'd stolen from my mom. Depression, anyone? Yes, six tablespoons' worth, thanks much. Three songs into the CD and one whiskey later, I envisioned a three-way with me in the middle, getting tickled by Methuselah's beard and Willy's wondrous willie. Willy must have caught something in my glances toward Methuselah, because he pulled me into the kitchen and said,

"Jesus, Clarity, you need to lighten up on the whiskey."

"Don't worry, Willy. No one ever touches—"

"Yeah, yeah."

"Uh, what?" Methuselah asked, being just tipsy enough to have followed us in, not thinking that something private might be going on.

"You explain, Willy. I'm too frazzled for deep philosophical thought."

He grunted. Then, in his own lovable way, waving his creamy yellow palms about, Willy told Methuselah about my No One Ever Touches Anyone theory. I'd never told Willy what had started it—not that there truly was any one thing. For all I knew, maybe the delivery room doctor didn't give me a butt-slap to initiate proper breathing patterns, though from what I hear from girlfriends, the act of birth itself must be traumatic enough.

We were back at the table and could see the fraternity's jack-o-lanterns. Under the porch a guy and a gal walked out and began kissing. On the CD, Leonard waltzed alone in the living room with "Famous Blue Raincoat." Rain pit-patted on my back patio's awning. Across the way, kissing turned to writhing. The guy had picked her up and she had wrapped her legs about his waist. How innovative, how masculine.

"You see," Willy offered, tapping on my window and nodding at the show. "Everything and everyone touches everyone."

"She'll likely run off with his big brother next Derby Day and the two of them will be killed in a car wreck. No touching. Ever."

"Jesus, Clarity."

So I told them. My first confession about what had happened with my roommate and my boyfriend, and here it was, being broadcast to two damned males. Ee-e! Monkey meat! Monkey meat!

"Uh, maybe you need to see a shrink to work through all this," Willy said after I finished. Methuselah tugged his beard, as usual trying to connect it to his navel.

"Well, I have one for a landlord, so—" I hit my forehead. "Damn, am I stupid. God, am I stupid!"

The two men stared while I cursed, so I stood to walk toward the secretary that had conveniently propped itself against the stairwell the day I moved in, a perfect fit just like the entwining couple at the fraternity house. I started to open the lid, but light filtering down the staircase from the bathroom glowed terribly dark—for light—and I flashed on the cab driver's face and the petite artiste's wail. My hands skittered on the secretary's dark cherry wood. Had someone planted something awful inside?

"Willy? Methuselah? Would you two come over here please?"

Because of my voice, they did so right away. I noticed that Willy had his hand inside his sports jacket holding his pistol and glancing up the stairwell.

"Thanks," I whispered. Taking a breath I opened the lid, but no gory head or severed body part gaped, no fine anthrax powder trail trailed—only inglorious, unpaid bills jeered. Those and a manila envelope that held the color copies of the petite artiste's sketches I'd handily made from our snazzy office Xerox. What my department chair didn't know wouldn't hurt him, bless his uptight structuralist bones.

Carrying the Xeroxes to the table I turned on another light, effectively blocking out the couple under the awning, whose staying powers were beginning to interest me too much. For some reason, Willy hadn't seen the Xeroxes. That reason being that we'd argued on and off all spring and summer. Not that there was anything he'd learn from looking at one more rendition of Gina before bad luck came her way. Still, he gave a low whistle when he saw the sketch of the head on the dormer, with the hair flowing down to root into the front yard. Had it grown on its own since I last looked at it? I found myself glancing out the window, imagining the fraternity boy pulling an ice pick from his back pocket and jabbing it into the girl's larynx.

We shifted the sketch this way and that; then we looked at the other sketches and the pastel of the creep that I was willing to bet was *he*. What if *he* had rented this house, what if *he* was the creep who prevented Dr. Kiefer from ever renting to students again? Wouldn't it be simple enough to show her these pictures and ask?I ran my thought by Willy and Methuselah. In response, either the boy or the girl began a loud chirping on the fraternity patio that carried through my windows and the rain.

"Guys," I finally said. "Enough's enough. I need to go dream of something pleasant. Both of you are welcome to stay. The couch is there, and there are blankets in that closet." I nodded toward a closet near the secretary. "Willy, could you at least come tuck me in and check the upstairs once more?"

"Uh, go on, you two. I'm going to have one more drink and watch the show over there."

"A regular endurance race," Willy half-whistled. "Wonder if they'd let an old high yellow nig pledge in that fraternity?"

"They couldn't stand the competition, sweetheart," I said, giving his butt a squeeze as Methuselah concentrated on pouring whiskey.

A wash of rain against my windows awoke me. With all this rain I should have turned the heat on; instead I covered my nose with a sheet. Willy lay next to me, so I slid toward him for warmth. The aroma of coffee wafted up the stairs: I realized that I'd been smelling it for over an hour, though it was barely light outside. Stretching for the alarm clock I held it to my forehead to be sure: ten till six. Was this Methuselah fellow a Trappist monk?

"Damn guy's crazy," Willy said, making me jerk.

"I didn't know you were awake."

"Felt you moving."

I pulled closer and rubbed my hand over his hipbone.

"Nu-unh, Clarity. I gotta be at work in less than an hour."

"No One Ever Touches Anyone," I mumbled.

"Not when they gots to work mornings for Massa Cap'n Jackson, they doesn't."

I narrowed my eyes, even though he likely couldn't see them in the lambent pre-dawn, and I shook my head. "Keep talking in patois and I'll make you my sex slave, boy."

"Nu-unh, pretty miss. Massa Cap'n Jackson don't 'low that miscegenationally stuff 'twixt slave ownahs and yard niggahs."

I lunged for him, but he was too fast and was out of bed. Damn cop training.

We walked downstairs to find Methuselah yo-yoing a magnifying glass back and forth as if he were a snooty waiter pouring French wine.

"Six more faces," he said. "Three male, three female." As he took a sip of coffee, I wondered if he drank it with as much sugar as Willy did.

Willy walked to the table, but I headed for the coffee. When I went by curiosity got me and I stopped to peep over Willy's shoulder to look into the magnifying glass. Sure enough, six camouflaged faces were embedded in the oil painting of my house, the painting without Gina's head on the dormer, though now that I looked, I could see that a tan outline had been laid down for what would surely have been another Gina. Willy pulled the magnifying glass farther back to enlarge the view. No wonder I didn't see any faces. One was hidden in the tree, one in what would now be my bedroom window, one in a bush, one in what I'd taken to be a flower pot in front of the garage, and the last in what I'd thought was a cat sitting near the house's left corner. Well, it *was* a cat, but this cat had a human face. The faces all must have been drawn at the Petite Artiste's home under a similar magnifying glass: there was no way she could have stood in front of my house and painted such tiny detail. It wasn't a Fabergé egg, but close enough for Kentucky.

"The males all look like the reconstructions, plus the Gibson guy," Willy said.

The Gibson guy was the friend of Thomas's dad, the one who'd been in law school. I agreed with Willy on that. Photos we obtained of him showed red hair, a thin nose and equally thin lips—just what this painting revealed under magnification. The others? Well, maybe. But Willy was pushing things by saying they all looked like the reconstructions. Suddenly, it dawned on me: one of the males resembled the male bugaboo figure with all the hex signs. Before I could say this,

"Shit," Willy said, looking at his watch. "I still have to get you home and change before work."

"I can drive Methuselah home."

I'd been pressing a breast against Willy's shoulder blade, just to let him know what he was missing. He scrunched his lips. I knew this grimace meant "No way, sister." He was probably right. My hormones were twitching.

We agreed that I'd call Dr. Kiefer to make a late afternoon appointment, and we'd all meet at her office. I asked Willy to take the Xeroxes of the drawings with him, since they were beginning to creep me out. But I did shuffle back through them to ascertain what I'd decided moments before: sure enough, the hex guy's face resembled the face on the cat. And now that I thought about it, maybe the hex guy himself resembled one of the facial reconstructs, the construct from the super-large skeleton. This was too confusing without coffee, so I walked to finish my original mission of getting one mug for me and one for Willy. I handed him the self-serve sugar bowl because dumping as much of that crap as he dumped into his coffee made me sick, from sight, texture, and smell.

"Return the mug," I said.

"Don't I always?" He usually added sex talk like, "Complete with some sugar for your bowl," but either Methuselah or the painting or both had waylaid his sex drive.

As the two of them left I got a sweet nip on the lips from Willy and a swanky European hug and double-cheek kiss from Methuselah. Willy pretended not to notice that Methuselah's hands landed about my waist while mine landed just over his butt.

Walking to work later in a pleasant drizzle to teach my nine o'clock, I wondered how many rooms chocked with drawings, sketches, and canvas boards filled the poor petite artiste's house or apartment. More likely, she lived in a boarding house. I envisioned one room stacked with sketchpads and canvasses, a calico cat prancing over them, knocking them down or scratching them to use for litter. I changed the calico to black, not so much in honor of Halloween as the Petite Artiste's personality.

Dr. Kiefer agreed to see all three of us at four-thirty.

"For someone who believes that no one ever touches anyone, you get around," she said over the phone, referring to the two men who would accompany me. She indicated that she knew both of them, Willy in a quasi-professional status and Methuselah "just because he's as hard-headed as I am." *You don't know Willy too well then,* I thought, *if you're leaving him out of that category.*

On impulse I called Mildred and asked her to get in touch with Bill the campus cop. She asked whether this had something to do with the Gina girl , and I asked her if she had ESP. She replied that she dreamed about her the night before, and that I was in the dream too. My smart-mouth response was, "You don't suppose my latent lesbian tendencies are—"

She cut me off, not because she's a prude—Mildred reads plenty for a secretary, there's evidently no law against one being intelligent—so no, not because she was a prude, but she cut me off to say, "I'd rather it had been that tame—lesbian, I mean. What I dreamed was that I was looking through a shack's filmy window and saw that reproduction of Gina's head stored on a mahogany shelf, but blood was dripping from its eyes. And when I walked into the shack a thick Neanderthal male was placing your real head, also dripping blood, next to hers. I think you might want to be careful about your little artist friend that you cornered in the bookstore."

"Careful," I repeated stupidly. "Thanks, Mildred. I'm sorry you have to go through this; I imagine everyone wishes Professor Tyler and his arrowheads were still here."

"His arrowheads still are, dear. State property. But you've upstaged them with your bones and those reconstructions. I don't think anyone really wishes him back."

"Thank you," I replied.

"I just don't want you to join those bones prematurely," she added. "So take my dream seriously, will you? I'll bring Bill down when he gets here."

"Thanks."

I walked to the cabinet but hesitated at pulling out the key. I unlocked the cabinet and removed what I wanted to show Bill and Mildred—again—which was the facial reconstruct that looked like the hex man. They'd been so shocked with Gina that they'd barely given the hex man a glance. Grabbing through our store of wigs, I picked out an Afro to top the head.

When they arrived, I shooed two graduate students out to fetch early lunch, then led Mildred and Bill to the reconstruction cabinet. "Maybe," they both said on looking at the hex man. "Maybe. There were so many wild-eyed students roaming around in that time."

"Sort of like now?" I asked.

"Oh no," they assured me, "there were plenty more then."

I smiled my condescending smile, but Mildred said, "Dear, you should step back from forensics and look around your classrooms. These children are self-centered cream puffs."

When she and Bill left, I realized she was right. I looked at the clay head with its shaggy wig and tried to spin myself back into the early 70s by imagining the reconstruction to be that of a poet or artist envisioning the third or fourth coming, or even a political scientist intent on procuring, say, voter rights. But all I could imagine was a murderer.

It wasn't until I removed the wig and stood back to look at the two gruesome rows of reconstructed heads that I came up with the idea of carrying them all to Dr. Kiefer's. On a lark, I placed the wig on another of the facial reconstructions representing a young girl. I did a double take, for the black hair brought out a striking resemblance to Gina. I remembered Methuselah's story about the cult murderers picking victims that resembled themselves to guarantee immortality, how that story backed up Bill the campus cop's rumor. Well, if Charlie Manson could convince a bunch of California kooks to murder and torture a pregnant woman because the revolution was signaled by a Beatles' album, why not? I shifted the wig from the mystery girl to Gina and back again. Without the hair they were only two young women. With the black hair, something about their cheeks and chins turned them almost sisterly.

At a quarter after four I stood in Dr. Kiefer's office, where I'd lugged a suitcase with the five unidentified reconstructs, including Gina's and the hex man's. I was glad that the hillbilly woman wasn't there, though a young black woman twittered nearly as bad. "Zoom," she kept saying. "Zoom." She wide-eyed on seeing my suitcase, which was painted a suitable mortuary black. Dr. Kiefer walked out, gave an askance glance at the suitcase, then motioned the thin black woman in, holding up a finger at me to indicate that the interview wouldn't take long. Zoom. How long, I figured cynically, does it take to inject tranquilizer? This woman needed to come out of the trees, and that certainly wasn't a racial slur, just an observation on her as an individual. Momma hillbilly could use a good dose too. Zoom.

Willy and Methuselah showed up. They looked at the suitcase and I told them what was in it. Willy, being his curious self, hefted it. "Jesus, you really do lift those weights in the basement, don't you?" He shifted his frame to accompany the load.

I flexed both biceps, to their male amusement. "I've got something even more amusing to show you—not about my anatomy—but about two of the reconstructions." They leaned toward the suitcase, but I pointed to the clock. "Let's wait for the good doctor. *Amusing* may not be *quite* the right word." I was getting into the melodramatics, probably from hanging around a detective and a double pony-tailed hermit.

A bit later, Dr. Kiefer asked us in, offering coffee, which the men took and I turned down. I noticed that Dr. Kiefer had only half a dozen or so packets of sugar in her crystal bowl. Willy left one—out of Kentucky Colonel politeness, no doubt. But it was unnecessary since Methuselah drank his coffee black, wincing with each sip.

"I think I've told you about the woman who sketches the house?" I said/asked.

Dr. Kiefer, working her way into her chair, grunted an affirmation.

"We think that one of the eight bodies we found in that mass site a year-and-a-half ago was a student named Gina—Regina Mason." As I said this, Willy, in the role of stage assistant, placed the Petite Artiste's sketch of Gina's head perching atop the dormer before Dr. Kiefer. Methuselah, still wincing, was staring at the large red clay Mexican head on the shelf behind Dr. Kiefer, bonding in his own strange way.

"Isn't this my house?" Dr. Kiefer looked from the sketch to me, and I nodded.

"Do you recognize the girl?" Willy asked. Dr. Kiefer tilted the sketch and shrugged. "Twenty-five years ago she was an undergraduate, a first-semester sophomore. She was an orphan and—"

"Oh yes, now I remember. The child who disappeared then reappeared to ransack the orphanage."

"She didn't do that, we don't think. Maybe someone was pretending to be her," Willy said.

"Or maybe she did do it and was killed afterwards," Methuselah offered.

"At any rate, we think she was murdered," Willy said. "Dr. Kiefer, we want you to look at the reconstructions Dr. Circle brought with her, plus this one sketch." Once more playing stage assistant, Willy placed the hex man sketch on her desk.

Dr. Kiefer recoiled, pushing her chair away. I'd never seen her face pale before, but it did, and her bosoms heaved as she breathed. "George Adolph Barnes." She looked at me. "The renter from Bosch's Hell that I told you about."

Willy snatched out his notepad.

"What about the faces I found?" Methuselah asked.

I took the Xerox of the canvas board from Willy and placed it on Dr. Kiefer's desk. Methuselah, ever the Boy Scout, pulled out a magnifying glass and placed it over one sketched head. Dr. Kiefer shrugged. Then he moved it over another head, a male one, and she commented, "Maybe. That could be one of the students who rented with Barnes."

Screams came from the hallway where the receptionist was stationed. The outer waiting room door flew open and we heard the receptionist yell, "She has someone with her. You have to wait!" But there was no holding back the little woman from coal mining country as she burst through the inner door into Dr. Kiefer's office.

"They've got my boy! They've got him in the hospital all hurt up. It happened last night. You got to go see him."

"Have you seen him?" Dr. Kiefer asked.

"I cain't, because of what he did. He followed some college girl around. Her father and brother beat him up. I cain't go see him after he did something like that. My boyfriend says no way. He should stay in the hospital alone for a week and learn a lesson, is what my boyfriend thinks. But they'll be cancelin' my insurance at the plant, won't they? If he stays in the hospital? I just got my first promotion over the summer."

"They won't cancel your insurance. Why do you want *me* to see him when *you* won't?" Dr. Kiefer asked. I raised my brow in agreement.

"You need to tell him to stop followin', and be good. That's what you're supposed to do."

This was the fourth time I'd encountered this hill woman. The previous times she'd worn nondescript slacks and I'd thought she was Mildred's age, late fifties. But here she was in a blue and black pleated skirt that lifted above her skinny knees, topped by a red, loosely knit blouse that clearly revealed a black bra underneath. And enough perfume to back Willy and his hay fever close to a window.

"What *I'm* supposed to do, eh. And not *you*?" Dr. Kiefer's face not only regained its color but flushed deeply into a new merlot. I couldn't understand how she'd managed to live so long with reactions like those. Without having a heart attack, I mean. She grabbed the woman's elbow and hauled her from the office, shutting the door behind them. We could hear enough to figure that Dr. Kiefer agreed to go only if the woman would start coming in with her son to therapy.

"It hain't me that's sick," the woman screeched, her voice crawling under the door like a leech intent on blood.

Dr. Kiefer said something that shut her up. Or maybe she gave her a tranquilizer or a gift certificate to Victoria's Secret for another bra. Anyway, she walked back in and told her secretary, who was still standing as amazed as we were, to pull out the rental forms for her house on Lightstone for 1972 and 1973, then copy them for us. God bless doctors: they keep records eternally. Dr. Kiefer turned her aged jowls toward us:

"Help yourselves to more coffee. Willy, there's extra sugar in that lower cupboard. If you use more than a pound, I expect you to replace it. My secretary will shoo you out and lock up. I wish I could stay." She lifted her eyes toward heaven, a universal gesture even atheists share.

Mother's little darling, Greg, Gray, or Grady—some growling name—had gotten himself pretty bruised up, with a dislocated jaw, one broken rib, two broken fingers, twenty stitches, and various contusions—all earning him a two-day stay in the hospital to make sure he wasn't concussive.

And Willy had gotten himself three real names: the three males who in the early seventies had signed the contract to rent the house that I now did. Still, it took Willy until December to locate the hex man, who was a preacher near Bowling Green. He'd changed his name just enough to throw most of the computer searches, and the fellow used absolutely no credit cards—the latter activity being suspicious enough to land anyone on the FBI's list these days. One of his two past roommates also lived in Bowling Green and ran a computer store. And he employed the same identity evasions. I thought: Bowling Green, sure, they can still access young coeds at Western Kentucky University. The third remained just a name.

Willy had the Bowling Green police interview both gentlemen, and as a hint he also asked for a list of locally missing women from the past 24 years—the two men had moved there directly after graduation. Nothing came of either the list of 32 missing females or the interviews, and I could see from the way Willy's eyes shifted that he figured if he'd driven there he would have spotted a black Gina hair tangled in one of their shoelaces, or maybe a sliver of her breast still embedded under a thumbnail after 29 years, or that oddly missing tooth dangling as an earring. To top it, one of the missing women's middle names was "Regina," and this coincidence had Willy going for days until I forced him to drink a Maker's Mark shooter and stare at the half-frozen creek behind Adam's Rib for fifteen minutes of silence. It managed a gurgle; he managed a sigh. "I guess you're right, Clarity," he said when I pointed to my watch to indicate fifteen minutes had passed. "I guess I am forcing matters." I waited for a *but.* Bless him, one didn't come—not that night anyway.

The third male roommate's whereabouts eluded Willy longer, since this one had changed his name and moved to Seattle. It wasn't until January 29th, my birthday, when Willy heard from the Seattle police. And guess what? They told Willy that the guy had disappeared two weeks before. Left a wife, two children, four Dobermans, and a fine-paying job with a computer company. The wife, the Seattle police told Willy, reported that her husband had been acting strangely since around Christmas. That he would only tell her he'd heard from someone he hoped he'd never hear from again. That he took the largest male Doberman with him on the day he disappeared. Neither came back. This sent Willy hustling, and sure enough, both the hex man preacher and his friend had been out of town that entire week of January, from the tenth to the sixteenth. On retreat, and in Northern California, to boot.

"Retreat. I thought that was high-church stuff. Baptists do revivals. This makes the first Southern Baptist retreat I ever heard of, Clarity. What about you?"

I love the breathing room rhetorical questions offer.

We were at my house, cozying before a nice hot fireplace, enjoying Valentine's Day together for once—I mean no arguments, no dating around. Willy's caramel syrup hand was rubbing my thigh, working its way inward, caramel on white, my version of s'mores. The fire popped and I jumped like a rabbit.

"I haven't seen the Petite Artiste in a while," I commented.

"You don't expect her to be sketching in this weather, do you?"

True enough, though part of me figured that if she'd stand sketching in a lightning-filled thunderstorm, why should a foot of snow stop her? It had snowed so much on my birthday and the night before that the university cancelled classes, and that snow remained on the ground to be covered with a few more inches even as we were sitting before the Valentine's fire. As a gust blew a mix of ice droplets and snow against the windows, I leaned into Willy's shoulder, feeling his pectoral muscle push my cheek. No One Touches Anyone almost got itself buried.

Almost. April Fool's Day lay just around the bend.

On that day a student came up to me and told me his dad wanted to meet me. Once students became used to me, this had become the game: introduce the young single female prof to divorced dad. One girl who hated her mom's new boyfriend even tried to get me entangled. No, thanks, I don't take on other people's losers, just like I don't buy used Jeeps. So, as this male student told me about his dad, I smiled condescendingly.

"No, it's not like that. I mean, he is single and all now—he and Mom have been divorced four years. But he used to live in the same frat house I do, the one behind your house. He said he had some wild tales about your place that you'd get a kick out of. He said they called your house 'Blue Lagoon' in the early 70s because of all the light shows that came from the windows."

"The early 70s." I looked into the student's blue eyes and wondered if his dad would be my older type.

"Dad was a Vietnam vet. My mom was his second wife. They met at the frat house. They had me late."

"The early 70s," I repeated, thinking of the hex man. "Was he friends with the people who lived here?"

"He knew them, but I don't think they were exactly friends from what he's said. They were the wrong kind of hippies; everybody in the fraternity hated them."

The wrong kind of hippies. A delightful phrase. I agreed to meet this young man's father at The Demitasse, feeling comfortable enough since the weather would push us off the patio where every damned squad car in Lexington cruised by. They could cruise all they wanted to, because we'd be sitting inside. Besides, I was consulting a student's father. This was academic business, right?

Rhetorical questions. The pause that refreshes.

Larry McGavin stood six-foot three and had the bluest blues I'd seen in a while, outdoing his son by an Elvis/Paul Newman long shot. Despite the two wings of gray in Dad's coal black hair he pranced like a boxer, and laughed like a piano arpeggio. I didn't even bother telling myself he wasn't my type. Why fight it?

"I'm a drug probation officer in Louisville," he told me when his son and his son's erstwhile girlfriend went to busy themselves at the counter of The Demitasse. "I'm a damned good one because after Vietnam I tried every lie these kids can possibly think up. I eternally owe the fraternity and Tim's mom for getting me straight and graduated." Looking backward at Tim, who was edging his hand below the girl's waist, he chuckled.

"Like son, like father?" I asked.

His baby blues twinkled—not a bad sign for someone bordering sixty.

"You know, the cretins who lived in the house you're in now nearly tossed me permanently off track. They—" He looked to see his son and the girl coming back. "I'll tell you later. Tim's heard it, and I don't think he'd want this young girl to."

As easily as that, we were committed to a "later." For that "later," after a drink at the frat house—my first time in the place and likely my last considering how many decibels vibrated windows even in the afternoon—he wanted to go to one of the whitest restaurants in town, an old steak house that had been and still was the hit of every fraternity and sorority. So I wasn't worried about Willy. And it turned out that I was indeed conducting academic research, for Larry had met not only the hex man, but his two male roommates and his four female roommates.

"An interesting number combination," I said, stirring my Dago Salad, a house specialty, evidently from time immemorial. It consisted of lettuce shredded to coleslaw thinness, a tenth of a tomato diced into ten cubes, and enough oil and vinegar to slide everything down even during flu season.

"That was one of the enticements they dangled before me. A button-cute sophomore named Gina. I had her as my special assignment in an orgy."

"Gi—" I stared at my maroon nails to see whether my hands were quivering. "Just like that? They walked over to the frat house and asked you to sleep with a cute girl named Gina to complete their orgy?"

He laughed, about six notes, enough for a jazz riff. His fingers were ultra long—he'd already told me that he played saxophone in a band during high school and that those same long fingers had helped attain stretches that defied Boots Randolph. He was embarrassed when he had to explain who Boots Randolph was to the young prof—time catching up, I guess.

"No, not just like that. I was taking—you're going to like this—an anthropology class with Adolph and—" he played those long fingers on the table— "Jerry. That was his name."

"Jerry Vander."

"Yeah, how'd you know that?"

"My landlady said they were the reason she stopped renting to students." I had already decided to keep everything else mum. Willy's wily ways were catching onto me—like influenza.

Larry laughed. "Well, I can't blame her. Their eventual plan was for me to move in, make it an even eight—at least until Adolph hypnotized some new nubile and naïve girl and skewed the numbers again.—This salad's not as good as I remember it. Kindly greasy?" He held his fork up in the dim lighting and two drops of oil fell onto the table.

"Kindly," I agreed, catching his Kentucky-ism and holding up my glass of red wine to take a sip.

"Does that help?"

I nodded, and he caught the waiter and ordered a bottle of "Whatever she's drinking," pushing his beer aside. A blue-eyed man who could take a hint. Matters were improving.

"Tell me about Gina," I said as the waiter strutted off.

"I think that Vander was supposed to hook with her, the new girl, Gina, but I gather that she balked. Vander had a slouch eye and drank to the point of sloppiness. After Vietnam I was a pro who'd learned to disguise how much I drank, inhaled, and ingested, so I guess I was elected to break Gina in." He stopped, catching maybe a jerk of my foot at his phrasing. "If I seem callous about this, I'm just reflecting their attitude. It caught me off guard even after two tours in Vietnam. Yeah, two, so you know I was out of my ever lovin' skull. And I misspoke about breaking her in. I think that my role was supposed to be something akin to a handler—walk the mare, trot it now and then, keep it in shape for the jockey."

"The jockey being Adolph?"

"The jockey being Adolph. 'Dolphie,' he called himself. I'm six-foot-three.

At the time, that was pretty tall—before prenatal vitamins and all. Adolph was maybe an inch taller. I was out of Vietnam for just over a year, so I was pretty scrappy as far as weight. Adolph hit 260 or so. He kept barbells in the basement, right beside his photography lab. That's part of the power sway he held: talking these young women into nude and semi-nude photos. The other part was his size and his blue eyes—intense like . . . I don't know . . . you ever work with thoroughbreds?"

I shook my head.

"Intense like a thoroughbred stallion being led to a mating stall. Adolph was definitely someone you paid attention to, if for nothing else but self-preservation. Anyway, he and Vander showed me a picture of Gina in some slinky underthings—pretty enough, that's for sure, though a bit thin and not quite my type. "

I giggled like a sophomore at his phrasing. Fortunately the waiter showed with the bottle and did his wine presentation thing, so my indiscretion went unnoticed. Then we were back to the story:

"They sure didn't mess around, that group, with anything, from developing porn photos in the basement to arranging orgies. When I walked in the front door a small fire was already popping in the fireplace, and quilts were spread over the floor. I mean nice homemade quilts that you think your grandmother had folded away in a cedar chest. Later that evening I noticed the quilts' designs were a hodge-podge of hieroglyphics and phallic, so I'm pretty sure the four women were assigned to make them for the commune. That was a word Adolph—Dolphie—liked to use: 'commune.' 'Commune,' 'community,' and 'communion.' He did shy from 'communism'—I guess because of Vietnam. He'd picked up some lingo from Blacks, too, so he introduced me as 'Cousin Larry, who's thinking mighty hard of joining our communion, so we should show him just what a good spiritual time we can have.' With that, he pulled a large bong from behind a stereo speaker, and one of the girls filled it with half a fifth of sweet wine, probably Boone's Farm apple, which was what everyone was drinking then."

"Sugar and alcohol will do it every time," I offered.

Three students following a maitre d' wagged their fingers at me. Fine. As long as they weren't Fayette Metro cops with two-ways plugged to Willy I was okay.

But then Larry was a cop of sorts, wasn't he? But in Louisville, not Lexington. I glanced at him and swore his blue eyes glowed in the restaurant's lousy lighting.

"After a couple of hits off the bong, Adolph and his gal are making out to George Harrison's 'My Sweet Lord.' Then Vander and his girl, then the other guy and his girl begin smooching and dry humping. I look up at Gina and make a peace sign, taking a sip of wine. That gets a big grin from her, showing all her teeth that are spaced odd—like a cat's or something. I mean a pretty, wide-as-the-sky smile and all, but there's space between every tooth and they're sort of small. I still remember her big brown eyes. We wound up in a sort of corner where the fireplace jutted from the wall. I put my back to it and she put her hand on my knee. 'Jesus,' I remember saying as I watched Vander and the other guy crawl over one another and start in on a different girl, then Adolph pushing Vander away and taking the girl he'd just hopped on. 'Yeah,' Gina replied in a whisper. When I smoothed her black hair she asked, 'You were in Vietnam?' 'Yeah,' I said. 'It was something like this every now and then.' 'Really?' 'Yeah, but the bodies were usually writhing from napalm or shrapnel, not love.' She put her head on my shoulder and we started kissing. I went there four times altogether, and Gina and I wound up . . . making love all four. She was really clingy, and I found out that she'd been raised in a Catholic orphanage all her life, so that clinging of hers made sense. The third time I asked if she could meet me the next day at the student union. She showed up all right, but with Adolph and a wisp of a girl named Josephine. Josephine was with Vander, attached to him, I mean, though Vander didn't come that time. Not particularly what I expected, Gina being accompanied by two chaperones, but that was all right. Adolph, he was really pushing me to move in. He said that something big was right around the corner for the whole commune and that I was a necessary key. When I said I thought the house was pretty crowded with seven he laughed and said that was going to be solved because his girl's mother was going to let us live on her farm, move into an old mansion and remodel it."

"So, his girl's name was . . ."

"I can't remember. He wouldn't let people talk with her much. She was tall for a gal—five-nine maybe."

"How tall was Gina?"

"Gina? She was right in the middle between Josephine and Adolph's girl and the other girl. Maybe five-three or -four? Sharp nails." Larry laughed at himself. "That went with the clingy part. Anyway, Adolph was pushing and we talked for maybe two hours before Gina had to go to class. So we arranged that I should come to the house again that Friday. That fourth time was more of the same but with this switch: some mescal thrown in courtesy of Don Juan and Carlos Castaneda—was he any kind of real anthropologist? I mean, I've always wondered that."

"Don Juan may have been," I said.

Larry laughed and said that was about what he figured. "Anyway, this mescal and the marijuana and Boone's Farm were doing a number on me. I just wanted to fold into Gina and make love and be with some softness. That's what she wanted too, so we did. But instead of going with the after-haze and maybe—you know, we were young—going for more, we were hit by bright lights, because Adolph had other plans. He turned up the music and the lights and began preaching—I mean it would have been preaching if it hadn't been so crazy. He was going on and on about the Egyptian and the Tibetan Books of the Dead and Lazarus, how he thought he—Dolphie himself, that is—was on to a link to immortality, but that it had a cost. 'A big cost,' he said, 'the type of cost that Brother Larry here, who's going to be a Brother, we all can tell just from the way that he and Sister Gina are grooving, the type of cost that he's familiar with after Vietnam. But Brother Christ told us to give up our father and mother and follow him, so once that cost is counted, well, immortality's cost isn't much.' He went on and on, and Vander tossed on a Doors' LP after a high sign from Adolph. The guy was into orchestration and control, I'm telling you. So Jim Morrison rode the stereo banging out 'No one gets out alive.' I could feel that I was going to snap, so I pulled Gina to me and said, 'You just wanna go out and walk for a while?' It was pretty cold out, but not dead winter, still before pumpkin time and all. 'I can't leave,' she said. 'You what?' 'This is a communion night,' she answered. 'I can't leave the community on communion nights. It would make for bad karma.' Karma, karma, karma. She might as well have yelled 'Incoming!' Five minutes later I was out the door, listening to Morrison's guitar for about half the block in the cold. I woke up under an oak tree the next morning, my knuckles scraped, my left cheek swollen. I'd been in a fight with either a sidewalk or a person. I remember giving Gina my phone number, but she never called. That was the last I saw of her, and I only saw Vander and Josephine around campus one more time."

Our steaks showed up and we ate. The best part was the potato.

"Let's go somewhere else to have coffee," I suggested. We'd taken my car, leaving his at his son's fraternity house. When we sat down with our cappuccinos, I asked Larry whether he knew that Gina had disappeared that fall semester around Halloween.

"No," he answered. "I didn't know anything the rest of fall semester because I went into a dry-out tank, on probation after a car wreck and a couple of fights. Then Christmas holidays hit me hard. I only came back to school next year after a spring and summer job in construction. I joined the fraternity and met Tim's mom and got married. We had Tim seven years later in '80." He shrugged. "When he got his driver's license a few years back, she figured it was time for her to hit the road too."

"Is that a practiced line?" I asked.

"Worn, not practiced."

After cappuccino we started making out by my car like two teenagers, so I invited him over for a nightcap. We stopped to pick up his car and he followed me back. I felt his body stiffen when we walked into my house. "Yeah," he said, several times, remaining stuck by the door, letting in cold air. "Yeah." When I tugged him in and closed the door, we went up the stairs. At the top of them he tensed, explaining that he'd never been up the steps, not even for the bathroom, which he'd used in the back yard by the rose bush. In my bedroom he noticed a book on skull identification on the bed stand and he said, while taking off his shoes:

"That's right. My son told me that you're a forensic anthropologist."

Once in bed, Larry became surprisingly easy-going. I turned out the nightstand light and we could hear music from his son's fraternity. Larry sure didn't need Viagra; I could feel proof of that against my thigh. I ran my fingers down his spine in time to the bass guitar and drum; I like doing that—running my finger along a man's spine. Morbid, if you think of it in the forensic sense, but I figure it more like assembling building blocks or stones for a temple. I was doing this when he suddenly called out "Gina."

I flipped on the light. But his face was innocent of any Viet vet flashback.

"Gina," he said again as the song changed at the fraternity to a slow number. "I hope that's not why you were so curious about her. I mean, forensics."

"Do you want to hold off of that until morning?"

He shook his head, and I could understand. So I told him that Gina had been one of the skeletons in the mass gravesite we excavated over a year ago. His stare moved from my eyes down to a nipple. I rubbed his hair, thick and black like Gina's must have been. They would have made a fine match, evolutionarily speaking. I moved closer and he responded. I tried to figure out what was playing at the fraternity: it was a woman's high, sad wail. I could feel Larry's eyelashes blink against my right nipple.

"Would you do me a favor," he asked, his body stiffening again. The light was still on, so I pulled back to look at him.

"Probably."

"Would you slap me, hard?"

"Because of Gina?"

His nod was barely perceptible. I scooted up on my haunches and pushed him onto his back. Before I became too intent on his blue eyes I let him have it, thinking that maybe I could make up just a bit for Gina. He shook his head and rubbed his neck, where the impact had evidently popped a vertebra.

"You don't fool around," he commented.

"I didn't think you'd want me to, considering."

He nodded again and kissed the palm of my hand, the one that had slapped him.

"Did it help?" I asked.

"No."

"I didn't think it would."

"Neither did I."

LARRY WAS GONE WHEN I awoke. He left a note that he wished we'd met under different circumstances. He was a sweet, slow lover, and I wished the same. I sent a return note through his son saying that if he wanted to help Gina, at least in memory, he could contact Detective Willy Cox of the Metro police in Lexington, and he did this. Afterwards, Willy felt he had three sure-fire suspects, what with the story about immortality, the description of the weirdly spaced teeth, and other odd bits that Larry supplied.

"Three?" I asked Willy. "What about seven?" We were watching the fraternity boys cleaning up after winter, and they were planting flowers, believe it or not. I spotted Larry's son on his knees planting, his back to me. He had his father's butt.

"You mean the girls living with them? How can Gina be a suspect in her own murder?" Willy waved his arm toward the kitchen and I looked over my shoulder to see the dirty yellow tile that no doubt still carried stray molecules from Dolphie and all his crew. And Larry too? I turned to look at Larry's son, still on his knees, still practicing botany.

"No Willy. I mean the *women* living with them."

Willy grabbed my arm. "Okay, okay. So still, what about Gina?—And why the hell are you staring out that window, Clarity? Planning on mating with the fraternity?"

I shot Willy a look that told him not to push his luck or his jealousy. Larry had been tit for tat over some lawyer's blonde secretary.

"From what . . . Mr. Larry McGavin . . . said—" I was spacing my words so that Willy got the picture to leave our love life on hold— "maybe Gina balked at killing the girl who looked like her. That would be natural enough, wouldn't it, to pull back from killing your alter ego? There were two female skeletons of about the same height and build, remember—the teeth in the second one were small, too, remember, even if they weren't spaced as far apart as Gina's."

It was Thursday and Willy'd stopped over after work. He massaged my arm and sighed.

"Look, your friend McGavin said something that makes me want to check the basement and the attic in this house. But I want you and Dr. Kiefer to sign a note saying I can examine the premises."

"A search warrant?"

Willy shook his head and let go my arm. "Not a formal search warrant. Two computer geeks at the station think someone has been breaking into the Metro files over the past six months. So I don't want a formal warrant."

"What about this Saturday? Are we still on for the park and some bike riding?"

"Either that or the Sweet Petunia Men's Perfume Ball." He reached into his sport jacket and pulled out a folded paper. "Here, sign this. I've already driven over and gotten Dr. Kiefer to sign one."

I opened the form and signed it.

That Saturday after morning coffee we started in on the basement, where we found two cans of film developer behind the old central heating. It was nothing short of a miracle that the house had never burned down from their being so close to the furnace. There was also a roll of undeveloped film that must have rolled under the furnace. Even though it wasn't near the heat it was so old—the expiration on it read "Oct 74"—that we figured nothing would come of it, though Willy dutifully sent it to the crime lab for development.

Getting into the attic was nowhere near as easy as getting the crime lab's negative report on the film. Getting in required scraping away several layers of paint from the entrance door, including a layer of black and two of turquoise. Willy finally pried the door open. I lifted the portable spotlight that I used on all-night excavations and shined it up a narrow staircase of eight steps—narrow as in turn sideways to walk up. Willy's sharp eye caught flecks of purple and silver glitter, the two colors glued on Gina's skull. He dutifully snapped a photo then scraped paint flecks into an evidence bag.

Topping the steps we found that Dr. Kiefer had remained true to her packrat form: four trunks and nearly a dozen boxes neatly tied with twine faced us. Natural for anyone anal enough to keep rent records from over thirty years back. Willy became excited, thinking in his usual Willy terms of fingers of evidence interlocking to touch here, there, and everywhere. Even moi, the No One Touches Anyone lady, became mildly curious, especially after we opened the first trunk and found a Shirley Temple doll.

"Worth eight hundred bucks, I'm betting," I told Willy. "At any antique dealer in town."

"Not to me. I'd give maybe the price of a cup of—no, on second thought you never can tell when you might need the money for a cup of hot java."

This was in mid-April and we'd had some warm weather finally, so the attic was pleasant as far as temperature. A bird was fluttering in the eaves outside, building a nest. And since the floor was planked in, there wasn't the usual rafter hopping required in attics, so we could actually sit before the first trunk like kids. Underneath the doll lay a couple of board games, and under them a complete set of Bobbsey Twins books.

"Where's the train set?"

"She just had girls. Three, well four, but the fourth committed suicide. Paranoid schizophrenia."

"I didn't know that," Willy commented. Then he added, "Physician, heal thyself, huh?"

I shifted my butt, which felt like a splinter was trying to dig in. "I imagine it was tough on Dr. Kiefer. She told me that what her daughter had could now usually be controlled with drugs."

Two birds chirped in the far eaves, and Willy and I listened.

"Yeah," he said finally, "I like the old gal. I guess it was tough on her. You know, for every black kid that died it seemed like my dad had a hunk of flesh slapped on his shoulders. I told myself I wasn't going to be no crusader for the race like he was."

We scooted to the second trunk, which was filled with costumes. Willy held up a glittery fairy wand and a white visor. Reaching out with the wand he touched my forehead. "Poof and ala-kazam. You're a believer."

"What is it that I believe?"

"That everything touches everything; every race touches every race, every person touches every person."

Picking out a witch's pointy black hat from the trunk, and a warty false nose, I put them on. "No way, Mister Cox. Everything just leaks around everything."

Willy shrugged.

By the time we finished the trunks and reached the boxes, our enthusiasm was waning. The birds outside had continued singing in mating ritual, so taking heed I spotted a bedspread and logically enough spread it while Willy rooted in the boxes. Then I crept to him and looked over his shoulder as he read an especially interesting set of yellowed grade school report cards accompanied by equally interesting spelling lists: *hen, barn, fox, chixen. Chixen*? Dr. Kiefer's genes for intelligence evidently hadn't passed to this one daughter. I began rubbing on Willy while the birds fluttered their wings.

"Mmm. How do you spell *stud*?"

"Clarity!"

"Mmm. Too hard for you? Well, what about *hard*?"

That got things going, so Willy forsook the box for the bedspread, commenting on how convenient it was. Just as if it had been there all along, laid out ever since the house was built.

We'd been working the missionary position for maybe five minutes and matters were just heating up when,

"Shit!"

"What?"

I grabbed the spotlight and shined it up to the slat wood underside of the roof.

LIVE
EVIL

This had been burned into the wood.

"And this was a guy who's supposed to have a mesmerizing presence? I stopped writing Live-Evil in the eighth grade."

"You also never started killing people and cutting out their hearts," Willy responded.

I shined the light elsewhere to reveal faded stick figures and alchemical symbols, hieroglyphics, runes, Sanskrit. "A regular New Age hodge-podge, just like in the woods around the eight graves."

"So you're convinced?" Willy asked.

"I'm convinced. I feel it in Gina's bones."

Willy murmured that everything touches everything. *Live, evil,* I thought in reply.

7.

Princess of the Diaspora

Year 2002

(Miriam, Pebble, Gray)

I, Mirabelle Tennessee, being a Southern Belle of sound mind and adoring body, am lying belly-down busily perfuming and counting my mistress's continental pubic hairs. It is a task she has assigned me whilst she reads aloud from Sodom and Gomorrah, *a continuation of Proust's* In Search of Lost Time. *Supported by five silk pillows, my mistress intones perfect Parisian, and sometimes probes me with a question, which she well knows will make me lose count of her beautiful preserve of hair unless I very carefully use a memory device such as 'mother-father-hate,' whose beginning letters would indicate the number 1368, though I've yet to progress that far in enumerating her lovely private forest of chestnut hair. For she always, always, always poses a sly question, and always, always, always in my anxiety to please I forget the forest, so to say, for the hair. Again this morning, just as the sun pants its first love outside, just as I dab perfume on the sweetest of her curling pubes, she innocently intones, "At the story's beginning, Mirabelle, our young hero stands on a staircase happily awaiting the duke and duchess. He is happy the D & D are coming so that he won't have to watch tiny drudge waiters serve breakfast. Here, listen: 'Without that geological contemplation'—he means watching the drudge waiters—'I have the deliberation of a botanist, and can behold the petite shrub of the duchess and demand of myself whether some insect might improbably come along, by providential chance, to visit the virginal pistil so offered and abandoned.'"*

I know better than to laugh at Proust's blatant flower-power analogy, so I keep my finely manicured fingernail in contact with the lovely pube I just perfumed and counted. "Whatever do you think, Mirabelle, he might mean by 'geological contemplation'?" My mistress pushes her lovely yet harsh hipbone against my chin. In the ensuant tumble I espy her nipples, which treasure she rarely lets me suckle, though I so desire to, especially when mid-morning sun tints their aureoles the color of portabella mushrooms. Fearful any tardiness will be punished with losing the electricity of her body, fearful I might be tossed into the castle's cold granite moat to wash her silken undies, I squeak an answer:

"My Regina" —I address her by her rightful Latin name of queen— "by 'geological contemplation,' I think he means that all the earth is subsumed in the very moment when he awaits the duchess."

"Very good. What number are you on?"

"One hundred and . . ."

My elliptical pause angers her and she glances out the open window toward the morning sun. Is she going to leave me in languishment? But her lip curls and she tugs a thin golden chain attached to a ring piercing my own lower lip. She pulls my face into her labia, where I perform blessed penance by worshipping her shrine until she is relieved and the sun has roamed onward.

A door opens in the hallway, so I stop writing and lean back from the computer's screen. Gina's door? Snow has been tapping my window for thirty minutes—495 porn hog words—and I fully expected her to leave before this. But it isn't her, for a male coughs; then the communal bathroom door opens and other abhorrent male noises begin. Always, always, always I dream of a time when Gina and I live alone. Sanctuary.

In the gray-blue evening a woman dying of agedness wobbles off her porch in the neighboring back yard to peep into a bird feeder. For the past four months she's gone out just before dark to inspect her five bird- and squirrel feeders. Wiping condensation off my window, I see that this evening her hair is pulled into a silver bun so tight that it looks like an inverted bowl—of strawberries? From behind in the hallway come three clicks of deadbolts unlocking and a barely perceptible shuffle. Forgetting the nature-loving crone with the dinnerware hair, I jump for my coat and muffler, recognizing Gina's demure footsteps. Cautious and clever, I wait until the hall's front door opens and closes. Then I, Miriam Johnson, pen name Miriam Saturday, rush to follow.

As soon as I step outside, wind gusts my cheeks and my nipples erect despite bra, blouse, sweater, and coat. Gina is already at the corner lamp, crossing the street under its glare where snow shafts down like lonely souls.

I follow her throughout the surrounding streets and onto the brightly lit campus in what is so far the season's harshest snowstorm, with flakes the size of her sad gray artistic eyes. For an hour I follow her, through accumulating snowdrifts. Just when I'm on the verge of running to force her to seek warm sanctuary and protect her frail fifty-year-old body, she regally enters a bookstore that for some reason is open, despite the night and the hazardous weather. I stomp my feet outside as long as I can endure before finally entering the store to see Gina settled before a low round coffee table, sipping hot chocolate, her chestnut hair still holding three snowflakes that are turning into glistening diamonds, her pink hands clasping a navy blue mug with a yellow interior. She does not look up; her pink cheeks busily puff what might be some private counting game or even a wildly syncopated jazz riff. Avoiding her body space, I reach for a cup of the store's complimentary coffee, inhaling deeply in hopes that her skin's warmth will inch across the room and envelop me. "Exactly why I stayed open," the store's owner, a male buffoon buffoonishly named Zeno, intones. "In case three Eskimos needed an igloo to read in." Three? Is he counting himself? I hear a giggle and turn to see a teenaged waif with eyes the size of King Toad's and a figure to match Sir King Toad's front legs—the skinny, atrophic non-hopping ones, that is. "I'm interested in philosophy, not igloos," the waif insists, petulantly stomping her toad feet. A gust of wind spatters snow and ice against the door. "Then Plato's where you want to start. The history of western philosophy is a footnote to Plato," Zeno the bookstore owner sniffles this out like a professor pronouncing pronouncements. He bumps around the counter, his bulging penis no doubt ready to implant this waif who must have walked to the store seeking heat, for she surely isn't old enough to hold a driver's license, even if someone were able to drive through the snowy nighttime mess outside.

Feet, feet, feet. Cold, cold, cold. I decide to sit with Gina, maybe even offer to warm her toes in my bare palms. Or at least offer my heating pad back at my room, which is only one room catty-corner from hers in the student ghetto boarding house where we live. But to my dismay Gina is walking out the door, leaving its bell to jingle.

"Wait!" I squeak. Only the third time I've dared speak to her.

She turns, her eyes large and encompassing.

"Gina?" she whispers. Behind her, snow slants heavily.

"I know your name, I know—"

As if I were a ghoul thrusting a spade into her future grave she runs off, and I run out the door after her, leaving the waif to her own problems inside the pervert's igloo.

Gina slips and falls in the snowy street, but is up and away before I can reach her, and then I slip and fall three times. No charm though, for when I regain my balance she is out of sight, and though I run, run, run I am left to return to my room alone, for I hear her last two deadbolts collapse when I enter the boarding house's hall and stomp off snow. My heart pounds at another failure, and the warmth of my room mocks me even as I put on nightclothes.

Gina, Regina, mistress, forgive me.

The storm continues; I think I hear thunder. Can it thunder during a snowstorm? I suppose it can, since that is happening now. Mostly though, I hear snow and ice pelting my window and I envision Brownies dressed in an unlikely blue, chipping away at the pane. "Gina, Gina, Gina, Geen, Geen, Geen—my breathing halts in my esophagus and I cannot push out the second syllable of her name as I chant myself into the furry land of sleep. *With each chant she grows younger, her breasts collapsing until they are mouth-sized balloons under a blue blouse. "Geen, Geen, Geen," I moan, twisting to face her room's direction as if I could incant her out of its box and into mine. Against my eyelids, shapes are pressing until I think I will cry, but the friendly blue Brownies skitter over my face kicking away tears with their blue velvet slippers. "Look," they sing, dancing and pointing. Gina! Gina sitting yoga-style in a corner of a large yellow room! But her hair has gathered raven-darkness, the color of my hair. And something about her teeth—tiny, so lustrous that the Brownies must have spent nights and nights softly polishing them into perfect Pythagorean equality. "Zeno, Zeno, Zeno," the Brownies chant, laughing in a frenzied dance while pointing to where I now stand in the yellow room, my back against a chilled yellow wall. An orange and yellow fire combusts in a fireplace that appears without even a poof! "Careful!" I shout, for Gina is twisting to place a log, but it is much too long to fit into the fireplace and she has to struggle, wobbling onto her knees. Under the sheer negligee I can see her lovely Pythagorean cleft illumined by the fire . . . then a dark shape in a brown-gray straight coat swoops from the ceiling into the room to stand spraddle-legged. The blue Brownies run off—up the walls and out the windows or into cracks. All except for one who watches a blue-eyed moment, her face molting into male grotesquerie with a shadowy broken nose. An ember pops into the air, and as Gina looks up at the man—for indeed a man does inhabit that portabella mushroom straight coat—he snatches the log from her arms as if to hit her. "Watch out!" I shout, but it is really Gina shouting and I cower by the fire that offers no heat only cold and the man is holding a cold, cold log caked with icicles and snow, and blood is blotching the man's face which is surrounded by a black beard that also holds gobs of blood and that beard is puffing about his cheeks that are fat not like a Santa's but like a pig's and his eyes are staring blue, blue, so blue that electricity ripples the striates of his iris like waves on a stormy afternoon lake and his heaving breath smells like a sack of just-opened peat moss and his mouth is caverning until his peat moss breath blows cold and the log isn't a log anymore but an ice pick that he twirls in his hand, its tiny tine revolving like Pythagoras triangulating sharp stars on a wintry night and he points the tine toward my throat my throat my throat and my Adam's apple tries to shift so that the tine will not touch, cut, penetrate, pierce, and then a flood of electric heat rocks my body and then I die into dark night.*

And awake to scream, scream, scream, for a real man's face presses against my room's window, a real man stands outside in the two feet of frozen grass between the boarding house and the falling wire fence and the old lady's endless squirrel feeders. A real man with a black beard like the nightmare man in the dream. His face glows blue from the street lamp out front. Scream, scream, scream. He disappears, and when the landlady knocks and shouts and when I open the door my neighbors on either side plus the skinny hillbilly creep who rents the room across from the kitchen and next to the communal bathroom and the music major from downstairs who plays his trumpet at night—they all are standing in the hall. Only Gina's door stays closed. I tell them what I've seen.

"You weren't dreaming?" the landlady asks. She doesn't want to call the police—who knows why, maybe she's renting illegally. But a new girl picks up the phone in the hall that can only call locally and calls locally anyway.

Gina's door stays closed.

The three guys want to go out and catch the peeping Tom, but I cough hoarsely and shout, "What if he comes in while you're out?"

"Is the kitchen door locked?" one girl asks. While two guys run to check it, the landlady runs to deadbolt the front.

Gina's door stays closed.

"We . . . we need to see if she's all right," I say, nodding toward her door.

"That old obsessed artist? Who would want to—"

Her door opens. She stands with graying hair wilding in the doorway, a fairy queen in a white gown. I want to run inside her room and jump into her warm bed and hold her and let her hold me. Over her soft shoulder I see a new painting on an easel. It's like all her paintings, depicting a woman my age, my color of hair. It's almost me, but it isn't me, it never is me.

"Gina?" she says, looking at me and almost falling forward.

"There's a man outside. A peeping Tom."

"Who would do that on a night like this?" the skinny hillbilly shrills in his bird-voice, just like he knows what nights are good and what nights are bad for peeping. This confirms my suspicion that he presses his ear against the wall whenever I go into the bathroom. It's like I can feel the heat from his head pushing through plaster and old wood into my most private space.

"He's tall and has a thick black beard and wild blue eyes," I say, for some reason, still looking at Gina, still talking to only her. "The peeping Tom, I mean."

Gina slams her door and triple dead-bolts it. One, two, three.

We all—except Gina—go to the kitchen to drink hot chocolate that the trumpet player provides while we wait for the police. Snow and ice blow against the windows and we glance at the back door, expecting a black beard to loom in it, black whiskers to seep through the cracks and tug at the deadbolt to let in black, black blackness.

"She's a basket case with all those paintings," the trumpet player comments.

"Aren't they a fire hazard?" an anorexic girl asks. I think she's a Spanish major since I see her in the halls of Romance languages.

"Oh no, dear. Most of them are acrylic, like water colors sort of," the landlady says. "I make her store the excess in a shed." When we all stare at her, she adds, "I charge her extra for the shed."

"What's her name, anyway?" my left-hand neighbor asks.

"Gina's her name," I say. The trumpet player has stood to unlock his reserved cabinet shelves. He pulls out a package of Fig Newtons and passes them around.

"I don't think so," the landlady says.

"You don't know her name?" the trumpet player asks, chewing a fig bar.

"She pays her rent in cash three months ahead, and she doesn't like to talk." The landlady shrugs. I've never noticed how fat this landlady's arms are, hanging beside her body like two slaughtered animals. And her voice's hill twang resembles what I hear whenever I roam off campus into Lexington. She and the skinny hillbilly creep whose room adjoins the bathroom are probably inbred cousins, though they don't know it.

There's a knock on the front door. We can see blue lights flashing in the street. We all move to the hall and listen as the two policemen confirm that someone has been walking in the snow around the house, stopping at each window.

"Her window too?" I ask, pointing to the artist's closed door.

The two policemen nod.

"Can you tell her that?"

"I don't think they should," the landlady says.

"How do you think she couldn't know, with all this noise?" the hillbilly boy says.

The skinny policeman who is weighted down by all the silver equipment around his waist knocks softly on Gina's door.

"Ma'am, are you all right in there?"

A squeak emits and he nods, as if conferring with the wooden door or maybe a mouse underneath it.

"Just be careful. Someone's been walking around the house tonight."

Another squeak and he nods again.

"We're going to patrol the area for the next few nights. Just be careful."

And then they're gone.

Back in my room, I pull a shade, but it won't go all the way down, so I put two sheets over the window, since I can't spare a blanket, what with all the cold.

APRIL FOOL'S DAY, AND one would almost think that summer is here, with the warmth that moved in yesterday, the last day of March. A light rain is forecast for tonight, so I know she'll go walking. She always walks at night whenever it rains or snows. Two weeks back I bought a dark raincoat with a hood so I can follow her, protect her, watch her, talk to her and tell her how very much I . . .

I finish balancing my checkbook and realize I can open a savings account. I'm actually making enough money writing pornography to pay for school, plus. What would Professor Hart, everyone's philosophy guru, think? Even worse, what would Professors Leona Coutts and Sandra Tompkins think, since both of them profess feminism, with Coutts even inviting lesbian girlfriends to play guitar or flute in classes for "curriculum expansion"? But then, what would my stomach think if I stopped writing and getting paychecks? I turn on my computer and fall into the screen's ivory blue haze.

Queen Regina is entertaining two friends tonight, and I am to serve the trio dinner. She has just finished reading Proust aloud while I decant the vintage Lafitte Rothschild and polish three wine glasses. "Clean a small fruit jar for yourself. You will drink Mediterranean style tonight," she commands, adding abruptly: "What do you think of the last lines I read?" The last lines she read analyzed Jupien, a type of homosexual attracted to older men, and rich Monsieur Charlus, an older homosexual used to having his way. More stems and pistils had found their way into the text. So what do I think? Proust has a reputation for being obsessed with smells and madelines, but he must have really been obsessed with pollen, I want to snidely comment. Instead, I silently polish my mistress's glass and listen to its crystal ringing B sharp, better known as C, while I cogitate the lines, which went something like, "Mostly, the lack of contact between two actors calls forth those types of garden flowers that are impregnated solely by the pollen of a neighboring flower, one whom they never touch." *One whom they never touch: I sigh over that line and finally say, "I wasn't thinking of Proust, but only of how melodious your voice sounds." A slow smile works over Mistress Regina's face and she walks onto the balcony to perform a yoga Warrior pose as the afternoon sun glows. I am entranced by her legs and hips and of course the intersecting V which I want to nuzzle my being into, to let its moisture and warmth surround my hair, my ears, my eyes, my lips, my shoulders and knees. The pose throws her calves out—or do her calves tauten because she wears the golden stiletto heels whose thin golden straps I have adoringly closed and opened many a time? I touch my breast and nearly drop the wine glass I am polishing. My motion to prevent the glass's fall must peripherally catch her attention. "Let me tell you," she sings lowly, "what the lines mean. They mean that you will be a lackey like Jupien tonight. If Amelia's young flute-playing friend finds you interesting, you will do whatever she bids"—my mistress turns with a smile—"even if that bidding involves her flute and your most private body."*

Six dollars a page to start, now up to twelve, since I've proven my ability, agility, and dependability—the three-pronged god, my porn publisher wrote me early on, in some rhyming Freudian quackery of his own. I once thought that all the readers were male, but haven't been so sure since over Christmas break I visited a lesbian friend and found several of the company's yellow and black paperbacks littering the bathroom's magazine rack. All of my writing so far—eight adventures (dependability!) —has centered about Mistress Regina and Mirabelle Tennessee, though I naturally have to introduce new settings and characters on occasion (agility!). But I have as yet to introduce a male into the text—not even peripherally (non-agility?). I stare at my computer screen and think of *flute*. A word that inspires the perfect opportunity . . .

While I feather-dust the dining room, Mistress Regina exercises on the balcony. At one point she sends me downstairs into the garden to fetch a certain rose, pointing down from the balcony and leaning perilously—what will I do if she falls? Where will I go, waiflet that I am? In the garden in my bare feet, since I forgot to put on sandals, I feel loam squeeze between each toe. "Over there," my mistress commands, still leaning to make my heart skip. "No, over there." At last, after scratching my fingertips and the backs of my hands while sorting through the rose bushes, I pluck the perfect ruby red rose and carry it up to her, placing it in her hair. "You hurt your hands for me," she sighs, holding both my hands up. I let them go limp and momentarily believe she is actually going to kiss each palm, but she says, "There isn't time for lotion to take away the nasty raw and scratches. Go put on the leather lover's lace." "Mistress, please!" "Go!" she commands.

The leather lace serviette outfit is suffocating and vulgar. It has three connected parts. First, a leather mask covers my face and hair, leaving my right eye open, my left nostril open, and my mouth—not only open, but unable to close, for an adjustable strap connects with the leather halter to cinch my lower jaw into varying degrees of openness. The strap runs through the same pierced opening in my lip that my golden leash did. The halter is the second component. With it, my nipples are always exposed to whatever impudence anyone might wish to impose on them. Needless to say, my front and back privates are exposed in the same fashion as my nipples. To finish the outfit off a two-foot leather tail with an eight-inch solid leather dildo always swings gluttonously. Whenever forced into the outfit my body reacts in a bi-polar manner, sweating underneath the leather, goosebumping on all its exposed flesh.

This is the outfit I wear for the rest of the summer afternoon until my mistress's friend Amelia arrives in a closed carriage. As I approach the carriage door, multiplicitously aware of my sweat, I hear her laugh. "Here comes the little pet I promised you, trotting to open our door," she says. A dark chuckle emits from the coach and my right eye widens to see sharp white teeth surrounded by a coal black beard buried inside the carriage like a malignant, malformed infant haunting a woman's birth canal. When I open the door Mistress Amelia (I am under strict orders to address her as "mistress") sticks out a dainty foot and says, "Well?" She did this once before and I had not known what to do, which earned me several sharp lashes, so now I quickly kneel and kiss her five toenails. "A trained monkey!" the male in the carriage comments. "And with a tail too," Mistress Amelia adds, pointing out the leather dildo attached to my backside after she wiggles her toes as a signal for me to stand.

If Mistress Regina is shocked to have a male enter the house, she hides the fact and seems almost delighted when he bows to rub his beard against her proffered fingers, though I notice her wiping those fingers into the folds of her gown the moment his back turns. Had he licked her hand? Did his beard smell of cigar smoke, hunting dogs, or raw deer meat?

Dinner goes quickly, with an older woman and me serving the three. Then comes the promised recital, with the bearded one playing flute while I stand in attendance, ready to serve, once more aware of the hot day's stench under the leather. During a waltz that the bearded one and Mistress Amelia play on flute and pianoforte I begin to sway, but the leather tail thumps the back of my knees, so I stop. My own queen nuzzles against Mistress Amelia during the last part of the waltz. The old woman nods at some signal from my queen—I never catch these signals and fear that if I ever I do I will replace the old woman, who is never allowed the pleasures of my queen's body, though I can see in her eyes that she desires that same flesh ravenously. The old woman soon returns from the kitchen carrying three flaming liqueurs on a silver platter. The trio makes a toast. Through the leather mask's single nostril opening I smell burning hair: the bearded one has singed himself. He scowls at the old woman and me as if his clumsiness is our fault. Mistress Amelia and my queen smile: I have never seen my Queen Regina so radiant as she is tonight before the fireplace, facing her lover, her lover who is not I. She blushes as if her first sacred menstrual blood is oozing privately in a public place—the universal initiation of all females into the sisterhood of secrecy. Leaning into Mistress Amelia, she turns toward the bearded one and gestures toward the old woman and me:

"Count, either or both are yours. I ask that you not scar the girl nor break any of her bones. There is a room you may use down the hallway."

Does this mean he has permission to break Grunthilda's bones, rip her flesh, or burn her hair? I soon find out that it means precisely that.

—Hypercorrect grammar, Latinate vocabulary, adverbs galore, tintinnabulating, sibilant, and guttural reverberations peppered everywhere—these tricks afford the key to writing seductive porn. At least this is what my publisher praises me for, and surreptitiously, subconsciously, I slip into a silvery slick satiny sway as I scribe. Alliteration, yes that too gives the reader a lift, often inserting mild humor. "Miriam, you ride the words to new heights with every installment," my publisher wrote six weeks ago. And he wanted to know how old I was. He wanted to know whether I was a student at the University of Kentucky or Transylvania. Or perhaps, he added snidely, at Lexington Theological Seminary. Not likely, I thought to myself: I'm a woman and an agnostic. He had no doubt googled *Lexington, Kentucky*, where he sends each check, and found a list of these universities. Praise

Benjamin Franklin for post office boxes to thwart stalkers. From what I understand of Ben, ye olde foresightful first American postmaster, it took one to know one.

I push from the computer and stretch with my own yoga warrior pose. Outside, clouds are moving in, covering a setting sun. Soon it will rain as forecast and soon Gina's door will unlock—one, two, three deadbolts and two new safety chains since the peeping Tom—and Gina herself will step outside with her tattered purple umbrella. Since that night seven weeks before when the real bearded one prowled outside our rooming house she has shown more than her usual skittishness. Twice she hasn't gone out at all when light snow or rain fell—highly unusual since walking in snow and especially rain seems a ritual with her. Did she lose a girlfriend to a car accident on a wet road? Six weeks ago I persuaded a living girlfriend of mine named Emily to come out with me, and when she did she responded that I was acting like a male by stalking Gina. "But she's lovely and it's Valentine's Day," I replied. We were standing at a corner behind an oak tree watching Gina sketch a crazy anthropology professor's house in a snowfall. "Yes, if you like sad, worn-out rag dolls for a valentine," my friend answered. "Come on, this is too creepy for me, even in full sunshine, much less this snow." Then, just two weeks ago in Nyx's Bungalow, a lesbian bar, my same friend accused me of using my obsession with Gina to avoid involvement with another woman. "You being that woman, I suppose?" I replied sibilantly, snidely, snippingly. With stentorian steps she strutted off. *Oh*, I thought, *oh yes . . .* I haven't talked with her since, though we share a psychology class. But I have promised myself that I'll either speak to Gina the next time we're out on the street or I'll forget the whole delusion and admit my girlfriend was right. If Gina is to be my queen, then I must be her princess. So, in bad faith—hooray for Professor Hart my fave philosophy professor even though you're male!—so, in blatant denial of Jean Paul Sartre's good faith I knocked on her door thrice last night, asking for sugar or tea bags or hot chocolate when what I truly wanted was the Promised Land. She never indicated that she heard, though I could smell fresh oil from her painting. (Oil, despite what the landlady promised—what else would my own Regina ever work in, but the purest oils?) So on this night, April Fool's, if she should walk out I will . . . but I glance to my computer screen and see that my fifteen-hundred-word goal for the day is four hundred plus short. So I scramble to type, in case the rain begins early and Gina does walk out:

The flute player says he will be careful of the young one, and my queen and Mistress Amelia ascend the wide winding stairway. I am watching the backsides of their delicate, low cut gowns when suddenly my lower jaw is yanked hard enough that I hear it pop and feel my lip tear. The bearded one twists me around and I stare in horror at an exposed cherry-colored stick that must be some Chinese flute, it is so fat and long. "Kneel, piglet!" he commands, shoving me backwards into a cranny between the marble serving table and the granite wall. My hesitation costs me a hard slap to my blind side and even through the leather mask my cheek stings. "Old one! Crawl into the kitchen and bring back vinegar, salt, and red pepper while I teach obedience to the piglet." For the next ten minutes I am slapped and battered against the castle's stone wall and the leather cord at my lip is pulled so taut that my lower lip tears and the strap becomes useless, which angers him, so he pries my jaw open with his hands and lunges. Blood from my lip plus his hot male flesh fill my mouth and I have to fight for breath, especially when the single nostril opening in the leather mask is covered with the bearded one's stomach or his hand. My head is cocked at such an angle that my eyes roll. When the bearded one finally ejaculates I choke on the congealing stickiness that swells like undercooked cream of wheat. My choking angers the count and he shoves me onto my stomach to kick my backside. In panic I gasp for air. I cannot tell whether the remaining blows arrive to save my life or endanger it. Someone rips the mask off my face and I spend a quarter hour gasping, balled in a fetal position. When I at last calm down I realize that the screams I've been hearing are no longer mine, but those of the old serving woman who is stripped nude and sheeted in blood. Her hair is singed and her face is a mangle. She has fallen against a chair near the table. "Don't scream even one more time," the bearded one commands, "or I will puncture your larynx." He is holding an ice pick, a copper or gold ice pick. "I am not accustomed to repeating myself. Do you understand?" The serving woman nods. To my right sits a heavy pewter soup tureen. If I can breathe slowly enough to stand, I can use it to crush his skull and then . . .

My editor warned that though violence should always lurk, it should also always remain subsidiary to sex. With this passage, I may have overstepped the boundaries of propriety and subsidiariness at one and the same time. Still, I have to wonder: will Mirabelle Tennessee pick up the tureen and clobber the maggot count, or will she numbly-passively watch as he slides the ice pick into the old woman's larynx? Clearly he plans on forcing a scream just so he can do such. Where is this ice pick bullshit coming from? Well, Sigmund, you don't need to search long, skinny, and hard—no pun intended—to answer that. Mirabelle, Mirabelle, I wish you well.

No poetry. My editor has been adamant about that after I once appended a porno poem to a text. I personally think him wrong, I personally think that a sweet porno poem would enlighten the hogs, but he signs the checks. Mirabelle, Mirabelle, I wish you well. And she will pick up the tureen, and it will be filled with scalding soup for there will be a burner underneath, and she will first pour the soup on the count's head and then on his gorged Chinese flute of a pecker . . .

One metallic snap. Two. Three. Gina's door is unbolting. I pull on my raincoat and wait.

The rain is surprisingly warm, considering that nightfall has come and considering that it is only the first of April in Kentucky. Gina walks differently tonight, as if she has an actual purpose. Sometimes she'll stop in a small hollow that serves as a neighborhood park, and there she'll swing on a swing. I love to watch her do this, for her face will always turn radiant as it lonesome-lifts in rain or snow or moonlight. But tonight she only pulls the swing to her breasts, gives it a heave, and watches it launch loblolly into the air and stop after one ascent. Normally she'll walk to the front of the law school to stare at a statue of some pretentious, bearded male. She does do this tonight and even speaks to the statue, in what seems to be a series of questions. I move forward as much as I dare considering the little cover available. As I squat behind a bush, I see movement behind and to my right, as if the follower is being followed. I think of my friend Emily who got so angry and accused me of stalking Gina. Maybe Emily's now stalking me. Projection. A good Freudian term every psychology major should know. That tangling theorem nearly convinces me to change my major from French to psychology.

Gina walks for another half an hour, omitting several of her usual haunts, including a typical fifteen-minute stand before the student union building staring from window to window as if searching for a face. Finally she heads back in the direction of our rooming house. At first I think she's going to stop at Zeno's igloo, ye olde horny bookshoppe, but it has closed early, so she sticks her nose against the window, and then walks to sit on a wooden slat bench in front of the mom & pop grocery store that went out of business right after Christmas. Someone said the old guy died and that the store hadn't made money for over a decade. Well, it's empty now and for sale and not making money for this new decade either.

Just as I'm empty from not making, having, holding love.

I stop on the other side of the bookstore and peep around its corner. Gina is sitting on the edge of the bench and a bus slows to stop but she waves it on. The driver, a woman whose face is illuminated by the fluorescence inside the bus, looks pissed, as if no one has a right to sit on those slats if they aren't awaiting her bus. Gina ignores her and leans to look up the street to the left. Is she truly waiting? I've never ever seen her talk with anyone. Could she be waiting for a long past lover? I think of Emily mocking me for following this woman. Maybe if I go talk with her, and tell her . . . which her? I sigh.

Then I slip behind the bookstore. A dog from a house behind barks a Chihuahua-bark. I come upon a narrow walkway between the bookstore and the empty grocery, but that does me no good since it's filled with rubbish that at the very least would make noise as I stumbled over it. At worst, I'd trip in this rain and break something . . . a brain cell?

So I continue along the delivery alley behind the stores. Turning the corner to the grocery store, I have to push through shrubbery. Doing this nearly makes me laugh, thinking of Proust's young hero with his shrub-bumble bee analogy. But this very real wet and scratchy shrub runs the length of the empty building and will provide cover. If I'm very careful and very quiet I can get within two arm's lengths of Gina.

Which I eventually do, settling to watch her shoulders rise.

I hear the Chihuahua bark again and seriously begin to wonder if Emily is following me. Projection? Wishful thinking? If we were to meet in these shrubs could we share wet kisses, secret wishes? But I have no rhyme, not even slant rhyme. I have no love, not even slit love.

I look at Gina's slumped shoulders. Is Emily right? Is Gina a worn-out rag doll? But something keeps her going, doesn't it? With all those paintings and sketches, I mean. And the way she sometimes looks at me . . . if we did become lovers . . . I open my mouth to call her name, "Gina." But I dare not here, at night, in drizzling rain. She'd think someone was about to rape or rob her. Or murder her vampire style, sucking the little blood remaining. Behind in the alley, the Chihuahua yelps shrilly. Gina coughs and the sound carries through the wet rain as if she were whispering love-nothings. I make a movement to get clear of the hedges, thinking that I can sneak back along the delivery alley and around the building, then walk up on Gina as if by accident and talk with her. But a porch light goes on to my left so I freeze before I can enact my plan.

I count cars and barking dogs. Eighteen cars, one truck, three barking dogs (though not the Chihuahua), and a siren. The porch light goes out. A long dark car pulls up in front of the bench and its window powers down. I crouch lower.

"Get in," a male commands. Between twigs and leaves of shrub I see only the car and Gina's back.

"Gina's alive," the male says. "Get in and I'll take you to her."

"Gina? Alive?" This comes from Gina. I don't understand, then figure maybe they are both speaking metaphorically: the old Gina, the boyfriend's toy love, will come back to life, blossom like a Proustian flower.

"Alive and as beautiful as ever. Like she hasn't aged. She misses you. Get in and I'll take you to her."

"Alive?"

"And beautiful. She wants you. Needs you. Get in and I'll take you to her."

Gina stands and opens the door.

"Not the front. Get in the back, so you and Gina can be together." She does as he tells her, gets in the back, but leaves the front door open. "Stupid damn bitch," I hear him say. He scoots to close the front door and I inhale sharply, for it's the man who'd been staring in my window, the man with the huge black beard. He pauses and shakes his finger—at first I think at me, then I think at Gina, but she's already in the back seat, so I realize I don't know what he's doing—making a magical hex? He closes the door, the interior light goes off, the door locks snap shut, and they drive away.

"No!" I scream.

I'm out from the bushes but the car is turning a street corner onto a main road.

I UNDERSTAND WHY CHRISTIANS clasp three gods: that number gives impenetrable, triangular comfort. Three Wise Men, three crosses on Golgatha, death at three in the afternoon, resurrection on the third day. All so reassuring and lovely.

But Gina's been gone three weeks now and she hasn't risen. I tell the landlady she should call the police, but she says I shouldn't worry, that the lodger in room two is an adult. *What,* I want to ask, *about the one in number three, that's me*? But the landlady heads upstairs to more TV, her hip joints and the wooden steps each popping three times. The trumpet player, who's been listening, imitates a triplet riff with his pursed lips; then he reminds me that the artist pays her rent three months ahead. I understand: the landlady won't care until rent's due. The trumpet player is skinny like Gina, but he has huge lips and even huger light blue eyes—not ocean blue and mean like the bearded man, but sky blue and happy. If I were ever going to nest with a male, it would be this trumpeter, even if I had to endure his muted scales each night. I finish washing my cup and plate in the communal sink, then head to my room.

Three weeks, and I've hit a dry spell in my writing after the last porno adventure. In that one, Mirabelle Tennessee did indeed decant scalding oyster stew over the count's head. Doing so not only saved the old serving lady but her Queen Regina, whom the nefarious count and Amelia were planning on murdering to steal her fabulous jewels. Mirabelle accomplished what I could not. My editor wrote back that he'd give the violence a shot—even porn hogs need a change now and then, he commented.

Three weeks, and the smell of oil-based paint barely filters into the hall anymore.

Three weeks, and I received a C on a Proust test—my worst grade ever in college.

Three weeks, and three people have disappeared: Gina into the depths of a long nighttime car; my friend Emily into the arms of heterosexuality shaped as a Greek god whose father's a doctor; and me into staring out my window at the creaking old woman planting seeds in her back yard—radishes or some other tuber, what do I know?

One, two, and three. Fiddledy-dee.

A damned robin lands on the old woman's shoulder just like she's St. Francine of Assisi, and since my window's open I hear her coo and call the robin "little gal," as in, "Did you enjoy your stay down South where the boll weevils grow, little gal?" Then she asks, "Where will you build your nest now, little gal? The bad neighbors have cut down your nice blue spruce." She means my landlady, who had some wretched sweating male relative kill the tree.

My mouth opens as if I too can bird-tweet, as if I can incant Gina, Emily, and the blue spruce back, one, two, and three. Instead, I recall what I couldn't on the Proust test: the ending of *Sodom and Gomorrah's* first book, where the memory-laden Swann comments, *In any case, this day, before my visit to the duchess, I never dreamed so far, and I am sorry to have missed, by my infatuation with the conjunction of Jupien and Charlus, the impregnation of the flower by the bumblebee.*

By his infatuation. Yes. Yes. Yes. By *my* infatuation, I am sorry to have missed . . . one, two, and three.

8.

A Wicked Little Laugh

Year 2002

(Althea, Simon, Francis, Professor John Hart)

> "There have been men so mad as to believe
> *that God is pleased by harmony.*"
>
> — Spinoza

We three—Althea, Simon, and I—met that late spring.

And we two—Simon and I—met that early spring in a freshman philosophy class. The teacher was a graduate student—an idiot, we both agreed while walking under a blooming male ginkgo tree.

"His thinking process smells like this tree," Simon commented. Around us, robins and cardinals were singing, honeybees buzzing.

I laughed my sophomoric laugh, one that might occasionally slip to a bullfrog's croak, but would remain forever unable to belly-rip and knock you to the floor. I suppose this was because I never knew my father, being raised by my mother and her sister and my grandmother. But don't get things wrong: I was no limp-wrist petunia. I knew how to swagger, blow snot from one nostril, and spit. Those arts I'd picked up from Hollywood despite residing eighteen years in a female household. Simon, on the other hand, did have a father, an over-bearing physician, a urologist. This last fact offered Simon immense pleasure, the fact of his father dealing with the instruments of piss for a living. It was Simon, you see, who was the petunia. Or was he?

The gingko tree initiated our plans to leave the dormitories and look for an apartment, since Simon commented that besides stinking like our philosophy teacher's thoughts, the tree also stank like John Faust Hall. John

Faust was the oldest dormitory on campus, a post-Civil War atrocity reserved for Honors Students, such as Simon. I lived in a non-descript dorm whose name I couldn't remember when I lived there, much less now.

When we completed the philosophy class—Simon an A+, I a B- —and summer semester loomed, I convinced Simon we ought to check out rental houses—I have no idea why we went for houses rather than apartments, maybe the image of a back yard barbecue, maybe some ill-conceived need for status. So we two drove Simon's spiffy blue convertible Audi around town and finally did rent a house on Transylvania Avenue—vampire incisors, coffin dirt, and sepulchral skin. At first the street's name gave Simon goose bumps—actual ones, for it was a drizzly Thursday morning, a Maundy Thursday if you will, though Easter and the entire Holy Week ritual lay well over a month past and though Simon was Jewish. Goose bumps rose on his pale arm like graveyard headstones as he turned his Audi's leather steering wheel onto Transylvania Avenue. "I vant your bloodt," he intoned, though his high giggle made it funny, not frightening. The street's name made me curious: I wondered why it lay near the state university and not downtown by the private Transylvania University. Then I wondered why anything in Kentucky was named "Transylvania" in the first place. "Trans"—*across*; "syl"—*woods*; "vania"—*empty*? *meaningless*? My stint as an altar boy in a town that seasonally celebrated open-air Latin masses on a redwood dais failed me on that last Latin tidbit.

While I stumbled through my linguistic exercise, Simon spotted a For Rent sign and parked in a gravel drive, his goose bumps subsiding. Mine arose, for I spotted a round-eyed window glowering from the attic, a cyclopean god blinking fateful mandates.

"Simon, this is one big house. We can't afford it," I said as we crunched gravel to peek through a window into a hallway that promised to wind on forever. The house was unfurnished—odd for a rental near a university. Nonetheless, through a third window we spotted a huge walnut desk with flowers painted on the side facing us. Wilting flowers, if you can believe it. Why would someone paint a nice lawyer-sized walnut desk, and why with wilting flowers? Maybe those were the reasons it remained behind—the sad flowers and its size, for it was a bulky affair that would present a problem moving it room to room, much less out of the house with its labyrinthine hallway. Hearing a pigeon coo, I looked up to see if the Cyclops was casting a future. My fantasy deserved a terrestrial splat in the eye, but that didn't happen. Instead, the cooing pigeon alit from an eave of the two-and-a-half story Victorian with bricks baked so maroon that they looked black against chalky blue wood trim, and I became enchanted, like Icarus, as a flurry of wings caught sunlight and punched through overcast skies. Simon spotted a fourth window ahead, higher and with a broken pane. We hurried to it, and I tiptoed on an unsteady concrete block to spy a washroom with sagging green plywood shelving, a free-standing sink and the ugliest orange linoleum I'd ever seen. Psy-groapic Orange, Simon labeled it after he took my place on the concrete block. Althea would later offer to paint the linoleum with flowers—of the non-wilting variety, she promised—to diminish the blaring orange. But at that moment we hadn't met Althea, so Simon just sniffed from his tiptoe perch. Typically, his nose fixed on spices and odors like a bloodhound's. He bragged on his ability to detect, say, garlic on someone's breath or cigarette smoke on their clothes from across a large room. But after an exaggerated inhalation through his miracle nose, he didn't reveal what he smelled. Leftover morgue? Over his shoulder I could see that the washroom had a tongue-in-groove ceiling about eight feet high, with two bare light bulbs, as if the upstairs Cyclops had gained a second eye by descending nearer earth. Until this modest add-on room, the other rooms and the omnipresent hallway had boasted soaring pre-air-conditioning ceilings aspiring toward fancy plaster domes and chandeliers—a sort of domesticated heaven.

Simon hopped off the cinder block and we walked behind the house, passing a wooden porch just made for drinking cold beer while staring at a barbecue grill. And the back yard was enclosed by tall green hedges. The pigeon now cooed from the gutter of a dilapidated red garage. Unwittingly, I stepped on broken glass from two wine bottles—MD 20/20's finest vintage. "Francis!" they yelled in a breaking retort. "Whoa, Francis! Lookie down here, wouldja!" I jumped, replying, "Sorry." When Simon glanced back I shrugged, unwilling to admit I was conversing with two broken Mogen David bottles, kosher or no.

Rounding to the house's third side, we came on an abandoned gas stove lurking near the continuous green hedge. Capsized underneath the second floor's fire escape, this stove lay as if someone had tried to secret it out one stormy midnight to hock for the rent, but accidentally dropped it from the slick fire escape instead: *A shifting wind howls; the nearby water oak's branches scrape my face as I stare down at the falling and soon to be worthless stove. Sheet lightning strikes the night; rain pelts my scalp and pings the stove's sides. Now I not only have to cough up back rent, but I have to explain what I was doing in a midnight thunderstorm on this slick fire escape toting the landlord's stove . . .*

Simon kicked the stove—*Twu-u-ng!*—to create thunder, and I blinked off my fantasy to leap upward for the fire escape's iron ladder, momentarily causing it to creak and descend. I let go since I was dangling counterbalanced in the air, so with another creak it returned to position. From the neighboring white house's second floor window came pale movement: An angel? A Victorian ghost? A co-ed in a Jeb Stuart nightgown? Bisecting the window was a limb of the huge water oak, so I couldn't tell. I wiped fire escape rust onto the back of my blue jeans, unwilling to appear slovenly to angel, ghost, or co-ed.

"Shades of Dachau," Simon joked darkly, again rippling the stove's side. He punched me when I didn't laugh. Though surprised at the strength in his skinny arm, I kept scanning that window, certain a beauteous undergraduate would raid my heart as surely as Jeb Stuart raided the North.

The windows on this side of the house were all intact. The walls of the different rooms—something I haven't mentioned—continued their rainbow parade: mushroom gray, burnt cinnamon, chalk blue, and Texas lemon yellow. It was Simon who provided those adjectives. His Audi, for instance, was "mom and pop sedate blue."

"Simon, we can't afford this place," I offered again as we ended circling the rectangular house to stare at a battleship gray front porch complete with blood red swing—those being my wimp adjectives. "We can't afford it—first floor only or not." That's what was for rent, the entire first floor, which held at least three bedrooms, a kitchen, a dining room with a crystal chandelier, a living room with a ditto chandelier, and that labyrinthine hallway threading it all. Maybe there were sixteen bedrooms, who could tell?

I was resting my hand on a battleship gray porch slat when suddenly the nearby upstairs apartment's door opened and a guy with a beard and a gal with a ponytail stepped out. Ah, the second floor inhabitants. The guy put his arm around the girl as if Simon and I were going to steal her. No way, her face was pockmarked from acne and her forearms had sinews. She looked more like a boy than Simon did.

"You're the first people to look at it. If you're thinking of renting, the lawyer who owns this is pretty nice . . . for a lawyer." The guy twitched his pebbly, Jesus-sandy beard.

"That's because she's a woman," the girl added, running her fingers through his beard.They joined hands and counted to three to hop off the porch in unison and skip arm-in-arm along the street, happily heading to never-never land.

"It's kismet."

"The house?" I looked to the girl's swaying rear end. She at least had that part down.

Simon giggled. "No, those two. But the house, too. My dad'll bite. You watch. But let's move that stove out of sight. Mom will balk if she sees it. And we'll need to clean up those broken wine bottles."

We walked back and did that, then moved the stove into the unlocked garage that leaned as if a huff from a barking German shepherd would knock it over. It was painted raucous ruby red. Back to Simon's colorful adjectives. The sky cleared and we called the rental agent on Simon's cell phone.

Mr. and Mrs. Gidron, Simon's mom and dad, were flying in for the weekend to visit, and it turned out that his dad did cough up the extra rent. This was partly due to Simon's practicing the sweet names of his colors to impress his mother, a New Jersey Jew who'd rarely encountered Southern schlock—after all, few can schlock like Southerners can, unless maybe it's German Jews. Partly due to that and partly because his father thought I'd shed good male influence on Simon since I a) drove a pick-up, b) was majoring in mechanical engineering, and c) was raised Roman Catholic. If only Simon's dad had known that all three attributes were influenced by women: the college major from my aunt, who thought I should major in "something practical" as opposed to math or physics; the truck from my mom; and Catholicism from my grand-mom. So far they'd only combined to earn me a B- in philosophy rather than Simon's solid A+.

"None of this emotive Protestant goop," Simon's father commented during dinner at the Campbell House. "You Catholics at least stick to *some* of your good Jewish theological and philosophical roots." *Yeah, B- worth*, I thought. "Mechanical engineering," Simon's mom sighed. Simon was majoring in—you guessed it, philosophy. During the entire weekend Simon's dark-haired mom's main function seemed to be to sigh or fawn, and she did a fine job of the latter with Simon, some even extending to me in happy little gifts—a fancy French press coffee maker, a Karl Marx t-shirt. She and the old man had flown down once before to attend Keeneland's Spring Meet. He dropped a bundle then, but she evened things out, winning a cool grand on the horses and taking Simon and me out to eat that time too. Her raven black—I mean so shiny that it gleamed purple—long hair and icy pearl nails entranced me, but what I remember most about her—what I remember most is exactly what I hugely want to forget . . .

So we rented the house, and Simon's dad even left a check for five hundred bucks to fix the place up, "'Cause you kids are going to stay here for the next three years, got it?"

"Got it," Simon replied.

After his dad and mom drove off toward the airport in their rental car, our combined "Got its" echoed through the house for an entire week.

IT WASN'T UNTIL WE started decorating that I realized how old the house really was. Lexington, Kentucky, should you not remember from high school history, didn't get torched by Sherman because Lincoln had been smart enough to secure his birthright state early in the war. If not antebellum, the house was at least old enough to have real plaster walls and ceilings, and in the room that Simon chose as his bedroom, a trio of plaster Cupids clung to each corner of said plaster ceiling, peeping backward over their shoulders. If the name of the street outside didn't give me goose bumps, these twelve Cupids did. Their twisted smiles—what I could glimpse of them behind sagging cobwebs—grinned malevolent and toothy, and their chubby thighs and fat feet humped each corner of the ceiling. So: a dozen sex-maniac angels individually humping Onan's love while gazing down to some central point on the floor where Simon would perversely situate the head of his bed. This room, by the way, lay on the side of the house that faced the neighboring white house, the one with a ghostly feminine nightgown in its window. Naturally I'd wanted a clear view of that second-story window, but gave in since Simon was so enamored with the Cupids and since they so creeped me out. I couldn't imagine sleeping under their gazes, even if a gaggle of cheerleaders pranced behind that second-story window every night.

"That's the Puritan influence," Simon said, meaning the malevolent Cupids. "Love decays the flesh. Think of Hawthorne."

"You think of him. I've had enough philosophy."

"Literature, you golem."

"Literature, philosophy, what's the dif?" I offered, tossing a manly interpretation of all the male movie stars I'd watched.

"Got it!" Simon countered.

Back in Bardstown last summer, my mom had bought me the pick-up that had so impressed Simon's dad—it was a robin's egg blue—even Simon had to agree on that clichéd color. The truck's upholstery still smelled of Nelson County's corn mash, and it was a Dodge and a piece of crap, but it fit my—and Simon's dad's too, evidently—TV image of manhood. So we used it to haul two beds from a second-hand store, a dining room table and chairs, a temptation green couch, Simon's stereo, and my TV. I threw my hands up when I figured what Simon was doing with the head of his bed: centering it under the collective gaze of the twelve Cupids. Was he practicing Hebrew/Puritan/Pagan mysticism? When we shoved the bed another three inches to the left and he checked the Cupids with his own malevolent grin, I made a production of shielding my eyes and executing a sign of the cross over the headboard.

We two decided to share the strange desk, leaving it in what should have been our dining room, since it was so large that it stymied us as far as relocation. How did anyone ever get it in here? Did the house get built around it, beam by beam, slat by slat?

"Being Jewish and Catholic scholars, we can stare one another down as if anticipating a scriptural debate," Simon said, setting up his computer.

"Or we can have a food fight," I offered, stowing Cheetos and peanut M & M's in a desk drawer. I opened a pack and tossed a yellow M & M at him. He rolled his eyes.

WHAT LITTLE SCHOLARSHIP I might have garnered from the desk lasted until the second day of summer semester when I met tall redheaded Althea in a second philosophy class that Simon badgered me into taking. Althea added the class a day late, and she was gangly and from Covington, across the Ohio River from Cincinnati. While her red hair didn't fit my specific fantasies, her long legs and a lanky laugh wobbling from her shoulders to her hips crippled me.

Though claiming to be Methodist, Althea really didn't seem much of anything—maybe a neophyte atheist, to judge from her comments during the opening days of class. Still, we three were working up a real ecumenical council: we needed only a Buddhist, a Hindu, a Muslim, and a Holy Roller or snake-handler to round out our search for truth.

Simon and Althea were taking a second class together, physical anthropology with the new professor everyone called "Dr. Bones," since she did consulting with the Metro police on skeletons and bodies. So it seemed natural—kismet, if you will—that the three of us trotted out for a first date to a movie. The university was showing *Vampyr* and Simon ate up the opening scene of a merchant ship floating silently into a canal to disgorge its load of rats onto the wharf of a quaint, unsuspecting European city. As Simon squirmed and let out an "Eeew," Althea didn't even blanch, but simply leaned in my direction. A big city girl, all right.

A weekend later she came over for dinner, once more all three of us convening—with classes, espresso in the student union, and Jean-Paul Sartre intervening during the weekdays. In this second philosophy class we had a real professor, by the name of Hart, and Professor Hart was a throwback devotee of existentialism: surely there was something more chic one might espouse after the millennium's twisted passage other than a leftover World War II philosophy—that being not my judgment and phrasing, but Althea's.

"Even Sartre forsook existentialism for communism—why can't Professor Hart make some modern, up-to-date move?" she asked rhetorically. "But you know what," she added, "I bet that Dr. Bones would be right in there with him, with her 'No One Touches Anyone,' line." Althea was leaning against a wall in our mushroom gray kitchen, watching Simon cook beef burgundy, at least that's what he settled on calling it after I botched its French name too many times. The previous day, we two had purchased a bottle of red wine through a friend with a fake ID. But when Althea arrived, we three had to return to the liquor store and buy a corkscrew, Simon being used to kosher twist-off-top wine and me used to the same from Bardstown bourbon, though I really wasn't much of a drinker. It was Althea who set us straight, saying that opening wine was one more thing she'd learned in finishing school, claiming that her dad was priming her for Kentucky governorship or the senate. "For real," she added as she demonstrated with a flourishing *Pop*!

"Professor Hart and Professor Circle are both right in holding to what they believe," Simon said, calmly stirring gravy—roux, he called it. "Maybe Monsieur Sartre was too much like some other people in jumping on modernity's passé communist bandwagon—living in *mauvaise foi*."

Mauvaise foi, Bad Faith, was what Professor Hart had been harping about during this entire second week. Whenever he mentioned Bad Faith, I thought of Roman Catholicism—since half of Bardstown professed that faith simply to gain prestige from attending the gorgeous cathedral built by nobility fleeing the French Revolution.

"Well what about an anthropologist holding that? I thought they studied the community of man . . . and women," I added lamely, looking at Althea's majestic red hair.

"She's a physical anthropologist," Althea commented.

"And she works on murder cases," Simon added.

"Murder seems to indicate touching well enough," I said, not willing to be beaten.

Simon poured himself another glass of wine and stared archly at me. Or was he staring wall-eyed at a single Cupid just visible through the hallway to his right? Althea, judging from her red face, was rising to our verbal bait. In preparation for counter-attack she twisted what looked like an antique ornamental knob, and what had seemed nothing other than shelving sprang to reveal itself as a door. Just like on the creaking vampire ship—at least just like I imagined during the movie—cold air rushed into the kitchen. I dropped the silver corkscrew I'd been playing with. *Thunk, clatter.*

Now, when we were first renting the place, Simon's dad had revealed an odd quirk: he insisted on placing a flashlight in every room, plus two extra for front and back entrance doors. So we had ten altogether, all Confederate Gray or Go Kentucky Big Blue. He even assigned these flashlights the names of angels in a type of Kabalistic ritual, and though Simon responded with an exaggerated sing-song that echoed off the bare walls, I could see that he deep-down believed, even when he later told me the ritual was a mishmash of Kabala and abracadabra his dad had learned from his own dad and that dad's dad—all the way back to when candles and not flashlights were used. Simon's mom held her tongue and looked on with her purple black hair, helping with salt, wine, water and whatever was needed for the ritual. *This is love*, I thought as she doled out pinches of salt to Simon and his dad for each flashlight assigned an angelic post.

So as the shelf cum door sprang open, one of the flashlights named after some angel wobbled. I grabbed it to shine down skinny steps built for a midget or maybe a tiny, vitaminless American Revolutionary War hero.

"What's there?" Althea asked.

"Whoooooooo?" Simon moaned, his wine-purple lips contrasting with his white teeth to create a ghostlike countenance.

I felt Althea's warm breath on my neck, her cool fingers on my shoulder. This was as intimate as we'd gotten, for Simon'd been our chaperone everywhere. In fact the two of them saw each other more, because of the physical anthropology class. "What's down there?" Althea asked again, seeing steps and slightly revising her question.

What was down there looked to be a small room with boxes and jars and either a concrete or hard dirt floor—and a dozen black Norway rats scrabbling over that floor as the flashlight's beam hit them.

"Boxes and jars," I answered.

"Let's go look!"

"Uh, and rats. There were some, anyway."

Simon let out an "Eeew." He was still preparing roux; I could hear the whisk click against the pot's side. Althea, however, grabbed a broom and nudged me. A big city girl, as I said. The steps were steep and narrow, imparting a feeling that I was going to plunge headfirst—Althea pressing behind didn't help matters. With each downward step, enough mold sifted through my nostrils that I figured I'd need Dristan for a week.

Once in the basement we could see that the room had been intended as a combination storm cellar and cold storage. The residual scurry of rats pushed me and Althea closer. Yellowed newspapers were piled in open boxes with chewed and decaying sides. I shined the flashlight on one paper and read a headline about U. S. troops advancing into Germany. A scattering of rat pellets on the body of the article quelled my curiosity, and a skittering of rat's feet made Althea nudge me to shine the flashlight atop some jars capped by what looked like lead lids, though surely not. Whose brain could live through eating preserves canned with lead? Was that what lost the war for the South? Anyway, all the jars held something akin to purple murk, so no one was going to eat anything from them, even if the lids were made of Teflon. A glitter atop one attracted Althea and she picked up a ring.

"A woman's wedding band," she said.

"Where's the diamond?"

"That practice only became, after World War II—it fits," she announced. I shined the flashlight on her hand to see that the ring did indeed fit.

Cornball that I am—keep in mind that my whole male life was forged from movies and locker rooms—I tried to kiss her and mushed a ruby earring and her earlobe instead of her lips. She tittered and turned to give me a full kiss. How, I wondered, could lips be so soft?

"Just that one, Romeo," she said. "Remember the rats and our ankles."

"And me."

I jumped. It was Simon, halfway down the steps, with his own flashlight beaming into my Bad Faith eyes.

After Althea left that night, Simon confided that he couldn't stand the thought of kissing a girl. While this came as no surprise, it was the first time we'd hovered around his sexual orientation. And his statement really left the question open, for I came away presuming what I'd to date presumed: that Simon was one of those rare birds that were truly asexual, a modern day

Saint Anthony without his hermit's cave. Women, painted or unpainted, tainted or untainted, would faze him no more than might men or racehorses.

Naturally we called the landlord about the rats, though we didn't tell her we'd seen them in the cold storage room, since we suspected she didn't know about it. "Nice" or not, as our upstairs neighbors claimed, she was a lawyer and would want to search for family heirlooms, even though it wasn't her family's house. While we figured Althea had lifted the only heirloom, we still wanted to explore for ourselves.

The ring stirred a good deal of conversation the following Monday after philosophy class. On its outside was fancy tooling that Simon said looked like Hebrew, Althea said looked like Wiccan runes, and I said looked like advanced calculus. What we did agree on was the engraving on the inside: R T & A J T – forever. That tooled script flounced out "forever" so finely that it turned nearly illegible.

"Why would she leave it down there?" Simon asked.

We were sitting in the student lounge, drinking cappuccino in air-conditioning, like every other student on campus. My Aunt Grace always told me that this campus was a hotbed of protests during Vietnam. I found that hard to believe looking around at all the lifted pinkies and espresso demitasses—and this barely eight months after September 11th.

"Maybe she was mad at him," Althea answered.

"Him?" Simon asked.

"She?" I asked, thinking of Aunt Grace dropping a placard over some frat boy's head.

"The wife. Her husband." Althea spurted her words like a cappuccino machine frothing cream, then held up the ring to give it a twist.

"Uh, maybe she was having an affair and took the ring off out of guilt," I offered.

"Down there?!" This was one of the few times that Simon and Althea agreed, and their joined voices caught the attention of surrounding tables, turning faces toward us. Rule One in Contemporary University Life: Don't show emotion unless you're attending a sportball game.

"Sure, why not?" I said after the collegiate faces returned to their Styrofoam demitasses. "If they used that cellar for canning and other food storage, they would have kept the rats away with a tomcat or traps. And if she was having an affair in the summer, the cellar would have been . . . fruitfully cool."

Althea and Simon laughed. So I'd scored in humor, after a bazillion failures in philosophy. The three of us continued inventing details about the mystery woman and her ring. We wound up concocting a murder/suicide combo that shocked the Commonwealth and left the house in disrepair—remember the broken window? Such was our millennial idea of disrepair, despite 9-11 and the World Trade Center, which already seemed an eternity away to our frothing 18-year-old minds.

We three decided to go on a picnic and take along Jean-Paul et al. (Nietzsche, Marx, Rawls, and Singer—"Why don't we study Spinoza?" Simon once asked in class. Professor Hart was getting a workout between Simon and Althea, I can assure you.) So along with our favorite philosophers we drove to a spot called Indian Falls, where my Aunt Grace had trekked during her student days. A local church group had bought the land and fenced it off, but that couldn't keep three enterprising philosophy students out.

Immediately within sound of the falling water, the trail became slippery and thin, so the three of us clung to one another like the kids we were, giggling as a loose rock plummeted 150 feet.

"Aunt Grace says that hippies used to trip on acid out here," I told Althea and Simon when the foaming, cascading water finally slipped into sight.

"Here? Drugs? How'd they ever get back?" Althea asked.

"She says some didn't, which is why the church group fenced the place off."

We sat on a ledge above the falls to hear and watch white spray gush over speeding water, whose only verifiable color was dark. And though it was only a bit past noon, we'd descended far enough into the gorge that the vegetation took on a shadowy patina to match the water. I pointed out a lilting black and orange butterfly crossing the gorge, bouncing its own waltz—*one*, two, three; *one*, two, three. Even as it flew out of view, I felt a wave of wildly dancing photons linking it to me. Or was that a stream of anti-neutrinos? Clearly my own brain matter stayed too dark to muddle through an engineering degree, despite Auntie's wish. Ether, the universal goop once conjectured to fill all space's emptiness, that's what I was searching for.

Over the ever-gushing water, shouts dropped from the gorge's upper far side, though they faded before we could figure whether they indicated glee, anger, or distress. Simon said something and Althea laughed, her gums fulsome and pink. I calculated the tilt of her chin: the angle of repose. Nothing could ever slip into oblivion as long as she laughed. She turned to catch me watching and gave an uncertain blink. I soared, as if my beating butterfly heart were hovering above—well, not the entire globe, but surely above the city of Lexington, the county of Fayette, and the Commonwealth of Kentucky. Back on the path we'd just descended, a cardinal chitted while cascading water below boomed around three rock shelves before rushing off to the Gulf of Mexico and the great mystic sea level. Sea level, isn't that where the sun's heat sent Icarus?

Pushed by a breeze, a white flower brushed my face. I sniffed but couldn't detect an odor, so I plucked it and turned to ask the expert nosologist. But my head quivered on seeing his hand on Althea's ankle, and my throat swelled along with the gushing water, for other than that awkward kiss in the storm cellar and one good night peck, I hadn't touched Althea. Now here the two of them were comparing ankles. As water gushed, I plummeted: down, down, toward the Gulf of Mexico and sea level.

I tossed the virgin white flower in a carefully careless manner toward the falls below where four old people, one of them a black guy, were searching for arrowheads or their past lives along the creek. "At night all cats be gray," I offered mysteriously.

"Huh?" Simon said.

"Party pooper," Althea commented, staring at me with a pair of blue eyes.

They were both right, so we stood and hiked past the slippery falls to find a grassy spot upstream where we could picnic amid patches of sunlight and shade, where we could study philosophy, make rhymes, and wade like the four old people—well, two of them anyway, the black guy and the white woman—had started doing below.

"Hey, I think that's Dr. Bones down there," Althea said. "I bet she's searching out some murder mystery clue with those men."

"I bet she's searching out a mate," I commented. "Maybe the black guy that's wading with her and just put his hand on her shoulder."

Althea leaned over. "Aww, that's sweet. He's keeping her from stumbling."

That night in bed, I thought about Icarus: could a bucket of Kentucky Fried or a hit of acid just as easily have dropped him from the heights?

ON THE OTHERWISE UNEVENTFUL day of June 3, a certain personage was born. That personage's two best friends baked him a red velvet cake soaked in rum, bought him two round-the-world pizzas from the famous Joe Bologna's pizzeria, one case of Heineken beer, one pint of Old Forester, and one three-foot concrete statue of Saint Francis of Assisi with a squirrel perched on its right shoulder, and its two open palms beckoning suffering, buffeted birdies to land and poot.

We three sat on the floor in the living room, whose walls were painted "heartbreak ochre," according to Simon. Waiting for nightfall, we were watching Francis Ford Coppola's *Dracula* and playing Trivial Pursuit. Every time Winona Rider strolled onto the screen I'd lose my train of thought. It didn't occur to me until halfway through the movie that Simon and Althea were timing my questions just at Winona's appearance. We were watching *Dracula* because the three of us had vowed to see every vampire movie ever made before summer was over. We were on our third, having recently screened Frank Langella's steamy version.

"A Trivial Pursuit question up for grabs," Simon said.

"Bram Stoker," I blurted, causing Althea to elbow me. As she did, I got a whiff of her perfume, which made me think of Winona Rider.

"Eeew, close. But this one's a real stumper: what do you think that the Marxist interpretation of the original Dracula myth is?"

"May I call Professor Hart on your cell phone for a prompt?" Althea teased.

Peripherally, I caught Winona, in her virginal white nightgown, tending her friend Lucy in the garden. Lucy, in her own virginal white nightgown, was confessing disturbing sexual dreams. It was time for another beer. I unsquatted and walked to the kitchen, overhearing Althea and Simon talking around the movie's music. We three had already situated the St. Francis statue in the back yard by a half-dead rose bush. In the red haze of sunset I could see what looked like a mouse on St. Francis's outstretched left palm, where Simon or

Althea had placed cheese, arguing that it would do until we bought birdseed. I heard Althea and Simon again. Althea had a deep voice for a teen, very sexy. In the cafeteria or the classroom, you could spot male heads turning when she talked, and that red hair of hers egged them on. Now her voice bounded along all the colors of all the walls, and I pressed against a cabinet, feeling my prick harden in nineteen-year-old kaleidoscopic abandon.

At the beginning of that week some frat boy with perfectly slick black hair straight from a Mafia movie had offered to sell me "date rape" pills. I'd said "No," but then asked how much they cost. Watching the mouse that began to look more like a baby rat crawl over St. Francis's palm, I pictured the frat boy's perfect dental smile replying amid his perfect Florida tan, "Twenty bucks apiece, personally guaranteed. The cheapest whore you'll ever buy." My hand had twitched toward my wallet, even though I knew I wasn't carrying but a ten. Anyway, I didn't want or need that kind of help in losing my virginity, so I shook my head. He shook his in turn and moved along. A few yards away, he glad-handed some blonde whose face barely looked as if she could legally drive, though her body would sizzle a jet pilot's license. She smiled prettily as he ran his hand along her bare shoulder.

"Francis, grab me a beer, please," Althea called, her voice's sine waves glowing violent red, envy green, blues blue, and mushroom gray. The result wasn't a mockingbird cacophony. No, it was like Indian Falls, where the screams, the butterfly, the flower, the hurling water, the four stumbling old people, and Althea's smooth, white ankle coalesced into an easily graphed differential equation. Graphing solves all of life's mazes, for with Descartes' handy number axis every bump shows, predictable and acceptable. I closed my right eye to wink at the ceiling: *I'm onto your tricks, you malevolent Cyclops, you.*

Giving a gratuitous peck on the window to scare the baby rat, I opened the fridge and took out a second Heineken for my red-haired princess. The Heinekens opened with a satisfying pop, and I carried them out to the living room while sniffing the hops.

"I've just learned that Marxists think that Dracula represents the old aristocracy preying on the poor," Althea said, reaching for a Heineken.

"Praying?" I asked.

"With an 'e,'" Simon said.

"Preying," I replied stupidly.

Simon won the first game just as Winona was escorting Dracula inside his mountain enclosure, readying to mercy kill him and earn him Christian redemption and a happy ending. "Praying," I silently observed, getting a laugh from myself.

We started a second game, a second pizza, and a second six-pack of Heineken, each judiciously throwing in a shot of Old Forester—if "judicious" and "shot" don't form an oxymoron. After my shot I remembered a box of science fiction books Abe Townsend's dad gave me in the seventh grade because his son was more interested in sports than boy-o science fiction. When I read one book and figured out that *Arret* was *Terra* backwards, I knew I wanted to be a nuclear- or astro-physicist. I told Simon and Althea about the seed of my physics major.

"But you aren't a physics major," Althea pointed out when Simon left to take a whiz.

"Too abstract," I replied. "Mechanical Engineering is something I can dig my teeth into." I snapped my teeth and glanced at Althea's perfect gums, her perfect breasts, her perfect arms, her perfect ankles. Since I was birthday boy, it only seemed right that—

"*Arrêt!*" Simon shouted from the hallway's blues blue. He was returning from the Grendel green bathroom. "*Arrêt*, not *Are-it*, like you've been saying. *Arrêt* in French means *stop*."

"Suiting for a negative universe," Althea commented.

Simon squatted on the floor and my prick momentarily took a backseat as we all three wandered off into a wonderland of philo-, socio-, politico-conversation.

By eleven-thirty, Simon and Althea had each won two games since we figured a way to speed it up. I'd won one by cosmic default after we tossed Bela Lugosi's *Dracula* into the DVD and its black and white film footage put Simon and Althea on autopilot. My Aunt Grace had shoveled those old non-color films down me left and right.

"Come on, this is the perfect time to go snoop in the storage cellar," Simon offered after I won.

I was for this, since I figured it would get Althea near me. Althea was for it—I don't know why—because she was looking for a mate to her wedding band? At any rate, we each grabbed one of Simon's dad's angel flashlights and lit out in Go Big Blue and Confederate Gray sincerity. Good Faith, here we come. Terra, terra, terra; go, go, go—not stop, stop, stop.

There weren't any rat corpses in the cellar because the pest control guy promised he'd use something he called "two-step," which meant that the rats would live long enough to go searching out water. They evidently lived long enough to reproduce, too, if what I'd seen earlier in St. Francis's palm was really a baby Norway. But the storage cellar itself was devoid of life other than the three of us and maybe a spare ghost. While I searched for Confederate stashes of money and Althea for more gold rings or old books, Simon plundered the newspapers.

"*Oy vey*," he called out.

Althea and I walked over and shined our flashlights on a yellow newspaper showing the gaunt faces of a young couple posing with grim, forced smiles. Over their photo, a headline read, "Camp Refugees Killed in Freak Accident." It turned out that the two had lived through Dachau and immigrated to Cincinnati to work at a German restaurant, only to be killed in a fire when the restaurant's deep fry ignited. The man had tried to pull her to safety but slipped in the burning grease.

"*Oy vey*," I agreed, for I'd lifted some of Simon's Yiddish phrasing. The date of the paper was June 4, 1947. "Fifty-five years ago tomorrow," I pointed out.

"Today," Althea said. "It's midnight."

So my birthday was over. Nineteen and still a virgin. But then, I was nineteen and still alive, which was more than that Jewish couple ever got to say.

NEXT WEEK, MY MOTHER called. Aunt Grace was dying, she said. Well, she might be, she corrected. Well, she thinks she is. Could Aunt Grace be having a Bad Faith crisis? Still, I agreed to come Friday. Simon and Althea both wanted to travel with me. Suddenly I was ashamed of Bardstown and my home and Aunt Grace with her holy cards, my grandmother with her snuff, and my mother with her job as a loan officer in a small town bank. (For though Bardstown had grown into a Louisville bedroom community, everyone still looked on it as a town; everyone still bragged about the bullet holes in Talbot Tavern that Jesse James had supposedly drilled into the wall, and everyone still revered the cathedral's paintings given by French nobility fleeing their Revolution not very long after helping us in ours.) So I fended Althea and Simon off and drove home alone, paying my tolls on the Bluegrass Parkway.

"The whole time I went to UK I paid tolls on that damned thing," Aunt Grace complained when I arrived.

She didn't sound or look sick to me. She was lying, however, in bed propped up on four pillows, so I just nodded.

"And now that I don't need it, it's nearly free." She let out a groan, what I'd been expecting since I stepped into the room.

My mother smiled—I could make out her polished teeth from the afternoon light at the window where she stood. She and Aunt Grace often passed for twins, though four years separated them. They both still had hair as black as a crow—that dark black that's almost purple, a Mrs. Gidron look. That's odd, because my hair was a dirty sand blonde.

"Grace wants you to carry us to the cathedral, so Father McKenna can hear her confession—"

"He won't give me last rites," Aunt Grace cut in. "He says I'm still kicking too hard." To demonstrate, she gave a kick that scared her Siamese cat off the bed and knocked a pillow onto the floor. She calmed after that, remembering that her immediate goal in life was to die.

We drove to the cathedral, shoulder to shoulder in the seat of my robin's egg blue pick-up like Three Musketeers in search of a rainbow color. About thirty years back, someone—from Louisville or New Albany across the river, every Bardstowner always claimed—walked into this cathedral and razored down eight of the valuable paintings. They were eventually recovered, and since then the cathedral has kept them under a light/sound/motion security system supposedly designed by the great grandson of the guy who built New York City's subways. While I can't attest to the truth of that last fact, I do know that two groups have since been caught by the system before they even pulled out their razor blades. If this system had been on those four jets, the World Trade Center would still be standing, the Pentagon intact, and that Pennsylvania field still growing corn or whatever it grew, not sprouting charred corpses.

Before I could check the walls for the age-darkened paintings, I saw Father McKenna waiting before the communion rail, hands clasped atop his mid-section, dandruff flecking his hair and eyebrows. He looked just as he had when he walked into the classroom and we all stood to sing-song, "Good morning, Father McKenna!" Once every two weeks he insisted on teaching us the Greek alphabet. This always amused me in its uselessness, but frankly, it's the only thing I remember from grade school other than trouble. Dandruff whirled as he nodded at my mother and me then shook his head at Aunt Grace, who'd walked—strolled!—in, feigning to wobble a moment too late to be convincingly dying. When my mom first called about Aunt Grace, I thought: *Bad Faith.* But now, looking with a pigeon's-eye view from the arched cathedral ceiling, I took in the eight dark paintings secreted out of France, the rows of penitent pews, and the four tiny people bobbling over the granite floor, and realized that it wasn't Bad Faith, but just time to offer tiny Aunt Grace a little special attention, a little relief from her duties as a social worker for abused women and children. So, fine. So we would nod and sway and Aunt Grace would carry on an individualized confession in a confessional booth that had seen minimal action for over twenty years, plenary confessions and reconciliation becoming vogue before I was in grade school.

Father McKenna limped more noticeably than I remembered as he unlocked the confessional. I heard Aunt Grace tisking at the fact that the confessional had to be kept locked, and I saw Father McKenna grab a rail inside the cubicle to ease himself down. My mother clucked empathetically. These were the people I was ashamed to have my friends meet? Speaking of Bad Faith, I trundled a mountainload. I eyed two single amber votive candles burning before a statue of Saint Joseph, complete with lily and stem cradled in his arm. Why not a hammer and carpenter's square? I walked up, lit two more candles, one for Simon and one for Althea, then dropped in two nickels, since their clunks would match those of quarters.

In five minutes, Aunt Grace emerged from the confessional, radiant and ready to face another fifty years of life. "He wants *you* to come in." She handed me a holy card with my namesake Saint Francis kneeling before a boulder, his eyes uplifted to some torch-like affair in the night sky. Where were the infamous talking animals? There! A mouse (Mickey?) stood on its hind legs beside the saint's sandaled feet. "Flip it over," Aunt Grace directed, as if mind-reading my blasphemous thought. On the back of the card was the old form of private confession, with appropriate blanks: *'Bless me, Father, for I have sinned. It has been ________________ since my last confession.'* And so on.

My mother was nudging me, too. "Are you going?" I asked her with as much accusation as I could muster.

"I haven't been away to college, I don't need to," was her blithe answer.

With a roll of my eyes I glanced at the card, then entered the confessional and knelt. Someone, probably a school kid, had been using it as a smoker's haven, despite the locked doors. I sniffed just as Father McKenna slid back the divider, and I could vaguely make out his chin resting in his hand.

"Good afternoon, Father."

"Didn't your aunt give you a card to follow?"

"What—oh yeah." So I started out, barely able to read the card by holding it to a crack for light. Father McKenna'd gotten my goat with his curt remark, so other than lusting in my heart (seven lucky times) and drinking too much (one unlucky time) I told him that I was guilty of "mauvaise foi." He didn't stumble in the hunky hillbilly way I expected, however. Why should he, I realized. He's Irish.

"Bad Faith? Are you having doubts about Christ and God?"

"No, Father. I've been guilty of acting in Bad Faith towards my family and friends."

"How's that?" he asked, unwilling to let me off the hook.

"I've been a typical college kid thinking that my family wasn't good enough for my friends, and . . . and I haven't always been good enough for my friends, either."

"What you're saying is that you've been thinking too much of Francis, and too little of others."

I had to swallow saliva at that. To top it, I heard the heavy thud of quarters out at the votive candles and realized that nickels wouldn't match their sound at all.

"You're in college now. Instead of rattling out prayers for your penance, what I want you to do is read a life of your namesake, Saint Francis. There are plenty around. Chesterton has a good one. And come tell me about it the next time you're in town, understand?"

"Yes, Father."

"Good. Take your Aunt Grace and your mom out to dinner. That's what you three are up to, isn't it? Driving to Louisville?"

"Yes, Father."

"And tell your-r-r Auntie Gr-race how pr-retty she looks. You know women love that."

"Yes, Father." He was slipping into brogue, so I tried to rush matters before he started talking about milk cows, shamrocks, and Patrick's banishing of the snakes. But instead of telling some hunky Irish story, he slid the confessional shut and began mumbling. When I stepped out, I saw that my mother had changed her mind, and had gone in on the other side. There were still only four amber candles lit. Who'd dropped in the quarters to make up for my skinflint nickels, Aunt Grace or Mom? Did it matter? *Mauvaise foi.*

That night we did drive to dinner at a fancy place outside Louisville where a waiter kept flirting with Aunt Grace, letting me off the hook.

In this manner was completed the saving of Aunt Grace, who could live another year or two without once more drooping into her erstwhile death-bed. I drove my robin's egg blue pick-up back to Lexington and forgot about Saint Francis.

WHAT HAD COME TO be my life returned to me, akin to a fine calfskin driving glove fitting a hand. I knew that feel because Simon's mom had bought him driving gloves for his sporty Audi.

Though I was stupidly comfortable in my life, as if I'd reached forty-nine instead of nineteen, Simon hadn't made it to my coasting stage. Under pressure from his parents and grandparents he joined a Jewish youth group. The group was aggressive in its stance toward Israel and the Arab question—"aggressive" being a mild description since two of the group's members owned an arsenal of semi-automatics and handguns between them. Simon stopped counting at twenty-three at one guy's place. This didn't sit well with Simon and Spinoza, whom Simon told me was a Jewish renegade expelled from his synagogue with a horrific oath invoking angels and fire, starvation and bones. And the semi-automatics sat entirely too well with Bad Faith. Simon visibly squirmed in philosophy class as Professor Hart spoke.

"Spinoza . . ." Simon started one morning as we walked toward class. We had to pass the same gingko tree, and its spreading male seed had become downright disgusting. *Please axe me, I'm a male and can't help it*, someone—no doubt a feminist undergrad—had tacked in pink paper onto the tree.

"Spinoza?" I asked after we stopped laughing about the note.

"Who?" Simon was evidently distracted beyond conversation. We walked on in silence, and I pictured Spinoza bent over lenses in some cavelike room, grinding away until his lungs filled with enough glass particulate to kill him. What if he'd been converted by Francis of Assisi? If they had lived in the same country and century that is. What if they'd met and formed a pantheistic order of Judaeo-Christianity? Maybe 9-11 and the World Trade Center would never have happened, maybe . . . the pleasant thing about being nineteen is that you have the willingness to believe any blather. That *should* be the pleasant thing about it anyway, shouldn't it? I mean, shouldn't every teenager, male or female, Jewish or atheist, American or Palestinian, Muslim or Buddhist, Hindu or Christian, animist or capitalist, have the opportunity and leisure to believe in blather? Instead of dodging bullets or worrying over the next slice of bread, I mean.

It so happened that Simon had a meeting with the Youth Group on a Friday evening, the beginning of the Sabbath. Althea and I were becoming cozy and planned to study in the house alone, together. It wouldn't take Spinoza, Sartre, or Yosemite Sam to figure out where *that* would lead my just-turned nineteen body and mind.

Now, one of Professor Hart's favorite examples of *mauvaise foi* came from old Jean-Paul himself: a woman is sitting on a couch with a man she's recently met. He drapes his arm around her, over the couch. She doesn't like this, so she pretends it isn't happening, that she doesn't feel it, that maybe it's an automated massage feature of the couch, say, or maybe a cat that's jumped up, even though she doesn't have pets. She makes herself believe this instead of confronting the truth and telling the masher to remove his arm and listen to what she's saying about culture and ideas. She makes herself believe that he's interested in her as a human, not as a lay.

"Jean-Paul Sartre wasn't much on social reality, was he?" Althea commented in class upon hearing this example.

"On the contrary, he fought in the French Resistance," Professor Hart replied.

"Then he should have been more attuned to social amenities," Althea shot back, "because there are times to stand firm and times to bend." She sat behind me and I could feel her breath on my neck.

"Existentialists never bend. Duty is a false imposition to an existentialist, even the so-called duties of friendship or social amenities," Professor Hart replied, not quite knowing what to do with the chalk in his hand. This was one thing I greatly admired about the entire philosophy department—no Power Point presentations.

"Could that be why there aren't any more of them around? Pretty much like the Shakers over in Danville with their virginity and separation of sexes and all. A self-defeating philosophy."

Professor Hart gave a smile. I think he was developing a crush on Althea. Or was I projecting?

Althea and I weren't Shakers. We weren't particularly acting in good faith, either, for instead of sitting at the lawyer's desk with the wilted flowers to promote study, we plopped onto the temptation green couch. Semi-recumbent is to intercourse as erect posture is to good study habits. Still, we fought the urge in good Bad Faith style. Once by going into the mushroom gray kitchen for Cokes, and once by going down into the storage cellar to see if we could find the match to the woman's wedding band and solve the mystery.

Instead of solving a mystery, we opened one.

Someone—Simon—had moved a mattress onto the middle of the floor, covering it with an expensive purple bedspread. And he'd started going through the stored old newspapers, cutting out articles pertinent to the uncovering of the Holocaust and the ending of World War II. Half-burnt candles were placed in front of the articles, including the one about the unlucky couple in Cincinnati that we'd read earlier.

"Haven't you smelled these candles burning?" Althea asked.

I answered that I couldn't smell much of anything because I'd been raised within the haze of Bardstown's whiskey distillery corn mash since I was a baby. "It used to be a dry county, no alcohol sales," I commented.

"Bad Faith," she replied, shining her flashlight around the room. "Make it, but don't drink it."

"Yeah."

A box of matches showed in the flashlight's beam, so I lit a candle, which cast a ruby hue through the votive glass that held it. Althea lit four or five more and turned off her flashlight. "The rats are all gone," I said, putting my arm around her. A lie, for I'd seen more babies besides that one in St. Francis' palm. We sat on the blanket and stared at the lit candles. The last one she'd lit illuminated another young Jewish couple who were supposed to immigrate to New York after the war. They'd died in transit, in the collapse of a Polish train trestle that had been weakened by resistance saboteurs but had never collapsed during Nazi occupation. It was almost as if the universe were having a wicked little laugh of galactic Bad Faith against the Jewish race.

"Spinoza," I announced, "died alone, without a family, because he'd been declared anathema by the Jewish community."

"He had to polish lenses for a living, because no one would let him teach or write in his chosen profession."

I blinked, looking into Althea's frank eyes, wondering if she were meeting Simon on the sly. But no, it was stupid of me to think that I'd come up with anything philosophical that she didn't know. I turned off my flashlight, and my nineteen-year old hands began to roam from her shoulder to her right breast. I felt her nipple harden as I concentrated on the ruby votive candle, pretending that my hand had maybe just slipped.

"I'm a virgin," she announced, unbuttoning her blouse and unhooking her bra. "So be nice."

"I am too," I said.

"Nice?"

"A virgin."

BOTH ALTHEA AND I were too embarrassed on Monday—from what we'd done in the one-room cellar—to directly bring up discovering Simon's personal Holocaust shrine, though Althea did start in about Jews and pogroms on the patio beside the student union cafeteria. She seemed so intent upon eliciting some lurid confession—*I, Simon Gidron, admit to harboring murderous anti-Arab fantasies in the cellar*—that you'd have thought she was the Roman Catholic, not me. We three were sitting on a low brick wall that boxed a bed of marigolds, which of course attracted yellow jackets. Still, if Simon and Althea were willing to sit there and drink espresso, I could forsake calculus and also brave the wasps and ultraviolet from the depleting ozone. Since Simon remained unresponsive to her talk of Jews and pogroms, I started about Spinoza being exiled by his own people, a subject Simon'd spent the last two weeks explaining to me. Could it be that you, Simon, view yourself as a teenage Spinoza, I wondered aloud. No response. Then Althea piped in about desert fathers, about their holing up in caves to study and meditate. Where'd she come up with that, I wondered.

"Look, you two. I know you were down in the storage cellar and saw the shrine." When we gave him our amazed and innocent looks, Simon pointed to his nose. "I could smell what you two . . . that someone had been down there."

I studied his hooked nose flaring, which evoked the thought of my jism intermingling with Althea's virgin blood, clinging in molecular clumps to permeate the damp cellar air. Althea had wanted to take the purple bedspread upstairs to wash, but I'd pointed out that we really didn't have enough time since Simon was due back in an hour. I'd also promised that I'd wash it early next morning when Simon went to the library. But next morning I lazily convinced myself that the basement's darkness would overcome any stains. I hadn't considered Simon's wondrous nose, which even now might be harboring molecules of my jism and Althea's virgin blood.

"Shrine? Is that why you go down there?" Althea was bulling through the sexual implications of Simon's dangling words, but Simon opened that subject directly:

"I don't go down there for the same reason as you two, if that's what you mean. Why didn't you just use Francis's bed?"

Althea blushed so sharply that I thought she was going to slap Simon. I could feel myself flushing too, but the only thought I had was, *Now you see what it's like to be on the outside.* I was remembering the cozy ankle-holding at Indian Falls. Now the only thing that saved a free-for-all was Professor Hart's ambling up.

"Well, well, my three favorite students."

Professor Hart conveyed—despite a middle-aged paunch—a contagious energy wherever he went. In front of class, he'd flip chalk and pace, popping his finger toward a student to ask, "What do you make of Singer's contention that animals should not be subjected to painful research, Ms. Jackson?" Rumor had it that he'd been in the Marines and fought in Nicaragua, which explained these drill-sergeant tactics, though hardly his concern for ethics. Or maybe it did. That's what he was like, making you ask questions when you thought you had only answers. Even now as he shifted from one leg to the other, it was hard to stay seated on the brick wall.

"Is your presentation moving along, Mr. Gidron?" He turned to Simon in a wide-legged stance. Althea and I looked quizzically to see Simon blush as heavily as Althea had seconds before.

"Ah, he hasn't told you two?—Keeping it a surprise, Mr. Gidron?"

Simon shrugged. One thing I'd learned about Simon was that he could take on a tremendous cloud of pouting and retain that overcast for hours on end.

"That's okay, the secret's over because I've decided that the only way I can keep the three of you off my back is to assign each of you a class presentation, so it's serendipitous that I find you in companionship with flowers and gentle bees." Professor Hart paused to laugh, and we laughed with him—who knows why? The wellsprings of Sartre's *Being and Nothingness*, stage 1. "Ms. Jackson," Professor Hart continued, "since you represent the flower of this trio, you might want to give us a presentation on Simone due Beauvoir's case for feminism, especially as you're such a fan of Jean-Paul Sartre." Althea's shoulders rolled loosely at his tongue-in-cheek comment, but Professor Hart turned to me before she could respond: "And Mr. Willett, I'm thinking that a presentation on your namesake, St. Francis, and his blending of mysticism and Christian charity would do just fine."

It was an iteration of the butterfly in chaos theory. I mean the bit about St. Francis emerging from a dormant cocoon not even two weeks after Father McKenna doled out reading his biography as a penance. So it was my turn to blush, for I hadn't completed that penance, which of course meant that my sins weren't yet truly forgiven. I could have died any time and gone to hell. Stung by yellow jackets and dropped into anaphylactic shock. But hell was where I was headed anyway after Friday night in the storage cellar with Althea. Intercourse, course, course . . . outside, side, side . . . matrimony's holy sacrament, ment, ment—I could hear a bevy of nuns sibilantly delivering their chorus from the Student Union's third floor windows or piping it through sewers all the way from the closest convent five miles away, via the storage cellar in our house five blocks away.

"This will be like Dante's descent into hell," Simon announced, twisting the knob that opened the cellar's door. He'd already been down there "setting the scene" in his words, while Althea and I steamed cappuccino from the expensive machine Simon's mom had sent him—well, him *and* me, since his mom insisted that I owned a half share. This was very un-Jewish of her, Simon had informed me, that is, her extending wealth not only outside the family but to a goy to boot.

But for now he was busy with theatrics and intoned as he held the cellar door open: "Midway on life's humble journey . . . I found myself lost in a woodsy cellar . . ."

"Not Dante! You're Immanuel Kant!" Althea burst out, being right up there with Simon on philosophers.

"No. You're a Kentucky basketball coach after an NCAA investigation!"

"Boo!" Simon and Althea hissed, turning on me.

It was a sham on my part, the sports talk, just like the mechanical engineering major. I really wanted to delve into physics or astrophysics, press my eye against a lens too large for even Spinoza to grind, or maybe press my ear against a nuclear accelerator out at Los Alamos, but my aunt, as I said, held sway for the moment. Odd, someone whose life's work had been helping alcoholics and abused and battered women and children insisting that her nephew undertake a practical college major. I'm not saying this out of meanness—even dear old Aunt Grace admitted that statistics showed she was beating her head against the Great Wall of China as far as effecting true recovery or healing. Which is why, my mother and I long ago concluded, dear Auntie underwent her ritual death throes every few years.

"After you," Simon said, tugging the door open.

"Said the spider to the flies," Althea responded.

"Oh no, Francis is the spider; we're just the flies."

Miffed at Simon's comment, I charged down. *Bump, bump, bump*—our three pairs of shoes clunking against the cellar's wooden steps; *slush, slush, slush*—our cappuccino splashing in all three cups. I spilled some and burned my wrist on the fifth step when I spotted a cacophony of flickering lights that tiers of candles were casting on that shelf of purple preserves. "Cacophony" is right because there was so little other sound—not creaking steps nor my hay-fevered froggy breath nor the slush of the cappuccino—so little other sound, except for candles guttering, that I momentarily thought the house on fire.

When Althea and I stepped below the floor joists to take in the entire room we exhaled deep "ah's," like kids at a firework display. Simon had cleared out most of the preserves and now there were—I don't know, I'm not autistic with the gift of instant tabulation—there were maybe a couple hundred candles. So many that the storage cellar had warmed. So many that for the first time I could see that the walls had long ago been painted a blue that had turned chalky from seeping limestone.

We three quit the steps to sit on the mattress, Simon assuming a yogi's lotus position over the purple bedspread—the washed and ironed purple bedspread!—while Althea and I squatted like good Kentuckians. Behind each candle stood picture frames of variously colored metals and woods, many holding newspaper articles on Holocaust survivors. Collectively, the glass from the frames reflected the guttering candles, creating the illusion of an endless hallway, just like the one above us. The weirdest part was that about half the frames stood as blank sentinels to the universe, waiting to be filled. I thought of a poem—or maybe it was a story—by Edgar Allen Poe about the masque of the red death, how death stalks people at a ball, silently strolling through the hallways of a great palace and pouncing upon them as they caress an illicit lover or drunkenly sip champagne or cower in a dark corner. Or maybe as they stoop to pet a poodle's manicured noggin.

"They're all so thin," Althea said, leaning to study a newspaper photo of someone who'd made it to America from a concentration camp, only to step in front of a car.

"None of them ever gained weight, even those who succeeded in some small way," Simon replied. "It's as if growth hormones had been exiled from their bodies."

While he whispered I spotted ten huge bullets of more military than hunting caliber, standing upright. Upright bullets, just like Mr. Gidron's ten flashlights, just like the ten angels that guarded the throne of Y----h. These ten were guarding a framed red posterboard sign done up in gold glitter that outlined a careful script that read (once I leaned so no shadow obscured it),

"The essence of faith
is awareness of
the vastness of Infinity."

Feeling Althea's edginess I knew she'd spotted the bullets too. All one hundred and forty-four candles were sputtering and flickering. I had downsized the candles to a particular number, so maybe I *was* autistic.

"Don't worry," Simon said, "I haven't given in to fanaticism, though the people who passed me those bullets certainly have. They wanted me to enshrine them and think of revenge every time I heard or read that a Jew was killed in Israel. 'Ten lives for one,' they shouted. 'Ten for one.' "

The candles guttered erratically, like leaking heart valves.

"I thought it was an eye for an eye." Althea's voice had lost its sexiness and was rasping.

"Post Holocaust, post World Trade Center thinking is changing that," Simon answered flatly. "That quote," he added, "the one about infinity, is by Abraham Isaac Kook, Rav Kook. For me, it's an antidote to the bullets and post World Trade Center thinking. I sit here and tap my knee bones like a Hindu yogi, substituting *faith* for *revenge,* and I chant that faith is ten borne to the tenth, to the tenth, to the tenth, to the tenth, to the tenth, to the tenth, to the . . ."

Simon, nodding, was hypnotizing himself.

"To the tenth, to the tenth, to the tenth . . ."

The candles seemed to join his mantra, sputtering . . .

"To the tenth, to the tenth, to the tenth . . ."

As Simon continued his candlelight chant, I could see tears glittering on Althea's cheeks, and I thought about old Deutschland father Friedrich Nietzsche's vision of eternal return. You'd only know life was eternally returning if you stepped outside of it, I'd argued with the graduate student last semester. And if you did step outside, then it wouldn't be returning. He'd given his usual blink and I'd thought him a fool. Now I wasn't so sure. Maybe you didn't need to step outside to know futility, maybe you didn't even need Aunt Grace's statistics or a history book about the Middle East. And maybe if you did manage to step outside, life would step right along with you to keep returning despite your coy intellectual chess move. Keep returning like a play about two star-crossed lovers sifting through violence and laughter and love to end . . . just when, where, and how you always knew they were going to end: atop a catafalque with poison on their lips and a dagger in the breast.

"To the tenth, to the tenth, to the tenth . . ."

Summer session was scheduled to last eleven weeks. We were nearing July and had passed midterms: Simon and Althea, an A+ apiece; young Francis, a B, up from last semester's B-. So there was hope, prehensile thumb and all, if only Brother Sun and Sister Worm could help. Yes, I'd begun reading Saint Francis's *Little Flowers*, for what good it did me—or him, since his Canticle of Joy praising God through "Brother Sun, Sister Moon, Brother Water, and Sister Mother Earth" seemed a sad prelude to the terrible stigmata that he suffered. In fact, I was holding a paperback copy of the *Little Flowers* in my hand, preparing to counter Simon's Spinoza when—

"She's pregnant," Simon said. We were sitting on the back stoop, taking in summer sun, which didn't feel very brotherly with all the heat it beamed down.

"Who?" I asked stupidly, stupidity being a recent occupation even in my calculus and chemistry classes since I'd taken a part time job as a short order cook.

"Althea, of course."

My heart pumped. It had been three weeks since our liaison in the storage cellar, in Simon's Holocaust shrine. *Liaison:* such an adult word.

"No way."

"She is."

"Did she tell you?"

"She didn't have to. I can smell her changing hormones. She may not even know herself."

"Bullshit, Simon. Bullshit."

"What if I'm right?"

I went inside for two beers and brought them back out. Brother Sun hadn't moved.

"Who the hell was it who made the sun stand still?" I asked, sitting down.

"Joshua."

"I thought he blew down the walls of Jericho."

"He did that too."

"Busy guy." I gulped beer and looked at the statue of Saint Francis, which had a fresh coat of pigeon shit.

"Yeah, he was a real schlepper."

I first thought Simon said "sleeper" and wondered whether he was right about Althea. But virgins can't get pregnant. I mean, not with all that blood and struggle. I mean, she was in pain almost the whole time, though she insisted that I go on. I looked at the sun and tried to envision Althea sitting behind me during yesterday's philosophy class. Had her cheeks been rosy, her breasts swollen? Isn't that what happened to pregnant women? But did it happen within three weeks? Within three days over three weeks? I couldn't very well ask my aunt or mother. I gently lay the *Little Flowers* on the wooden step. I couldn't very well ask St. Francis, either.

July Fourth fell on a Tuesday. Althea invited us to her condominium for a cookout. She'd lost her roommate after the spring semester, but her parents told her not to rush to find a new one, to take her time and be certain of getting a good one that wouldn't ruin her studies and that they'd cover the difference in the monthly mortgage payment. Mortgage, not rent—imagine that for a college student. I was hanging around with the best, all right.

Althea'd bought a leg of lamb, thinking of Simon, and she had even gone to great lengths to clean one of the community grills so there'd be no pork residue. So she was under the same misapprehensions about his devotion to religion as he was about hers; to me, they both teetered on agnostic at best, despite their weekly attendance at services. And from what Simon told me of his hero Spinoza, that philosopher's oddball brand of theism wouldn't impress Methodists or Catholics any more than it had his own Jews.

"Simon, explain to Althea and me just what Spinozian aspect of godhead those three jocks come under." I meant the three jocks barbecuing an immense amount of meat—immense even as judged by someone raised in Bardstown—on a nearby grill while three females dangled their jewelry and arms near the fire and smoke. The females were all blonde, two of the jocks were white and one African American.

Simon gave a plum-grin and lifted his pinkie: "Prince Charming, Prince Charmin, and Prince Charred."

An hour and a half later we were inside when Althea said, "Why don't you two carry our cooler up to my sunning balcony? I'll meet you there in a couple of minutes." Her sunning balcony wasn't a balcony at all, but a fenced-in area on the roof. There were only five of these in the complex, and to hear Althea tell it, each added ten grand to a condo's price, but her parents argued it would help resale value. The right people, as I mentioned earlier. Me, hanging around them.

Simon and I obligingly took the cooler up to the roof without any questions, and began setting up chairs. Thinking Althea was planning on coming right up, I'd left the door open, and upon hearing loud voices, I walked toward it.

"Where's the two faggots who were laughing at us?"

"They left. Out the front door." There was a pause. "I have two, you know. Doors."

"Yeah?" This was from a different voice. "So maybe the three of us should come in this door and make ourselves at home. Entertain you. Lock your other door. Teach you who to hang out with."

"Not faggots."

"Just go back to your blonde girlfriends, fellas."

"We're in the mood for redheads."

"Yeah, we wanna see if your cunt hair's as red as—"

There was a gunshot and a howl just as I was starting down the steps.

"Bitch! You shot his foot."

"That was rat shot, the rest are hollow points and I won't be aiming at feet but balls. My father was a Marine and he taught me to shoot. Get out of here and be happy I don't call the police and press charges for forceful entry and attempted rape. Coach wouldn't like that, would he?"

Althea's sliding door heaved shut with a thud and I could hear her latch it. Simon and I were already off the roof and could hear through her open second-floor bedroom window as we ran through:

"Goddamned bitch shot his foot!"

"What the hell will Mary say?"

"Mary? You better worry about Coach and hope that rat shot all comes out."

We ran down the last flight of steps to see Althea waving a red scarf at us, holding a pistol in her right hand. She started to cry and dropped the pistol on an end table when we reached her. I jumped, thinking for sure it would go off. Simon went to the sliding door and pulled its curtain closed. "They're over at those three girls' place," he reported. "Arguing. One of them is shoving one of the girls."

"Great," Althea muttered.

I could still smell gunpowder, and through the plate glass before Simon had pulled the curtain I'd seen a trail of bloody splotches.

"Just like Rehab," she said, giving a nervous laugh, "red scarf and all."

"Rehab?"

"In Joshua. She was the harlot who saved his two spies when they went into Jericho. She sent them to her rooftop." That came from Simon, who still stood watching.

"You're no harlot," I said to Althea, finally doing something useful and putting my arm around her.

"We'll see." She pulled from me and placed the black pistol in a drawer.

The police arrived an hour later, but not because of Althea's gunshot.

After all, there were plenty enough fireworks banging and Althea assured us that only a quarter of the shot actually hit jock-boy's foot. No, the cops arrived because the three girls called them to toss the jocks out of their condo. Or maybe a neighbor made the decision for the girls.

"Your dad was a Marine?"

"He was a lawyer in the Air Force. He retired a full colonel. Mr. Straight and Narrow himself. Super Dad."

We two were sitting in the student union, drinking hot green tea this time, treating ourselves to an antioxidant. Simon'd been roped into doing something for the Jewish youth group—transporting hand grenades, he had joked. Simon's group of "Jews Against the World"—his name for them—was becoming ever more militant after several car bombings made the news, and of course this was after bin Laden had toppled the towers of Babylon, as he no doubt thought of them. Two of Simon's group had already quit the university to go to Israel, just like that Walker fellow had quit to go to Afghanistan.

In a far corner, a gaggle of students were playing video games. Occasional whirring noises bounced off the low, dried-blood brown tile ceiling. We two tried to look outside at the gorgeous sunny day.

"So you lied to the jocks about your dad being a Marine? That's great."

Althea plucked out her tea bag. "I lied to you and Simon, too, because I saw the jocks coming through the kitchen window. They were drunk and looking for a fight."

"But—"

"I overheard them talking earlier, when you two were carrying in the platter and cooking utensils. They finally figured out that the three of us were laughing at them. They weren't very nice: they said all three of us needed an ass-fucking. So when they walked over I sent you both up to the roof to avoid a fight." She flipped the tea bag onto a plate. "Great strategy, huh? Instead of a fist fight, I wind up in a gun fight."

"You didn't have any choice; they were going to—"

"I should not have answered the door. Even stupid jocks aren't stupid enough to break through a plate glass door. They weren't that drunk."

"Maybe," I said.

"Look, let's change the subject. The three little blonde weird sisters are avoiding me like I'm rabid, so everything's settled. And I'm really not into remembering. How's Simon handling the Jews Against the World?"

When I bit my lip and looked into her blue eyes, she glanced toward the video games. "I'm worried about him," I replied. "He openly spends time—lots of time—in the cellar, burning enough wax that I can smell it, despite my allergies. Yesterday he taped quotes in pastel ink on pastel paper all over the house: on the desk, on our refrigerator, on the front and back doors. Most from Spinoza, but not all. One from Einstein, one from Albert Schweitzer."

Two video games intensified their whirring business, while students cheered from the television room across the hall.

"The milk of human kindness," she said, adding cream to her tea. "Mother's milk." She laughed, but it wasn't a funny laugh, more like one of the video games announcing with a belligerent electronic cackle that you've just lost.

"Do you want to go out and walk?" I asked.

"It's too hot. The heat's killing me lately."

"Hah. We're in here, in air-conditioning drinking hot tea, and—"

"Humans are full of contradictions."

I looked at the video enthusiasts. Maybe that's where I really belonged, with a gaggle of laughing, backslapping students. I turned to Althea: "Simon taped one really weird quote from Spinoza the semi-pantheist on our refrigerator." Althea shrugged, so I continued: " 'There have been men so mad as to believe that God is pleased by harmony.' I read it this morning when I got out eggs. If he keeps taping up Spinoza, I may resort to frying bacon and pork chops."

Althea didn't laugh, but said, "There's harmony, all right, the harmony of chaos warbling an old, sad refrain, like in a country song.—Would you like to go to Indian Falls this Saturday, just the two of us?"

I was processing the country song and chaos, but recovered, "Yeah, I guess. Sure. What's up?"

She knocked her tea over. The video games and the TV shouting some sports drivel were getting on our nerves, so we left. We both had to go to class anyway. My calculus class was on the far side of campus, Althea's Shakespeare with *Romeo and Juliet* nearby.

"Wouldn't it have been nice for Juliet to wake up two minutes earlier, just before Romeo comes in?"

"Then it wouldn't have been a tragedy."

"You're so right about that, Francis."

So we went to Indian Falls again. It was Saturday and Simon was committed to the library besides having been roped into a service at the synagogue, and we were once more alone, sitting in the same spot where Althea and Simon had traded ankle measurements. That seemed like a year before, so I could laugh at it—to myself, anyway. There were no shouts from above this time, no mixed race old couples wading in the water below; instead sunlit photons pressed in a solar wind that heated my brain and coated my tongue with oil, something sludgy that I might find in my grandmother's 1964 Impala. I stole glances at Althea's breasts: they were larger, I was sure.

You'd think we two would have been hopping in bed every chance we got after breaking our dual virginity. But that wasn't the way it was. In fact, we'd only talked about it once a week afterwards when Simon had sent us out to swap Dracula movies while he cooked Red Baron pizza:

"I'm sorry it hurt you so much," I'd said, studying a red stoplight as if it were the most important innovation in the last thirty years. "The other night, I mean."

"It sure wasn't as much fun as I'd been led to believe."

"It smelled."

"What?!"

"I mean the whole thing, doing it. It smelled like a mushroom farm."

Althea had pointed a long finger at me: "Mushrooms. You're getting like your roommate."

"At least I'm not counting hand grenades."

The light had changed and we drove on to the video store to rent another *Dracula.*

Althea pulled a really strange one off the shelf: a cowboy Dracula. *What's this darkly dressed gunslinger's secret? Why is he invincible in a gunfight, even when he fires two shots later than his opponent*, the DVD liner read. Althea was reading this in her mock stage voice, still sexy.

"Francis?"

I'd turned to see Paula Ammons. We'd dated in the fall semester for nearly a month. Paula was my fantasy, with her crow black, raven black hair. She was from Louisville and majoring in computers, and had milky pale, almost translucent skin to prove it.

"I've seen that one," she said, looking at Althea. "He's a vampire, of course, and he finally gets killed by silver bullets molded with a cross on their tips.—Hey," she said, still talking to Althea. "Don't think I gave anything away. Not if you're as smart as I guess. Francis always dates smart girls—don't you, Francis?" She executed a perfect about-face and walked away.

"My, my," Althea had commented. "You'll have to tell me all about it."

"She dropped me," I said. "I don't see why *she's* mad."

Althea then threatened to go ask her, and the threat almost came true because Paula was the cashier who checked us out. We three stood somberly when we realized there was no other choice. Then Althea began laughing, and then Paula began laughing. Being the only one who didn't get the joke, I pulled a five-dollar bill from my pocket and laid the DVD on the conveyer.

"Mushrooms," Althea pronounced, looking at Paula.

Paula blinked, handed me the change, then answered while looking at Althea: "Provolone. Do I win a prize?"

Althea only laughed, which started Paula up again, too. Sisterhood. When we got into my truck Althea commented, "You really were a virgin. You weren't kidding."

"You couldn't tell?"

She answered with another laugh. When we went back to the house, Simon had of course put mushrooms on the pizza. Althea picked one off a slice, held it to the light and sniffed it—much to her own exaggerated amusement.

But that was the only time we even talked about it and here it was a month later. We'd kissed plenty, of course, but whenever my boy-o hands wandered even to Althea's shoulders, she'd stiffen. Mostly my hands didn't get a chance to wander, for we committed to a threesome with Simon and stuck to our usual political and philosophical balderdash.

So on the ride over for this second trip to Indian Falls my Bad Faith self speculated not about Spinoza and pantheism but Sartre's concept of mind, which seemed to involve a wellspring of nothingness. Hence, his book, *Being and Nothingness*. My Bad Faith boy-o hormones were springing well enough all right. Even as my Bad Faith mouth yammered about Sartre, my hormones speculated that if gushing water made people want to tinkle it might also make them want to fuck. Indian Falls here I cum.

And once we reached those Falls, my bad faith mouth blubbered that Sartre's nothingness offered as good a definition as anyone had for free will. Meanwhile, my fingers caressed Althea's ankle.

"Free will?" Jerking her ankle away Althea shouted this so loudly that her voice echoed from the cliff across the falls. "'Free will,' he says!" With a lunge she tossed a pebble over the side of the gorge.

I blushed. "It's like Heisenberg's electrons and the uncertainty principle."

"Francis, let's stop talking about Sartre and physics. Let's eat and listen to the water."

She tugged at her knit blouse, a hunter's orange mesh, and we spread things on the cliff's narrow path. She'd made sandwiches from pita bread, goat cheese, Greek olives, and some type of Italian ham. On the last picnic my choice had been Colonel Sanders fried chicken, Original Recipe. The right people, all right. I was hanging around them.

"Simon and I email about you," she said minutes later, watching me study the sandwich as if awaiting instructions from a helpful maître d'. Should I cut it with my pocket knife? The info about her and Simon emailing put a picture in my mind of her and Simon playing with one another's ankles. She rarely emailed me. I pictured them down in the cellar, among the candles, naked. That image faded into Simon sitting in a yoga pose before the Holocaust shrine, then one of him hunched over the black computer on the desk with the wilted flowers, reading Althea's emails.

"About me?"

"Actually . . ." she broke off, distracted by something below. "I swear I saw a snake swimming in the water down there. A fat one."

"They do that. Swim, I mean. They can strike in the water, just as well as on land. And the fat ones are almost always poisonous." I looked where she pointed, but I couldn't see anything. She pinched me hard and I yelped.

"What are you doing?"

"Checking for fat content."

"Ha-ha. Is that what you and Simon talk about, putting me on a diet?" I'd gained ten pounds since I'd taken a part time job at a greasy spoon cooking hamburgers and dropping French fries into a deep fryer with an emergency extinguisher built into its exhaust hood. So while I safely gained all the weight that the Jewish couple in Cincinnati never could, my grade point seemed to be thinning of its own free will.

"What we talk about is how you're our alter-ego. Like what you just said: knowing that snakes can swim, knowing about the fat ones. You a mechanical engineering major, the two of us majoring in philosophy."

"I thought you were in pre-law."

"That's what I tell my mom and dad. Philosophy, that's what I'm into. And telling or not telling people things to make them happy, that's what I'm into."

"What do you mean?"

"I'm pregnant."

The water below rushed so hard that even Joshua and Wynton Marsalis together couldn't have blasted it into stillness, with all the trumpets in the world. Stupidly, I pictured Althea and Simon holding ankles.

"Is it mine?"

With a lurch Althea's leg knocked the picnic basket off the rock shelf, sending it bouncing somewhere below. She was standing when I looked up from watching it fall.

"I have to go now."

"Althea, I . . ."

But she was half a dozen steps up the path, hanging onto vines. Something else fell, or maybe she threw it. I heard a metallic ring on a rock below as I tried to catch up.

A LINE OF TORNADOES moved across the state on Monday afternoon. Simon hadn't talked to me Sunday, the day after Althea ran off at Indian Falls. And she wouldn't talk on the drive back, but just kept turning up the radio if I spoke. Then she hadn't shown for philosophy class Monday morning, though this was before anyone knew anything about the tornadoes, which caught even the weather people off guard. The uncertainty principle.

"I'd think you'd at least try to call her," Simon hissed, breaking his own silence and walking up beside me after philosophy class. "Or email her. Do something. She's not doing well."

Professor Hart came from behind his desk and grabbed my elbow before I could reply. He asked how St. Francis was coming along. Simon continued walking and I heard him snort a laugh. Professor Hart raised his brows and looked at Simon's thin back and birdie shoulder blades as they passed through the classroom door.

"Fine," I told Professor Hart. "I'm reading all about Brother Sun, Sister Moon, and Brother Worm."

"The worm's the one you have to watch out for," Professor Hart commented, going back to gather his notes and book.

I must have raised my brows, for he added, "At your namesake Francis's age and at my age, the worm means that delightful creature we encounter in our coffins. At your age, though—" he broke off with one of his patented guffaws, the one I was so jealous of because it held the world at bay. I turned to see two blondes blocking the door, smiling dentally. Were they selling date rape pills? Simon was well out of view.

"We just—" one of the females started.

With preternatural acumen, I could hear Simon starting down the steps. I nodded to Professor Hart and hurried by my dental classmates, trying to catch up. But his footsteps were already echoing off the marble landing two flights below. I started to run, but dropped a book that picked this time to lose its binding, so I had to gather loose pages. When I got outside, Simon was nowhere in sight. Just as well, I thought, feeling an unexpected chilly gust and looking up at the still mostly clear and hot sky. Just as well because I had to get to class and pull up my grades. My mom and Aunt Grace had promised to send an extra two hundred a month if I quit the short order job and concentrated on my grades, which were faltering. Althea's telling me all that stuff Saturday hadn't helped that problem any more than Simon's wanting me to email her. Or his damned hand-lettered pastel signs on our refrigerator.

At a summery 4:20 p. m., Simon and I were both home. Sirens were howling throughout the city because of tornado warnings, as in multiple sightings. I stepped out onto the back porch and sat down despite the sick green, purple, and black sky. Behind me, Simon opened the door as hail pelted the yard. He'd been sitting at the computer when I walked in from engineering and had barely talked to me the two hours since.

"Maybe we should go down to the storm cellar," he said. Hail was pelting St. Francis enough for snowballs to accumulate in his two open palms.

"Down to your shrine? I thought you said that God wouldn't keep people from falling off a cliff at Indian Falls, so why should he keep them from tornadoes?"

"That doesn't make any sense, and you know it," Simon pointed out.

"So what else is new in life?"

"I think you need to ride over and see Althea. She's more than upset."

"In this weather? Anyway, she won't talk to me."

"God, you really are a golem."

He left the door open and stomped back in. I heard his bedroom door slam. True to my golem mentality, I remained staring at the sky, betting with each gust of hot or cold wind that the rust red garage was going to tip over. Quarter-sized hail pelted the ground. St. Francis faithfully kept his palms up against the hail. An ice-cold gust whipped my face, then a hot one. Distant sirens howled as if every cop and ambulance driver in town had decided to play an afternoon chorus. Suddenly, the wooden steps I sat on trembled and the statue of St. Francis levitated. A loud roar vibrated from my haunch bone through my neck. When I shook my head I was sprawled stomach-up in the yard where the Saint Francis statue had been. I twisted but couldn't see it. The garage had gone down, and when I looked back at the house I saw that the huge oak tree had split, to crash into the roof, crushing it over Simon's bedroom.

I ran inside, but the right-side door from the kitchen to the hall was crushed so I had to detour through the dining room, clipping my hip on our wilted-flower desk. I yelped, realizing that my other hip was sore from landing in the yard. Leaves and broken glass were scattered about the hall and I slid on them to collide with a branch that had punched through the top of Simon's closed bedroom door. I yanked the door, fighting it, yelling out Simon's name. When I forced it open I was blown back by a gust of rain. Half of Simon's outside wall and the ceiling were missing. More rain pelted me. Part of the oak tree blocked my view and a bright blue recliner I didn't recognize lay upside down underneath it—from the upstairs apartment, I realized. Then I saw the fire escape twisted and stuck out from Simon's bed at a fifty-degree angle.

"Simon!"

Overturning his dresser I climbed over it to see one iron foot of the fire escape running through Simon's chest, pinning him and the bed to the floor. His eyes bulged and he heaved, forcing blood from his mouth. His hands held the ladder as if he were getting ready to climb. "Simon!" At my shout, his hands dropped, the left one's knuckles hitting the wood floor with a crack. I stared at rain running blood in rivulets over his arm onto the floor.

How soon, how late was it when there was pounding at the front door, when a policeman and two medical techs pushed me against a bedroom wall left standing? One of the techs moved from me and leaned for Simon's wrist—I guess to take his pulse, though that seemed a waste. I focused on the tech's blue pants and the rain falling through the ripped roof in white sheets. A moaning wind threw hail and leaves into the room. There was a tornado's thump, thump, thump—at least I thought there was.

The cop looked at the sky, clearly visible through the crushed ceiling and wall. "Let's get into another part of the house quick," he said. I thought his voice came from the cellar or the attic, or from something black strapped to his hip. Then I was being moved past the tree limb, pushed and pulled into the hallway then into the living room where we three had played Trivial Pursuit. A gold DVD lay on the floor. Another Dracula. It was supposed to go back to the rental shop yesterday. But no one had talked yesterday. More howling wind, more thump, thump, thumping, and something flew through the room, part of a tree limb that exited through a broken window, a cruise missile intent on a target. We four crouched in a corner. Air pushed and pulled my face. By the front door I saw a Cupid, a foot-long length of jagged ceiling molding attached to it. For a moment it looked as if it was crawling, but a black Norway rat edged from beneath, turned to stare at us, then ran toward the broken window, managing to jump clear by climbing the couch.

"Christ, the damned student ghetto," one of the techs offered.

A few minutes later, the thump-thumping and thunder were heading downtown toward Transylvania University.

The medical techs looked at me. "Do you hurt anywhere?"

"No." I winced as I moved my hip.

One held my wrist and pointed a small flashlight from his pocket into my eyes. I blinked twice.

"Anyone else live here?" the other asked after a moment.

"Just Simon."

"Simon?"

I gestured toward Simon's room.

"What about upstairs?"

"They left for the weekend. I saw them drive off."

"Does Simon have any relatives in town?"

I shook my head. "New Jersey. Springfield, New Jersey."

The second ambulance driver walked in the front door, pushing a shiny metal object that looked like a wheelchair. I hadn't even noticed him walking out. So maybe it was the cop who'd asked if anyone else lived here. He was a huge black guy. How couldn't I have noticed that? The first EMT was pushing back the oak limb that partially blocked Simon's door. His partner had to help him. Then he and his partner unfolded the wheelchair thing into a stretcher while I retrieved our address book for the black cop. It was lying where it always was, under one of the ten blue and gray angel flashlights that Simon's dad had bought. Why was I so cold, when the flashlight was so hot? And what was it the ten flashlights guarded? Paradise or the Ark of the Covenant or the throne of the Almighty? My shoulder hurt, both shoulders hurt. The ten angels, what were they guarding? Not Simon for sure. Not our house. Paradise? I handed the address book to the cop, who already had Simon's wallet and his identification out. Where'd he get that? I looked at his black hand shaking, but realized it was my own white hand shaking.

"They have to take him to the hospital first," the policeman said.

"He's dead."

"I know, but they have to take him to the hospital first. A medical doctor has to say that."

My arm quivered.

"You sure you're okay?"

"I'm okay. I wasn't even in the house."

"Do you know your roommate's parents well enough that you want to call them, just to tell them what hospital—it'll be Central Baptist, that's the closest—he'll be in?"

"I . . . never met them," I said.

The cop looked up from the phone number I'd pointed to, then nodded. "Your neighbor called us. Said she was looking down from her room and saw your roommate get hit by the ladder."

I nodded. Good for her, I thought.

And then I was standing alone in the living room. I heard the cop outside telling the two EMTs as they loaded Simon, "I think he knows this kid's parents. I think he's afraid to call."

"He's young. A college kid. What do you expect?"

"Walker's young. Does that mean he had any business playing footsie with bin Laden?"

"Come on, Jerry. Lighten up. The kid's just lost his roommate. He's in shock."

After they left, I spotted Simon's cell phone and noticed the computer was on standby. Miraculously, the electricity had never gone off. I fiddled with the mouse as I punched in the first auto-dial number in Simon's cell phone. I was surprised to hear Althea's answering machine: "Lady Sophia here, aka . . . well you should know who you're calling anyway, shouldn't you? Leave a message. Ta-da." She'd taken to calling herself "Lady Sophia," Simon "Spinoza," and me the "Daimon," as in Socrates' guiding voice. I opened my mouth to speak, heard a gust of wind and flinched, pressing disconnect before I even exhaled. Simon's email was minimized. Maybe he'd left it that way on purpose. I clicked it open to see a response from

Althea. "*I don't think so,*" was all her note said. I scrolled down to Simon's preceding message: "*He might come around. He's a good person at heart, like his namesake.*" Wind howled and I thought of Simon's patented "Eeew." I scrolled more to see that the email replies went on forever. It was a wonder the two of them hadn't passed the file limit. I absently pressed the second auto-dial and reached who I'd expected on the first—Simon's mom. "Gidron residence, Ruth speaking." There was no wind, only that odd silence that groans over telephones, a silence as deep as stellar echoes of the Big Bang. "Simon? Is this you? Simon? Francis?" How could she—of course! Caller ID. "Simon? Francis? Francis, is that you? . . . Oh God, it's Simon . . . something's wrong. I know it. Something's wrong!" I heard the phone drop and I heard a long wail that ascended a scale of notes, Joshua's trumpets bringing down Jericho. Mr. Gidron's voice came into the background, asking her what was wrong. I still hadn't said a word. I looked at the computer screen, with all those messages; then I noticed the blue "unopened message" icon. I double clicked it: "Ten to the tenth, to the tenth, to the tenth, to the tenth, to the tenth, to the tenth, to the tenth," was all it said. It was a new message from Althea, at 3:44, maybe half an hour before the tornadoes moved in. I grabbed Simon's car keys off the desk.

OUR STREET WAS A tangle of fallen tree limbs. To avoid them I had to drive Simon's Audi onto the curb twice. Once I was off our street, though, there were only twigs and leaves. A drizzle was falling, pleasant almost. With my hands firmly on the leather steering wheel, I thought how I'd tell Althea about Simon, how she'd want to go to the hospital and see him. We'd clean up the house. I'd put my arm around her. We'd stay in philosophy class with Professor Hart and listen to him guffaw. We'd get married and we'd name the boy "Simon." Or if it was a girl, "Simone." I envisioned Althea and me sitting at the huge desk that we'd buy from the female lawyer. Althea'd paint new flowers on it, ones that weren't wilted. Althea could paint; she told me she'd had to learn that and piano because Super Dad insisted. We'd install a portable roof on her sunning deck and move the desk up there, so we could overlook the whole city of Lexington as we studied and rocked the baby.

At a stoplight, I thought of a book Althea told me about from her French class. It was about a man who killed someone on the beach because the sun jarred his eyes. No other reason, just that the sun hurt his eyes. If the sun, why not dropping barometric pressure? *Ten to the tenth, ten to the tenth . . .* Spit caught in my throat. I ran the stoplight.

By the time I reached Althea's condominium, I'd passed a dozen ambulances and police cars heading back toward the university, so I was jolted to see two police cars and an ambulance in her parking lot. I pulled in five spaces away from them and walked toward her front door, where a cluster of people stood. I recognized the three bimbos, their blonde hair glimmering emerald in the evening's weird light as another line of thunderstorms threatened, as the sky once more took on a sick green cast. The bimbos were talking with two policemen. I cupped my ear, pretending I was itching a flea maybe.

"She was crazy. She shot her boyfriend in the foot." One blonde nodded toward the blonde next to her.

"That's right," this blonde said. "We poured three bottles of peroxide and alcohol on it."

The cop said something—his low voice wasn't carrying, for some barometric reason.

"My boyfriend said not to. He's on the football team and thought he'd get in trouble with the coach. Little pellets are still coming out of his foot."

Blinking and taking a step forward, I looked at the black cop who was talking. At first thought it was the same one who'd been at our—Simon's and my—place half an hour before. Then I thought maybe it was the guy who'd been wading in the water at Indian Falls. Lightning sheeted the sky and everyone looked up. Not me, though. I was watching a gurney bumping down Althea's front stoop. It supported a body covered with a white sheet. A third cop followed, holding something in a clear plastic bag. The pistol. I belched and could feel sweat on my neck, or maybe rain. Since I was close to the ambulance, I moved toward its vitamin C orange and gravestone-white paint job, its flashing lights. Some noise was click-clocking, the lights maybe. The gurney hit a bump in the sidewalk and I could see where the head was under the sheet. A blotch of blood appeared on the sheet. Did they run out of body bags, with all the tornadoes?

Both the EMTs glared at me as I watched them push the gurney into the ambulance. I stood so close that I had to move when they opened the door wider. Althea's purse was propped by her hips. It was the one that Simon and I bought her; it had a figure holding her hands in a Hindu pose. If my arm contained a robotic extender, it could reach and touch the leather. It could reach and touch Althea.

"Get an eyeful?" the woman tech asked as she slammed the back doors shut and walked to the passenger side of the ambulance. She gave a hefty horse's wheeze that belied her wavy honey hair and cherubic red complexion.

"I didn't know her," I replied.

"Exactly. You missed your chance." She got into the ambulance and gave me one last glare before her partner backed up and left the parking lot.

I DROVE INTO THE countryside. In the distance, a funnel cloud touched down, a ballerina performing twists; then it lifted to disappear into a bank of dark clouds. I was so mesmerized that the Audi wandered onto the shoulder and hit a large rock, bouncing a foot in the air. I pulled over to check for damage, but couldn't find any. It occurred to me that the police would have called Simon's parents and that maybe I should get back. I had to be out before they arrived. I couldn't look at Mrs. Gidron's ivory nails, her raven hair, her brown eyes. I couldn't watch Mr. Gidron slam a flashlight onto the floor, I couldn't hear him curse in Yiddish. Hearing Mrs. Gidron wail over the phone lines had been plenty.

A sudden image of the blood-splotched sheet covering Althea returned and I fell over the Audi's hood and started crying. After a while I realized I was humping the hood—my crying had turned to blubbering. A car passed and slowed. I stood up. It was nearly night. I had to get back.

Of course my fear of encountering Mr. and Mrs. Gidron was ridiculous—no one would be landing at Blue Grass Field with the weather the way it was. And if they drove, the trip would take twelve hours minimum. Still, I sped back, passing four utility trucks in our—our! *Our*? We three's, we two's, we one's?—neighborhood, their yellow lights revolving. At the house, the electricity was off like it should have been three hours ago. I felt for one of the ten flashlights perched by the front door. It stood, stiff and alert, just as if it were truly some muscular guardian angel. I walked toward the kitchen, and the flashlight's beam hit the computer where one of Simon's Spinoza signs hung, pink paper with Simon's elaborate handwriting in purple marker: "There have been men so mad as to believe that God is pleased by harmony." When had he moved this note from the refrigerator? It had to have been this morning, since I'd used the computer for homework Sunday night. But I used the computer three hours ago, when I read Althea's and Simon's email messages, and I hadn't seen it then. I shivered with an image of Simon's ghost tossing the iron ladder aside and rising from his bloodied bed after I took off in his Audi. *Stop! Traitor! Thief!* Wind gusted through the house and I heard noise from Simon's wrecked bedroom. Were the remaining Cupids helping Simon's ghost clean up? But a ghost would indicate harmony, as in life ever after, as in retribution. *There have been men so mad* . . . It was only an errant tree limb scratching some chaotic pattern. Or a rat.

I rubbed the pink note, wanting to read it aloud to counter the scratching. But the damp paper ripped and both pink pieces landed on the keyboard, caught in my flashlight's beam. *Harmony.* Seeing that word I gave a bullish bellow that dropped me to the floor. Which is where I cowered, listening to wind, sirens, and pelting white rain. Occasionally, I laughed a mushroom bellyful.

9.

The Petite Artiste

Year 2002

(Clarissa, Willy, Dr. Bug)

Willy did some searching and came up with two disturbing facts: Josephine, Vander's supposed love-mate according to the lovely Louisville probation office Larry McGavin, had drowned in a boating accident in late spring of 1974. And Adolph's girl, evidently named Kelly, drowned in the very same accident. The girls were supposedly playing some kind of dare game that capsized the boat. Willy learned this from the sister who'd sold the farm where the bodies were found. It turns out that Kelly was her niece from yet another sister who had "died of heartbreak" three years after her daughter drowned. Both girls had been autopsied and both showed high alcohol content along with traces of marijuana and a couple of other drugs. In Tennessee we called results like that an Elvis autopsy. To seal matters, evidently neither girl could swim. And to seal matters even more, guess who was piloting the boat? Adolph and Jerry Vander, who both could swim. The deaths were ruled accidental.

"Are you going to exhume?" I asked Willy.

It was Derby Day and Willy'd pushed his growing seniority around and gotten off. We were at the patio bar of Adam's Ribs, listening to pre-Derby blather. The bartender strolled over, winked at Willy and jiggled a fishbowl of names, flashing his fingers to show that five bucks was the price to enter the pot. Willy and I put our hands in together and pulled out a horse named "*Nole me tangere.*"

"God. Latin," Willy said.

It looked familiar from my abandoned English major, but familiar was the best I could do these days, since it wasn't a biological phylum.

"'Don't even think about touching me,' is roughly what it means," Willy said.

I crinkled my brows at Willy, who crinkled his back.

"A scholar," the bartender commented. "A scholar," he repeated, pointing Willy out to another customer, a lawyer I recognized. Then the bartender gave Willy a Cheshire grin and added, "Just too bad you ain't a gentleman to boot."

"Watch it, Rocky. I've still got friends in traffic. You could be using credit cards to pay tickets off for the next three years."

The lawyer laughed. Rocky grinned and walked away. Not my type, I mouthed, watching his ass as he put his tanned arm around a waitress.

"Remember I told you how Dad sent me to this high-priced private school?" Willy leaned toward me so I could smell his cologne. "Three other blacks went there, an even number, so we could watch all four directions and cover one another's black backs."

I sighed instead of laughing. "What if you just got permission to exhume and just waited to see what happens?"

"You're referring to our department's two computer geeks who think that someone's tapping the police computers, you're thinking that someone might be Jerry Vander who owns a computer store? Well, I don't think Vander's smart enough. But it might be Adolph."

"Dolphie."

"What? Oh yeah, Dolphie, the sweetheart of Sigma Paw."

"What about the fourth girl, Willy?"

"Fourth?"

"Counting Gina, Josephine, and Kelly. There was one more."

Willy shrugged. "Any of your neighbors living here back then? Mrs. Walburn?"

There'd been a royal turnover in the neighborhood since the seventies. But Mrs. Walburn, the woman living in the white house across from me, had lived in her same house then. She was an octogenarian and widow of over a decade. Just this spring we'd helped with her rose bed—we meaning Willy while I drank Diet Pepsi and poured hot tea for her, coffee for him. It was an experiment in multi-generationalism, multi-culturalism, and multi-cuisine.

"We could ask her right after we win the Derby."

Rocky had moved nearby and laughed when I said that. "Fat chance of your two's winning. That No-Eat-My-Tangerine horse is so bad that they won't even let him in the field betting. I think the odds are 40 to 1, plus they throw in a free mint julep for every sucker's five-dollar bet, and the track still comes out ahead."

Rocky the bartender was right: No-Eat-My-Tangerine, aka Don't-Even-Think-About-Touching-Me, finished a blah eleventh. Not even an inglorious but memorable last.

We had no better luck with Mrs. Walburn after we drove back to my house. For all she knew, the fourth girl could have been truly named No-Eat-My-Tangerine. About medium height, sandy hair, medium build. Mrs. Walburn never got close enough to see her eyes, commenting that she'd seen the tall guy's once and didn't want to inspect anyone else's who lived in the house.

"I'm betting she drowned or was in a car accident," I told Willy that night. "Just search the newspapers."

"Already have," he said.

I should have known. "Hey Willy." I batted my eyes like a freshman at sorority rush. "What would 'Think about touching me' be in Latin?"

"*Vole me tangere.*"

"Whatever you say, master. I'm your Latin slave."

"*Amo, amas, amat,*" he instructed.

WHEN WILLY MADE NOISES about an exhume order it was mid-May. I hadn't seen Petite Artiste all spring, since meeting lovely Larry in fact. Could Larry have . . . I shook my head, realizing that by connecting the Petite Artiste's disappearance and Larry I was showing serious signs of contracting Willy's Everything-Touches-Everything virus.

The last day in May I received a call from Methuselah, with whom I'd gone out drinking a couple of times—though always in the company of Willy, after that first rendezvous at the Demitasse.

"Do you know what today is, Dr. Clarissa?" This was one of Methuselah's adopted Southernisms, combining a formal title with a first name. Really too Deep South for Kentucky, nonetheless charming.

"Other than the last day of May, a week before summer session starts, and a time when I should be vacationing and hiking in the mountains of Georgia instead of talking on a phone, no. So tell me, Methuselah."

"Today is the Roman Catholic feast day celebrating the, uh, Queenship of the Blessed Virgin Mary."

"Virgin, and you thought of me immediately." I stared at the receiver, contemplating dropping it on the floor to give his ear a good shock.

"It's also the feast day of, uh, Saint Petronilla, another virgin *and* the daughter of Saint Peter. Let me read you something from *Butler's Lives of the Saints*." Before I could do as much as roll my eyes into the vacant air of my bedroom, he started: " 'Saint Petronilla lived when Christians were more solicitous to live well than to write much: they knew how to die for Christ, but did not compile long books or disputations, in which vanity has often a greater share than charity.' –There, you see what you missed by not being raised Roman Catholic?"

"I weep."

"So did Christ. You two have that in common. And you're just about the age he was when he died."

"Is there a point to this phone call, Methuselah? Otherwise, I'm beginning to understand your name."

Silence. Just as I was ready to comment that I was only joking he spoke: "The Petite Artiste's landlady, uh, reported her missing."

"Oh no. How long?"

"Evidently two months."

"Two months!" I walked to the window of my bedroom and stared down to the sidewalk, as if I could incant the Petite Artiste bending down there with her purple neurasthenic hunch.

"Her rent was paid ahead and—"

"And now since it's due, she calls the police? This landlady gives new meaning to the word 'bitch.' "

"Yeah, well. Anyway, the police are going over there at two, after they get a search warrant. It would be good if you came along. You know her better than anyone."

"Better? . . . I—"

"Think about her personality, Dr. Clarissa. You talked to her several times, which is a good deal more verbiage than anyone else likely exchanged with her. Hell, she even paid her landlady in quarterly installments to avoid talking. The cop who took the call said the landlady had to check her books to remember Petite Artiste's name. But you chased her down the street, you sat and drank coffee with her."

"All right, all right." I remembered that the Loquacious One, a.k.a. the Petite Artiste, had been drinking hot chocolate not coffee. Then I realized I, too, didn't know her name, any more than Methuselah knew what she drank.

"Want me to pick you up?"

"Willy—"

"Willy's in Bowling Green chasing down everythings connected to everyones."

"You seem to do a good enough job of that yourself, with your Saint Pedrilla."

"Saint Petronilla."

"Yeah."

"Yeah, pick you up?"

"Yeah, pick me up." But no eat my tangerine, I thought as I hung up, even though I suspected that Willy was seeing an-ex student of mine, a bottle-blondie, as my mom used to say, who was working in the courthouse. I changed my blue blouse for a tan work shirt from Sears, one that I wore when excavating shallow graves. I also changed to a sports bra that nearly strangled me, and a pair of boots. But on rethinking Methuselah, I figured work boots might turn him on in some kinky way, so I changed into tennis shoes.

It didn't do any damned good. Not a bit more than rooting through the Petite Artiste's obsessive paintings and sketches and pastels of Gina—stacks and stacks of them under the unmade bed, on either side of an old desk, under the room's single window, in front of a bookshelf filled with poetry, behind that bookshelf, on top of a dresser and nearly covering its small mirror, in all four corners like talismans, and inside a closet in three separate foot-tall piles. Amid that chaos and the lingering hint of incense I did chance on a painting depicting whom I took to be the four women who lived in my house in the seventies along with the three guys, the ones Larry had described. Petite Artiste had drawn them standing before a barn, each holding a skull against their stomachs. The same barn where we exhumed the skeletons? I couldn't be sure. For once, Hex Man wasn't exaggerated, so I took this painting to be in the realistic mode. What was the Petite Artiste's connection to this sad crew? Other than Gina, that is? Had Gina somehow managed to keep in touch with her despite Adolph?

"How much does this room rent for?" I asked the landlady when we finished. She'd stood in the doorway the whole time, sucking tisk-tisks through her teeth.

"Ninety a month. You share the bathroom."

One of the policewomen snickered, and when I turned to smile at her we had a brief communion of eye-rolling. I turned back to the landlady.

"I'm going to give you a check for ninety dollars. You keep everything here, in case she comes back."

"I was going to raise the rent to a hundred and twenty since she left." The old hag gave me the rheumy-eyed treatment.

The woman cop spoke up: "You had a fire inspection lately? I was just wondering because I didn't notice any fire extinguishers in the hall."

"Ninety dollars will be fine," the landlady said.

Not one damned day later, twenty-two hours, Willy came back and figured out—magically, I supposed, or maybe through cop radar—that Methuselah and I had made the beast with two backs along with other zoological treats. So Willy and I were once more on Dr. Circle and Detective Cox terms. Consequently I drove to Helen, Georgia, alone, hiked mountains for two days then drove back, alone, listening to Gregorian chants. The boys made up within a week, but I was the scarlet whore of Babylon. *C'est moi, c'est moi*, as Lancelot sings in *Camelot*.

Willy and I did see one another, though, because while Methuselah was rummaging through some abandoned farmhouse near the river he discovered a bizarre double-suicide, a couple we immediately dubbed the "lap-top dancers." Once or twice when we were working on this, Willy seemed ready to give in, but mostly he kept seeing my ex-student, so I kept seeing Methuselah until he took up with a classical guitar-playing sweetie.

Then in mid-June I finished my lecture to a freshman physical anthropology class—something I only taught during the summer now because the forensic unit was taking so much time—and Mildred handed me a note and added, "Detective Cox left a phone message for you, Doctor Circle." Mildred was hep to Willy and me, and she could always translate the current mood between us in code so that no nosy bodies could decipher. Then she reached and wiped away lipstick that I'd smeared while blabbing about bones. "You're just never going to get that extra deduction on your tax form this way, dear," she added.

That was the last time I laughed for about a week.

Some pre-pre Fourth of July revelers had found a body in a gorge over in the next county, on property that belonged to a church, the note on Mildred's violet, lined and perfumed paper read. I should expect the body today at 1 p.m., the note read. It was 11:30.

I wiped down a gurney we kept for any bodies that needed to be steamed clean of flesh. We were holding another skeleton of a black man in his mid-twenties with a single shot to the back of the head courtesy of a nine-millimeter. He'd been identified as a Louisville drug dealer courtesy of Larry with the bright blue eyes, and we were getting ready to give his corpse a last go-over in the unlikely event that his murder came to trial.

At 1:35, I received a phone call informing me that the ambulance carrying the body was on campus. I told the driver—a female! Vive la revolution!—where to meet me, and I walked down to the basement. A pasty young man with post-adolescent acne was also working the ambulance, and judging from their sour faces neither was too happy as they wheeled the body onto the ramp. Even though the corpse was enclosed in a thick plastic body bag, a faint odor followed the gurney; this odor turned stifling in the elevator and the young man let out a groan and rolled his eyes. Fortunately, the ride was fast since I had a key to bypass the first floor. A secluded entrance to the lab was planned, but still under construction with its filmy thick plastic, so Mildred had warned the few academics hanging around. Plenty of doors stayed closed as we left the elevator and wheeled the body through the halls. Mildred gave a toast as we went by. Her special medicine?

"Can't tell you nothing about it," the male said, hiccoughing as we entered the lab. "Might be male."

"Might be female," the young woman countered. "Luckily, we don't need to find out."

I'd notched the odor hood up an hour before, and the solution was beginning to steam. They stared at it when I told them to shift the body onto a nearby stainless steel gurney.

"That going to do what I think it's going to do?" the male asked, referring to the steaming unit.

"It's going to steam off the residue and flesh."

"Gag me with a maggot," the girl said.

"Those will be steamed off too—presuming that you or one of your colleagues took entomological specimens at the site."

"Et-em?" they asked simultaneously. I expected that, since I'd already received three bodies from the sheriff of this county. So I knew the answer to what I was about to ask before I asked it, since this county's coroner was happy to pass along any corpse over forty-eight hours old, over twenty-four in a hot midsummer.

"Entomological. Bugs. Maggots. Flies. They're used to ascertain the time of death. Were any bug samples taken from the ground, from remaining clothing or flesh?"

"We had to do this last evening, facing a double shift. Other than what fell on her shoe we didn't keep nothin'." The male gave a nod to his partner, who grimaced and rubbed the top of her right shoe with the sole of her left.

"You used gloves, didn't you?"

"Well, duh."

I signed four forms; they signed five. Then they were gone, and I was left alone with the unsexed Doe, 12-2002. I posted a "*Lab work in progress: do not enter*" sign. Then I called my favorite bug doctor on campus.

Look, I know I say this all the time—that he's not my type, I mean. But Professor Burt Wilson isn't. My type. For A, he's married. For B, seventy percent of his conversation revolves around some or other bug—I understand that students love to get him lecturing on preying manti, just to watch his unique black-belt demo of that bug's fighting skills. He evidently broke a microscope and two cases of slides demonstrating this in one early morning class. Professor Burt is tall and lank, with a shovel face and a pair of horn-rimmed glasses that likely were attached to his nose in the birthing room, for I've never seen them off, even for cleaning. And that concludes with reason C, considering his occupation.

He promised to be over within half an hour. "Record the temperature in your lab right now, would you, Clarissa?"

I started to ask why, then realized that the lab would count as "bug-breeding time" and that he'd need the total of growth-warmth hours in here, too. Seventy-four Fahrenheit. Someone had been tinkering with the thermometer. I resisted turning it down and just unzipped the body bag.

It wasn't like an abundance of skin, clothing, or hair samples were left. From the scant report, the body had been buried fifty feet—twenty meters—from a creek. When I tilted the pelvis—no pun intended, Elvis—scads of maggots squirmed. I took a sunshine break to stare out the window. Just when I walked back to start again, an abrupt knock nearly sent a scalpel through my left index finger. It was Burt. He gawked on in, a preying mantis lanking straight for the prey, in this case a corpse.

"Buried?" he said.

"I've been doing pretty well, Burt." I sighed melodramatically. "Busy. How about you?"

"Sorry, Clarissa, but I've got a two-thirty class, my wife just told me she's pregnant, one of my male colleagues has been accused of sexual harassment—with another male—and a PhD candidate seems to be doctoring her research and stealing drugs. But I'm glad you're doing well. Was this body buried?"

I reached up to give him a pat on his tall skinny shoulder. "Yeah, buried. Under a solid rock overhang, twenty meters from a stream, in a hollow in Indian Falls over by Nicholasville."

He pushed his glasses against his snout. If, as the folk belief goes, that nose kept pace with his penis, no wonder his wife kept dropping litters. As his head bobbed, I knew he was taking count of the critter colony in the pelvis and elsewhere. "At least a dozen instars," he said. "It's a she, right?" he asked, pointing to the pelvis.

"Very good, Burt. Yeah, most likely a she."

"Considering the on-and-off hard freezes we've had into early May and the burial, I'm going to say March or April. Let me collect and I'll get back to you.—God, Clarissa, what is that crap playing on your tape cassette?"

"Gregorian chant. Are you a non-believer, Burt?"

"That's no heavenly choir, Clarissa."

I grinned and Burt collected, pulling what looked like several glass pill vials from his pockets and briefcase. Once out in the open and free air, the maggots caught the spirit and began to squirm with the Gregorian chant.

"She's all yours," Burt said, closing the last vial and snapping his briefcase shut. "Salt and pepper her up, boil her down."

"Burt . . ."

"Laughing's a hard job, Clarissa. Someone's gotta do it." He strode out the door, his bones shifting stiffly as if he were coated with exoskeleton rather than skin.

"You're all mine," I told the corpse, flipping over the cassette tape. Then I started again.

While the body had been buried under an overhang, unfortunately for the murderer, the nearby creek had swollen just enough to expose a "leg bone," and four god-fearing picnickers spotted it just after fried chicken and gravy, just before cherry tarts.

"I thought the Nicholas County Church of Holy Flying Paracleters didn't picnic on Sunday." I was addressing the skeleton, which was held together by skin and mud. Being crumpled on its side skewed the body and left its skull staring at the table's stainless steel lip. In answer to my statement, a snail crawled over a clump of what I figured to be hair. It was a dull honey-colored clump. "Dear heart, one thing for sure: you furnished a good reason to keep their future picnics on church grounds." I turned up the Gregorian chant, thinking the corpse and I could meditate on everlasting possibilities while we were sharing cozy time. Nodding with the monks' up-down notes, I gathered myself and switched the chant to earphones then turned on the tape recorder.

Considering the snail, the clumps of hair, and the small amount of remaining flesh—10 percent of the brain and about the same for the buttocks and stomach, plus part of the right heel—I was more liberal than Burt and estimated anywhere from two to five months in the ground, given last winter which had been on permafrost starting around the middle of January. I'd have to go to the site and get a feel for that, but being under an overhang would have kept the corpse cold—maybe through most of April. I counted backwards: June, May, April, March, February. No one could have been patient enough to hack out a grave from frozen ground then. The ides of March through April five had bought on rain and a warm spell. Okay, Burt, let's say April one, then. Hell, let's say the day I met Larry. Uh-oh, here we go again: everything touching everything, everyone touching everyone. God bless you, Willy, Happy April's Fool Day.

I turned to the corpse. From a preliminary examination of the pelvis the Doe truly was a Jane, a small Jane, but a Jane. The skull was intact—no damage from gunshot or impact. Taking forceps I searched the flesh mass while church bells rang and pious monks sang. Rhyme . . . I'd have to make sure I didn't mouth any into the autopsy tape or I'd be seeing Dr. Kiefer. I looked from the body toward the window to consider that I could have been an academic poet, could have settled with the cute philosophy professor, instead of trying not to beat him by too much in tennis. Umph. An entire fingernail. I carried it to the examination light and that's when matters started sliding downhill.

"No," I said to the fingernail. I snapped off the recording I'd barely started. "No," I repeated. Under the magnifier, not fingernail polish but flecks of oil paint: purple, red, green, yellow, which is likely what kept the fingernail from dissolving. I looked back to what was left of the corpse. Strands of honey brown hair showed occasional streaks of gray. I went and measured a femur, something I'd done often enough working on my dissertation to have the correlation in height memorized: five-foot to five-foot-one. I spotted a patch of purple cloth, a one-inch square; the cloth had paint splotched on it, too. "You're not who I think you are."

It was a futile statement. I walked to a window. Pressing my head against the windowpane I luxuriated in the summer heat. In my right ear, the monks were going at it —the convenient thing about Gregorian chant is that it always sounds like a funeral march, if you so desire. Once more I realized I didn't even know the Petite Artiste's name, despite the fact that I'd plundered her rental room. Her landlady kept calling her "the odd bird." That or The Petite Artiste or The Loquacious One stood for her three aliases. Was Jane Doe 12-2002 going to be her fourth? Walking back, I restarted the autopsy cassette.

The phone rang and I ignored it. It rang again, six, seven, eight times, going through that many voice mails. I gave up and pounded over in frustration, answering, almost wishing for a telemarketer I could curse, but really wishing for Willy or even Burt. I got none of the above.

"I'm happy that it's you who's taking care of my art angel," a rasping voice said. "Are you going to shelve her with the pretty heads? You're really pretty, too. Stay that way."

Then a disconnect.

Ever since Willy and I started going out, he decided—logically enough—that there should be an automatic trace on all phone calls into the lab, so we installed a caller ID that logged every call as well as automatically recording it.

I phoned Willy.

"Willy," I said when he answered.

He huffed into the line, letting me know we weren't yet ready for first names.

"Willy, damn it. Listen to this." I played the tape about the art angel and the pretty heads.

"I'll be right over. Get campus security there now."

"And that's not all—" But he'd already hung up. I was happy that he cared. I was also scared. To fight that off, I went back to Jane Doe 12 and began probing, turning the cassette back on. *All the pretty heads.* I remembered the girl with the camera last September 11. And the open cabinet. Damn it.

I'd had just about as much digging around in bones and mud and flesh as I could stand when my forceps hit something hard and loose where something hard and loose shouldn't be. I figured it for a river pebble, but what I pulled out was a small tooth. I looked immediately to the mandible and skull. No missing teeth. The tooth in the forceps was a left canine, and it was smaller than Jane Doe 12-2002 would have had anyway. Abnormally small, though adult from its root size. Small, small, small. Familiar, familiar, familiar. *All the pretty heads.*

I again switched off the cassette. Lots of bathroom breaks, I'd have to explain. I steamed off the left eyetooth. *Parva, parva, parva.* Wasn't that Latin for small? Regina, Regina, Regina—Latin for queen, Willy told me. Christ, had the Petite Artiste carried around Gina's tooth? Did she murder Gina, then? Or had the Hex Man force-fed it to the Petite Artiste while murdering her? It had been where her stomach was. Had he found out that I talked with her? Is that why he murdered her? *Did* he murder her? No One Touches Anyone, I assured myself, while carrying the tooth to the case that held Gina. I cradled her skull and gently nudged the tooth—a perfect fit. One of the few carie-free teeth Gina'd ever had. It had finally wandered back home.

"Shit!" I exclaimed, as the lab door burst open. I bobbled the skull most unprofessionally as Bill the campus cop and his female shadow stared.

"Willy told us to get over here with lights and siren. What the hell's up?"

"What's up is that I wish I'd gotten a degree in English lit. Bill, there's so many things up that I don't know where to start." I gave the tooth a tug and out it came.

"Start with why we're here with sirens and lights."

I set down the skull and played the tape. Then Willy showed up, evidently having fanned policemen throughout the building. He'd already had the phone number traced. It came from a phone booth in Nicholasville, the town closest to where Jane Doe 12's body had been found. I looked at his sweet, thin lips that I hadn't kissed in too long.

"Jane Doe 12 is The Petite Artiste, Willy. I'm sure of it."

"I figured," his lips said.

"You figured! Well then why don't you bring the son of a bitch in?"

"He's been in once already. He's admitted to following her ever since he moved in her boarding house over Christmas, after getting beat up by some irate father for stalking some young daughter. Claims he's now protecting only older women. And guess where his mother lives? In Nicholasville. We're looking for him."

"Wait. Who's this *he* you're talking about, Willy?"

"The same kid your pal Dr. Kiefer's been treating, the one who got sent to the hospital by the angry pop."

"God, Willy. Not him. How'd you get on him? Adolph. It's Adolph. Look." I went to Gina's skull to show him and Bill and Bill's female shadow, and Mildred and the chairman, who'd just walked in, how neatly the tooth fit the upper jaw. So neatly that I had trouble dislodging it this second time.

Willy tugged his moustache.

10.

The Silver Platter Matter

Year 2002

(Gray, Pebble, Miriam)

A's ugly roommate Raven-Satan barely missed pepper spraying my face, just because I was walking by their deep-creep place, and I hadn't eventhenyet (doesn't that word ring swell?) peeped up to their stupid four windows. I told her that how else was I going to get to work and she said, "You don't go to friggin' Joe's Pizza by this street."

"How do you know I work there? You been following me?" I screamed, sneezing from the pepper and rubbing my eyes. I bent for wet leaves and mushed them on my face to get the spray off.

"No, but the cops have ever since you came back. It's called a restraining order for a reason, you know. How come they let you out?"

"It's a free country." The wet leaves were helping.

"Not for dickheads." She pointed the spray again, but I threw leaves at her and ran.

So I really was like bin Laden hiding out in caves.

None of that mattered though, because I finally realized my mistake all along. An artist woman lived in the front right room of the boarding house I had caved up in since after Thanksgiving. Her door was open Monday in the third week of Advent right before Christ's Mass and I walked by and saw paintings, paintings, paintings, sketches, sketches, sketches. Thenafter I smelled not only patchouli oil but artist's balm oil whenever I passed her room.

I realized my mistake because she was older like a forlorn pale princess who needed a kiss—not young, tan, and pampered like A by her Raven-Satan roommate and her parental Dad and her gorilla Bro who did lots worse than pepper gas. So theneverafter all winter and early spring I flew true to the artist, treading behind whenever she looped in circles around the campus, whenever she stared at a parking structure and its stinko ginkgo tree. This last was weird, until I found out that the English Department used to be there until eleven years ago. Maybe she had been a professor or something, though I thought she was too young for that, so maybe she had been a graduate student like my stupid new English teacher who keeps giving me D's because I make up words like "thenafter" or "thenever." I bet if I was Black she'd just say, "That's fine, little Sambo Akeema, you're expressing your sweet Ebonic culture." So I thought that this was another reason—besides the Twin Towers of Babel—that bin Laden got things right about Amerika, where cops follow good Christians around while artists piss on Jesus for art and government money. Fart art.

I realized all that after my pepper spray experience with Raven-Satan, A's roommate, (I don't write or even say her name anymore, I just print out "A," but you know whomof I mean, that she-person of the still lovely bending neck despite her gorilla father and brother, the still sad lifelong cardinal mate I'll never have), anyway I realized after my pepper experience that I didn't want to scare the patchouli artist, so I kept a really long way away whenever I guardian-angel followed her. Sometimes so far away that I lost her, but guess what? Someone else was following her. At first I thought it was the girl of whomee doomee the patchouli artist kept pictures hanging and lying all over her room. Then during the last week of Advent, just one week before Christ's Mass, two old people that I bet were the artist's parents came and said, "We need to talk, Grace Ann." As soon as I heard their voices I peeked through my peepyhole. They stood at her number Two door and repeated, "We need to talk, Grace Ann. Open Up." When she did, they took her elbows and her into the kitchen, the communal kitchen whereinwhich I keep hoping to fate-date-mate-meet her, but can only everthere eat-meet the stinky trumpet guy who rooms in the basement and lives on Fig Newtons. When her parents dragged her elbows, she left her door open, so whenas I heard them talking to her in the roach haven kitchen—she hardly wouldn't talk back to them—I sneaked into her room and stole a painting of a bunch of people—seven people—I can count, you know. One painting person looked like the girl who was following the artist, the girl who boarded next to me in number Three, but it was just the black hair and the eyes that made it look that way. The painting girl had thin teeth and no breasts. The girl boarding next to me has breasts like Dr. Kiefer's though only two crawfish could scoot between them, not a whole catfish with its whiskers and all like could swim through Dr. Kiefer's two holding tanks, which I try to never stare at whenon I'm in her official officarium.

Three plus Five (my room number) plus Two (Grace's room number) make ten, which is not a square. Five plus Two isn't a square either, but it makes Seven, a lucky number, so the titty lesbian girl living in Three needs to get lost.

You know about the Twin Tower of Babel, because I've told you somewheretime before. Well, bin Laden got that much right, but he messed up because he did not listen to the reed shaking in the wind. That's John the Baptist, who foreran before Jesus the Lord Christ. That man John the Baptist was born a Nazarene, which means he never used a razor or brushed or conditioned his hair, but always let it grow. I know they didn't have hair conditioner back then; they used egg whites and patchouli oil. I'm not stupid.

Grace's mother started crying in the kitchen after I tiptoed back with the painting into my room. I don't mean she saw me take the painting, I just mean that she started crying. Some things just happen together without meaning anything. And some things happen together meaning everything. This is like my mother's insurance drying up and me getting out of the nut cage past time to visit on Turkey Day with my mother and her cum-soaked boyfriend, but in time to pay rent on my room and celebrate Advent in Church and get my pizza job back because all the students left on break. The spheres were circling.

"Why don't you go back to school, or at least come home to Cincinnati to live with us? You can paint there. We're just so worried about you here," the mother of Grace said.

I think Grace said "Gina" in reply. That didn't make sense, and for a while I wondered if her parents got her name wrong by calling her Grace Ann. I mean, I wouldn't be surprised if my mother called me Ishmael or Aardvark, especially after she's been drinking and smoking and whoring with her creep-deep boyfriend whose hands are like lobster claws. Maybe,

I thought, Gina is Grace's sister. Or maybe she's a friend. But I never-ever have seen anyhoodle person everwhen visit, other than these old folk parents, and they only came once in December. So Grace was her name and she was named right. You'll see why.

Here's how Grace became my Grace: I kept following her far-far away, like a good guardian angel. That's how I saw that the girl who lives next to me was following her too. This girl calls Grace *Gina* all the time, like maybe she only heard the first letter of her name and has forgotten the rest, and of course Grace is too polite and doesn't care about this pervert lesbian girl anyway, she wants a Christian man, so she lets her call her Gina. What does she care about names, right?

But I learned for sure Grace was her right name on this special April One night I guardian-angeled her. Here's the happenwhen: The lesbian number Three girl was also following her. After far-following maybe an hour I saw Grace sitting on a bench when I topped a small rise in the sidewalk, and I panicked because I didn't want to frighten her. There were two buildings near, a bookstore and an empty store for rent. I walked behind them both into an alley, wherewhen some dumb-ass tiny dog began barking. There was a broken concrete block that I picked up and threw, sending the dog limping off. Maybe I broke its stupid back leg. Barking gives off bad karma.

So I sneaked by three garbage cans and stopped at a row of hedges. Across the street and through another back yard, A's and Raven-Satan's second floor apartment with its green sheen shades faced Grace and me with its four whore eyes. This was like a sign: the dwindle-dwarf past framed by the artist-queen future. Where'd they ever get those silly shades, anyway? But I didn't have to worry about stupid college girl taste anymore, just like I soon didn't have to worry about bin Laden anymore, because Grace was ready to descend.

Then when I spotted the lesbian number Three girl from down the hall: she was almost breathing on Grace's neck, though she kept hidden behind a pile of wood and shelves probably from inside the store now for rent. Do lesbians rape one another? I mean, with a red dildo or piece of raw vegetable or wood? I'd knock the shit out of the lesbian to protect Grace if they did. Guardian-angel her.

For maybe half an hour I crouched ready to spring a guardian angel wing. Then I heard this car slowing. It was a long car like they used to make—I don't mean a limousine, but a long car. Like a hearse, but forest green or blue, so I knew a preacher or prophet was driving, and when it slowed in front of Grace, I saw a cross proclaiming on the dashboard. I bowed my head for Jesus and looked up to see the passenger window roll down like smooth nighttime magic. I heard the preacher/prophet proclaim something. I had to get nearer, so I practiced cave-breathing and scooting the same way I figured Bin Laden was doing.

"Gina." I heard. Grace was the one who'd said it, and once more I was confused, but it only lasted a second.

"Gina's alive. She misses you. I'm going to take you to her. Get in."

Write that down four more times in your mind, because I don't want to. That's what I heard five times, and that's what Grace and lesbian girl who lives next to me heard the prophet with the black Nazarene beard and straggled hair say five times, like the number of my room.

"Gina's alive. She misses you. I'm going to take you to her. Get in."

His voice was deep, like the voice maybe of God, one you could trust because it sang little notes. *Alive* went up, *misses you* went down, and *take you to her* tumbled like a creek in summer. *Get in* came out just how I figured Gabriel or St. Peter might say, wheneverafter they arrive-drive in a leathery limousine to tote me to heaven.

Finally, Grace did as the prophet foretold. She got in the car, though he commanded her to get in the back the minute she opened the front door: "Get in the back, so you and Gina can sit together and talk." She did, but this is where true Grace descended, because the front door was still open and when the prophet leaned to close it he looked right at me with dark sacrificial eyeball eyes and wagged his long white-in-the-night prophet finger.

I had been anointed by the Nazarene.

He slammed the door and the key to my life turned: Women are not mothers; they are Jezebels. All of them. Some day my head would be served on a silver platter or maybe I would be crucified; how I died wouldn't matter, it would be because of some cunty woman.

The car drove off. A silver cross on the back dashboard wobbled like one of those no-barking dog's heads. The tit-filled lesbian Jezebel girl who lived next to me tripped over sticks and shelving and fell out on the sidewalk to scream at the disappearing long car, "No-ooo!"

Rainy night air began cleansing the world, so I, newly anointed, placed my head against cool concrete blocks to whisper,

"Ye-esss."

11.

Zeno Approaches the Unapproachable

Year 2003

(Zeno, Clarissa, Harriet, Willy, Methuselah)

At the very instant and point that Professor Clarissa Circle entered my bookstore, sweet musk glissaded from her bosom toward my lungs. Like an ice pick, the door's chime tickled a lump forming in my throat, and my love spilled on out. This demi-goddess (I did not yet know her name) stood five feet seven with her loopy blue-gray eyes contrasting an emerald green sundress. She bestrode me like the Colossus once bestrode Rhodes. Or like the twin towers once bestrode Manhattan.

"Come," the demi-goddess chanted from the Social Sciences section, only to hold me off with a raised, pure palm when I attained half-distance to her lean body. Seeing my disappointment—perhaps when my sorrowful turtle countenance teetered over a warp in the oak floor—she cooed, "Oh come here, my little Zeno." So again I halved the precious distance to her selfdom. Again and again was I coaxed, not only with words but also with wafts and undulations, until her pungency vibrated an inhalation away.

She waved a book she'd taken from a shelf, a dense monograph on bone classification, and asked where I'd gotten it, explaining how she'd heard from a graduate student that I had it in stock. I explained how I'd recently bought it and a baker's dozen off someone claiming to sell them for a guy named Methuselah:

"I laughed when he told me that, but sure enough, that name was inscribed in all fourteen books."

"There's always someone breathing oxygen, nitrogen, and argon who thinks he's Methuselah. What would it matter if he were? No One, not even someone who's inhaled earth-dust for nine hundred and sixty-seven years, Can Ever Touch Anyone. Ever."

Her odd, sharp answer and her intense eyes thrust me right into Everland; oxygen, nitrogen, dust, and Methuselah all be damned. She stood so commandingly close that her perfume's pheromones burrowed beside my pelvic cradle, scientifically bypassing nostrils and lungs, just as they were designed to do.

"Thanks," she said.

It took me a moment to realize she was dismissing me. Back to my point of origin an eternity away, to be shelved with Methuselah? I sauntered to my counter, where I pretended to read, though I did nothing but whiff stray pheromones.

Harriet, a high school student who'd haunted my shop ever since a snowstorm over a year ago, strutted up to the stunning woman and said something curt, instilling puzzlement on the demi-goddess's face. Harriet then crossed the hardwood floor to toss a tattered gray paperback copy of Sartre's *Nausea* on my counter.

"The title fits," she said, giving a melodramatic grimace and a lithe twist of her lithe hips. "Just remember your friend Heraclitus from the Isle of Obscure: 'Eyes and ears are evil witnesses, if you don't have a soul to understand their language.'" She leaned over the counter and crooked a bitten fingernail at me. When I neared she whispered, "Methuselah, you likely remember, lived nine hundred and sixty-*nine* years. You'd think she'd at least have gotten the *sixty-nine* part right, considering her slut perfume." Pulling out a five-dollar bill to pay for the paperback, Harriet rubbed it over tiny, pert breasts. "I create my own musk." With a disdainful green-eyed glance she tossed the bill onto the counter and swayed out my front door, not even waiting for her change.

"My, my," the blue-gray eyed woman called from across the room. "Quite the *enfant terrible*."

"You don't know the half of it. What did she say to you?"

"'The kingdom is a child's.' Whatever could she mean?"

It was more Heraclitus, which Harriet had been reading the week before last. Though I knew exactly what she meant, I only shrugged.

"And just what did she whisper to you?"

Her question approached me in undulations, much as the infamous, impotent arrow purportedly wobbled unendingly but persistently from the shaft of my Greek namesake, halving its distance toward an unnamed goal with each undulating instant. Always, always, always halving, never ever, ever reaching, just like his infamous tortoise and hare. "I couldn't catch it all," I lied.

Fortunately I didn't have to answer more than that, for an anorexic college student walked in and nodded at the blue or gray-eyed woman whose name I soon learned was Professor Clarissa Circle. I rarely read the newspaper, or I might have recognized her name from the summer before.

Five minutes later I sold two elongated black candles to this student, who, unlike Harriet, awaited her change while I broke open a roll of quarters. Ms. Anorexia impatiently tapped the candles against one another to form an X, remindful of how a priest might ease them around your throat on Saint Blaise's feast day to ensure tonsils and adenoids one more safe annum. Just over two anni before this evening I'd opened my store, Zeno's Used Books, in this up-and-coming section of town near the state's flagship university. I was twenty-seven then. One month after opening, I began selling these dark, witchy candles that a friend of a friend made, taking them in on a lark. By the time I turned twenty-eight, her black candles and another woman's prurient scarlet ones accounted for a fifth of my sales. And just one week ago, a guy approached me with wind chimes he made from collected junk. *Jim'd-chimes*, he called them, a bastardization of his first name and a long lost pun.

Before these Jim'd chimes was where Professor Clarissa Circle now moved. Each chime got named for a theme: Vanity Fair, constructed of old combs, compact mirrors, and lipstick tubes; Techno Chimes, made of gaily painted circuit boards and obsolete RAM; New Mexico Chimes, made of beads and holy-card portraits of Virgin Mary shellacked inside sardines-with-jalapeno cans. With a finger-plunk to the latter, Clarissa laughed at their tinny sound.

"Come back soon," I said to the college girl, who smirked as I handed her the quarters she'd been awaiting. Smirking, you should know, serves as the prevalent attitude of current university students. As she walked out the door and across the street, I glanced at Professor Clarissa's long demigoddess legs and spoke:

"I took in eight of those homemade chimes you're looking at, halving my poetry section to make room. Poetry doesn't sell, even near campuses, though a third of this area's college bars hold open-mike poetry readings."

"I've been to one. Reading just a tad more of what they pretend to write might help matters."

"Exactly." I watched her backside fill and her emerald sundress lift as she bent to nudge a different Jim'd Chime. Over the chime's resulting clatter, I called out, "What if everyone who played piano or guitar never listened to piano or guitar music?"

The chime she tapped was called "Pearls Before Swine": forty strands of pearls, each with a small plastic pig clacking at the end. It wound up that she would buy a chime whose ascribed theme was "Memento Mori," consisting of shellacked bones inset with costume jewelry. She also bought three books, including the bone tome, but still, that meant two Jim'd Chimes sales inside one week. Between the chimes, candles, and smirking university students where would my store end up? A lip-gloss boutique? I'd planned to run a quiet used-book store, dealing in fine intellectual volumes, distributing fingers of knowledge to massage the population out of its millennial angst. A place for enlightened humans to encounter one another, if only through furtive glances and shared coffee or tea in real china cups surrounded by old Garamond and Clarendon fonts. But just moments before, I'd chased off one of my best customers, if Harriet's comment about nausea went deeper than her anger at my not returning her months old crush. But she was seventeen and I would soon be twenty-nine, not all that long before the age when Buddha sat meditating under a plane tree and Jesus began his mission. Jesus wound up crucified, and Buddha evaporated. How would I wind up? Mummified in a lip-gloss boutique and alone?

After Clarissa bought her Jim'd Chime and three books, she revealed her Rumpelstiltskin name and once more intoned, "Come closer, Little Zeno."

Ahem, I thought, *mummified maybe, but perhaps not alone.* So I closed shop and we went out for a single martini . . . well, a single double martini. Or two. They should name the juniper berry the chokeberry whenever I'm concerned. Or maybe the mistberry. Still, a fine summer's eve presented opportunity as we sat on the patio of a nearby café watching the precious spot between buildings where the sun was setting. I looked into Clarissa's gray-blue eyes—I still hadn't deciphered their predominant color—as she bit an olive. Cars passed and I leaned toward her aquiline nose, her high cheeks. "My house is only five blocks away," she offered after our second double martini. "Let's walk. Follow me." She could have added in a whisper, "And discard your cloak, your shoes and pants, and your parents." I would still have followed.

FROM THE BONE TOME I surmised that Clarissa was a professor, so I wasn't surprised to discover that she lived on the fringe of the student ghetto, in a sizeable two-story granite-block house with a wide front porch.

"Physical—actually forensic anthropology," she said as if reading my mind as we walked up her front steps. She pulled the memento mori Jim'd Chime from its bag and tiptoed to hang it on a hook in the porch's tongue-in-groove ceiling, but couldn't. "Boost me, would you?" I blinked as she and her quivering lips faced me, but did as she requested, clasping and lifting her until she hung the chime, her leather purse twisting on its strap to intercede between my nose and her navel. When she patted my head to indicate she was done I eased her down, trying to inhale her mid-section discreetly, being human and not cur.

She unlocked her front door and stepped inside; then she adjusted an elaborate burglar system with emerald green lights. Finished with poking the lights, she tugged me up curving oaken steps to a bulging, turret-like corner bedroom. Blue and red lights twinkled like stars the instant we entered—by motion-detector? She was suddenly lounging in an armchair, one leg angling to coolly, bluely reveal her thigh while I stood in lust's lumpish red glow.

"Take off your shoes," she intoned in singsong.

I did, thinking of Moses overlooking the Promised Land, chanting Kaddish.

"Take off your . . ."

I stripped before her, before I even realized I was doing so.

Under those twinkling blue and red lights, music began—I supposed this also electronically arranged since I never saw her touch a switch or dial. A Bach fugue burst from an organ whose mammoth pipes must have nearly pricked whatever arched cathedral ceiling they stayed housed under, for even their CD digital projection vibrated cavernous and eruptive. By then I'd stripped to my blue polka-dotted briefs. When Clarissa's fingers gave a commanding twitter, I removed those too, dropping them to the floor and nearly tripping on a polka dot, for I'd caught sight of what appeared to be a large, elongated bone peeping from under the chair she lounged in. Following my glance she stood, a sudden glass of red wine in her hand, which she pressed against the small of my back while she pressed her loose, short, and silken emerald sundress against my front, the dress that had so caught my attention in the bookstore. Well, it and the long legs under it. And the blue-gray eyes over it. And the pheromones about it.

We danced around the bed to Bach. Of course one can't dance to Bach, so we ground against one another, the silk of her dress coolly interrupting the bounce of my prick, which neighed in mid-air like . . . like a half-open book in an avid reader's clasp? My metaphors became as entangled as I was. Whenever I tugged to suggest the queen-size bed so very close by, to take the book and speed-read, so to speak, Clarissa proffered a sip of red wine and we would climb another fugue. I felt like an acolyte following a grisly crucifix, whereon hung a sad, bug-eyed Christ with an ultra-high forehead and thin, thin lips that hissed "Follllow mmmmmeeeee."

Until that night I accounted myself a blues-folk-acoustic man. Until that night I accounted myself an Ancient Age man, typically drinking that bourbon on the rocks. But blues drifted to *Organ Fugue in Stratospheric Major*; bourbon drifted to gin and lust-red wine. Between climbing and descending fugues and sips of lust-red, I heard the clunk of one high heel, another, coming after she'd stumbled on my instep twice, the second time with the point of a heel. But on the third stumble, it was her bare foot releasing moist, cool warmth gathered from the wood floor, not leather grinding like sandpaper or a heel puncturing like an ice pick. Veins in my foot pounded, yearning. Our skin almost touched. But then an interrupting, untouching, halving distance resulted from her suddenly blasting air conditioning and ensuing goose bumps. And then a callous on the bottom of her foot interposed impenetrable padding. And what else? Did eight or so hairs atop my own foot intervene between our fleshes? Whatever, as surely as her purse had intervened on the porch, something interposed to prevent true contact.

"My little Zeno," Clarissa sighed, as if reading my cosmic, sad thoughts.

At last we lay in the bed, swaddled by the room's tiny red and blue lights blinking like demonic—or angelic—eyes. My head swirled from her perfume, from the gin, from the taste of wine—rare Medòc—and from the lipstick off her lips. Just as I sank into a pillow and closed my own too-human eyes to envision crimson nebulae and ice-blue planets, there came a clatter, like bamboo wind chimes, like bones, and I felt something pounce on my left foot.

"Aristotle! Miaow, miaow," Clarissa cooed.

In the strange blue and red lights, a dark gray cat arched its back, its purrs jabbing at my skin like a seismographic needle.

"Will Plato be coming along?" I quipped.

"Why, yes," Clarissa replied. Her moist breath condensed on my ear. "Plato will no doubt also climb up tonight, my little bookstore man, my little Zeno."

Overhead, those red and blue lights danced like constellations hastening through millennial rotation to arrive at . . . entropy? Big Bang? And then, five nails dug at my hip—Clarissa's or Aristotle's? Plato's? And then we did our business, using a prophylactic, which at the time made sense, though it was ribbed.

"I've never used a ribbed one before," I said, thinking of the old saw about not wearing a raincoat to bed. It was the one useful thing my father told me before running off with a hooker. And of course, the one useful thing he'd told me was useless: witness his death of AIDS six years later in Seattle. Raincoats, they do keep off the rain.

Sensing how Clarissa remained urgent after my petit mort, I tried a different tack, for I pride myself on leaving women satisfied. Working downward with my tongue, I licked her belly button and blew alternating hot and cool air with each descending, each ascending motion. Outside, these things happened: 1) a trio of sirens rushed by, 2) a bottle broke, 3) two students yelled obscenities, 4) street lamps hummed. Assiduous as ever, I continued downward into the silk of her thighs until her hips lifted and I heard a gurgle, or maybe a purr. Giving respite, I rubbed my cheeks against those soft inner thighs, alternately blowing hot puffs and inhaling perfume, which seemed to owe its origin to her softly shampooed pubes. My tongue, pilgrim before a shrine, unleashed itself to roll and curl about her labia—and when her breath pulsed I pressed onward, sucking her clitoris like a child working a tiny pull of vanilla taffy. This elicited moans, and her left hand tugged my hair, then my right ear. Suddenly there came a pop! Something considerably harder and larger than a kernel of corn had shot into my mouth. But her thighs pressed so tightly against my ears that I couldn't disengage without a good deal of will and force—neither of which I possessed.

She let out a sob and a dark laugh. As I mentioned, I pride myself in satisfying women . . . so I spit out what I imagined might be part of a shield or diaphragm or rib from the prophylactic, and I continued tongue massaging until Clarissa chirped enough to bring in Plato, who joined Aristotle in kneading the backs of my knees.

Afterward, in the calm of Pachelbel's "Canon," we lay side by side. I was too embarrassed to mention the piece of diaphragm or whatever, and anyhow, the mood ebbed into serene. Mechanical matters could keep.

Not sunlight—I've never been sensitive to sunlight like people who can't sleep once dawn arrives as if they were cloisterers intent upon the work of the Lord—so not light but a ringing phone startled me awake. I'd been dreaming about Harriet the high school nymph, about dancing with her in a field while she sang out her poetry, but I awoke to that ringing. And then to the motion of a mattress depressing near my cheek to tilt my glance toward Professor Clarissa Circle, physical anthropologist. Then I heard her voice.

Her foot, clad in a silken blue high heel, was propped on the mattress, its ankle before my left eye. I watched her fingers strapping the heel while she talked on a cell phone held between cheek and shoulder. When I scooted to kiss her instep she smiled, even though my turtle lips touched only blue leather. The multi-colored lights had been extinguished.

"All right, I'll be there at 8:30 . . . Yes, I know that gravel road. Fine.

I'm picking up a new assistant . . . Zeno. That's right, Zeno . . . it's a Greek name, a philosopher . . . Yes, Willy, I'm well aware you know all about philosophy . . . No, he's much less thin-skinned than the last." I heard an electronic beep, and with a hop she leaned to place the phone on her dresser. I thought I saw a skull reflected in its mirror, then realized it was one of the candles I sold out of my store, a hefty dusky gray one shaped like a skull. So she'd been in before. How could I have missed her beauty?

"Well, hell. Undo my straps for me, would you, Zeno," Professor Clarissa sighed, again propping her right foot on the bed.

She had to point for me to understand that she meant the straps to the high heel she'd just fastened, for I had become entranced by the two patches of dark beneath her skirt, foresting either side of delicate blue bikini panties, patches which I had a sudden memory of pressing my ear against last night. Chthonic rumblings had trekked to and fro; underground gremlins and witches had drummed my tympanum in frenzied Walpurgisnacht incantations. Had they fabricated the homunculus that had ejected from Clarissa's womb? And just where was that homunculus now?

No time to search, for sans high heels, sundress, and panties, Clarissa was transformed from love-nymph professor into a field hand, complete with beige work denims and waterproof boots. Out of the bed and nude, I zipped her up. Had women's jeans always had their zippers in front, like a man's? I thought about mentioning the . . . homuncu . . . whatever it was that had been incanted and ejected but—

"Now you," Clarissa insisted. When I started for my clothes, she said "No," and pointed to a closet behind the bedroom door.

"Pick something assistatorial. We're going to the river. You'll like it. I'll make us coffee."

"Tea," I said.

"Coffee. You're going to need the caffeine."

She pulled back the bed covers, giving them a shake. In the middle of the mattress I spotted what must have popped into my mouth last night—but surely not. It was a molar. She saw it too, bent to study it, then shrugged and tossed it into a brass tray where it gave a rattle. Had I spotted the instance of a smile?

"You need to hurry and dress," she said. "We've only got an hour to get to the river. Two lovers stumbled onto a body last night and the police want me to ascertain its age and how long it's been there."

Glancing at the molar in the brass tray, I ran my tongue along my upper and lower teeth. None was missing.

Our musical diet while driving—in an extended cab pick-up with a red camper shell—to place a "temporarily closed" sign on my storefrontwas Gregorian chant.

"It helps me concentrate," Clarissa said as I scribbled a note for my door. I nodded and taped up the sign, then got back in her truck to watch my store diminish in the passenger side mirror. Half a league, half a league, half a league o'er. It certainly seemed easier to leave than to approach. Did my Greek namesake ever say anything about that? If goals could never be attained by approaching, could they come to fruition through leaving?

Half an hour later we were descending toward the Kentucky River, driving through patches of fog not yet lifted by the morning's sun.

"The su-u-un it gi-i-iv-eth, and the su-un it taketh a-way-ay-ay," I mumbled alongside the Gregorian chant, fretting over the mechanics of settling and lifting fog, over morning customers evaporated by a taped sign and locked door. But not many at this hour, unless they were searching for lip gloss.

"Mmm," Clarissa answered, as if she too were worrying over my bookstore, or the dissipation of earth's moisture, the onset of sun's heat. Reverse entropy, if you will.

With that "mmm" and Gregorian chant reverberating, I settled into my bucket seat to watch for any wildlife that wasn't roadkill. The life count came thinly considering how close we were to the river: a cardinal, a blue jay, five squirrels, what might have been a weasel in a small stream, and my two favorite animals—a rabbit and a tortoise.

"You are destined never to meet," I mouthed into the window as we drove by the tortoise, some hundred yards farther along than the rabbit. As if heeding me, it tucked into its shell for a little nap, just to coax ol' cotton bottom fruitlessly hopping behind to try and catch up.

"What did you say?" Clarissa turned off the chant when the road dipped steeply into a bend toward the river.

"I didn't mean to speak aloud. I was trying to let you concentrate."

"I have," she replied. "I'm prepared. So what were you saying?"

I explained about my namesake's theory of the tortoise and the hare, how the rabbit could never catch the tortoise's head-start because it would always have to cover first half the distance to the turtle, then half the remaining distance, then half that remaining distance, then half that . . . unto infinity.

"Zeno. Well of course." Clarissa popped her purse closed. Had she taken a pill? A breath mint? Smeared on lip gloss? Had she brought along the molar? "Of course," she repeated, glancing at me before turning back to the road's curves. "Your namesake was exactly on target. In this mess of a world, Nothing Can Ever Touch Anything."

"You said something like that in the bar last night. It sounds like 60s existential rhetoric." I thought of my father and how easily Clarissa's pronouncement could have served as his slogan during life, then thought how easily he could now rebuke that argument were he not dead, for the efficient cause of his death had been intimately touching. I also considered that we were going to investigate a skeleton that very well might be the remains of a murdered victim. If so, it-she-he could also convincingly argue against Clarissa's romantic existential platitude.

Clarissa had no time to defend her statement, for a policeman waved us onto a gravel road, then got into a cruiser and followed us. After a half mile, the area thickened with gendarmes, some with their heads bent to the ground, others seemingly bird-watching cardinals or blue jays in the surrounding trees.

"Are there always this many policemen when a skeleton's discovered?" I asked.

"Only when it's by the river, and even then only on sunny days. I knew there'd be a mass cop picnic here, so I figured you could pass as my graduate student."

Well, sunny it was, though the sunlight came in patches now that we entered denser forest. And most of the policemen were carrying coffee and laughing, so the picnic part was right too. After we parked precariously on an embankment, a wiry black man of butterscotch complexion approached Clarissa. When she introduced us he nodded curtly at me—at least I *think* he nodded at me and not at some skittering squirrel. I soon figured that he carried a crush for Clarissa and viewed me, if at all, as competition. I also had a crush on Clarissa, so I engraved his name—Captain William "Willy" Cox—into my skull and promised myself to run it through a computer check when I got back to the bookstore to learn whether he'd clocked any bad eBay buys from porn dealers.

"Did you listen to your chant on the way here?" Willy Cox asked Clarissa. When she hummed a bit he laughed. "Good. You're going to love this then: two college kids, maybe you know them—" he consulted a pad and read off two names, to which Clarissa shook her head— "anyway, these kids were out here screwing when the boy—he's politically correct and on the bottom, right?—when the boy feels something poking his back and pulls a skull out from under his butt."

"Alas, poor Yorick," I said.

Clarissa snickered but the detective just narrowed his eyes.

We started walking toward a clump of cops who were smoking and in general lollygagging. When they saw us, the smokers cupped their cigarettes and scattered while the remainder began searching the ground.

"I told them to leave the gravesite alone," Willy said, snorting at the suddenly busy police. "I told them the Goddess of Bones was coming and to keep their stupid paws off."

"Thanks."

"Anything for you."

I wanted to cough at the cop's ironic tone, but held back when Clarissa threw an elbow at me.

"There," Willy said, giving a nod. "The male kid placed it there so we 'could be sure and find it.' " The detective snort-laughed and pointed to an oil drum that managed to capture a shaft of sunlight. Atop it perched a piece of plywood, and atop that a skull.

We walked over and Clarissa rubbed her thumb along the skull's brow, bending to look at the upper teeth, most of which were still there. "Adult," she announced, "likely in his or her late twenties." She pointed to a molar near the back, a wisdom tooth erupting from the upper jaw. Realizing that I had one in the same spot that had been troubling me for a month, I ran my tongue over it. Then she bent closer and gave a smell, then shrugged. "Touch it, Little Zeno."

I did. Sudden choral music sang in my ears, nearly toppling me onto the dewy grass.

"How long?" Willy asked.

"Forty years or so. No flesh, no grease, no smell. Still nice and white, though."

The detective grunted. "Grave's over here." He squelched the two-way at his side as we walked under a canopy of trees. Just as we reached the grave, there was a gunshot and Willy took off. "Don't worry—probably a snake," he said. "I don't suppose any murderer's still hanging around thirty years after the fact."

"I don't suppose," Clarissa agreed.

Still wobbly from the singing skull, I watched the cop stumble over a root; meanwhile Clarissa squatted to survey the shallow grave, which made a slight depression instead of the mound I expected. With her trowel, she pointed out a torn package for a rubber. Un-ribbed. I blinked and squatted too, ripping the back pocket of the pants she'd loaned me because I'd left my loaned trowel in it.

"That sassafras tree over there made it through the flood three years ago. It's about ten years old. That crushed oak sapling at the head of this grave, on the other hand, the one the environmentally enhanced student couple crushed, came well after the flood. That's what brought the skull up, most likely."

"The flood? Or the oak? Or the coupling students?"

Clarissa didn't answer, but began to dig. Two hours later, she'd cleared a good part of the dirt to reveal a nearly intact skeleton, both tibia resting across collapsed rib bones as if the skeleton's owner had fallen asleep like Rip Van Winkle—except this owner had never awakened. What gave the lie to falling asleep was a crudely machined knife in the pelvic cradle—still partly standing, since it had penetrated the bone. "A male," Clarissa said, rubbing her ring finger along the pelvis. "And with that knife penetrating the pelvis, I'd say we have a homicide from jealousy. Lot of angry force to drive it that hard."

"What about the folded arms? Would an angry murderer fold the arms of someone he hated?"

"Cain did."

"Beg your pardon?"

"Cain. Don't you read your Bible? 'And Cain foldeth his murdered brother's arms to be receivèd by warms.'"

Warms? I narrowed my eyes and Clarissa laughed. A rhyming joke. Still, when I reached for the coffee that the good Willy had left us, I heard her murmur, "Maybe Cain did fold Abel's arms. The last touch ever."

It was creepy, as if Clarissa was envisioning Abel's murder and burial. Was she kin to Adam and the mysterious Methuselah? Or just to McTeague, Frank Norris's grotesque dentist who could extract molars with his bare hands?

On the drive back from the river, the rattling boxed bones made me wish for Gregorian chant.

"You were lucky," Clarissa commented. "A lot of times the skeletons have partly decayed flesh clinging to them. That's why I prepare myself with Gregorian chant—this one was grisly enough with the knife. It will stick out too."

"No pun intended."

"My little bookstore man," she cooed.

Her little bookstore man was very late opening that day. But despite the skeleton, Clarissa invigorated me for the next three weeks whenever I visited her office as she pieced the skeleton together, though I had to get a hepatitis shot to do so. The No One Ever Touches Anyone rule evidently didn't apply to viruses and corpses. I also had to sign in with a secretary with a ramrod back who listed me as a "special observer." This woman, I suspected, was guest lecturing the ubiquitous Abusive Etiquette 101 class that taught so many students the fine art of smirking.

My morning visits came frequently, and not entirely because of my growing infatuation with Clarissa, for whenever I touched the skeleton, music filled my head, just as it had that first morning by the river when I touched the skull on the barrel. After the second week, just nearing its open case was enough to start the music. One evening I brushed against the homemade knife, still fixed in the pelvis bone, and awoke on the floor of Clarissa's lab, there had come such a tympani. Fortunately no one was there to see me pass out—not even Clarissa, who'd run off to find a reference book. It was like the skeleton was my long-lost twin, dead at birth but still trying to tell me something. Carpe Diem? Grab Clarissa while you can? But she was not only the Goddess of Bones, she was the No One Touches Anyone Lady—at least emotionally and spiritually, for as much as we rocked, as much as we rolled, something lingered untouched. The mission bells tolled, to complete a rhyme worthy of young Harriet, whom I had only seen three times over the last three weeks, lurking across the street from my bookshop.

The skeleton came to my height, exactly: five feet nine inches. Well, the reconstructed bones really came to five feet seven and a quarter inches, but Clarissa assured me that flesh and gristle would fill out the extra one and three-quarters inch.

"Flesh and gristle fills out a lot," I commented, rubbing her flank while the graduate student helping her busily scribbled notes. Clarissa rubbed back. I knew we were in for another night of Medòc and purring cats after I closed the store.

There were other oddities about the skeleton—or rather, about me. Clarissa had originally dated the skeleton's age by the wisdom tooth angling down from its left upper jaw. Upon cleaning and piecing the skeleton together in the lab, she spotted a lower intact wisdom tooth on the mandible and had to revise the murdered victim's age upward: Now she guessed the man had been in his late twenties.

"Twenty-eight?" I asked, pulled by my affinity for the skeleton.

She shrugged. "Why not? Sure. Twenty-eight."

I didn't tell her that a wisdom tooth was just coming in on my upper left jaw and that two already graced my very own mandible. Anyway, Timmy Doe, as we'd come to call the skeleton, had only the one on his lower jaw, his mandible.

Or so I thought. For one late night while I was fetching coffee I overheard a graduate student, a young woman of twenty-two, ask if she and her boyfriend could drive out to the river and dig for the missing wisdom tooth. Clarissa told the student she'd be wasting her time, whether she was looking for a tooth or someone to touch by a romantic river, either one. "Impossible odds never keep *you* from trying, do they?" I heard the student ask. With a sigh, Clarissa started up her Gregorian chant.

That night over gin, I confronted her: "You didn't tell me that Timmy had both his lower wisdom teeth."

"Why on earth would I?" She leveled her cool gray or blue eyes on my arm and said, "I didn't tell you that he'd broken his right forearm as a child either, did I?"

My hand flew to my right forearm, which I too had broken as a child; simultaneously, my tongue rubbed over my upper left jaw where that third tooth was working its way in. I did a quick recap: had I ever told her about falling off my bike?

Need I add that the graduate student never found the molar, though she did find a strand of thin blonde hair and a rabies tag, both of which Clarissa showed me. My hair is thin and blondish. And though I've never owned a dog, I imagined Timmy Doe walking a Doberman on a leash. That's certainly the dog I'd walk near a river if I feared being murdered.

Two nights later, I filched the molar that had popped from Clarissa's feminine darkness out of its resting place among earrings in the cupped brass hand. And one morning later I furtively fit it into Timothy Doe's mandible, where it made a perfect match. I studied Timmy's forearm, where Clarissa had indicated a break in the . . . tibia? I consulted a nearby chart. The ulna. But I couldn't spot anything indicating a break without Clarissa near to point it out. Anyway, had I broken my ulna or . . . my radius? On my right or my left arm? I was no longer sure. Eyes and ears are evil witnesses, unless you have a soul to understand their language. Thank you Heraclitus. Thank you, Harriet, whom I'd again spotted staring at my shop from across the street, an angry, desolate, unrequited waiflet.

Sex with Clarissa had permeated the scale of kink from that first night's male strip tease act and eruptive cunnilingual molar. Remembering the long bone under her chair, I'd never acquiesced to her banter about handcuffs, but we'd drifted through a dozen *Kama Sutra* contortions, tonight's coming with the addition of a pink ostrich feather and a blindfold.

"What did you do with the molar?" she asked, tickling my ankle. Lying on my back, I lifted my head cautiously. Through a slit in the blindfold I studied her backside and its vertebrae.

"The one on top of the dresser," she persisted.

"I took it . . . it fit in Timmy's—"

She interrupted with a laugh. "Of course it fit; that happens all the time."

"No, I mean that it really fit."

She twisted to look at me. I moved my head back and forth to convince her I couldn't see. "Everything touches everything, huh?" she said, in a half-mocking whisper.

I shrugged. She twisted to tickle my nipples with the pink feather. Then she sighed and lifted my blindfold.

"Two of my students died on this date one year ago," she said, waving the ostrich feather idly.

My head jerked. Despite what poets claim about death's intimate connection with sex, death presents a less than pleasant topic when one is conducting the venereal process.

Clarissa put her left hand on my chest and leaned. "The girl student put a bullet through her brain. Althea Tompkins. And the boy was killed when one of the tornadoes that hit near here dropped half an oak tree into his apartment. They were friends. He was New Jersey, Jewish. She had the prettiest red hair I've ever seen—long and flowing like a river. I'm not sure if she killed herself because of Simon—the boy—or . . ." she trailed off, still waving the ostrich feather whose pink reminded me of . . .

Red hair. New Jersey. "I knew them," I said. Clarissa had been staring at a mirror to her left. She turned to me and dropped the feather, which oddly enough clattered on the floor—from the quill, I realized. Her eyes were blue today. "They used to come to my store regularly, I'm sure of it. I remember her red hair and his New Jersey lingo. They always came with a muscle friend named Francis. I remember his name because he bought a book about Saint Francis."

Clarissa's buttocks settled onto my stomach. She'd taken her panties off, so her sex felt moist and warm. "I think Althea was pregnant. Her cheeks were always flushed; her skin was changing. She may not have even known it, but likely she did."

Clarissa hopped off, picked up the feather, which she placed on the dresser, before plunging her hands through a bottom drawer. While she did, I almost said, *Pregnant. One more proof that someone can touch someone else.* But I let it go, since we'd argued the tortoise-hare-nothing-ever-touches-anyone thesis all last weekend. It was fortunate that I kept quiet, for Clarissa pulled out a box, ripped at it, and produced a cherry red dildo, which she strapped on, turning to smile at me. "Let's change the subject, my little bookstore man. Sex therapy."

She was upon me, thrusting her tongue into my mouth while rubbing the dildo against my prick and thighs. When at last she began to glide upward along my chest from my stomach, I thought I understood its purpose.

"Open wide," she said.

What the hell, I thought. But a penlight, not the dildo, went into my mouth.

"Just as I suspected," she said.

"What?"

"You're nearing twenty-nine, you have two lower molars already in, and a third upper one pushing at a twenty degree angle on your left upper, the same angle as the upper molar in Timmy Doe's skull. Did you really break your right forearm as a child?" She nudged my chin with the dildo.

"Did Timmy Doe really break his?" I asked.

She rubbed the dildo against my chest, unstrapped it, and leaned to kiss me.

"Enough erotica for one night," she said.

DURING THE FOURTH WEEK with Clarissa, I found two notes taped on my store's door. The first came from the detective I'd met at the river: "Please call Detective Cox." That and a phone number. Down at the river, I hadn't told him I owned this bookstore. So unless Clarissa told him, why wouldn't he have just believed I was a doctoral student helping out like she said? The second note was from Harriet: "There would not be right without wrong." It took me a minute, but I realized that was another fragment from Heraclitus. I thought about Harriet, then about No-One-Touches-Anyone Clarissa with her changeable eyes, her two dead students, her weird living students, her wired corpses, and her jealous cop friend. Something was bothering Clarissa other than two dead students. She'd almost brought it up several times, with a "Did I tell you . . ." I was beginning to feel more like a therapist, a "sex therapist," as she said, than a lover. So I taped a large blue note for Harriet on the window that read, "The kingdom is a child's." This was really Heraclitus's commentary on time and its whimsical tosses of the dice, but since Harriet had usurped his meaning when she mouthed this to Clarissa, I would too.

With a second cup of coffee I walked to the computer to google "William Cox" on a computer search, something I should have done the first day we met as I'd planned. Around 6000 entries showed, and I pitter-patted until I'd narrowed twenty-one to Lexington's Detective Willy. The usual cop crap: fingerprinting diploma, forensics school, excellence award for civic duty. Member of the American Philately Society. I double-checked. How many cops are stamp collectors? How many blacks are stamp collectors? For that matter, how many women are? In America anyway, it seems to be a white male spectator sport—no doubt due to the anal retentiveness native to the hobby. But here perched Willy, the exception to prove the rule. Three years ago on a lark I'd bought a stamp collector's album full of worldwide and American stamps off a kid for what seemed to me to be a generous price, since the kid's cotton top reminded me of my youth. Two weeks later I was offered ten times that amount and of course took it. The kid and I were both probably robbed. Staring at the screen's search results, *American Philately Society,* I remembered a small red book titled *The World's Rarest Stamps—and Their Stories*. I fetched it and called good old Willy, believing in starting out aggressively.

Willy, however, was into aggressive one-upmanship: he entered my shop even as I was put on hold at the cop place. I lamely cradled the phone and waved the book.

Taking the book from me, he flipped through it, but had to dampen his two-way's squelch, whose blare sent a balding English professor backwards into the low table holding my coffee machine, though no damage was done. Willy chewed some false pity and shook his head at the clumsy professor. Then he leaned over the counter and whispered hoarsely, as if he'd taken up smoking to make up for losing Clarissa:

"It's a crime to ferret away murder evidence. A felony."

"I don't—"

He waved away my excuse, opened the stamp book, and slapped it on the counter. I stared at a photo of two black stamps depicting Washington's bust. A price tag of thirty-five grand hung on the stamps, littermates, evidently. Thirty-five grand? It would be the proverbial cold day in hell when I'd dish out—MY GOD! My eyes slashed to a drawer in my desk, then back to the photo. Was this duo what had fallen out of the album the day I sold it for what I'd thought was a steal of a price, ten times what I'd paid the cotton-top kid? Had these two Siamese twin black ten-cent Washingtons fallen on the floor when the buyer yanked the album from me even as I tried to wrap it? I hadn't noticed them lying face down until an hour later. And ridiculous fate on top of ridiculous fate, I almost tossed them when I'd picked them up!

"Pay attention," Willy said, tapping the bottom of the page. So I read: *A pair of the eighteen extant mint issues of this stamp, still connected to one another from the original printed sheet, are rumored to have caused the death of a rare book dealer, though his body was never found.*

With the oddest urge, I fantasized licking the adhesive gum off the back of the—I had to look at the book—the 155-year-old pair of stamps that lay in my drawer. They would taste—

No, my little Zeno. Their gum would never touch your tongue. Nothing Ever Touches Anything in this wretched world. Clarissa's voice sounded so clearly that I glanced behind the detective to see if she'd walked into the store.

"This chump," Willy turned the page to where the story continued, "lived in Boston. He stole the paired stamps from a company called H. E. Harris Stamps and was going to sell them to a private buyer. The last place he was seen . . ." Willy read upside down to find the city of Paris, Kentucky, and tap it with his pinkie . . . "was on a horse farm in Paris, just twenty miles from here."

Outwardly I shrugged, inwardly my heart thumped.

"Besides his being a bookseller like you who probably knew zilch about stamps, guess how old he was? And just guess when this happened?"

I looked into Willy's eyes, a delicate butterscotch that you sometimes see in black people.

"Twenty-eight years ago. And he was twenty-eight."

"Jesus," I started, but took a covering breath. "Jesus was thirty-three," I commented in non sequitur.

"Jesus didn't deal in rare books or stamps. I want that damned tooth."

My eyes cut to the drawer, not for the tooth, of course, but for the pair of stamps that still lay there. The guy had never come back to claim them like I thought he would. And I had no idea that they might be worth nearly forty grand or they would have been as long gone as dinosaurs.

"I don't have them—it," I said. "The tooth," I added, hoping that the detective wouldn't think of the stamps. But of course he wouldn't. Would he? But then, how had he thought of the molar? Clarissa? Was she playing us both for fools?

Willy followed my glance to the drawer and tapped the wooden counter. "You know, I could get a search warrant and turn this place into a shambles. Your nice house on Woodlawn, too. Probably cause you a week's worth of business, if not more. Cops are pigs about things like books."

"Look . . ." I didn't know what to call him: Detective Cox, Pal Willy, Willy the Weeper, Willy the Wasp. "Look. The tooth sings to me. I can't explain that. It sings to me. You've got a whole skeleton, what's a damned tooth more or less?"

The English prof walked up with seven books. Willy looked askance at him, then at me, then rolled his head over his neck bones, creating a popping noise. Flinching, the prof pulled out three one hundred-dollar bills. A couple of the books were nice first editions, an Updike and a John Nichols' *Milagro Beanfield War*. At the sight of the three hundreds, Willy ground his vertebrae even more, popping them enough to make me drop one of the bills.

When the prof left, Willy looked around to make sure the store was empty. Then he shouted, "It fucking *sings* to you? Jesus, pal, you need to be dating a shrink, not a physical anthropologist."

He pocketed the rare stamp book and gave a big grin. He had a tooth capped with gold. How had I missed that? Probably because he'd never grinned at me before, only scowled.

"I don't even need a search warrant. All I need to do is tell Ms. Professor Clarissa that you think a tooth sings to you and that will be all the hair pie she ever slices your way. The professor's pretty high on order and sanity, if you haven't noticed."

"She thinks that Nothing Ever Touches Anything Else, that No One Ever Really Touches Anyone."

Willy laughed sharply, something of a burp.

"Why do you want the tooth, anyway? What could it possibly matter?" I persisted.

"You're right about one thing: she does think that no one ever touches anyone." Willy's face contorted and his gold tooth glinted. "But she's still a mess after last summer, and I'm the one who's right, and she's goddamned wrong. Everything matters. Including molars." He leaned over the counter to tap the drawer with the two ten-cent Washingtons in it. "Is it in there? I'll sneak it back to you after we've identified this Boston stamp thief's corpse. Then you can serenade it or it can serenade you until the cows come home."

"Do you promise?"

That laughing burp again. "I promise." He stretched to open the drawer, but I stopped him.

"It's not in there. That's just for cigars and labels, pens and crap." I opened the drawer half way and offered him a cigar, which he snatched so fast that I decided I'd say something about the stamp book in his pocket. But first things first: "The tooth's at home. I'll bring it tomorrow."

"At opening?"

"At opening," I agreed.

He nodded while looking around as if searching out something. I don't know: maybe that's the way all detectives are, but it was unsettling.

"Officer . . ." I pointed vaguely at the book in his pocket and he gave a golden grin.

"I'll trade you this for the tooth, tomorrow—I may even buy some books. I've got a three-day weekend coming and I'll need some reading since my dating life's been the pits lately. I wonder why." He glared at me. "Pick me out three or four classic mysteries. I always solve the new ones halfway through." He was already at the door. "The lovely professor, she's wrong, you know. Everything touches everything. In her line of work how can she not see that? After last summer, how—" He broke off to stare at the sign I'd left up for Harriet, fingering it as if he were going to haul me in for pederasty. "How everything touches . . . everything." He placed his palms together with fingers spread. "I wouldn't be surprised if you found that very pair of stamps in this store, those double Washingtons. You're a bookseller, right? –Do you have Boston connections by any chance?"

I shook my head.

"Your parents, grandparents?"

I shook my head again.

"Still . . . maybe you ought to search around, see if those paired stamps show up." He flicked a bell attached to a disposable plastic syringe on the Jim'd Chime by the door and walked out. The Jim'd Chime was entitled "Happy Endings." It consisted of syringes and oral and rectal thermometers with bells attached to each. As perverted as life.

OF COURSE I WAS lying about the tooth. It sat in that drawer near the Siamese twin stamps, which in their turn sat inside a small plastic case, where I had blithely let them rest for three years, considering them representative of my Abe Lincoln honesty. Now that I knew they might be worth forty grand with inflation . . . well, what is honesty? chortled jesting Pilate. I eased the drawer open to find the stamps, and I accidentally touched the tooth. A high-low wail ran across my clavicle just as the phone rang.

"Zeno's Books."

"Don't give it to him."

"Clarissa?"

"Don't give him the tooth."

"He said he'd give it back."

She laughed, not a burp but a sneeze. "Look, I'll bring you another. He'll never know the difference because . . ." she paused, as if someone had walked into her office, or as if she'd just tired of playing at whatever she was playing.

"Because Nothing Ever Touches Anything anyway?" I guessed.

"My little bookstore man. I'll be over this evening. Don't give it to him."

She hung up. I stared out my front window, watching a UPS truck stop at a traffic light. As usual, Clarissa had sidetracked me. But if nothing ever touched anything and if no one ever touched any one, I couldn't see how giving Willy the Creeper the creepy tooth could matter. But if nothing ever touched, how could UPS stay in business? For the first time, I really considered how the tooth had spawned—if you will—directly from Clarissa's womb. From her *belle chose*, as the Wife of Bath would say. Her beautiful thing. Not just improbable, but impossible. Was it all a trick? But what kind of elaborate trick would that be? And why?

As the light changed and the UPS truck drove off, I spotted Harriet across the street, and I again realized how much Clarissa had distracted me if I could forget that bright young girl whose hips and lips wouldn't quit, whose eyes, always bulging anxiously, would grab at me with their emerald green. Yes, pro-simian and nocturnal Harriet, who since first stepping in my shop during a fierce March snowstorm one year and a half ago had spent her nights and days reading, reading, reading—matching me book for book, rarely lagging behind, often leaping ahead. Harriet, who since before the beginning of this summer, for nine weeks, had been asking where she could get her poems published. Her poems, a pervert's—sigh!—delight. Where anyone—from Emily Dickinson to Robert Penn Warren—could publish pornographic poetry was beyond me, though I'm not claiming my hands are pure. Like every used book dealer, I keep a selection of "art" books behind my counter. But "art" is art and poetry is poetry, and the twain remain twain. Never touching, not even halfway.

"Nice blue sign. In your window." Harriet announced, standing under the tinkling Jim'd Chime as she held the front door open. I grinned to keep from falling over the counter, and she walked closer, staring with those emerald eyes. At last she popped her feet together as if she were coming to attention. "I'm going to turn them all into stories. My poems. I've already started." Had her bosoms matured since our five-weeks-back spat? They carried a roundness that reminded me of morning's lambency. *Lambency*, I thought, forgetting molars and stamps. "Stories will sell better," Harriet continued, conjuring her right hand from a nascent mammary to the top of her bare shoulder.

I sighed.

"And I'm going to write a new story, too, one about a handsome old guy who runs a used bookstore and sighs all the time and falls in love with a virgin nymph."

I laughed and she laughed, handing me a yellow lollipop she pulled from her tight yellow jeans.

"Piss-colored," she said, as if she could read my mind. "In Japan, they sell girl's pre-worn undies in vending machines for all the busy, busy salesmen to smuggle into motel rooms. Do you think we could manufacture virgin, piss-flavored lollipops and export them?"

"Harriet, I just don't know."

"So, back to your message in the window, the Heraclitus quote. Do you want to marry me yet?"

"Are you eighteen yet?"

"Last month."

"You said that last month."

"Just checking to see whether you'd Alzheimered out from hanging around with older women."

Placing both hands on her derrière for my benefit she walked to the philosophy/religion section, turning coyly and slapping her flank. "Think about the lollipop angle—that one's okay, by the way."

"Do you mean okay virgin, or okay piss-flavored?"

She only grinned.

Two other customers walked in, and this calmed Harriet down. She typically turned sedate once she wandered into the books. Her routine had been to buy two or three a week, come back and harass me about their meaning after reading them. The child was an absolute wonder that American public education hadn't been able to cripple. A dozen more like her and I'd never need to sell another black candle or a Jim'd Chime.

Once everyone settled in to browsing, I was able to return to the stamps. When I pulled them out, they certainly looked like the ones in the book. But since Willy the Wonder Cop had lifted that source, I had to go online to ascertain whether the pair of ten-cent Washingtons was really worth forty grand or whether I'd just mistaken matters.

It turned out that there were two issues of this stamp, one in 1847, another in 1875. From my computer screen, dismaying mumbo-jumbo about the right edge of Washington's coat pointing to the "X" in one issue and to the "T" of "Ten Cents" assailed me. I'd need a straight rule plus a voltage regulator to figure it out. And get this: my internet source stated that in the 1875 reproduction issue, Washington's eyes look "sleepy." Practicing a Washingtonian yawn, I lifted the stamps from their plastic box and began angling them this way and that when—

"Uh, excuse me."

I nearly tore the damned things in two, which presumably wouldn't have done much for their value. And when I looked up, I nearly dropped them on the floor, which would have performed ditto squared for their value. The guy standing before me was preening a salt & pepper beard extending way past his vestigial nipples—should they ever choose to reveal themselves from behind his Navajo dream-catcher shirt done up in earth-tones. His backward-frontward ponytail of a beard was bound on its bottom by a purple hair-band, which he tugged. There was a pink hair band midway too. In keeping with the Navajo theme, wrinkles crisscrossed his forehead like cracks in a dried Arizona riverbed, and a scar over his left eye made him look like he'd gotten in a fight with a chain saw. Guess who won.

"Uh," a tug at the ponytail beard—"do you have a book—a new book, just, uh, reviewed in *Newsweek* . . ." The guy wagged his riverbed head, either to knock the book's name loose or to get a shot of Harriet, who was grinding her hips as she read from a philosophy book that looked vaguely like Nietzsche's *Thus Spoke Zarathustra* from where I stood. I noted something swinging behind the guy's head: damned if he didn't have a bleached blonde ponytail that equaled his beard in length. Maybe he was a traveling scholar visiting UK's campus: The Amazing Hirsute Professor. Where do they dig these characters up? Campus Comedy Circuit?

"In . . . I, uh, think it was *Newsweek*, anyway . . . about this scientist guy."

"Do you know his name? Or the name of the book?" I really didn't need to hear the aging hippie's answer, because I knew he was talking about

Stephen Wolfram's *A New Kind of Science* since I read *Newsweek* every week, like all good Americans. Magazines made the cut; newspapers didn't.

"No, uh, but it's a big book. Like *Ulysses*, I think they, uh, said."

It was tempting to see how many *uh's* this guy could mutter before noon, only an hour away. But I wanted to get back to the stamps, which he pointed at, giving a smile, to say:

"Issue two and issue four. Very nice, but a thirty-nine thousand dollar difference in price. Or, uh, maybe someone's cleverly found a way to dye the 1947 CIPEX issue from orange to black and conjoin the two stamps. If so, what you just picked up off your counter is, uh, worth about a, uh, half buck."

Frowning, I put the stamps back in their plastic case and snapped it shut. "The book you want is Stephen Wolfram's *A New Kind of Science*."

He clapped his hands. "You're right! Do you have it?"

"It's only been out ten days," I said. "This is a used book store."

"But since it's about science, philosophy—"

"I've heard about that book!" Harriet exclaimed.

"Of course you have." The aging hippie tugged his beard and gave her a smarmy smile.

I wondered, *Should I offer him the yellow lollipop*? Then I realized that if Harriet had heard us, the other two customers had heard us talking about the stamps. I pulled the drawer open to hide them and their plastic case, but I accidentally brushed the tooth, and the first five notes of Tchaikovski's "Marche Slave" shivered my fingertips to my clavicle. I looked for Harriet, but one of the other customers, a female in her forties wearing a slinky gray dress with a white stripe running down its side, suddenly stood by the register, holding three books, one of which fell to the floor on my side of the counter.

"How much for all three?" she asked as I bent to pick the book up.

I piled the books and opened them. The prices were fifteen, thirty, and ten. "Fifty-five, plus tax," I said, smiling at her while surreptitiously reaching for the plastic case and easing it into my pants pocket.

"Let me think it over. Do you have change for a hundred?"

When I nodded she moved to the coffee pot to pour herself a cup.

"I really have heard about that book," Harriet said again, as insistent as any teenager.

"Everyone's heard of it, and everyone's buying it," the old hippie replied. "But owning a book and, uh, reading it are two different matters—though I'm certain, my dear, that *you* are a reader." He gave Harriet a small bow and she actually blushed. Then he turned to me. "And since it's, uh, about science and philosophy as I said, I figured someone in this city—some college student who recites poetry at a bar maybe, would have already traded the book in on soft porn or a guitar collector's guide. Can I leave my name, uh, so you can call when you take in a copy on trade?" In answer, I indicated a pink pad where customers list their wants, and he moved to it. "There's a certain charm in buying a partly unread used book, the challenge of succeeding where one person has already failed."

"Put my name down too!" Harriet called out. "It's Harriet."

"Cellular automata!" the guy shouted in reply. He looked to the ceiling as if a spider web had given him that clue. "*That's* one of Wolfram's principles." He finished writing his name and phone number on the pink pad, then Harriet's name. He looked at me. "Could you say that this entire conversation is working by some 'cellular automata' principle?"

I'd gleaned enough from the *Newsweek* article to know this was one of Wolfram's proposed axioms, that nature constructs itself upon a simple principle involving contiguous cellular automata. "Personally—" I turned to lovely Harriet— "I think it's been working in a rather Pythagorean manner, say squaring the hypotenuse: 3,4,5." With my little finger I pointed to him, Harriet, and me. Then I surreptitiously patted the plastic case in my pocket. 3, 4, 5 and 40 thousand.

The hippie tugged his ponytail beard until I thought he was going to chew it like cud. He pushed the pink Want Pad toward me and straightened to become taller than I first thought.

"It's too bad that Pythagoras never wrote down *his* wonderful axioms. Humanity's first great systematizer. Just imagine: *Orpheus's Musical Spheres: Bean Soup for the Soul,* by Pythagoras from Samos."

Harriet laughed at his theatrics, for he'd tossed his hands this way and that, ending by swinging his ponytail beard to the right and his ponytail

ponytail to the left. Campus Comedy Circuit for sure.

The woman who'd brought up the three books rapped her coffee cup against the table and said, "Interesting how males individually systematize while women do it communally. If you're looking for the very first human systematizers, Wiccans are a likely choice."

Out of the corner of my eye, I could see Harriet shimmying her hips and sticking out the tiniest bit of her tongue at me, awaiting my predictable pet-peeve response:

"*Wicca* is a twentieth-century word, you know," I said. "It's derived from *wicche*, an obsolete form of *witch*, according to the *Oxford English Dictionary*, which was and is a communal work systematizing the English language. That dictionary, by the way, is over a century old, and it was gathered mostly by males."

The woman let the cup of coffee drop to the table, where it broke and spilled. "No wonder you have to sell candles and wind chimes to stay in business." She strutted out the door and tried to slam it, though the spring was too strong, so she turned to glare and stumble along the sidewalk.

I caught movement: the other gentleman who'd walked in previously. Evidently he'd been either cowed or annoyed with all the conversation and had hidden in a corner with the literary criticism. Now he was roaming the shelves again, gathering books. I looked at the broken coffee cup, then to Harriet.

"Where's the guy with the ponytail and beard?"

She shrugged. "Maybe he left when that woman dropped the cup."

Maybe, I thought. It's too bad Clarissa hadn't been here. She could have assured the woman that Nothing Ever Touched Anything and that dropping the cup served only as a futile gesture, just as she could have assured me that my snide remark about *wicca* would fritter away into the semi-reality we label *air*. Willy the Weeper, on the other hand, could have lifted the woman's fingerprints off the cup's shards and shape-shifted her into a prime suspect for the murder of the wayfaring Boston stamp thief. He could have conjectured that as a child she'd been brainwashed into pulling the trigger—oh no, it was a butcher knife that killed the wayfaring stamp thief. Or, she might have been an adolescent witness strolling the riverbank, and the recovered rabies tag might have belonged to her puppy, Out-Out-Damned-Spot.

Curious, I looked at the hippie's name and phone number. "Hales u'Htem." Greek? Arabic? Wiccan? But then neither his phone number nor his address contained the number of the Beast. Patting the plastic case in my pocket, I opened Harriet's yellow lollipop and took a lick. Bless her perverted heart: it tasted of brine.

Half an hour later I gave Harriet 25% off on *Einstein's Dreams*, *Sophie's World*, and Nietzsche's *Zarathustra*.

"You're not going to get through those in a week," I said.

"Watch me. I'm like that old front-and-back-ponytail hippie guy who just left—I love a challenge. Oh, by the way," she said, stretching to tug the lollipop from my mouth, "Next week I really will be eighteen. My birthday's Tuesday." She giggled and stuck the lollipop to my nose, which is where I left it until another customer opened the door five minutes later.

By four-thirty, I had amassed over $800 in the till, easily the best summer weekday I'd ever had, and not a black or red candle nor Jim'd Chime among the lot. Maybe I would hire help if this kept up, someone young and vibrant who knew her books . . .

The phone rang before I could pursue that thought.

"Zeno's Books."

"The rabies tag."

"Excuse me?"

"The rabies tag that Dr. Circle's real assistant found, it belonged to a third cousin of one of your uncles."

"I don't have any uncles."

"You had two; one is still alive. Your dad just never told you about them."

As I've mentioned, the only memorable thing that Dad ever told me was not to wear a raincoat to bed, ridiculous advice considering his demise, so Willy's news seemed entirely plausible.

"Talk about your basic *deus absconditus*, your old man was the gem of them all, *Pater abscondtitus*."

"Is this Detective Lieutenant Willy Cox?" I had to ask this, since the

Latin threw me. But then, so had the stamp collecting. Don't pigeonhole is the moral.

"Don't pigeonhole and you'll discover a lot more connections in life," Willy said as if he'd read my mind. Then he gave his infamous—with me anyway—burp-laugh. "I'll be over in an hour for the tooth—I know you've got it there, there's no sense in waiting until tomorrow. You ever find the paired stamps?"

"Stamps?"

He laughed again and hung up. I patted the plastic case and smiled my own silent laugh.

Fifteen minutes later, Clarissa herself walked in, wearing a maroon blouse cut to her navel and patent red heels straight from Victoria's Secret. I mean, I had to inhale to keep my spine from shivering off my back and pogo-sticking across the floor. She pulled a molar from her purse and shoved it toward me. When I took it, I thought I heard the makings of Ravel's "Bolero," but that dissipated. I could, however, still smell Clarissa's perfume and see her cleavage, so at least two of my senses were working. I put the tooth to my ear to make sure it didn't sing, and Clarissa drummed her fingers on the pink Want Pad still lying on the counter. Giving it a sudden twist, she laughed out,

"That frizz-brained petunia's been here?!"

"What? Who?"

She pointed to where the hippie guy had signed up for Wolfram's book, and I gave a foolhardy attempt at pronouncing his handwritten name, which now looked Jewish. With a snort-laugh reminiscent of some molecular cops I've known, Clarissa pulled a compact mirror from her purse and slanted it before the name.

"MetH'u selaH," I stuttered aloud, reading the mirrored image. Linear B? Then it dawned on me. "The guy whose books I bought? Methuselah?"

"He wishes," she commented. "Two ponytails, right?"

"If you count his beard." I glanced at the mirror's image again. Anagrammatized backwards, the oldest trick in the book. Detective Cox would have been disappointed. I might as well hand over both the singing molar and the deaf-mute one too.

"He used to braid that silly beard into two pigtail strands. A real master of disguises. Our friend Detective Cox theorized that the three braids of hair—counting his real ponytail—might contain a code for either the Trinity atomic bomb test site or the local Trinitarian church. I told him that they didn't have anything to do with anything, that the old fart was playing him like a Jew's harp. Boing, boing, boing."

She tilted her head, those eyes of hers a Guinevere Gray. Again, their color shifted: Atlantic Ocean Blue? "He's a double-negative hypocrite. He knows damn well just like I do that Nothing Ever Touches Anything, but he still collects thousands of books, filling his house as if he owned a miniature Library of Congress aggregating factoids that some day will coalesce into Einstein's Unified Field Theory."

I waved a customer at the door on in, but he caught sight of Clarissa's red high heels—exactly where his eyes settled—and let the door push him backward. He scurried off as fast as his three hundred pounds would let him. He was a porno regular. I'd have sold him Harriet's poems long ago if I weren't afraid he'd find out who wrote them. What I mean is that he didn't like women. At least it seemed to me. But he did like porn. Go figure.

"Uh, Clarissa, you, uh, collect books," I said, returning to the subject.

"Crap, it's contagious. You're sounding like *him* with all the *uh's*. The books I collect are about bones. Dead, gone, good-bye, adios, so long. Buried."

I had to catch myself from saying, *uh*. "How is he a hypocrite? He says he reads the books."

"Boing, boing, boing. Feisty today, aren't we? He reads them to torture Detective Cox and me. Cox is a good guy, you know. Don't get jealous, but we have our fling now and then. But a fling's all I can take, probably all he can take, though he doesn't think so. What I told you about him trying to decipher the ponytail and beard pigtails only scratches the surface. Get this: Once he walked into my house and told me my banister was made of the same burled walnut that they recently found on this walking stick that was used as a murder weapon. And so he wants to know who built my house. So, down at the Courthouse Annex he finds the builder, and then on the internet he finds that the victim's grandfather and the builder were both founding members of the next county's Lion's Club. Meanwhile I'm in bed polishing my toenails violet or blue, listening to Bach." She batted her bi-colored eyes. "Oh my little Zeno, you at least had enough sense to parade me around to those wonderful fugues. We almost touched several times, didn't we?"

I knew better than to answer. I placed the tooth she'd handed me to my ear. "This one doesn't sing to me."

She wobbled in her high heels, catching herself on my counter.

"It's a tooth, not Barbara Streisand."

"The other one sings—"

Fortunately for my reputation, a chuffy, curly-haired college student walked in, a kid I'd heard at my one and only open poetry slam in a nearby bar. "Third eye is blind, third eye is blind," he kept chanting as refrain to his grandiloquence while the audience politely waited to chant out their own marvelous poems. "Third eye is blind, third eye is blind!" That warbled refrain made the most sense of anything he read. "Read it out backwards!" someone had shouted. "I am," he'd replied.

Now my own third eye was operating on a higher yoga plane, for I decided *No* to both Clarissa and her tooth, *Yes* to Harriet and her bright wit and lovely musk. The student with the dim poetic genes who'd just walked in held up a thick book, and with immediate insight I knew it was Wolfram's *A New Kind of Science*. He placed it on the counter with a resounding thud.

"Trade," he said. The most poetic sequence I'd heard him utter.

"Made," I answered, tossing in rhyme for his learning benefit. While he walked to the music section and picked up a picture essay about the Rolling Stones, Clarissa read Wolfram's back cover.

"'Cell automata?' They never stop, do they?"

"They?"

"Systematizers. Frazier, Levi-Strauss, Moses. Even Einstein and his Unified Field Theory. Maybe you could write a book systematizing singing molars. *The Fossils Speak*."

"Been written already," I said.

"Singing molars?"

"*The Fossils Speak.*"

"That's right," she said. "It has." She dropped the sarcasm and her face softened, a Hollywood superstar preparing for a romantic scene. As the camera lost focus to soften her face further and concentrate on her glistening gray—no, blue—eyes, she asked, "Do you know who my favorite scientist is?" With fortitude, I looked away from her eyes and her lips and her bosom and her bare shoulders, and I flipped through the Wolfram book: unread and stiff, just like the Methuselah fellow predicted. I could toss an extra couple of bucks onto the price. I looked up at Clarissa and shrugged to her question.

"Heisenberg," she said.

"The Uncertainty Principle."

"Zeno, my little bookstore man," she cooed while reaching to almost touch my cheek. Maybe, maybe, maybe her fingers even brushed my six o'clock shadow.

"Mother of Lord Jesus in heaven!" I yelped. "It's Willy, parking outside!"

"Quick! The molar!"

I pulled the tooth from the drawer and thrust it in my pocket, hearing it click against the plastic case. I placed the faux molar Clarissa had given me into the drawer in its stead. Magically, when I looked up, Willy and the college boy were standing side by side at the opening in my counter, blocking my exit. And at that exact moment, something niggled in a rear compartment of my mind, some grand absence.

"The tooth," Willy said.

I opened the drawer to hand him the fake one, but he raised his palm and stared at Clarissa. "I know you, Professor. That's why I came this evening instead of tomorrow. You've substituted another molar. But it doesn't matter. We've ID'd the corpse."

"The stamp thief?" I asked.

"No, of course not. It was a man accused of raping a seventeen-year-old girl. He was acquitted for lack of evidence. The girl killed herself before the trial. It was the rabies tag that gave it away."

"The one that—"

"That's right. Belonged to a third cousin of your uncle."

"Are you going to press charges against *him*?"

"Not yet."

"So it's still an open case, as usual," Clarissa interjected. "Molar or no molar."

Willy pulled the red stamp book he'd taken out of the shop from his sports jacket and waved it at her. "Not quite. It's closing in on getting closed, because said cousin worked for the horse farm where the stamp thief was last seen."

"Stamp thief?" Clarissa asked.

Stamps. My eyes widened. I tugged at the case in my pocket, careful not to pull out the molar. I held the case in my right palm, where it burned like a driven nail. I turned from Willy and looked at the clear plastic case: it was empty. Snapping it open I pulled out the black foam: nothing under it, either. I looked to where the three books still lay. The Wicca woman! Had she filched the Siamese twin stamps from the case when I picked up her dropped book? Had she dropped that book on purpose? As I lifted the trio of books she never bought to search under them, I tried to picture where she'd stood, I tried to remember whether I'd heard her moving as I leaned. I didn't think so. In fact, I think she'd started down for the book too. I riffled all the books, wondering about the double ponytail guy. Were his arms that long? Could he have snagged the stamps and hidden them in a ponytail? I looked on the floor behind the counter. I looked on the floor in the opening of the counter. Then I walked and leaned over the front counter—had either Willy or the college kid been standing on them?

Meanwhile, Clarissa and Willy of the Winding Ways were arguing while the third-eye poetry kid stood between them.

"What makes you so sure that all these supposed links you're discovering are going to lead to this humbug stamp killer who's anyway turned into a rapist who was maybe murdered by the girl's father or brother or lover, who may have been Willy's uncle, whose dog may have just gone stray down by the river?"

"Life."

"Well, well. Say the secret word. Guess what? That's the same thing that makes me sure they're meaningless. Just like that damned molar."

"The stamps . . ." Still leaning over the counter I studied their feet, their trampling evil feet and the cruel, punishing floor.

Willy lunged at me. “I knew it! You have that pair, don’t you!?”

“I . . . I may have. But they’re gone. Someone may have stolen them. Uh, would both of you mind moving back just a bit? Easy and not scuffing your feet?”

“What are you two talking about?” Clarissa asked.

The kid and Willy obliged, and when Willy and I explained to her, Clarissa rolled her eyes, taking off her red heels one at a time in a strip tease mimic. “No stamps here. No stamps there.” She put her heels back on. “Hey, do you mind if I make some evening coffee?” she asked. “Unless you have red wine or gin . . .” I shook my head, so she walked to the pot, stepping on a shard of the broken cup. This sent her to her knees, in good physical anthropology style—a reflex reaction, I suppose. While she swept her hands over the floor for bone splinters, Detective Cox motioned me near, giving a glance back to Clarissa.

“You say that the three-bearded one was here? Methus . . . Methus . . . him?”

Had reverence, hatred, or fear kept Willy from pronouncing Methuselah’s name? When I nodded, moving to again to check the floor and watch Clarissa, still on her knees, Willy reached for the pink pad.

“There’s one way to find out if he took the stamps,” he said. “Do you mind?” He indicated my phone and I shrugged.

“By the way, tell him the book he wanted just came in.” I looked for the college boy, hearing movement near the gardening section. Peripherally, I caught a yellow wisp across the street. My heart skipped a beat, my groin tightened. I looked to Clarissa in her tight black jeans and red high heels, her rear end still swaying over the floor.

“What are you looking for? The stamps?” I asked that and at the same time confirmed that the yellow wisp was indeed Harriet returning in the evening summer sun, with an intent gait. She stopped to cross the street, being a good girl and looking both ways.

“Nothing! I’m looking for nothing! I’m touching nothing!” Clarissa shouted, still sweeping her hands meticulously over the wooden floor.

On the phone behind me, Willy of the Winding Ways gave a burp-laugh, this one sounding near a snort. He and Clarissa—why fight it? They were star-crossed from Day One at the celestial star-making trough.

I heard squalling brakes and my heart dropped. Flinging myself through the counter's opening, I saw Harriet and her yellow jeans sprawled on the street. I ran out toward a hump-backed black car from the fifties, one of those gangster types, its grille snarling over Harriet like a Mafioso.

More squalling brakes as I ran across the street. "Harriet! Don't move!" She was trying to sit up, and waved me off, patting the grille beside her and reaching for a book on the hot blacktop. Another book lay flung nearby, and I picked it up. It was one she'd bought hours before.

"Harriet! Careful! Are you hurt anywhere?"

She looked at the book in her hand, then at her legs, then at her palm, which was bleeding, and she started crying. Squatting next to her I put my arm about her shoulders.

"I, uh, just called an ambulance. I, uh, was talking on my cell phone to Detective Cox."

I looked up to see Methuselah and his beard. "This is *your* car?" *Keep calm*, I told myself. *Don't scream. Don't upset Harriet in case she's hurt worse than it looks.*

The pony-tailed hippie nodded, bending to inspect Harriet. Then he walked to pick up the third book. He handed it to me, and when Harriet caught my movement, she started caterwauling.

"I wanted to surprise you on my birthday. It's tomorrow, not Tuesday. You can check my driver's license. I wanted to surprise you. I was going to speed-read them all. But . . . but someone tore the last two pages out of Nietzsche's *Thus Spoke Zarathustra*."

Methuselah—for lack of a more pronounceable name—and I both gasped, but a voice behind us shouted,

"Step aside!"

It was Willy of the Winding ways, who bent and looked into Harriet's emerald eyes. "I called an ambulance," he said. "How do you feel?"

"Better than the tightrope artist. Not as good as Zarathustra."

Methuselah and I chuckled, and Harriet gave a brave grin.

"I think your car barely tapped me. I slipped as much as anything."

It appeared that that was true. Harriet's lithe body could have boomeranged off the grille. I kissed her palm where it was scraped.

"You're so sweet," she said.

"Very paternal," Methuselah commented.

Willy gave a burp-snort and pulled at his crotch. "Paternal, huh? Good thing Professor Clarissa's still inside your shop searching the floor for plenty of nothing."

"Still!?"

"Who's Professor Clarissa? Not that—"

"The kingdom is a child's," I said, placing a finger on Harriet's lips.

Willy, Methuselah, and I affirmed Harriet's notion that she was all right. The ambulance crew maintained professional demeanor and refused to comment. This is what our wretched legal system has accomplished: the people whom you need to comment are afraid to. At any rate, the ambulance left empty, Methuselah parked, and Willy, Harriet and I strolled inside my bookstore.

"In Dolores Cemetery in Mexico City they dig up the bodies every seven years," Clarissa announced upon seeing us; rather, she half-sang it in modernized Gregorian chant. She was still sweeping the floor with her hands. When Harriet leaned on me, Clarissa forsook chant to blurt, "And in America, the average first marriage lasts three years. A person gets more rest being dead."

"Someone's been tearing pages out of books in here," Harriet said, twisting to look at me, recovering from both the accident and Clarissa.

"Did you find the stamps?" Willy asked Clarissa.

"Well? Is *that* what you're looking for?" I yelled.

Clarissa stopped brushing her palms back and forth to glare at Harriet, then me. "I'm looking for nothing. Nothing, nothing, nothing."

Hearing a cough from a corner I remembered the curly-headed college boy. Pages out of books—Harriet's words hit me. Could this curly-headed would-be, word-lacking poet be tearing pages out of the books? No, I'd never seen him in here before, only at that one poetry reading. Harriet, still leaning on my arm, cooed. Willy walked toward the coffee pot and began to make what Clarissa supposedly set out to do half an hour ago. The front door, having caught on something, remained open. The Jim'd Chime called Happy Ending tinkled in a breeze and I inhaled evening summer air. Someone must have just cut grass. A sudden vision of the Siamese twin stamps floating out into the street and into freshly mulched grass sent me lurching to close the door.

"This tea . . ." Willy said suddenly.

As I slammed the door, he held up a box of tea I kept for non-coffee drinkers, a box Harriet brought in five weeks ago, before the terrible non-touching Clarissa interlude. Harriet had claimed she was prescribing me antioxidants so that my "hot blood wouldn't turn crank-case old on her." The kingdom is a child's.

"This tea comes from Charleston. The only tea plantation in America," Willy added.

"So?" Through the window I scanned the sidewalk for the stamps. Nope.

"Charleston's where your uncle's third cousin went two weeks after the victim was listed as missing." Willy completed three revolutions scanning the room before adding, "Those stamps are still in here." He looked down at Clarissa, who'd returned to rubbing her hands across the wooden floor. She'd gathered a hodge-podge of articles on the low table holding the coffee pot: a penny, a dime, a hairpin, half a pencil, a pile of lint—I leaned closer: a stamp! But it wasn't the Washingtons, just some recent commemorative of Bugs Bunny. Our forefathers would cringe.

Willy, completing his coffee pot duties, began moving books about, picking them up and riffling the pages.

"Willy, uh, might be right," Methuselah said, bending to look under a display counter by the window.

"Oh for Pete's sake. There's nothing anywhere! Nothing!" But even as Clarissa inhaled she added a piece of lint to the pile, picking out what looked like a splinter and dropping it atop the dime.

Harriet let go of my arm to walk to a shelf, where she eased out a page from under several books. From her face I could tell it didn't belong to the Nietzsche book she'd bought. I looked back: Methuselah was on his knees just like Clarissa. Then Willy went down too, inspecting shelving. I heard movement in the back: the curly-headed student emerged with a book from the gardening section.

"He's coming to tell you to tend your own garden," Harriet whispered. She'd read Voltaire's *Candide* two months before.

"He wouldn't dare." Would he? If he did, he'd likely speak it backwards. *Garden own our tend musk each we*. Mus*k* we? I gave Harriet a sniff. O sweet youth's goddess whose musk mocks the perfume industry!

The college kid eyed Harriet, who entwined her arm with mine. Then he nervously looked at the three creatures scrabbling about on the floor. The coffee began to perk, which understandably made him jump.

Harriet and I walked ensemble to the register. "That the book you want to trade?" I asked. The kid nodded and handed it to me. It wasn't about gardening, but about guitar collecting, just as Methuselah had predicted. I subtracted trade-in for the Wolfram book from this guitar book's price. "Three bucks," I said. The kid handed me a fifty. Where do they keep coming up with their money? I flicked it toward the light to ascertain the threads then handed it to Harriet, who did the same. When I nodded toward the cash register, she smiled, took the fifty, made change, counting it backwards like she'd seen me do, and sacked the book.

Sack in hand, the kid walked outside. He leaned over the curb to look into the traffic as if he might take a suicidal leap to outdo Kierkegaard. Then he looked back through the glass door at the trio on their knees, still scrabbling amid the coffee cup's shards for the double stamps. I felt Harriet's warm left hip touch mine. The hell with the stamps, I thought, figuring they were the 1947 CIPEX dyed black anyway.

"Third eye is blind, third eye is blind, third eye is blind," the curly-haired kid chanted, his voice penetrating the glass. Playing air guitar, flapping the sack up and down, he ran across the street.

"You were really going to read all three of those books this afternoon?" I whispered to Harriet while the trio scooted over the wooden floor, gargantuan mice.

She undulated, giving a wide grin so that the pinks of her gums showed. I remembered, from weeks—centuries—ago, Timmy Doe, the skeleton Clarissa and I had dug up. All the gum reconstruction in the world would never get Timmy back in shape.

"Skim them," she said, batting her eyes. "Layered learning. Remember that I told you about that from a psychology book I read?"

Hearing shuffling I was momentarily discombobulated, having been so captivated by Harriet's eyes, which dazzled like King Tut's emeralds in the evening light. The shuffling came from the trio on the floor, looking for the blessed stamps.

"Tomorrow, you say? You'll be eighteen?"

"Midnight tonight. Mom told me it was thirty seconds after midnight."

"Midnight?" Willy asked. "We'll stay here till three in the morning if we have to."

He was pouring coffee. I watched as he dumped an unbelievable amount of sugar in his cup. Then he was back on the floor, placing his head on it to stare at either the planking or Clarissa's red high heels propped against the coffee table.

"It's just like the ending of a comedy," Harriet whispered. "I mean, everyone coming together."

She was right. Clarissa had sloughed her red high heels and was scooting across the floor. Willy brushed her foot with his hand and she looked back with a grin. I remembered what she said about him rubbing her banister's wood and linking it with some murder. I remembered hobbling to Bach fugues with her, and I remembered the tooth. I touched it in my pocket, but there was no music, just a bookstore owner playing air molar. I remembered Clarissa's shouting insistence that nothing ever touched anything. She would be as impossible to live with long term as Willy. And Methuselah?

"Uh, is this it?"

"A stamp! We're looking for a pair of stamps, not a dime!"

"We're looking for nothing!"

Harriet giggled, and we looked one another in the eyes.

"Here's where we keep the front door key," I said when we finally had a chance to blink. "And here's where we keep all the reference books about first editions and what books are in and out of print. Soon enough, you'll be able to just look them up on the computer." I knelt and showed the books to her, taking time to straighten one that had been kicked out of place. I felt her tugging my hair and looked up, but not before I spied teasing toe rings on each foot, one emerald, one garnet.

"At the end of every comedy, you know, there's a wedding." She offered both hands to help me up, bravely ignoring the cuts on her palm.

"That's right. There is."

I looked at the store clock. It was midnight. How? I narrowed my eyes. Had Harriet slipped over to change the clock while I was straightening the reference books and blathering? She swayed her head and smiled. Or had time slipped in Einsteinian happiness?

"Here's how we work up credit card charges." I pulled out my wallet and placed a credit card in her hand. Together we ran it as a test card through the scanner.

"Zeno Randall Dioniskon," she read from the card. "I never knew that your hands were so soft and warm. Zeno Randall Dioniskon. What are your lips like?"

I bent toward her, she tilted toward me. In spite of intervening lip gloss, we approached, closer than anyone ever came to touching.

12.

Tilting the Blame R

Year 2004

(Willy, Methuselah, Clarissa, Callie, Harriet, Zeno)

It beats it all, like that horse Afleet Alex stumbling in the Preakness, but racing on to win. Clarity and I go dine outdoors last night, Clarity throws one of her No-One-Ever-Touches-Anyone tantrums, and I'm left staring at Morris The Stamp Man four tables away. So I sit alone and stare instead over the railing to listen as the nearby quaint white-folk stream gurgles its gargles, and on the twenty-dozenth gargle I look back again to Morris The Stamp Man. He has a date! And not only a date, but the widow of Fayette County's last sheriff before we consolidated into Metro. All this is what beats all. Synchronicity must be pacing just upstream, biding its time. Do I think this because my friend Methuselah has been lately filling my head with a long dropped dead psychologist named Jung? Maybe.

And now it's noon today and here I am, pulling in to Morris's Stamp and Coin Shop, searching out synchronicity. For five years, Morris has been a widower. I've known him for seventeen—well, more truthfully I've been a customer and we've talked stamps and weather for seventeen years, ever since I became gainfully employed with Lexington's finest. Looking back, I must have started philately in the sixth grade just to see what it would be like to be white. Like a taste for Scotch whiskey, the habit grew.

I've been patronizing Morris's shop more frequently during the last four years, ever since I started dating Clarity. Clarity's not the first white woman I've dated, but damned if she isn't the most intriguing, white or black. And the most frustrating. But she's had an excuse ever since the Adolph Barnes crap happened two years back, which I partly take blame for. Anyway, truth be known, I've been visiting Morris's for the not-so-friendly reason that he's remained so thoroughly widower-y and down in the dumps that he pulls me up whenever Clarity drags me down. Bad boy, I know. Not much of a friend to Morris. Which takes me right back to where I started.

But today Morris's balding skillet head and his cute little earthenware butt—that last a Clarity comment from when she met him a year ago—are bobbing and wiggling happily. From my car window through to his shop's window, I watch him gyrate. Then I smell the onion rings next to me and my stomach grumbles. Is my bad boy guilt why I stopped at McDonald's for two Big Mac Happy Meals? To share with Morris, I mean. But with that skillet head bobbing the way it is, he doesn't need Ronald or me to cheer and grease him up today.

Still, hope springs eternal, so toting my Ronnie Mac bag, I open Morris's shop door, hoping his gloom will reappear, to compensate me for last night's fight with Clarity. A yellow and orange shop bell ding-a-lings—something Morris's wife painted a ladybug on. Though I never met the lady, he talked about her a good deal when she was alive, and he continued to talk about her for over a year after she died of lung cancer. I mean: someone who never smoked a pack in her whole life dying of lung cancer. Her doctor thought it was because of the factories in her hometown, Ashland, Morris said. Well, it's not like our Ohio Valley air can claim the President's Clean Environment Award. I've breathed it in land-bound Fayette County—Lexington—all my life. Anyway, our present President, W, likely doesn't believe in clean environment awards—likely considers them vaguely un-American or at least un-Texan. God bless him, though, he's cleaning up everything else. My three Black Muslim friends have been lying low with their Detroit horseshit ever since September 11 three years back, and that suits me and plenty of other blacks I know fine. A.M.E.'s the way to be.

"Willy!" he says as I walk under the ding-a-ling. He being Morris. "You sure were having a rough night with that woman."

"You got that right," I think I say, getting angry all over again at Clarity. I shake my head clear: "Here, I toted us some lunch. I want to see that fancy collection that you stole off that poor widow." That's another thing that brought me here: the rumor that Morris just bought some ass-fabulous stamp collection that stretched his little shop's budget. I'm thinking, along with plenty of other local collectors, that he'll be wanting to unload some on the cheap.

He smiles, and an inverted triangle of wrinkles works along his bald head, oddly leaving his damned eyeglasses gleaming under the store's fluorescent lighting. "I gave her a fair price," he insists, jutting his chin.

"Uh huh." I set the Ronnie bag on a clean spot of counter, and his eyeglasses turn like radar, though he's really more interested in justifying himself than keeping grease off his countertop.

"It's true. The only time . . . well, times . . . I've ever cheated anyone have been accidental. Here, let me show you something that I nearly got that way a couple of years back but had to pay out the nose for recently." He sniffs at the brown bag. "You really did bring me lunch?"

"Yep, white boss, sho'nuf really did."

He shakes his head at my Uncle Tom. I can't blame him. I'm getting worse and worse at it. When Dad sent me to a white private junior high and high school as one of the advance invading black horde, I could perform a righteous passable job, though.

"Well gee thanks, Willy, but let's hold off on loosing the grease until we look at the stamps I'm talking about."

"That good, huh?"

"That good. To tell the truth, I admit that these two stamps would have tried my moral constitution since I only paid a hundred and ten dollars for the whole collection they were buried in several years back, like I said." With a nod of his skillet head, he motions me away from the McDonald's bag to the end of the counter where he clears off space. Then he pulls out a thin blue album with tiny gold stars on it. Inside on black vellum lie two black-and-white stamps, connected. Connected without any perforations. I whistle on an inhale, for this ten-cent pair are the first American stamps ever issued, though they're officially known as Number Two in Scott's catalogue because it was a co-issue with a five-cent orange, that stamp being listed as Number One. And here these two lie, connected, uncut, sweet, and prim. I whistle again. I'm guessing forty grand.

"About fifty grand," he says. "Retail."

All of a damned sudden it hits me. "You didn't buy these off some bookstore dope named Zeno, did you?"

"The one and the same. The woman I was dining with last night is his mother-in-law."

Of course. I'd forgotten that I'd seen her at Zeno's wedding. But then Clarity and I'd only gone to his wedding on a bet with Methuselah. I do remember the underage slink he married. Sultry blue eyes and Paris lips, a real beauty. Zeno perched at nearly twice her age. She reminded me of a youthful and sane Paris Hilton. "The son of a bitch found them," I say, returning to the stamps.

"In a philosophy book, according to his mother-in-law."

"I slink, therefore I am."

Morris laughs, but then says, "What's that mean?"

"You should see the little sweetheart the chump married, is what that means. Is he the one you almost brought them off of for a hundred and ten bucks? Hey say, how come his mother-in-law's doing all the dealing on this?"

Morris shrugs. Then he sighs, looking back to the stamps. "Yeah, he's the one, but they were originally hidden in a collection I bought years back and must have fallen out. I'm conjecturing about this, by the way." He looked up with a shrug. "This time around I paid plenty for them. Nineteen grand I've got to Fed-Ex them to H. E. Harris in a day or so."

"Is she a good lay?"

"Who?"

"The sheriff's widow, the mother-in-law."

He looks at me with those eyeglasses glinting from hell, so I sing, "Hey say Morris, you wanna have some fun?"

Again with the eyeglasses.

"Let's go visit the bookstore chump's store tonight. He hasn't ever seen you because Momma-in-law's been doing all the dealing, right?"

"Yeah," Morris says, but he makes that *yeah* hesitate into about seven syllables.

"Come on, Morris, get out, have some fun." I bend over the stamps to give them a last look. Damn, fifty grand. And just like the time when we pulled in a half-mil worth of cocaine connected to a screwed drug deal murder, I inhale. This dumb cop's never gonna see this quantity of quality money, unless I hook Professor Clarity in a pre-nuptialess contract nuptial after her newly endowed chair in anthropology.

"Have some fun. That's what Robin always tells me, too."

"Who's Robin?"

"The woman you saw me with last night. The ex-sheriff's widow, Zeno's mother-in-law. She's a cyclist, a bi-cyclist. Get out and have some fun, Morris, she always says."

For a moment I try to see behind those glinting glasses and peer into that shopkeeper brain. Jesus preserve us, do I really want to be white?

So we set a time to meet. I'll drive by after your shop closes, I tell Morris, and pick you up. I whistle and walk out of the store. I owe this Zeno bookstore turkey one because he and Clarity made the beast with two backs together a bit over a year ago, right before he got married, no less. Revenge served cold makes the best platter. Or something like that. Let's see . . . Attila the Hun? Ben Franklin, first United States Postmaster? One of the two said it. A fine icy coldness will come of this bookstore excursion, more chilly possibilities than even Jung the psycho would allow. As I drive away from Morris's shop, I contemplate calling Methuselah and pulling him in on the act, but decide against it. Then exactly one hour later, lo and behold, Mr. Synchronicity himself calls:

"Willy. Heard you and the professor had a hard time last night at Adam's Ribs."

"How the hell'd you hear that, Methuselah?"

"The mouth of Fayette County."

"I always thought that was you."

"Nope. Lauren."

"I didn't see her there."

"She's lying low, dating a twenty-year-old."

"Male or female?"

"She hasn't sunken quite that deep into the local horse manure. Male. A journalism major from Pikeville."

Methuselah is 56 and living with a 29-year-old, so he doesn't have much room to shift in, but I let that go. "Yeah," I say, "she went into another rave. I tell myself to be patient. I mean, you know . . . after Mr. Adolph Barnes and all."

"That's exactly what you *should* tell yourself. The professor's a catch, Willy . . . uh, she went a little nuts the other night over here, too, during her guitar lesson with Callie."

I sigh. I'm talking to Methuselah on my cell phone, driving by the Saratoga Bar. Time was when the only way a nig like me could get in there was the back door, washing lettuce. On impulse, I pull over and park. "What'd she do at your place?"

"That's not why I called, Willy. I had a dream about you. You'd written a book."

"A book?"

"Yeah, it was called *Tilting the Blame R*."

"What the hell's that mean?"

"That's what I asked you. The R was real fancy like, with a curlicue foot."

Two white coeds with legs that could stride Fayette County in five steps walk by, being led by a cocker spaniel on a leash. I can't see a rabies tag, and think about jumping out and giving them some grief, but let it go.

"I don't follow you, Methuselah."

"In the dream. That's what I asked you in the dream: 'What's that title mean?' "

"Jesus."

"You really need to stop calling on him, Willy. He couldn't help people while he was alive: got them poor, confused, and got himself crucified. What can he possibly accomplish from a two-millennia-old grave?"

"Jesus," I say again, this time because one of the coeds bends to untangle the cocker from its leash and she's wearing a hot pink thong.

"We just went through that. Willy, what are you doing tonight?"

"Got a date," I lie, still watching the pink thong. It's skinnier than the damned cocker's leash. Her girlfriend catches me staring and says something to the thong-girl, so the thong-girl gives her butt an extra wiggle for the old black cop perched in his virgin white car. Though surely they don't realize the cop part.

"I thought you were going to give Clarissa a break?"

"I am, Methuselah. The date's with Morris the Stamp Man. We're going over to play a practical joke on that bookstore geek, Zeno, maybe get a free peek at his young girl bride bending over to shelve books. Fresh, eighteen-year-old pee-pee, if you can remember what it smells like. That interest you?"

"Well, maybe I'll see you there. What time?"

"Around six-thirty."

We disconnect. The college girl with the cocker is still bent over, though she's now turned her attention to untangling something from the dog's paw. On impulse, I shut the engine down and hustle toward them, flashing my badge like a packaged condom. The girl with the cocker straightens up. Even twenty feet away her blush glows as pink as her thong.

I hassle them for five minutes for not having a rabies tag on the cocker, until my cell phone rings. I wave them on, with a "warning." It's Methuselah again on the phone. I notice that neither girl puts much sway into her walk; they use a move-it-along business pace. The cocker's got more swagger and shake than either of them now.

"What's up, Methuselah?"

"I just wanted to tell you that Jung wasn't like Freud. He thought that dreams could indicate something actual about the future, not just past potty training mistakes or wish-fulfillment."

It takes me a minute to realize he's talking about his Tilt-the-blamer dream. "Jung also thought that every person in the dream is an aspect of the dreamer, didn't he?"

"So well read. No wonder you made captain in the police force."

Methuselah needs to take some ginkgo for memory retention, because he's already forgotten that he told me all this Jung crap before, and now I'm just spouting it back. That's what he gets for smoking reefer as an undergraduate. Speaking of which, the girl without the cocker smelled vaguely of hashish, though she tried to cover it with five ounces of perfume.

"Yeah, I've been reading him in the original French."

"German," Methuselah said. "He was Swiss."

"Yeah, that too."

"Well, just remember what I said about the future, and think over that book title of yours: *Tilting the Blame R.*"

"Good-bye, Methuselah." Maybe his live-in girlfriend Callie has cut the old guy off sexually, or maybe she's wound one of her used guitar wires around his nuts. I can't think of any other reason for him to be so weird. The whole day on top of last night makes me want a whiskey in a white man's bar, so I jaywalk over to the Saratoga.

"Hello there, Captain Cox."

I stop at the second booth from the door and situate the guy speaking by cuing in on his blonde moustache and blue eyes: he's a realtor. Six years ago his wife found a dead baby wrapped in a lemon yellow blanket behind one of the new houses she was trying to sell. We found the mother within two weeks, a sixteen-year-old meth-head. Her ex-boyfriend turned her in, thinking there'd be a reward. Twenty, thirty bucks or so, he thought. The realtor and his wife are divorced now. He was clean-shaven then, the realtor, not the boy. There's a connection in all that, but then there always is. Synchronicity, you just have to search it out. I'm doing a line-dance in my head, with a doo-rag chorus clapping and singing behind me, *Syn-chro-ni-ci-teeee! Slip, slide and search for me!*

"See your billboards everywhere," I say, which is how I recognized the moustache and eyes. "Business must be ripping." Business has been ripping in Fayette County ever since Toyota moved in to Georgetown when I was still in in high school playing Uncle Tom.

"It is. My new colleague and I—" he indicates the guy sitting across from him—"were watching you talk to those two leggy girls."

"No rabies tag for the dog," I say.

"Well, you should have run the one *without* the dog in. If the KKK ever comes back to this county, it will be because of her father."

"Really?" I remember the marijuana smoke clinging to the second and blonder girl. For some damned reason, I feel sorry for her and her peroxide. Poor screwed-up kid.

"Here, let me introduce you two: This is Tom Jenkins; he just started with my company. Tom, this is Captain—as in three months ago, right?—Captain William 'Willy' Cox. Homicide."

The Tom Jenkins guy is realtor-slick, with coal black hair and a goatee. Evidently facial hair is SOP with this guy's—Mark Abram, that's his name—with Abram's Realty.

"My daughter owns a pet shop," the goateed guy says. "Land, Air, and Sea."

"Wasn't that one robbed by Red Jack about two months back?"

"She was petrified. And when the guy threw down a red Jack of Hearts, all she could see for ten minutes after he planted a kiss on her lips were the white gloves he wore. The asshole. You all any nearer to catching the creep?"

I shake my head. A waitress comes up and asks if I want to order. I tell her I'm going to the bar, and Jenkins and Abram make a half-serious invitation for me to sit with them, but the table is covered with realty brochures, so I pass and head on up to the bar. I didn't tell this to the Jenkins guy, but his daughter was lucky. We've been expecting Red Jack to escalate the game, and he obliged us just five days ago, leaving a woman comatose with razor slashes. His calling card Jack of Hearts was spattered with blood. He's made a habit of catching female cashiers alone, robbing them, and then—at first—asking for a kiss. It escalated to two kisses. A touch of breast. A nibble, a bite, a bruise . . . the guy is a real master of disguises: a goatee one time, white gloves, black gloves, no gloves, blonde hair, red hair, ponytail.

Speaking of blondes and masters of disguises, at the bar sits a blonde I used to date from the courthouse, her butt overstuffing the bar stool. They're everywhere, blondes, that is. She's one of Clarity's ex-students, which caused a good deal of tension that took an entire summer to dissipate. But I was getting back at Clarity for sleeping with my good friend Methuselah. Revenge on the platter. Then came along Adolph Barnes, and he made all that soap opera seem like Cracker Jacks. I nod to the blonde; she screws the corner of her mouth and twists to nuzzle her Daytona Beach-tanned boyfriend, as if I'm going to drop with jealousy. Hey, darling, you weren't all that hot in bed.

"A South of the Mason-Dixon Maker's Mark, pretty please Massa," I say when I pull up a stool five spaces away from Blondie. Again with the faux Uncle Tom, more for Blondie and her boyfriend's sake than for the bartender's. Snowy doesn't have a racist bone in his body: as long as you tip well you could be a polka-dotted penguin.

Snowy leans in good bartender fashion. "Thinking about buying a house?" he asks.

After a double take, I realize that from up here he can see the front tables and all those realty brochures.

"Yeah, Snowy, In fact, I'm considering one on your block."

He shrugs. "As long as you keep your front lawn mowed."

"I knew that's how you'd feel."

"Well, one more thing, too," he says, handing me the Maker's on the rocks.

"What's that?"

"You've got to promise that you'll never—I mean never—consult Honest Paul on your love life or any of your cases."

I just have the whiskey to my lips and nearly spew it out. Honest Paul's this old guy apparition who's been chanting predictions on the courthouse lawn for nearly a year. The fine ladies and gentlemen of Fayette County are obviously in need of entertainment, since there have been days when actual lines have formed to ask him a question and receive one of his patented non-sequitur answers. But he doesn't panhandle, and there's not a law against bull crap. "No problem, Snowy," I reply. "I keep hoping someone will lose a horse racing bet on his ridiculous advice and pitchfork him. I need some good honest business; murder's been slow lately." Snowy gives me a wink and walks off to wait on two women who just showed up. I didn't know the guy had it in him: humor that is. And now he has the two women laughing. Maybe he's grooming himself for politics. What else could it be? Surely he's not eyeballing Honest Paul's place as our local soothsayer.

I listen to Snowy hit on the women until it's a quarter after five. If I have one more whiskey the rush hour traffic will fade, and I'll be primed for Morris and Zeno. What a combination. I flag Snowy away from the women, and just as I get my drink, damned if Methuselah and his girl Callie don't walk up behind me. There's an empty, though dirty table nearby, so the three of us pile all the glasses on the bar, retrieve a red wine for Callie and a Heineken for Methuselah and sit down.

"Uh, Callie said she wanted to get in on it," Methuselah says. "The bookstore prank, I mean."

"Why not?" I say while trying to figure if I'd said something on the phone about coming here for a drink. I turn to Callie and her hound dog eyes. "Hey Callie, what is it that Clarissa did the other night?"

Callie gives a glance to Methuselah, who tugs his ponytail beard. He's got two pink hair bands in it tonight, so I roll my eyes and look to Callie's brown eyes and long fingers that won't quit. She reaches those fingers to give Methuselah's salt and pepper beard a good tug before turning to me:

"For about five minutes she just kept banging the guitar strings. When I got her to stop, she said she could smell her father in the guitar."

Clarissa's dad had sent her the fancy guitar before he offed himself with drink. We all three stare at a cigarette-burn on the tabletop. Smoking's been banned in Fayette County restaurants for over two years now, so the burn holds nostalgia, even for a non-smoker like me.

"Is that possible?" I ask. "That she could smell his cologne or something?"

"I suppose," Callie says. "I mean, it's wood. I heard she jumped hard on you last night. This is just a phase, Willy. Hormones or something."

"Jalapeño and sardines," I say, thinking of a suicide case in New Mexico. Hell, I'd suicide myself too if I ate that for lunch.

"She's basically been doing pretty well, you know," Callie insists. "Considering."

"I know, I know. That's why I've got a date with the original stamp dealer nerd and not some bimbo blonde." I say this loudly and give a glance to the bar, then look back to Callie and Methuselah. "They're a lot of bimbo blondes floating around," I say, bimbo-ishly.

"I figured out Methusy's dream." Callie swirls her wine like a fortune teller sifting tea leaves—speaking of soothsayers.

"I can't tilt the blame?"

She looks up in surprise. "How'd you know?" she almost shouts.

"Uh, that's not the damned title," Methuselah says, leaving a swath of beer foam in his beard. "It was *Tilting the Blame R*." Callie gives him a look and he wilts back into the booth. This young gal's got the old pecker trained.

"He thinks he's going to write songs lifted from that geezer sitting in front of the courthouse."

"Honest Paul?" I ask.

"The same. Methusy's been obsessed with him when he's supposed to be writing a history of Fayette County." Callie gives Methuselah a glance, pretending to look down through the bifocals she doesn't wear. "So . . . what he really dreamed was, *I can't tilt the blame there*, but shifted it to *you* so *he* could keep wasting time at the courthouse. Maybe he's hoping to run into an old girlfriend."

Methuselah blushes, and oh ho I know why. One time when we two met while watching the courthouse soothsayer, Methuselah really did run into an old girlfriend, but she shivered him an iceberg shoulder. "You don't have anything to worry about there, Callie," I offer sweetly. "All his old girlfriends betrayed the hippie movement to become lawyers or CEOs. Or marry lawyers or CEOs."

She grins, and Methuselah places his elbows on the table. My mom would swat them off, white or not. "When my book of wisdom gets published, neither of you can expect a dedication page," he pouts.

The blonde at the bar gives me a delayed glare for my bimbo comment, flops off her stool and swings her ass all the way to the front door, draping herself on the slicked-down Ken doll, who's evidently got just enough IQ to figure there's something between me and Blondie, because his face flushes with anger. That's a good sign for me to wait for one more whiskey before picking up Morris the Stamp Man.

"He's not here tonight. Every Tuesday is his night to ride out and buy book collections from people."

The slink, who's only become slinkier since I'd last seen her at the wedding, is telling us this. "So you watch the store by yourself?" I ask.

"I get to read," she says, showing me a thick book, *Plato's Dialogues, Volume One*. She's halfway through. "The only trouble is that I can't underline or write in the books—I recognize you," she says of a sudden. "You're the detective who likes old mysteries and collects stamps. You should write a mystery about a stamp collector. And you came to our wedding with the witchy professor and the funny double ponytail guy. My name's Harriet. Old people never remember young people's names." She gives a green-eyed blink. "But then, young people never remember old people's names either."

So twice in one day, my sentimental side tugs at me, just like it did with the perfumed hashish coed with the KKK wannabe father. "My name's Willy Cox," I say, "and this is Morris."

"Hello, Mr. Morris." Harriet does a little curtsy from the middle of last century. The Greek philosophy must be getting to her. Then she turns on those big green eyes—no wonder the chump wanted to bag her with a wedding ring. "Have you read Wahloo?" she asks me. "He's old and cynical. A good mystery writer." She springs from behind the counter after carefully placing a bookmark in Plato.

"How many volumes does Plato have?"

Before she can answer, and before I can glom my eyes too thickly on her hips—I notice Morris doing the same—Methuselah and Callie walk in.

"Detective Cox, did you hear—"

"Save it, Methuselah. He's not here." I turn to Harriet and say, "We were going to play a joke on your husband."

The little charmer giggles and damned if she—within ten short minutes—doesn't saddle all four of us with a book apiece that we wind up buying. So the joke's on us. Then she's busy selling some bronzed Adonis with long blonde hair and an equally blonde goatee another book, though he appears to be a good deal more interested in her body than her mind.

"You're some type of salesman. Your husband should leave you in here alone more often," Callie comments as we leave.

So that the night won't be a complete loss, we head to the corner espresso/martini bar. It's Clarissa's absolute favorite hangout, and I feel my shoulders rise as we park, wondering if she'll be there. Morris and I get out of my car to meet Methuselah and Callie. Callie's paying attention to something in her hand—her cell phone. Ah, she's text messaging while walking. The younger generation can perform miracles. When we sit down, she grins smugly at me.

"You passed your test, Willy," she says.

"What test is that?"

"You didn't fall over yourself while talking to the young bookselleress."

“Harriet’s her name,” I insist, remembering Harriet’s comment about older people never remembering younger people’s names. “So, do I get a diploma?” I ask, while ordering a Bombay gin martini with double olives in honor of the absent Clarissa.

“No, but you do get a bonus . . . a surprise,” Callie adds when I raise my brow.

The waitress, one more college cutie to round out my Clarissa-less day, drops off our drinks, Morris keeping to the conservative espresso route while the rest of us go martini.

Not five minutes later, a bombshell blonde in clacka-clack blue high heels struts in and every male mouth drops the length of their dicks. She heads towards us and,

“Clarity!” I half-laugh, half exclaim.

She grins. “Callie called and told me you were here.” She points to her newly dyed hair, “I’m acting out. Had it done this afternoon while you all were drinking at Sar—”

She doesn’t get any more than that out, when I jump from the chair. “The bookshop creep! He was disguised!” I grab Clarity’s arm in passing, “I love it. Your new blonde hair! Callie, Methuselah, call the police station. Olsen and Tyler have that neighborhood. Tell them to meet me at the bookstore, sirens on!”

I run to the car and tear out, popping a portable police strobe on the roof as I head to the store.

When I get there, the front door’s locked, even though it’s only a quarter to seven and the store hours go to nine and all the inside lights are on. No movement inside. I flash back on the blonde Adonis sitting next to my ex blonde bimbo girlfriend. I try the door again, rattling it a bit. No movement inside, still. I’m positive the Adonis was the same guy we saw in the bookstore, except for his long wig and that fake goatee. Ms Bimbo is just weird and stupid enough to start dating a creep. Another rattle of the doorknob. Now I see movement and hear a yelp from the back. Three books fall off a rocking shelf. Another yelp and young Harriet’s leg gets slammed down onto the floor. There’s a concrete smoker’s oasis by the door, and I lift it to smash through the glass, jumping through and pulling my Glock.

The blonde creep, khaki pants half down, scrambles around the corner with a gun pointed at me, and he fires. I fire twice, dropping him.

There's a loud moan.

"Harriet?"

"Yeeesssss," more moan than word.

I run back, kicking the creep's revolver far off. His wig has snagged on a bookshelf. When I round the corner I see Harriet clutching her yellow blouse, blood on her face and hands.

"Are you okay, Harriet?" I give a glance to the creep: he won't be moving again.

"He was cutting me with a straight razor. He told me not to yell or—"

Blue lights flash out front. It isn't Olsen or Tyler, but a woman officer I recognize who peeks through the broken glass, pistol drawn. "Get an ambulance here pronto! I'm Detective Will Cox! Everything's . . ." I lower my voice, remembering Harriet. "Okay. Everything's okay." I remember the woman's name, Brandi Thomas. "Brandi, come on back here. There's a young girl—Harriet's her name."

I LEAVE THEM ALONE and stand halfway to the front. Where the hell is Brandi's partner? Brandi steps out to confirm what I suspected, since Harriet's pants and tennis shoes were still zipped and laced as when I first saw her: "No rape. He didn't have time. How'd you wind up here so fast?"

"A little synchronicity," I say. "And a little luck," I add.

"She wants you to call her husband. Says his cell phone number is taped to the register." Brandi turns back to Harriet, kicking the creep's leg out of her way. I notice she places her hands on her holstered pistol, like he'll try to grab her foot, even though he's far beyond that.

As I go to the register I see Methuselah, Callie, Morris, and Clarity standing outside gabbing with some guy who'd been on the force in St. Petersburg, Florida, and moved up here to join with Fayette last year. *Well now, I at least know where the creep's bullet hit*, I think, spotting a hole in the register. I phone Zeno and tell him he needs to come take care of Harriet. I have to calm-talk him all the way to his car to keep him from panic, telling him that she's basically all right. But just when I have him calmed, an ambulance brakes outside the bookstore, its siren whining, and Zeno starts screaming all over again. From the noise over the phone, I figure he must have run up on a curb and hit something hollow and metal, a trashcan or newspaper rack. Brandi walks up and tells me that Harriet doesn't want to go to the hospital, that they don't have insurance.

"We just sold nineteen thousand dollars' worth of stamps!" Zeno yells. "Tell her she can go. I'm coming right there." I hear another empty clonk before he hangs up.

"She doesn't really need to go," Brandi says. "The creep's dead and you shot him, so there's no legal issue. But still . . ."

"But still," I agree.

Somehow Callie and Clarity have horned their way inside and are back to Harriet before Brandi or I can stop them. They're on either side of the girl, their arms around her, cooing and turning her away from the creep. Brandi joins them and I see Clarity pull out her "Ma Mildred" flask and give Harriet a sip. That Ma Mildred flask, always filled with cognac, is usually reserved for especially vile forensic cases when even Gregorian chant won't cut the mustard.

Jim Warren, one of the department's two photographers, arrives to photograph the corpse. "Can you do it without a flash, Jim?" I ask. He looks up at the store's lighting and shrugs. "Harriet's still back there. They just got her calmed," I explain. "She's the victim." He nods and places his camera on the counter and notices the bullet hole in the register. "Your handiwork or his?" I tell him it was his, and Jim says he'll get a picture of that too after he fetches his tripod. "Fetches" is the word he uses; Jim's a bit strange.

Zeno, rushing in, barges into Jim going out, knocking him into the doorsill hard enough that he grabs his hip. The women are leading Harriet out past the creep, who gets kicked two or three times. Harriet sees Zeno and runs to him, her torn yellow blouse coming apart to reveal tiny breasts still bleeding from the creep's razor.

"It's the guy from when we were all here an hour ago, isn't it?" Callie says as Zeno and Harriet hug.

I nod.

"It's my fault. Right before we left the bookstore I said something about her husband not being here and he heard me. Remember?"

Instead of answering I look at poor Jim Warren: just as he's coming in the door with the tripod a crazed woman rushes by and knocks him into the sill, opposite hip. When his mouth and both eyes open into a squadron of O's, it's like he's providing comic relief. The crazed woman is Robin Holland, the sheriff's widow, Harriet's mother, the one who sat chowing down with Morris last night. She ignores Morris, Jim, and her son-in-law Zeno, to glom onto her daughter. Zeno takes the opportunity to walk back and look at the creep, with Callie and me following.

"I recognize him. He's been in here three or four times. Always staring at Harriet, never buying anything except a black candle."

"Candle?" I ask.

He nods toward the front of the store. "I took them and those wind chimes in to help with sales." Of a sudden he kicks the creep hard enough to knock his body into a shelf and topple five paperbacks. That kick nudges the little bookstore man up several notches in my estimation; it also dislodges something from the creep's pocket: a red jack of hearts, confirming my suspicion. I bend for the card, but on hearing Jim Warren clunking about, attaching his camera to a tripod, I straighten and tug Zeno's elbow to lead him to the front so Jim can finish without anyone else bashing him. He only has two hips. There, inside the front door, the young ambulance duo shift their feet. Bookstores must make them uncomfortable.

Jim's evidently forgotten about not using a flash, so whirrs, clicks, and strobes create a miniature lightning storm in the shelving. When Harriet turns to look she bleats, so Clarity holds out silvery Ma Mildred again. Harriet takes another sip, to the consternation of Brandi and Harriet's mother, but the cognac works and young Harriet looks from Clarity to me, to her mother and Morris, to old front-and-back ponytail Methuselah, who no one could ever forget, and she says to her husband, "Just like the ending of a comedy, everyone coming together again. Someone should get married." Then she bawls and giggles at one and the same time, in great gasps as Zeno clutches her.

Clarity bites her lip and walks over to snake her arm around my waist. She must be thinking of the night Adolph Barnes tried this same crap on her. I put my arm around her and we lean. Brandi stands by her partner, the St. Petersburg guy. The two medics are bumping shoulders like rock stars. Morris and Robin are holding hands, as are Callie and Methuselah. Even Jim Warren and Red Jack are performing a stylized dance, for as Warren tilts the camera atop the tripod Red Jack's body convulses. For a moment it seems that Harriet's right and we'll all step off a fancy, intricate, comic minuet. But no, we're circling in man-made lightning like hell-bent Druids, so comedy's out. I take in the scene: a bookstore. Could we co-author a tragedy? Call it *Tilting the Blame R?* Why the hell not? The only difference between comedy and tragedy is that in one the bodies laugh and dance; in the other, they weep and get buried.

13.

Amo, Amas, Amat

Year 2002

(Clarissa, Willy, Dr. Bug, Methuselah)

Dr. Bug, Methuselah, Willy and I drove to Indian Falls, where the Petite Artiste's remains were found. And she had a name at last: Grace Ann MacAuliffe, a teaching assistant known as "Pebble" according to a retired English professor Bill contacted. So even in real life she couldn't settle on one name. What if I'd simply bothered to have Bill run a campus cop check on the files of past English Department graduate students? What if I'd walked up to her in the used bookstore and said, "Pebble, I'd like to talk with you, 'cause I used to be an English major, too"? What if, what if.

We drove my new red F-250 in as far as we could after shifting to four-wheel drive, then hiked a quarter mile in. I was proud to note that I led the way, despite Dr. Bug's long legs. Which proves that desk jobs'll do it to you every time.

Yellow police tapes were still flapping at the overhang where the body'd been found, even though Willy'd asked that they take them down if no one was going to guard the place. No sense in inviting the curious. Even with first glance we saw two pieces of purple cloth strewn on the ground. Willy laid them in a box he'd brought along, just in case. An odor still clung to the soil, since much of The Petite—since much of Pebble—Grace Ann—had soaked into what wasn't limestone. Dr. Bug pointed out that insects were still working the fatty residue and other remains. Happily, it seemed. Their writhing sent Methuselah to the creek. I watched him bend and splash his face and realized how hot it was. With a final glance to the area, Willy commented how that wasn't a bad idea and joined him.

Puttering around, I spotted a woman's gold ring, a wedding band, surrounding a disarticulated finger bone. What a bang-up job cops and the ambulance crew had done. I bagged it, all the while knowing just who that wedding band had joined despite death, despite righteous laws against lesbian marriages, despite time's laughter.

Eventually, Dr. Bug and I joined the others at the creek, showing them the ring and the rubber sole of one tennis shoe. Dr. Bug said that an animal had likely carried off the other sole, and Methuselah recovered enough from the body parts to comment, "If that, why not something else?"

So we walked along the cave side of the creek toward the actual falls, which Methuselah, historian, geologist, and geographer, assured us lay not more than one half-mile ahead. About halfway through that half I looked up to spot a familiar shock of red hair on the opposite cliff.

"Can I borrow your binoculars, Methuselah?"

I just knew he had a pair in one of his nineteen pockets. He handed them to me and I saw that indeed the red hair belonged to a student I was teaching, a young woman named Althea. A New Jersey kid whose thick Yiddish slang remained, but whose name I'd forgotten was sitting next to her. For the world, they looked as if they were comparing ankle sizes. A third boy, no doubt another student, pretended to gaze at trees but kept stealing what I took to be angry glances at his two mates playing touchy-leg. Beware the green-eyed monster.

Willy found the rubber sole to the second tennis shoe. It was hot and we'd stupidly drunk coffee driving over, so I hoped this item would be enough. But no, Willy of the wandering ways insisted that we complete our trek to the bottom of the falls. Well, he was right, after all. I wouldn't give up and toss seven bones that didn't quite seem to fit into a garbage pail just because it was time for lunch.

As it turned out, we found a man's belt buckle with about one centimeter of leather remaining. What made us keep it was the shred of purple cloth entangled in it.

"Christ, you don't suppose whoever did it beat her—"

"Damn it, Methuselah!" I yelled, loudly enough that an echo popped back at us from the cliff on our right.

The three men had rightly shut me up on the way over when I speculated whether Adolph or Jerry Vander had made her swallow Gina's tooth in some weird communion ritual before killing her. Now it was me who didn't want to hear any speculative torture scenes about Grace Ann Pebble.

The falls themselves were entirely too steep; no animal would bother carrying anything up those slick rocks. So, turning back, I suggested we wade the stream. The guys looked from me to the boulders around the falls. They raised their brows in a silent chorus.

"Not up. I'm not suicidal. But back there again. In the actual water instead of just on the bank." I sat to remove my hiking boots.

"All four of us wading in there would stir too much muck and reduce the visibility."

"Cowards," I chided, stepping in, but giving a shout at the cold water.

When Methuselah offered to join me Willy speedily interjected, "No, it's my job, I'll do it." And he was in the water, next to me, shoes and all, suppressing an exhalation at the cold.

Beware, beware, beware the green-eyed monster.

"PRESSURE, PRESSURE, PRESSURE," WILLY kept chanting as if he'd been transported to a hilltop monastery in Italy. We were sitting at Adam's Rib and he was considering ways to make either Adolph or Jerry Vander panic.

Now, despite TV, there's only so much you can do with a belt buckle and a shred of purple cloth. The CSI shows would have Willy Lear-jetting down to Bowling Green to check out the stores by asking, "You ever sold a buckle like this?"/ "Oh sure, we're the only store in Bowling Green that carries that brand of man's belt buckle."/ "Is that so? Sell many of this particular style?"/ "Oh no, we've only sold two in the last nine years." / "Well, do you keep records of your belt buckle sales?"/ "Just let me see. (A flash of the computer screen) Why bless me! We sold those buckles just eight months ago to a preacher named Adolph and a friend of his named Jerry Vander."/ "Thanks, that's very helpful." (And with a tip of the Sherlockian hat, the case gets closed. Lear jet back to Lexington with maybe a swank female forensic anthropologist who's serving gin martinis on the plane and who, because of her yellow stiletto heels, keeps falling into the detective's lap with every air pocket.)

That hadn't happened. Nothing had happened, other than my assurance that Pebble was strangled, since there was a broken bone in her neck. The weird hillbilly kid rooming in her boarding home—his name was Gray Billingsworth—had alternately claimed he'd shot her, strangled her, drowned her, electrocuted her, and frozen her to death by exposing her to the snow we didn't have on the day she disappeared. I mean in a freezer, he'd added. On a farm. In a pizza restaurant I work at. At some people's house where I was house-watching. Someone finally called Dr. Kiefer, who convinced the child it was time for a little R & R at a local mental health unit.

"United we stand, divided we fall," Willy said, inspired by a cardinal's chit-chit, as it landed in a tree across the creek from the restaurant's patio.

Cardinals being Kentucky's state bird, I said, "Is this a civics test, Willy? State motto, right?"

"Yeah, state motto, right. But true, too. What if I have the Bowling Green police pull in Vander and grill him—hard? What if I have him conspicuously tailed? What if we pull his store records and business and personal checking account for auditing? And what if we just ignore Herr Adolph?"

The cardinal was perched in what I'd been told was a mulberry tree, though I'd never seen any berries. Supposedly they came around the end of April and would drive everyone working the outside bar nuts for ten days, and then they were gone. I spotted the dull brown female cardinal and thought of Vander and his dull eyes.

"Willy, you do realize you just might be giving Jerry Vander a death sentence, don't you?"

"You mean from Adolph the executioner?"

I nodded.

"The only better person it could happen to would be Adolph himself, but Vander doesn't have the cajones."

"Or the brains," I added.

Sure enough, my prediction came true. Not a week later, after the Bowling Green police put on pressure, Vander was reported as missing by employees who showed at his computer store two days in a row with no Jerry Vander to open up for them. And on June 20, his body was found in a lake, pretty much under the same circumstances that the two young women who'd lived with him and Adolph had been found twenty some years ago; that is, his blood showed quantities of alcohol and marijuana, adding Xanax as the latest drug of choice.

"He's gonna slip yet," Willy said, speaking to himself over morning coffee at my house, and of course meaning Adolph.

I walked to work and told Mildred, whose sole response was, "Let's just hope this slipping doesn't involve you, dear."

A month or so later and Willy and I were supposed to go—at last—to Helen, Georgia, over the July Fourth break. I dutifully announced to the sophomore class, which had taken to skipping Fridays despite the quizzes I threw at them, that I would not be in my office Friday through Tuesday, since I was going hiking in Georgia with a friend. The female students lolled their heads romantically while the males woke up just enough to ask whoever sat next to them what I'd said.

But murderers and their victims don't cooperate with vacation schedules. Wednesday night two bodies were found in a shallow grave on a horse farm in Paris, of all places. The two had been executed drug style, hands tied, a single shot at the base of the skull. Horse farms in Paris, Kentucky, don't come cheap, in case you're unfamiliar with the territory. In fact, they probably cost, acre for acre, not much less than land directly outside their city's namesake in France. Consequently, to placate the wealthy owners my Thursday was spent at the gravesite and my Friday was spent steaming off what little was left of the flesh and examining the skeletons. I identified one as being from Lexington, which made matters worse, for now Willy was involved. To assure ourselves that we were still going to Helen, Georgia, Willy and I drove to eat at a small Italian place Friday night. It always amazed me to watch Willy put down spaghetti. He never, and I mean never, stopped at one plate, no matter how loaded it was.

"Tmml I'll ghoh to hoffice in—"

"Willy, Willy. What would your sweet momma think? Chew, then talk."

A waitress delivering coffee to the table behind us giggled. Willy sulked up but did what I suggested. What he was trying to say was that he'd go into the office early tomorrow—Saturday—finish the paperwork by nine and we'd be on our way. Great. And to assure his getting to the office early, he was going to be a good boy and go home. Which meant that I had to be a good girl, alone. Not so great. No one was going to touch anyone Friday night.

So, a shared last glass of Chianti, and then homeward, to perform a quick peck at my door, since we both knew better than to French slobber, as that would undoubtedly lead to the beast with two backs.

"What's that smell?" Willy asked just as he was about to turn and go.

"I burnt French toast this morning."

"I thought you didn't cook breakfast."

"My morning consolation for having to work with the two bodies when I thought we'd be on our way to Georgia."

He nodded, gave me another peck, and then walked back to his car. I climbed my stairs to change into a sexy red teddy, all the evening consolation I was going to get.

Fifteen minutes later I was half-dreaming, oddly enough picturing Gina's mouth missing that left canine tooth shouting something urgent. Mildred stood behind her, shouting just as urgently. The dream came too late, as did my hearing an unmistakable noise in the attic. When I bolted up in bed a harsh flashlight blinded my eyes.

"You're just as good-looking a bitch as I've heard," a voice said. "I bet your cunt's as sweet as apple blossoms."

My new nine millimeter, which was Willy's old nine millimeter and had replaced his older .38, lay two feet away, since I'd rolled to the middle of the bed.

"How *are* all my eight pretty babies? I keep a picture of them from your lab right in the middle of Revelations."

"Adolph?"

"Very good. Obviously I wasn't wrong in coming here. But call me Dolphie. I want us to be friends."

He'd moved by the bed, on the side where the pistol lay between the mattress and the box springs. He was shining the flashlight lower now, playing between the sheet I was clutching and the teddy's red strap and my face. Crap, I first thought, wondering what had possessed me to wear the teddy to bed. Then I said,

"We can be friends. Would you like to talk?" And I moved the sheet down just a bit to reveal more of the red teddy, thinking to buy some time or buy some something, I don't know.

Whatever, it was a wrong move, for he hit me with the flashlight and I fell backward to flip off the bed, grabbing a pillow as I fell. He lost me in the dark long enough for me to grab a jewelry box off my dresser and throw it at him, spilling earrings and necklaces over the floor. He caught me by the hair just as I made it to the top of the steps, and he yanked me back hard enough that I lost my footing and he lost his grip on my hair, falling on me. I scooted toward the bed on my back, using my elbows and heels. He grabbed the teddy and somehow rolled me over onto my stomach.

"You're going to pay, cunt. I'm going to ram your ass full of cum then have you lick my dick clean and beg to let you live through the night."

Grabbing my buttocks with his hands and digging his fingernails in, he pulled me apart and rammed his cock against me. My head hit the bed-side table and the clock radio fell, turning on WVLK's soft rock. "Pretty Woman," by Roy Orbison was playing. Outside, the fraternity started its own music, the few brothers remaining on campus getting into the July 4th spirit. Music wasn't what mattered; Willy's pistol was what mattered; getting Adolph off me was what mattered.

"Dolphie, stop." I coughed then started again. "You don't have to do this. I'll do whatever you want."

I was within reach of the pistol, but he'd retrieved the flashlight and was shining it on me, so I didn't dare move.

"You'll do more than whatever I want. You'll beg and you'll cry."

I could hear and feel him spitting on my ass for lubrication. When he thrust, I edged forward a bit, half on purpose, half because his body shoved me. Willy's gun, the gun, the gun. Adolph spit again, but it landed on my spine.

"Daddy! Please stop, Daddy!" I shouted.

"What'd you call me, cunt?" He bashed my kidney with the flashlight and I inhaled in a wheeze.

"Dolphie, let me suck you good and wet," I said when I caught my breath, barely believing myself, gambling one more time.

"You really are nothing but a slut-ass cunt, aren't you, *Professor*?" But he was easing off, rethinking his game maybe. My face was smashed into the floor and I felt my nose tingling and filling with blood.

"Beg to suck me. Beg."

"Please, please let me suck your sweet prick. Please, please." *Daddy don't, Daddy, don't,* kept echoing through my mind. How could I equate this asshole with my father? How?

"That's what I want to hear," he said. "But I'm going to have to give you a good whipping first so I can see pretty pink welts on your pretty white professor skin. Welts always feel so soft against my hipbone."

I could feel him sitting back on his haunches and heard him undoing his belt. When the buckle jingled, I reached under the mattress and pulled out the pistol, which Willy always told me to always keep safety-off, because if I wanted it, I wanted it.

I wanted it.

I rolled over between Adolph's damned knees and began firing, the muzzle flashes playing like a private and skewed Fourth of July. I didn't stop until I'd emptied the clip. The flashlight skittered into the hall and wound up shining into the room across from mine. Quiet. Then I heard a gargle from the floor at my feet and I wound up sitting on the radio, not even noticing it cutting into my haunches.

"Clarity!"

It was Willy, downstairs.

"Willy! Adolph's up here. I shot the sonofabitch and hope to hell I killed him."

I heard Willy running up the steps, then stopping. A beam of light played on blood spattered across the floor in front of the bathroom. I saw what looked like a gob of flesh.

"Clarity, baby, it's me, Willy. You got him, all right. Are you okay?"

I was laughing and sobbing. Under my buttocks Roy Orbison finished wailing out "Pretty Woman" while Willy's flashlight did a dance, showing more blood and what looked like a dead mouse or patch of hair.

"Clarity, baby, are you okay with me coming around the corner? You're not going to think I'm him and shoot, are you? He's long gone dead, my hot shot gal."

"The pistol's empty Willy. I fired it all, like you told me to."

"That's good, that's good, my sweet gal."

His voice wasn't rebounding anymore, and his flashlight played over Adolph, who had been thrown backwards by the bullets and was lying on one bent leg, the other sprawled toward my window and the fraternity. His arms flayed at 45-degree angles like a misdirected Jesus.

"I'm going to turn on the lights, Clarity. Just look up at me before I do, look where my voice is. Don't look at the floor, okay?"

"O-tay." In my calm, play-doll voice. "O-tay." Was I talking to Willy? To my father? To . . .

Willy had come back because he realized about ten blocks away that the smell he'd smelled in my house wasn't burnt French toast, but marijuana and incense. And he knew damned well that my drug of choice was red wine or an occasional whiskey. Adolph, we learned, came there to retrieve eight jelly jars of dried blood and pieces of hearts from under the attic's floorboards. Methuselah and I speculated that this was part of some ritual used to assure eternal life, that the dried blood would either form a hex or keep the dead spirits guarding Adolph. You can't look for too much sense in psychotics, other than what internal logic they seem to squirrel away. After Adolph's death, the Bowling Green police went to his farm where they found the skeletal remains of seven women, most of them BSU coeds missing over the years. They were buried inside three horse stalls.

In the movies, an experience like this glues a couple inseparably. In the movies, Willy and I would have driven to Helen, Georgia, hiked in sunshine, and eaten lobster by a gurgling mountain stream while the credits rolled and some sweet rock love song played.

But it didn't work that way.

Willy and I cancelled Helen, splitting the fifty-buck no-show fee. We were obliged to see one another for some official reports, or at least to glance at one another. Willy hugged me once, but he could tell by the way that I tightened that it wasn't a good idea. Of course he testified about Adolph. That and the testimony of the two women cops and the nurse who started the rape kit and accompanied me to the emergency room got me off any charges. I stayed at Willy's apartment that first night. We sat on the couch, listening to a cough I'd developed—no music. Saturday at noon I got it together enough to call Mildred, who offered her house, who in fact met me at mine with Willy and helped pick out enough clothes for a week. The radio was off, I noted as soon as Willy unlocked and opened the door. No "Pretty Woman." Willy walked up the stairs to de-spook the place, ran some water in the tub and bent over the doorjamb. I realized that he was wiping up blood, either Adolph's or mine. Mildred put her arm around me.

"Want me to stay up here or come down?" Willy asked.

I shrugged so imperceptibly that he couldn't possibly see.

"Come on down," Mildred replied. "We won't be a minute."

When we walked up, Mildred, bless her, didn't even balk at the blood spattered on a wall, where Willy and forensics hadn't seen it. Willy waited downstairs quietly, except for the Mr. Coffee machine he started. The smell of coffee was a lifesaver, for the iron smell of blood pervaded my bedroom. Mildred packed me and we three were out of the house with our coffee.

By the time I saw the photos of the gash over my eye where the asshole'd hit me with his flashlight, I could barely feel a bump other than the stitches. The other wounds eased up after Monday, my second day of non-stop walking. On those walks I avoided anyone's eyes and listened to Gregorian chant on a Walkman.

July Fourth passed with firecrackers and no Willy, though Mom drove up from Tennessee. At the sound of the first firecracker around noon, I skittered back to Mildred's house and locked myself with Mom in the guest bedroom. For me, the most disturbing thing really wasn't Adolph. The most disturbing thing was what I'd shouted: "Daddy! Please stop, Daddy!" I'd always told myself that all that ever happened when my father got drunk was that he would occasionally cuff me hard enough to knock me backwards. In Tennessee, this is good child rearing, Dr. Spock quality even. Once, he had beaten me with his belt, two straps on the buttocks. But I couldn't get straight in my head whether I'd shouted "Daddy" before Adolph started taking off his belt or after. Had my father done something akin to rumors about incestuous Appalachia? Had I repressed this?

I'm not sure whether Willy or Mildred contacted my mother. She drove up to stay with me that July Fourth, bravely keeping up with my daily peripatetic through suburban streets, though I'm sure she was relieved at the firecrackers sending me skittering back to the house. There, as she drank Crown Royal, I closed my eyes and smelled Daddy's whiskey-breath leaning into my face. I felt his rough, unshaven cheek. No, I decided, giving a cough and opening my eyes, I can't ask my mom that, in a stranger's guest bedroom, especially a bedroom with blue-flowered wallpaper. She had to get back to work anyway, having the first decent job she'd ever held in her life, with medical benefits and all. No, I can't ask her before she has to make a three-hour drive back to Tennessee. So she left, promising to come help me move in a couple of weeks, for it was clear that I'd have to leave Dr. Kiefer's house. No, I can't ask her, I thought while staring at the exhaust emitting from her car, and then after going back into the guest bedroom to close the blinds, still faintly smelling her Crown Royal from the evening before. I can't ask her—ever. No One Ever Touches Anyone. I was going to live with that, wasn't I? And now it reached far beyond a car wreck and a drunken lover's betrayal with a drunken roommate. In the kitchen, Mildred's husband, the chiropractor, tuned in a country radio station. I inhaled Crown Royal fumes and heard twanging guitar chords and tried to picture daddy's smile, his tobacco-smoke yellow teeth. They were nice teeth. He had a nice smile. An always-sad smile.

MILDRED KNEW OF A house for sale, and since I was a shoo-in for early tenure, why not? Driving to it on Thursday got me off the peripatetic routine—much more sidewalk-pounding and I'd have to teach in the philosophy department or coach track.

The house was a lovely granite two-story just a couple of blocks from the Demitasse. I touched the hard stones, hewn eighty years before, during the Roaring 20's. I didn't even bother haggling; I just countered the asking price with the asking price. Dr. Kiefer surprised me by dropping by Mildred's that evening. When she commented on how thin I looked, Mildred told her about my peripatetics, as we'd come to call them.

"Way-ell," Dr. Kiefer said, giving a fake—or maybe not—mountain drawl, "at my age I can't ramble with you like some fool Greek philosopher, but if you want to talk at my office, you can pace the floor just as hard as you like for free. It's got six coats of polyurethane."

The next day the real estate agent told me my offer had been accepted—no surprise there—and that the seller was going to pay all the points and fees, which was a three thousand dollar surprise. I later found out that Dr. Kiefer was behind this, knowing the dean who was selling the house and shaming him into some concession considering my recent troubles.

One day short of a week after July Fourth came a Blue Monday that consisted of a line of tornadoes moving through Kentucky, three hitting Fayette County. That marked the end of my week off. I informed Mildred and the two graduate students who'd been filling in for me that I'd be back a day early.

So before my ten o'clock Tuesday class I took a peripatetic around campus, having to step over and around fallen limbs and trees left from the tornadoes. In front of the used bookstore I spotted a newspaper and learned that one of my students had been killed on the previous night by a tree limb driven through his chest. His house was eight blocks away from Dr. Kiefer's, about ten from where I then stood. I bought the paper and read on the second page that another student of mine, Althea Tompkins, had killed herself the previous night. Like a bursting dam, the memory of the two of them at Indian Falls playing footsie flooded me. I envisioned them through the binoculars, his pale hand on her pink, sunburned ankle. I walked into the bookstore and asked for change for the pay phone outside. My cell phone was still at Dr. Kiefer's rental house, and damned if I'd go back before I had to. The bookstore's owner, Zeno, once more not recognizing me, barely looked up from a book he was reading. I walked out and placed a call to Willy, since he'd likely know about them both—or at least the girl who'd killed herself. As I dialed, I envisioned her lovely red hair.

What are the odds, I egotistically thought as Willy's phone rang, of one professor losing two students—two star students—in one night, in two separate, isolated incidents?

"Clarissa," Willy said, answering his cell phone. How, I wondered, did he know—and then of course I remembered caller ID. But I was at a pay phone.

"How did you—"

"Hell, I've been answering every damned call I get with your name for the last two days. I tried to call last night, but Mildred's line was out from the tornados. I drove by your old rental house before work and it looked fine, without any damage, so—"

My face went red and I fell against the booth's plastic hood hard enough to crack it. "God, Willy. I'm not going to stay there. I've already made an offer on another house. I can't believe I haven't told you that I'm going to move."

"I figured you'd want to."

"Willy." I stopped. "Willy, I'm calling about two students of mine."

A sigh. Willy'd never sighed before in his life that I knew of. Then he spoke: "Don't tell me that—"

"Yes. Remember the redheaded girl and the New Jersey kid we saw at Indian Falls a couple of weeks ago? Through Methuselah's binoculars?"

"Jesus."

When he said that word it sounded more like Gregorian chant than blasphemy.

"Jesus," he chanted again. "Something kept niggling me about the girl's red hair when I went out there."

It was my turn to sigh, but I inhaled loudly instead.

"Clarity, are you sure you want to know the details now, after—"

"Yes, I'm sure." I softly hit my forehead against the phone booth's plastic, which in turn sharply reminded of the stitches. "Yes. I owe it to them."

The odds, I calculated while watching a female student trying to parallel park a blue SUV in a slot that would barely hold a blue motorcycle, the odds of a screwball professor losing two star students in one night were about as astronomical as the odds of any two people ever touching one another on this planet Earth. The odds of a country music song offering sincere insight. The odds of Dentyne cleansing a two-pack a day cigarette habit off buckteeth.

"Clarity? You there?"

"Look, Willy, I'm returning to work today, a day early. I've . . . I've got to go in and teach soon or . . . hell, if not, I may never return . . ."

I shook my head. Damned if the girl genius didn't fit her SUV in the slot, though she had to use her bumper to scoot a second car back several centimeters, speaking of astronomical odds. So. So maybe two people could at least nudge one another, maybe it could happen, maybe it happens all the time.

". . . But Tuesdays this summer semester are light for me, and I'm out after mid-morning class. Screw the grading. Willy, can you get off? Willy, can we meet at The Demitasse for a martini lunch? Can we . . ." *Touch*, I thought, listening to the SUV's door slam and the girl's heels clacking down the sidewalk.

"The Demitasse at noon. I'll meet you there," Willy replied. "*Amo, amas, amat.*"

"Yes," I whispered, remembering the Derby and our silly bet. "*Amo, amas . . .*"

"*Amat*," Willy filled in as the girl's heels clicked on concrete. "*Amas, amat*. You love. He loves, she loves. Noon."

"He loves, she loves," I repeated, hanging up and leaning into the comforting heat of the bookstore's brick.

14.

The Theoretics of Love

Year 2005

(Professor John Hart, Haley, Clarissa, Gray)

Five of them were gathered on the Student Union patio, drinking one cappuccino, one white wine, one Perrier, one iced tea, and one Coca-Cola. Haley was drinking the Coke. She liked it and menthol cigarettes since the combination kept her metabolism up and her weight down. The five had been talking about a lesbian professor but had drifted back to the heterosexual males.

"I hear that the only professor—male or female—in all of liberal arts who hasn't slept with a student is Hart."

"What do you expect, with that beard of his?"

Whenever Haley saw Professor Hart in Patterson Towers, she thought his brown beard was sexy, sort of a facial phallic extension. Somehow he managed to keep it trimmed so that it came to a point, like a goatee, but about five—not six!—inches longer than a goatee. It wasn't the longest, but it sure was the neatest beard she'd ever seen. Once on an elevator with him, she'd had to restrain herself from asking if she could touch it.

"I think it's cute," she offered in counter.

Her four friends gave mock groans, with Sue adding a slurp of her cappuccino as a topping.

"No one, huh?" Haley continued. "I bet that I can sleep with him by . . ." she put a thin forefinger to her temple and rotated her head, as if daring a migraine to come her way. "By the end of spring semester."

"Why not this semester?" Lynne asked.

"Because this semester is half over. And because I'll have to shift from poetry to at least one philosophy course, which is more than any of you dumbasses could handle." Haley gave an affected flip of her cigarette and grinned. She was older, if not wiser, than the others, since she would turn twenty-five in February. Tammy, who was drinking the single white wine before noon was, naturally, still underage. Lynne and Ellen hadn't been able to legally drink until two months ago, and Sue for only a year and a half . . .

All that was last fall, and here it was early June and here she was at twenty-five plus, moving into Professor Hart's two-story house on the fashionable edge of the student ghetto. And here she was, standing on his porch steps watching him pull a half-full dresser along the bed of his pick-up. She shook her head. For a forty-something guy, he held himself like an ox, though she kept waiting for a stroke or heart attack to send him rigid or limp.

"Weren't you in one of my anthropology classes?"

Haley nearly dropped the cuckoo clock she held, a keepsake from her Pike County grandmother, who supposedly inherited it from her German grandmother. Haley turned toward a dark-haired woman standing on the lawn, a professor whose name escaped her.

"I'm Professor Circle," the woman said with a nod. "Though I suppose I should just say 'Clarissa,' since you and my tennis partner John are evidently an item. The single most eligible bachelor in all of liberal arts. However did you manage it? You may turn out to be the solitary proof negating my theory that No One Ever Touches Anyone."

Haley grinned at the professor who kept her black hair slicked like an Indian's and whose gray eyes projected like lanterns at midnight. An inch or two taller and she could have been—still could be, probably—a model. And now Haley remembered her, haranguing a huge lecture class, insisting that culture's customs and mores—counter-intuitively, she had insisted—served only to prevent people from truly touching one another. She had waved her muscular bare arms and pressed her palms together in example, insisting that people were never really together, that some "ineluctable" space remained between them, just as such a space remained between any two human psyches, from those in the most advanced to the most elementary and crudest civilization. At the time, her argument had struck Haley as an extremely bizarre stance for an anthropologist, but then Professor Circle—Clarissa—had reminded the class that she was a physical, not a cultural anthropologist.

Haley heard scraping and turned to see John trying to move the dresser off the bed of the pickup by himself. She shouted for him to wait, setting the cuckoo clock on the concrete steps. Both she and Clarissa rushed to help him.

"You two've met," he said simply as they took the other end of the dresser.

"But not touched," Haley said, giving a lift of her brows.

Both John and Clarissa laughed.

"Oh, you'll do just fine here, dear," Clarissa said, turning to give Haley a wink as they toted the dresser. "Just fine."

MONTHS BEFORE, EASTER HAD arrived liturgically on time, though seasonally early; and John Hart was driving to see his mother in Louisville. He realized on the way over that visions of Haley Lambert, a twenty-five year old senior, had flicked before him with nearly every new hillside. Not pornographic visions, but visions of her laughing or jokingly placing her finger against her temple and rocking her head. That was no doubt the real enticement of youth: gaiety. After he'd undergone the same visions during the entirety of his visit with his mother and on the drive back too, he told himself he was obsessed, foolish, immature, warped—and just plain nuts. Still, after the very next class he took a good existentialist stance and asked Haley to come to his office. Naturally, she'd placed her finger to her temple and grinned, leaning against the classroom's professorial golden walnut desk.

"You're not a philosophy major," he stated simply once they were inside his office facing one another.

"English," she answered.

"And you're well over twenty-one . . ."

"Twenty-five," she said. "And I already have an A-plus all but locked in your class."

"Right . . . So how would you like to go to a bluegrass concert this Saturday?"

She'd blinked, searched her purse for some lip gloss, found it, but put it back without using it. "I'd love to," she said, oddly coming to attention before him by snapping her soft golden slippers together.

That Saturday she'd worn a gauzy yellow blouse that split along each arm from shoulder to elbow; it billowed whenever she raised her forefinger to her temple with that odd gesture of hers. The gauzy blouse didn't particularly fit bluegrass, but it certainly caught his attention. Haley herself immediately took to the give-and-take bounce of the banjo and mandolin, bobbing her head and getting lost in the music, just as he got lost in her. They were listening to a grandfather-granddaughter duo. The young woman burst into an *a cappella* "Oh Death," and Haley pulled her knees to her chin and sat perfectly still in her lawn chair, her eyes wide and her lips pursed as granddaughter and grandfather pleaded with death to spare them for at least one more year. After they finished singing, Haley commented, "In Elizabethan poetry, death signified the climax of intercourse." It was one of those things that John knew but didn't know. It made sudden, immaculate, and ineradicable sense.

They'd wound up in her bed that night, though he'd never slept with a student before, though he'd not slept with any woman at all since Thanksgiving, and she had been a visiting anthropology professor that his neighbor Clarissa had stuffed down his throat. They'd hated one another, which Clarissa took as proving her silly No One Ever Touches theory, which he on the contrary took as *disproving* it: they had, after all, very much touched—just not amicably.

But Haley, with her full-lipped smile, her thin elegant body, and her loomy hazel eyes . . . well, she was another matter. They'd stood in her kitchen clasping hands at shoulder level in front of themselves, elbow to elbow, entangling in that diaphanous yellow blouse, pressing forearms and fingers together like two preying mantises meeting uncertainly in a field of red clovers. When Haley lifted her face, her huge eyes—almost in incantation—dilated with green. They'd kissed greenly, bluely, pinkly, rainbowly. He'd concentrated on the feel of her upturned nose against his cheek, the smell of talcum mixing with lime perfume. And when he had peeked amid the roller coaster middle of that kiss, she was staring at him with great and loomy yellow-brown irises. His knees wobbled at the change in her eye color. She twisted so that he wound up against the kitchen cabinet, and she stood on his insteps. Her next kiss bit into his lips. Within ten minutes they were in her bedroom and he was hungrily mouthing her soft skin, ravenous as she giggled and pointed at spots she wanted him to kiss, then scooting away, leaving him to lunge. When they finally made love, her pelvic bones had driven into his like a pair of rivets. As far as he was concerned they were.

It was soon settled. She'd already applied for graduate school in English for the coming fall. She would live with him, read poetry to her heart's content, and if age didn't offer too great a barrier . . .

NOW, THE THREE OF them—Clarissa, Haley, and John—walked back outside after carrying in the dresser. They looked down at the cuckoo clock still on the steps.

"It's over a hundred years old," Haley said.

John expected Clarissa to comment that it was nearly as old as him, but she only stooped to lift one of the clock's miniature pinecones at the end of a golden chain and rub it between her fingers.

"Hand-carved black walnut," she said rubbing her bent knee. "Someone put an amazing deal of work into this." As she turned her gray eyes up toward Haley, John feared their gray and green irises would clash mid-point over the clock, blasting out muddy purple arcs. But Clarissa stayed oddly demure, just as she had about the age business between him and Haley. "You should take great care of it. The clock, I mean."

"I do," Haley replied.

"We . . ." John choked off what he was about to say, feeling it presumptuous. How could he, at this early stage of their relationship, lay claim to anything of Haley's that was so personal a keepsake? And how could anyone ever promise to take care of time, either in a mechanical cuckoo clock or in love's hungered tangle? So he wound up blurting, "I've always wondered if the Swiss aren't conveying some subtle life irony with these clocks and their silly mechanical birds."

That elicited two female groans and made Clarissa flex upward with an angular bounce.

"I'll leave you with him, dear. If his speculations and his irony and philosophy get too much, I'm three houses down, the one with the granite turret and the black trim."

Haley gaily tick-tocked her head and grinned.

From his room's window, he watched them barbecuing in the back yard behind his boarding house. He hated the professor, a godless atheist with a pretentious beard. John the Baptist had a beard, but it was for a reason: it displayed a Nazarene vow. And John had eaten locusts and honey, not shameful mounds of barbecued meat and bottles of wine.

He pressed into the window. He was positive that the girl was a student, a graduate student maybe, but a student. The whole university was a Sodom and Gomorrah—why should it surprise him that this professor of high-toned philosophical humanism and freethinking morality would practice the vices of those cities?

He studied her thin body and her short, dark auburn hair. She might as well have been a lesbian, since she didn't have any breasts. When she glanced toward his window, he backed into his room, to recite, "He that sitteth in the heavens shall laugh; the Lord shall have them in derision. Then shall he speak unto them in his wrath . . ." Losing concentration as the girl twisted, he restarted the Psalm from its beginning: "Why do the heathen rage, and the people imagine a vain thing?" –Why wouldn't she stop staring with those big eyes and lips? Did she want to drag him down into hell too? She held up a wine glass. Toward him? It might as well have been a huge red apple.

"Someone was staring at us from that house. I saw him pressed against the window."

John stood and looked to where her glance indicated. From the side, she watched his eyes, darker than caramel, always alert. It really wasn't his beard, but his eyes from that time on the elevator that had pushed her into betting her friends that she could sleep with him. And anyway, she had to keep up with the name her parents had given her, after some dead 50s singer named Bill Haley, whose claim to fame was a song called "Rock Around the Clock."

"John . . ."

"Second floor, corner window?"

"Yeah."

"My little Christian friend. If you take Christ out of the name, that is, and replace it with a capital X. My advice is to stay away from him."

"Why's that?"

"He's haunted. He's going to blow up a women's clinic, mass rape, or . . . something that doesn't have much to do with Christ, except in his mind."

"His own version of existentialism."

John raised his glass and took a sip of wine. "Touché."

Haley blinked. Dusk was coming on. She liked this time out on the porch because she couldn't see the wrinkles in John's brow, the crow's feet in his eyes. He was exactly twenty years and two days older than she was—two days since their birthdays both came in February and she'd missed being a leap year baby by three hours. He wasn't really old enough to be her father, he pointed out, since he remained a virgin until he was twenty-one. It was an oddball argument she accepted, just like his argument about living together before they decided whether to get married. Well, she had no intention of marrying him, and his argument was a complete bluff: if she produced a wedding ring from the hip pocket of her pajama pants right now he'd run it through his nose. Still, all in all they got along well enough, and most of her friends were graduating and taking jobs or getting married, leaving her behind to enter the English department's Master's program.

She thought she spotted a flame in the window that John had pointed out, like a candle. She was sure and said so.

"Let's go on in," John replied.

"Why? We can sit here in darkness. He cain't see us here under the top deck." Haley winced at her twang. She'd tried to cover the little town of Paintsville ever since she came to Lexington and the university. She'd tried to forget that she'd been a cheerleader for a bunch of lanky, pimply boys who wound up as car mechanics, miners, grocers, or drunks.

"I guess you're right," John mumbled, taking a seat after scooting his chair farther under the balcony's overhang.

Haley bit her wine glass, giving off a clink. John Hart might have crow's feet, he might have wrinkles, but he listened to what she said and had never once made fun of her hill twang. She moved her chair close to his and they stared at the coming night, at the candle that occasionally moved behind the window, flickering like an eye. Crickets began to saw their little legs. Blocks away, tires squealed. She could make out the hum of an electrical transformer on a nearby telephone pole. Though she loved sitting on the porch, she wasn't as comfortable with these periods of mutual silence as John was, and she certainly wasn't comfortable with the candle still moving in that window like a ghost in a horror movie. So she rubbed John's thigh, reaching under his loose shorts to close in on his sac. She felt him squirm when her fingernail caught it.

"You're right. Let's go in. That candle's creepy."

John inhaled the perfume Haley was wearing, which emitted one low pheromone and one high one: acid and base, or cayenne and basil, or lemon and whipping cream for all he knew. What he did know was that it yanked his nose as if it were clipped to a short metal leash. She typically didn't wear perfume because of her allergies and migraines, but tonight . . .

"Va-voom," he whispered into her right ear, eliciting a laughing hiccup.

He followed her thin twitching shoulders, watching her hands rub her flanks. The moment they entered the bedroom, without turning she bunched those fingers into fists and shouted, "Down on your knees! Now!"

He knelt and seeing that his doing so caught her off guard, he stared at her right flank as she emitted a titter. But she got into the game and undulated her hip to rub against his face. She'd worn blue silk PJs out on the porch so he started to kiss them.

She giggled. "No nuzzling, Friedrich. Restrain yourself or you'll have to crawl into a corner and read the New Testament aloud."

Despite himself he laughed. She did too, but then pirouetted to grab his hair with both hands and smack her lips in a tsk. "Laughing without permission, Friedrich?" The light over the bed shed enough brightness that he could see her grin. She pulled him to her mid-section, and in the air conditioning, the heat of her body ebbed onto his cheeks and he smelled the light musk of her period. When he leaned into that she pushed him back.

"Not yet. Strip first. Then go fetch me a Coke."

While she sat on a corner of the bed and placed her finger to her temple, rotating her head, he stood to take off his clothes. Already hard, he stumbled while shedding his underwear, to her amusement. When he finished and leaned toward her again, feeling his own heavy breathing, she held up her hand in admonition.

"The Coke?"

He sighed and turned for the kitchen, hearing her pull back the sheets, move books along the headboard, and get into bed.

They'd lived together for two weeks now. School was out, but she'd kept busy reading poetry and literary history on the balcony attached to the upstairs study, because she wasn't happy with her GRE scores. He thought they'd been plenty high considering her educational background from the eastern mountains of Kentucky. A good deal higher than his had been, for instance, if the truth be known. Maybe her hill origins prodded her toward perfection. Opening the refrigerator, he pulled out a Coke and popped the tab. He smiled, feeling the bubbles releasing through the thin can. The air-conditioning was running unusually cold because he'd turned it down on coming home figuring that would get them in bed faster so he could lie next to her slender, warm body.

Re-entering the room, he caught his breath: Haley had changed into a green teddy with tan platform heels. She wiggled her right foot and he felt his cock bounce in response.

"Very Pavlovian," she commented.

Vivaldi was playing low. Lately, Haley had been reading to 60-cycle music, ever since Clarissa mentioned that certain music enhanced the learning process. He handed Haley the Coke. Her teeth gleamed as she turned toward the light. After she took a sip she grabbed his cock and pressed the cold Coke can against it. With a silent lurch his penis lost its erection.

"Oh, Friedrich, you're supposed to keep more single-minded than that."

Her eyes, her eyes. Even with the light silhouetting her head he could see those huge hazel eyes. Jean-Paul Sartre had been fascinated by the glance of the other, but Jean-Paul had never seen Haley Lambert's eyes. *Being and Nothingness* would have been twice as long if he had. But then, if it were that long, *absolutely* no one would ever finish the book instead of *almost* no one . . .

She gave a mild kick, and a high heel fell to the floor. With her toes she rubbed his thigh and laughed at how quickly his erection returned. "You lovesick philosophical puppy."

John lifted her foot to kiss a silver toe ring, idly wondering if spittle would tarnish silver.

"That's nice," she said. "Maybe you should take off my other platform heel and keep worshipping until I get in the mood." She reached back for a book and scooted temptingly, but when he cut to look at her mid-section she wiggled her toes in his face. They were lovely, lovelier than the rings adorning them. He sighed and sat along the bedside, trying to see what she was reading . . . Byron. Maybe if she started *Don Juan* she'd pull him to her sooner. Didn't that poem get kinky right off the bat?

Outside in the neighborhood, summer students had started a party. Their music was anything but 60-cycle. Now Haley sighed, but John concentrated on her toes, taking them in his mouth and running his tongue over them to the tempo of Vivaldi until he felt her relax against the pillow. *Toe duty. A poor existential job*, he thought, torn between studying the tendons on her foot and catching sight of her lovely, lovely eyes.

The second season in Vivaldi started, and Haley shifted to say, "Free association." His brows arched quizzically, so she repeated, "Free association," and placed the book on her lap. "I say something, you respond." When she brushed his cheek with her ankle he nodded.

"Nietzsche."

"Friedrich."

She slapped her thighs in mock exaggeration. "John, this is supposed to be entertaining and informative, not insipid . . . Try again: Nietzsche."

"Freud."

"Libido."

"Vibrato."

They laughed.

"Vibrator, you mean, you lovesick puppy . . . Don Juan."

"Me and you'un."

"No rhyming, John."

"Why not?"

She moved a big toe to his nose and pushed lightly. "Because I said so, little boy . . . Don Juan."

"Truman Capote."

"Truman Capote?"

John shrugged.

"Clarissa Circle."

"Isolationism."

"Clarissa Circle."

"Walk garishly, yank little sticks."

"Is that an allusion?"

"President Teddy Roosevelt and his South American policy to keep Europe out. Walk softly and carry a *big* stick is what he said. Meaning troops and warships."

She momentarily spread her arms invitingly, then closed them to place her hands on her lap. "My own private tutor . . . Tudor."

"Shakespeare."

"Henry the Eighth."

John paused. Thinking of their backyard neighbor he almost said *religious fanaticism*, but caught himself and said, "British ale."

"British ale?"

"Sure, he's always pictured fat and red-jowled." John's back straightened to make a professorial point of sorts.

"You might have said pork, too."

"Might have."

She inhaled and looked at the closed curtain. He glanced there, and to his horror saw a half-foot gap. He jumped to close it and caught sight of the window in the boarding house behind them, where he thought he spotted a flash of fire, but it was so brief he wasn't sure. He leaned into the windowpane.

"He's still there, isn't he?" When John didn't answer, Haley continued, "John, I just turned to a poem by Byron entitled, 'When a Man Hath No Freedom To Fight For at Home.'" She laughed sharply, then asked in sing-song, "Can we agree that that's the case in this household, that you have no freedom to fight for at home?"

He remained pressed against the pane, gazing at that distant window, which had stolen the moment's humor and passion. Still, he replied that he would certainly agree to that proposition.

"Well, I've read the poem before and that's not really what Byron means. He means that when the home country is free a foolish man feels obliged to fight for freedom in other countries." He heard her shuffling along the headboard, presumably reaching for the book. "Here, listen:

'Then battle for freedom wherever you can,
And, if not shot or hanged, you'll get knighted.' "

John kept his grip on the curtain and turned to look at Haley, who said:

"If we changed 'knighted' to 'sainted' and mailed this poem to that faux-Christian sap in the window over there . . . is that what he's thinking?"

"He's hardly fighting for freedom."

"The British were hardly fighting for freedom in the 1800s, certainly not colonial freedom. But don't Born Again Christians claim that they give their will to Christ to find freedom?"

Whenever Haley thought hard she had a habit of tapping her foot—when she was deciphering poetry, for instance. John was surprised to see her doing it now, in the bed. It made him consider. Was religious fanaticism what he was undergoing? Giving his will to Haley Lambert, a twenty-five year old woman, in what might pass for idolatry, to find freedom? He'd volunteered to paint her fingernails emerald green the other night, and as he inhaled nail polish he had no worries about committees, about his book-in-progress, about students wanting A-pluses for C-minus work. But his Haley Lambert idolatry was a role, and roles are always momentary. Was their neighborhood berserker's role as firebrand Christian momentary? He'd been booted from campus last year for harassing a biology graduate student who mentioned Darwin. Would he carry his firebrand Christian role beyond momentary, carry it to his grave or to prison?

"What would rhyme with 'sainted'?" Haley asked, pulling John from his reveries. "Painted? Fainted? Hainted, as in ghosts, as in the Holy Ghost?"

"Don't mess with him, Haley."

She gave a mock kick of her foot. "Don't try to switch roles, Friedrich. I'm your Lou Salomé, and you're my slave. We don't want to pull out the whip and start potty training all over, do we?" With a grin she placed the book on the headboard and opened her arms. John walked toward her eyes, inhaling. "But don't worry, lover; this time I will surely take your advice. Christian or faux-Christian, I'm leaving him be."

Gray Billingsworth watched them enter the house, watched a light go on in the kitchen, another light in what he knew was the bedroom on the first floor. His eyes widened, for there was a gap in the curtain. Scanning both ways to make sure no one could see him, he stepped forward to again place his head against his room's window. But all he could make out was a slant of light with occasional shadows. It was just as well. He could imagine the professor shoving the young coed to her knees, slapping her and prying her mouth open, wallowing against her tanned face and her large innocent eyes to spray his lustful hot seed, making it fall on hard ground amongst thorns.

Then the shadow movements stopped, though the light remained. What was the heathen professor doing now? Watching his filthy seed drying on her lips and cheeks while he circled her kneeling body, yanking her hair, kicking her calves, stroking himself, and reciting some humanist slime? Staring at the smooth halves of her ass?

Father Williams said that humanists weren't the greatest enemies of Christianity, but that Christians were. How could he say that when his own younger brother had been killed by Charles Manson forty years ago after serving his country in the Marines? Manson listened to the Beatles, who were pop song humanists with their gurus and their fancy French horns. More popular than Jesus, they claimed. All their tapes and CDs should have been burned right then. Should still be burned. Father Williams said that protesting against abortion should be done carefully, so that women who were already confused and upset wouldn't become more so because of Christians. But the road of righteousness must be filled with swollen belly tribulation. The road of righteousness *was* tribulation.

Gray imagined dried baby skins hanging in the professor's bedroom. He'd be the type to get young students pregnant and make them bring back the dead aborted babies so he could hang them as trophies. Or maybe nurses from the university would abort the students in his bathroom, making them squat on the toilet or stretch their legs at forty-five degree angles in the bathtub or over filthy sheets clotted with old blood.

A shadow moved. Had the professor finished his spewing humanist cant and pushed her on her hands and knees to enter from the rear so that more seed would fall into stony places? Gray could see her spine in candlelight, its vertebrae prominent and twisted into waves of light and shadow from the professor's lunges. He heard her coughs and groans as the professor pushed her chin against the carpet to feel his manhood thrusting. Shove. Shove. Into the carpet to leave crisscrossing red on her face, for everyone to see. He shoved harder, harder until her head hit the wall.

Gray felt seepage against his pants and coughed heavily.

No man can serve two masters. Hypocrite! First cast out the beam out of thine own eye! He unzipped to see his erection, since he wore no underwear so his flesh might rub his blue jeans like sackcloth. Reaching for the candle he nearly dropped it because his palms were so sweaty, but then he swung the lit tongue of flame underneath his pubic hair, which flashed up. Stifling a yell, he dropped the candle and inhaled sharply, causing a low whistle. His belly button ached where the flame had concentrated. Some hair roots still glowed like coals. Batting back tears he stood to see that the bedroom drapes of the professor's house had been closed, so he rubbed his right palm over his sternum. *Blessed are they who hunger and thirst after righteousness: for they shall be filled. Ye are the light of the world. A city that is set on an hill cannot be hid.*

School would begin in two weeks and John was pushing for a vacation. Just last spring, with her girlfriends, Haley would have been the one pushing to drive to Atlanta or even Fort Lauderdale the very moment exams were over. Now she obsessed with preparing; she obsessed to improve her 3.86 undergraduate grade point to a perfect 4.0 in graduate school.

"Go, dearest one. Take him up on it. Don't be one more example that I'll be holding up to prove my thesis."

Clarissa Circle and she were walking back from the library. It was Ohio Valley hot and muggy, and Haley wished they'd driven, but Clarissa was an outdoor fanatic. Sweat was cupping in Clarissa's belly button, showing through her tight pink blouse. Walking into the library an hour before, Haley had watched every male eye turn toward Clarissa as her nipples erected from the air conditioning. Haley'd even recognized two guys she occasionally flirted with at the local bars in that gawking group. She had no particular desire to flirt with them anymore, and it wasn't because of John:

it was just that she felt that frivolous part of her life waning. Or maybe it *was* because of John.

"Where is it that he wants to go, anyway?"

"Some place called Helen, in Georgia. It's in the mountains. He says we can hike in the mornings, go tubing during the afternoons, and wine and dine at night."

"He's right, I've been there. The mountains are lovely and cool, especially considering this heat. You should take him up on it. What's the point in having a sugar daddy if you don't—"

Haley stopped abruptly in the sidewalk. She'd been cradling three library books about T. S. Eliot to her sternum; now she shoved them against her nipples. Having taken only one long stride, Clarissa turned and came back.

"That was my cynical joke, Haley, I'm sorry. I've watched you two enough to know that a great deal more than gold-digging is going on. Though I do suspect that John's the enamored one, poor boy." She paused and Haley blinked, her wiry calves tense. "Lovesick, my daddy used to say, like a pregnant sow before a trough." When Haley pursed her lips, Clarissa continued, "Oh yes, I'm straight from the hills, but not the hills of Kentucky. Tennessee." Clarissa raised her eyebrows and waited.

Haley thought of her own father, a mechanical engineer who still worked for the eastern Kentucky mines. He'd been born in Cincinnati, but by the time she was a teenager he'd lived in Paintsville forty-two years and was completely hillbilly-ized. The pregnant sow bit sounded exactly like something he'd say. He was sixty-four now and still worked. Having been raised by older parents made her comfortable with people like Clarissa and John. All this time she'd been staring at Clarissa, and it was the professor who blinked first. Haley exhaled.

"Haley, I've had a few sows at the trough in my time, if you'll excuse the sexual misnomer. Still do. There's a lovely chocolate detective whom I work with. At times, I suspect he'd jump into one of the shallow graves we investigate and let me cover him with topsoil if I told him that's what I wanted. Then, at other times . . . never mind. But you have John, and as far as I can tell the two of you are doing your best to ruin my theory about humans never touching. So . . . is my cynical comment about sugar daddies forgiven? Again, I'm sorry."

Haley nodded slowly, her chin touching one of the Eliot books. Then she took a breath. Clarissa Circle might be the loneliest person she'd ever met, despite all the men pawing at her. Haley smiled and could see that her smile lightened Clarissa, despite her cynical theory.

"Good. I really hope you don't put John through too many contortions. I saw him massaging your foot out on the balcony last night. He'd make quite a podiatrist."

Lowering her eyes, Haley grinned to herself and said, "Not too many contortions, no. He'd like it too much."

"Sharp girl. Sharp."

"It's a way to even up the age thing. We both agreed on that. We don't do it all the time."

"Roles."

"Yeah, but roles we both enjoy."

"But roles still."

"Professor—Clarissa, do you ever get tired of the no-touch thing?"

"Every night at eleven, Haley. Every night at eleven."

They waited on a traffic light. Behind them was a student bar. Haley heard someone shout her name so she turned. It was a guy she thought had already graduated; he held up a beer. She waved limply and turned back to watch the light. She'd dated him twice—one time too many. He was red-faced at twenty-three and likely to grow more so until mom and dad cut off the money.

"Cute," Clarissa commented.

"Yeah, but full of himself."

The light changed and they crossed the street. Fumes from fresh tar combined with the heat to send a wave of nausea through Haley. "So . . . this detective. Do you love him?" From the corner of her left eye, Haley saw Clarissa Circle's mouth twitch.

"I wish I could. I mean, I really think that I wish I could. He's a gentleman, he's bright, and he's a regular jalapeño in bed. A credit to his root and his roots."

"So . . ."

A car drove by and honked. Clarissa waved at the two male students, her bracelet jangling.

"So his name is Willy. Of the wandering ways, I call him. Willy's as obsessive in making connections as I am in dissolving them. We were investigating a corpse found by two students near the river, and he became convinced that this certain used bookstore guy had some stolen stamps lost in his shop just because a third cousin of the bookstore guy's uncle, who may not have been an uncle but only a half-brother to the father, that this half uncle had taken a train to Boston about the same time, that is, twenty years before, when said person by the river became a corpse by the river, and because Boston is where the stamps were stolen, and because the guy who'd stolen them supposedly drove from Boston to sell them on a horse farm in Paris, Kentucky, or maybe the other way around, and because this same third cousin of the maybe uncle had once worked on a couple of horse farms in Bourbon County." Clarissa's high heels hit against the sidewalk to punctuate her tirade. She inhaled theatrically to continue, "Then somehow Willy tossed in a virgin, underage hillbilly who'd become pregnant because . . ." Clarissa growled like a mad dog. "Because, because, because. It was a nuclear chain of events worthy of Los Alamos or Stephen Hawking's favorite emerging supernova."

After Clarissa's mock declamation, Haley perversely stepped on a sidewalk crack and made a wish that Clarissa would get involved and marry the detective. The woman was a walking can of gasoline ready to explode any male nearby. Supposedly John only played tennis with her and they'd never slept together. Haley wasn't sure whether that made matters better or worse. She blinked, realizing that she was suffering a bout of jealousy. So much for roles. Inspired, Haley said, "Sounds to me like you and the detective are made for one another. Yin and yang, opposites attract and all that."

Haley listened to Clarissa's high heels clicking on the sidewalk for at least a dozen steps. Clarissa wore high heels everywhere except on Indian digs and criminal investigations. She told Haley that the heels put her mind in one gear, while knee-high rubber or leather boots put it in another. With one last hard clop of a heel, Clarissa acknowledged what Haley'd said:

"Yin and yang, eh? Well, that's just it. More roles. We'd not see one another as Clarissa and Willy. We'd see one another as Professor Circle of the weird decomposition theory of human interaction, and Detective Willy Cox, of the weird gravitational theory of human interaction."

They were approaching a section near the campus that began an upscale swing, peppering meticulous houses with tiny meticulous lawns among student ghetto rentals. Two plastic hummingbird feeders separated by a statue of Saint Francis stood on a space of bright green grass that appeared to have been freshly cropped by a stable of racehorses. Haley stopped, despite the heat, to watch a blue hummingbird.

"They terrify me. They have since I was a kid." Clarissa closed her hand on Haley's left arm. "Too fast. I'm afraid they're going to poke out my eyes."

The hummingbird darted toward something—another hummingbird. They seemed to be fighting, though for all Haley knew they were making love. Clarissa's nails bit into her arm, but it was Haley who finally started them walking again. She then forced Clarissa to take a turn before their street, for she wanted to see the front of the house where the faux-Christian weirdo lived. The street was quiet, lined with large pin oaks, which was a bonus, since their own street was a busy thoroughfare devoid of shade. Clarissa let go her grip of Haley.

"I'll tell you the weirdest thing. He, the detective, Willy, was right about the damned stamp. Almost right, anyway. There wasn't just one, but two of them together like Siamese twins, and they showed up pressed inside a book in the guy's shop about a year ago."

"Is this the couple who started a pornographic poetry publishing house?"

"This is they."

Sniffing the Eliot books, Haley knew that very moment that she was going to write a pornographic poetry collection and send it to the bookstore couple. God, did that mean she'd have to start hanging around the English department's creative writing weirdos, the ones who yapped more than they wrote, certainly more than they read?

She and Clarissa were halfway up the street, with Haley proclaiming her inspiration to compose a pornographic poetry collection. Clarissa, bemused, became involved enough to promise a few tales about her many lovers. Suddenly Clarissa grabbed Haley's arm.

"Change the subject from sex. Don't talk about anything personal. Follow my lead. Trust me." Clarissa shifted her voice "Did you read the newspaper about the new suicide bombings?"

Haley glanced to where Clarissa had been looking and saw a pimply kid with reddish hair standing in a yard, staring at his bare feet. Clarissa elbowed her. "Did you read about them, the suicide bombings?" Haley said, "Sure" and offered a fictitious comment about forty-five people being killed the day before. She bit her lip as soon as she finished, thinking of John's age, exactly forty-five.

When she walked by the student with a t-shirt depicting a grisly bleeding Jesus hanging on a cross, her eyes widened and her breath caught. His feet were glistening with what must have been honey and they were covered with ants crawling up well beyond his ankles. He had to be the faux-Christian who'd been staring at John and her. He never looked up, though she heard a whimper as they passed. Neither she nor Clarissa could talk until they turned onto another street.

When Haley told John about the faux-Christian, he wanted to call the police.

"You're the one who said to leave him alone," Haley protested. "Besides, there's no law against standing in an anthill and whimpering." Haley looked out their study's window toward the boarding house. "When I told Clarissa how that guy is always staring from his window at us, she did offer to give me one of her detective friend's old revolvers."

"Guns," John said with a dismissive wave of his hand. "Let's just go to Helen. Maybe he'll be locked away by the time we get back."

So they left for Georgia early the next morning. Haley laughed when they walked into Helen from their hotel. "Mein Gott, Friedrich, you haf broughten mir to your faterland."

John reached for her eternally soft hand, and swung it as if they were Jack and Jill. "You're going to need to write several reams of Teutonic porno poetry after this visit."

Haley's porno poetry collection had captivated them on the drive down, and they'd swapped rhymes about *cock* and *rock, cunt* and *hunt, pudenda* and *mind benda*—no, no *prick benda*, one of them corrected.

"After our visit? I think not, John. During. While we hike, while we drink wine, while we walk around in the shops, while we make love. That'll add spice to matters."

"I'd say matters are plenty spicy already."

And they were. Because they'd left Lexington well before dawn, it was not even noon as they walked the town's cobbled sidewalk and took in its sham German housing and shops, its baskets and baskets of violet petunias and crimson begonias. They each breathed in the mountain air and thought . . . absolutely nothing. Or, Zen-like, they thought, *Mountain air.* Or, *I should smile. I should smile a whole lot at everything and everybody and . . .* so they smiled. *Guten tag, guten tag.*

On that first day they didn't make it out of the village, despite their plans to nature hike. An elevated park overlooking the town did attract them, however. Up there John pushed Haley in a swing until they felt their faces burning.

So downward to the drug store they walked, amazed at how the banality of obtaining, say, Coppertone sunscreen was elevated to the electrical. Or, say, of how buying two iced teas with lemon turned oceanic. Each of them felt like the new laser guns they'd heard about on NPR while driving down, impeccably pure lasers relentlessly seeking one another despite any and all worldly interference. With unusual tenderness Haley stood under an awning and rubbed sunscreen on John's beak of a nose as people walked by and smiled, stared, or turned away. She sniffled some scent in the lotion and worried that her allergies might deliver a migraine, but then her vision, her breath, her pores remained so clear and acute that she was sure migraines could never visit her again.

Later in a gift shop, spotting John on the other side of a display of German beer steins, Haley thought of Donne's poem "A Valediction Forbidding Mourning," wherein two lovers, bodily separated by distance, remained spiritually attached like the top of a two-legged schoolchild's compass.

While she thought this, John busily opened and re-opened the lid to a beer stein to let it clink. He was thinking of the clunky dances that Sartre put his false-stepping humans through whenever they promoted bad faith. Bad Faith was something John was questioning lately. He remembered an odd memorial notice in a Memphis newspaper where he attended a conference. A disturbing photo of a criminal-eyed black man in his mid-twenties was adorned by text underneath that droned: "I hate how bad you was and what evil things you did to your friends and family, but the bond between mother and son outlast a lifetime. We are soul mates beyond life. I love you and always will." No mention of the cause of death, no enumeration of just how bad this glaring son was. Sitting under a glittery poster of Elvis, John had flinched at the impoverished grammar and overblown sentiment of unconditional love. Now, well, now he wasn't so sure.

He spotted Haley inspecting a hand-blown glass frog. As her petite frame quivered with laughter in the nervous way she had, he smiled. But his eyes widened when she opened her purse and put the green frog in it. Shoplifting? A lump formed in his stomach. No, she pulled the frog out again with a fold of money and counted. With a small stomp of her small foot, she placed the frog back on the shelf.

He turned before she spotted him. He'd not held with that Memphis mother's ne'er-ending love. However fleetingly, he'd envisioned a headline in the *Lexington Herald* proclaiming, "Professor's Concubine Jailed on Georgia Shoplifting Charges." He remembered young Francis, a student from three years before, and how he'd seemed so enamored of the redheaded Althea who sat near him. But then when Althea blew her brains out on a tornado-filled Monday and Francis's own roommate died from a tornado in a statistician's nightmare that same Monday, Francis hardly missed a beat as far as attendance. Back by Friday, ready to give a report. Life drizzles onward. Well, maybe young Francis was right.

John Hart spotted a store surveillance camera. Had that stopped Haley? *Why, Zarathustra, did you ever descend from the mountain to the valley, where life grows so muddled?* Then, surprised, he felt Haley's warm hip against his. His hip burned. Slipping his arm around her, he rested a palm on her pelvis and closed his eyes. Breathe out. Breathe in. Were particles of Haley filling his lungs? Breathe in. Breathe in.

Later, they stopped before a jewelry store's display window to stare at a clock, just as an erratic spring shoved its cuckoo onto a wobbly perch. Three in the afternoon. It had taken three rebuttals, the magical three of any fairy tale, to make John stop offering to buy Haley the glass frog. Unknown to him, Haley remained adamant because Clarissa's accusation of "sugar daddy"—even though retracted—left her sensitive to the disparity of her and John's income.

The cuckoo seemed ready to fall off its yellow perch. John placed his ear against the store's window. "It's whistling," he said. He looked at Haley. "A whistling woman supposedly brings bad luck. But your whistle would bring good luck." Haley grinned and whistled "Hotel California." Matters would improve with the fall, for she'd have a paying research assistantship. Pressing her ear against the glass she stared into John's brown eyes.

Later, on that first evening while drinking beer from ludicrously tall pilsner glasses alongside a river, as vacationers tubed by in blue, yellow, or mint green tubes, time refuted itself in fairy tale manner. *Rumpelstiltskin*, each of them thought from their balcony table overlooking the river. *The magic word to capture a soul.* "Here," John said when Haley returned from the women's restroom. He pushed a bar napkin toward her:

The Theoretics of Love
Like Victorian ghosts we flash,
And though no ectoplasm stays behind
Our skins share a turbulent rash
As the heat we bear unwinds and winds.
So this is my theory of love:
It comes in squirts and secretions
It comes in coos of a mourning dove
It comes in cum, but never in depletion
It always comes—like cold breath on a morn
Or sweat in a hot afternoon sun.
It imparts lightness to be borne;
It offers a Milky Way to be run.
Thus thrives our love, a racer against time
A bard, whose eyes but glitter rhyme.

"A porno love sonnet!" Haley cooed, primly folding the napkin and placing it in her patent leather purse with a snap.

On the second day they drove to Anna Beulah Falls. Another fairy tale:

the lovely and sole daughter of a Confederate major who'd been widowed during the war. Buy the falls to name them after her, Daddy. Give her a chunk of the grand old South. Immortalize her beyond any convections that the next century's Einsteinian geometries might convect. Just so, in a photo reproduced from a daguerreotype, Anna Beulah remained serene, while her 1800s neckline tickled her stately chin; while her falls—actually two conjoined falls—cascaded, frolicked and frothed in the mountain air. But say, had Daddy glimpsed a vision of daughter—whose beauty so resembled Mamma's—and himself illicitly conjoined?

Did one of them, both of them, imagine that because of their age disparity? John and Haley, that is. Daddy and Miss Anna Beulah, that is. The water of the falls roared.

"Let's walk," one of them urged. And they did, for moving is more real than thinking. Heraclitus said that. Truckers have said it. Cowboys have said it. Willie Nelson and Waylon Jennings have said it. The philosopher Gassendi said it. Everyone but Descartes seemed to know its truth. "I walk; therefore I am." And so they walked and drank and danced and ate their way through a fairy tale town and fairy tale time. Rumpelstiltskin.

On the third day they let the river ease the late July heat. Tethering their rental tubes together they eventually drifted between a young couple having a water-gun fight with huge lemon-colored water guns that surely were modeled after lasers.

"*Mi abuelo tiene más.*"

John was so busy splashing the boy and girl shooting the water guns that he didn't hear one of the Mexican teens floating ahead blurt this to his three friends, who laughed, looking at John, then Haley. *My grand-dad has more*, a play on the suggestive colloquial expression *My man has more. That's right,* Haley thought, *he does have more. Screw the four of your pigeonholing minds*. It amazed her how liberal young people always judged themselves to be when compared to their parents, but how they inevitably thumped with their parents' rigidity, pushing it into a slightly different slot, like a youngster might painstakingly thump a cube of wood into a triangular hole.

On the fourth and last morning they walked so relentlessly that Haley wondered if maybe John *had* overheard the Mexican boy's comment from the previous afternoon and was consequently trying to prove his steady, sturdy health. Then she began to fret that he was working up courage to ask her to marry him. Surely not. She listened to her footsteps. It was so quiet that she heard the stream before she saw it.

John, well, John watched Haley rush toward a stream, take off her shoes, and dangle her bare feet. To his right, a rusted automobile door leaned against a rotting fencepost. If we walk this entire and full day, he thought, we can turn one day into two, or even a magical three. Our eyes and all our senses can store a great lump of matter that we can knead and fold to let quietly rise, so that in a future it will serve as proof to bond any argument, hurt, or misunderstanding. Yes, this discarded automobile door. Yes, the fence-post. And a secluded spot to make love. A bird alighting on our shoulders after a particularly passionate kiss. A bee stinging our elbows. Our tendons stretched and sore. We'll knead all that so we'll remember.

He inhaled with a hiss as cold water splashed his back. Turning, he managed to dodge another handful.

"Wake u-up," she sang. "Professor John is drifting far into philosophy-land again."

"Ambulamus, ergo summus," he replied, walking to the creek's bank and proffering a hand after stepping up on a flat boulder just above her.

"What's that mean?" She suspiciously appraised his extended hand.

"We walk; therefore we exist." He twitched his fingers. When she took them he pulled her up then abruptly sat on the boulder and yanked her over his lap to give her bottom a hard smack.

She twisted. "John Hart, I'm gonna beat you blue for doing that."

"First a kiss."

Still on his lap, she sat up and drove her tongue into his mouth. He thought he heard singing, or a kettledrum. Of course it was his heart. He reached down to touch the boulder, searching for Victorian ectoplasmic residue.

They stood and walked. Long enough that they both wanted not to make love but take a nap when they came upon an abandoned grove of what appeared to be plum trees. So they hid from sight and sun in the thickest part and slept.

Until one of them moved. Then they awoke to connect their lips as a cloud scudded overhead, and then they did make slow, side-by-side love, climaxing together—why not? It was a fairy tale time, despite the twigs digging into their sides. So why not? John was still partially hard inside her when Haley screamed: an orange-red hummingbird was darting over them. The bird paid no attention; it was concentrating on a trumpet vine growing on a nearly dead plum tree.

"I was never afraid of them until Clarissa said they could poke out your eyes."

John put his hand over her eyes, letting her peek through his fingers at the bird.

"Another contradiction from the good professor Clarissa. The bird would have to touch you to do that."

"It's just humans that can't touch in her world, John."

"She's brilliant but nuts, Haley. Abused as a child."

"Really?" Haley pulled his hand from her eyes, but put it back, for the hummingbird darted to a flower closer to them.

"I don't know. She once said something about an alcoholic father. She . . . well, you'll surely find this out anyway . . . she was raped about three years ago and killed the guy with an automatic pistol."

It was Haley's turn to inhale. "God, no wonder she keeps saying what she does."

"No wonder," John agreed.

Forty minutes later Haley spotted the notice of a bluegrass festival at the state park, just as they were about to leave for town. The festival was oddly labeled "Kitchen Instruments," which she first took to indicate Julia Child, or maybe how to boil down molasses with local artisan Johnny Jim Chipwood. But then she spotted a list: washbasin, washboard, pie pans, and spoons.

So they bought tickets and grabbed a blanket from their hotel room after filling their Thermos with hot tea to fight off the chill air during the Georgia mountain night. Luckily, they arrived early, for over five hundred people would eventually show. Twice they heard a rumor that Tony Rice was going to play because he was a friend of one of the bands. At ten o'clock, when the stars glistened in their full mountain splendor, this rumor proved true.

As Tony Rice sang “Molly and Tenbrooks,” the two of them leaned to touch heads.

Run old Molly, run. Run old Molly run,

Tenbrooks’ gonna beat you, in the hot mornin’ sun.

Above, the Milky Way swirled through planets, stars, galaxies, and black holes. Because of the Ohio Valley smog back in Kentucky, this was the first time either had been able to see it in years.

Classes had been in session for over a month. After prodding from both Haley and Clarissa, John again took up his book, *Nietzsche’s Contrarieties.* Odd, he thought, that Clarissa would show concern. Was she turning over a new leaf, Everyone Touches Everyone? As for Haley, he promised that he would dedicate the work to her, alternating between, “For Haley, my Lou,” in reference to Lou Salomé or “For Haley, my prod from peak to peak,” in reference to Nietzsche’s claim that his rarified ideas danced from mountaintop to mountaintop.

“That’s why,” John said one evening as they enjoyed sweater weather on their elevated deck, “that’s why Nietzsche is so filled with contradictions. It’s his concept of the necessary mutability of truth—”

“Necessary?” Haley interrupted. “Mutability? Truth?”

“Ah, to the quick. You, my lovely Lou, should be a philosopher.”

“No thanks. A porno poet cuts closer to the bone.”

Wind scattered early leaves onto the deck, and John cupped his coffee mug with both hands. He looked to the faux-Christian’s window, which had remained dark for over a week.

“I heard that he was recently escorted off campus after disrupting a sociology class in feminism,” Haley commented, following John’s gaze.

“He did a bit more than disrupt: he got into a shoving match with two students.”

“Female?”

“Egalitarian, one each. A year ago he spit at a young biology teaching assistant who mentioned evolution.”

Leaves rattled across the deck of the balcony.

"Why'd you buy this place, John? I mean, a house with four bedrooms."

"Three years ago, I was supposed to marry a math PhD candidate. She had an eight-year old girl . . ."

"Okay . . ."

"The girl was sweet. Ashley was her name. Huge eyes like yours, but bright blue. Mom was supposed to get a job with Lexmark working in computer security. That was the plan. But three weeks away from my tenure, she interviewed for a job at Michigan State. The lure of the big time, I suppose."

"Do you ever hear from her?"

"Not the mom. Can you believe that I get birthday and Christmas cards from Ashley?" John shrugged, remembering that he hadn't gotten one his last birthday. He'd been so wrapped up with Haley that lacuna had slipped by.

"Andrea was thirty when she had Ashley," he added.

LEAVES SKITTERED ACROSS HALEY'S foot. *Thirty*, she thought. John was pretending to look at his manuscript, but she could tell by the way he played with his beard that he was thinking, *Thirty*, also. Four-and-a-half more years, just when she would be maybe halfway through her PhD coursework. Women were having babies at forty these days. If a woman kept in shape, didn't smoke or drink too much, well . . . at her forty, John would be sixty. *Thirty-five then*, she thought.

A scraping came from the patio directly below. Through the decking, Haley saw movement; then she heard the sound of someone trying the sliding glass door.

"Stay up here," John whispered, handing her his cell phone. "Call the police." He grabbed the hammer that he'd been using to nail down loose decking and shouted, "I'm calling the cops! Get out of here now!" Haley dialed 911 and made a grab for John, but he eluded her and ran through the upstairs study to the stairway.

"Emergency."

"Someone's breaking in our house."

There was a crash of glass.

"I can't hear you."

"Someone's breaking in our house! 815 Woodland Way. Help us! John?! John?!"

GRAY BILLINGSWORTH HAD STRAPPED a two-and-a-half gallon can of gasoline to his stomach and another to his back. He had been letting his hair grow for the last two months, just like Samson. Even his pubic hair had started to grow back, he noted, taking that as an omen.

He was dressed in black, to fight the blackness of Satan. He'd even blacked his face with shoe polish, and its odor had combined with his two-day fast to make him visionary. After he crossed the fence he unscrewed the tops to both cans and felt cool gasoline evaporate against his stomach, felt cool gasoline evaporate against the back of his right buttock and thigh.

He stopped under a crabapple tree to see if he could hear the sex-talk the two of them were making. "Eight-year-old girl . . . blue eyes . . . Do you ever hear from her?" He grimaced, for the girl's voice made him spill more gasoline and some of it ran into the infection around his belly button, the spot he let fester as a reminder of his sins. This was no time to think of pain; no time to think of his leering, lisping hillbilly mother; no time to think of Father Williams and his weak Christianity. It was time to be a dynamic Christian, a Samson! The girl was the real sinner, she had seduced the doddering professor. Hadn't she seen the ants on his ankles? Hadn't she refused to offer help? Or to stop and pray? Love thy neighbor as thyself.

Running through grass to the house he bumped into the grill and bounded away, fearing it would explode him before he could reach the whore. But nothing happened. He pulled two lighters from his pocket, bent to spill gas on one arm, then the other. And gas ran along his spine with a chill, too. This was better than what the Muslims were doing. It was more pure, for he was bringing down an actual whore sinner. He tried the sliding door, but it was locked. Hearing shouting from above he picked up a potted plant to break the door then unlatch it. Once inside, he looked up to see the professor coming at him with something raised in his hand.

"Why do the heathen rage?" Gray shouted, trying to evade the falling hammer, which caught his shoulder anyway. "Not you, the whore," he pleaded, slipping on tile wet with gas and crawling toward the steps. But the hammer was in the air again. He flicked both lighters. One was wet with gasoline. One caught.

"MA'AM, YOU PROBABLY SHOULD move away now. They're about to bring him—"

"No. I cain't." Haley shook her head. "I can't," she corrected.

And it was true. She had to see John Hart's body. Burnt or not, she had to see his body. She laughed hoarsely then coughed from the smoke of her menthol cigarette mixing with the houses' embers. When the fireball had ripped up the steps to blow through the study onto the deck, she'd picked up her cigarettes and both her and John's manuscripts. The manuscripts had scattered as she ran along the roof and finally jumped, screaming John's name.

Her cough turned into a low laugh as two firefighters carried the body bag down the front porch steps. She leaned to touch John, but the thought of the warm, greasy-looking plastic body bag stopped her. Instead, she nervously jiggled her foot. She watched the body bag being loaded into the ambulance: its top sucked inward as it was tilted, as if meat and vegetables had slid to the bottom of a just-boiled prepared food pouch. Someone inside shouted that they'd found another body. Moments later she watched two more firemen carrying out a heavier bag.

"Was there a hammer near him, in his hand?" She pointed at the bag.

"A hammer?"

A fireman stepping behind the two carrying the bag said, "Yes ma'am, this one was holding a hammer. He must have kept one hell of a grip—" Another fireman coughed and the one speaking looked away.

The hammer that John carried down to hit the faux-Christian asshole. She could still hear that stupid hill twang screaming "Why do the heathen rage!" So the body that she thought was John's really belonged to the asshole. And she had been ready to touch it, to caress it. She stared at a fold in the black bag before her as it reflected a neon street lamp. She nodded at the two firemen who'd stopped before her; then her laughter punctuated the night air to break toward the harvest moon. A hand touched her shoulder and she remembered John's soft touch when he told her how light-heartedness went a long damned way in his book, then gawkily asked if she'd move in with him. She turned expectantly, though of course it wasn't John but a fireman her age with smudges across his forehead. She shrugged his hand off and kept laughing—for herself, for John Hart the existentialism scholar, for his lost book, for her silly scattered pornographic poems, for the asshole faux-Christian neighbor, for the young fireman, for the whole wasp's nest that called itself humanity. She laughed until her frame shook. "I almost touched that asshole, I almost touched that asshole."

Thinking she heard a voice saying, "Come home with me, darling; come home," she turned to see Clarissa walking toward her, carrying an Indian blanket streaked with red lightning and green prowling bears.

"Professor Circle. He's gone. Gone. I almost touched—"

"Yes. I know." Clarissa put the blanket around Haley, unsure whether she or Haley was trembling so violently. She looked to see Willy Cox writing in his yellow detective pad. "Yes, I know. Almost," she whispered.

15.

The Lover's Paradox

Year 2005

(Francis, Leigh)

I left the storm-splintered house just after dawn and walked until just a little before dark. Wind occasionally rattled a stop sign, but no more rain fell, no more lightning struck. Spotting two buildings, a bookstore and a sandwich shop, I walked behind them and lay down against a stack of tree limbs that some industrious soul had already sawed into logs after they had fallen from the tornado. What was left of the oak stood halfway into the back yard, ripped red and white like scarred flesh.

Lying there at sunset, I realized that my right hip and both legs were sore from where the tornado had tossed me. I guess that walking all day had kept them loose. Simon—or was it Althea?—once mentioned a philosopher who mocked Descartes by saying, "I walk, therefore I am." That thought came to me; I understood it until dark, and then I didn't understand it anymore. I just smelled the stacked logs and watched a full moon rising over an old apartment building. A light went on to reveal a couple arguing. She threw something at him. After a while, the light went off. The sky was clear, the moon kept rising.

When the sun came up I smelled bread baking in the sandwich shop and got mad at myself for being hungry. How could I be hungry when my friends were dead? So I walked. But just one hour later I had to stop and eat. And when I ate, I knew I had to go back to the house.

There was a note on the door: *Francis, we would like to talk with you. We are taking Simon back to New Jersey for burial. Talking with you would help us so much. And it would help you, too, wouldn't it? Here is our number.* The note was written in an elegant left-hand slant with tiny curls at the end of the *o*'s and slashes instead of dots over the *i*'s. Of course it was Simon's mother's writing: I recognized it from all the gifts she'd lavished on me and Simon.

The phone inside the house worked, so I stepped over debris to call—not Simon's mom but my mom. Aunt Grace answered.

"We've been frantic trying to get you. We—"

"Simon and Althea are both dead," I said.

"I'll be there in two hours, less. Can you stay there, or would you rather—"

"I'll be on the front porch."

But first I walked out to the back porch and found the Saint Francis statue lying in what remained of the garage. It looked like the two had met halfway in the yard for a slumber party. The girl from next door, the one who sometimes haunted the window that I sometimes watched, walked up with a tiny plate of cookies and a Coke. "I'm sorry about your roommate," she said. "I called the ambulance. An old couple came here an hour ago. They came twice yesterday afternoon, too. His parents. They left a note. These are for you."

"Thanks." I took the food. I wanted to lean on her and cry, but she nodded and walked away.

A + Ω

My aunt insisted that she should rent an apartment and that I should live with her until the end of summer semester. She also insisted that I go to a grief counselor. The counselor said that I should make a list of all the things that I liked about my two friends.

"Three," I said.

"Beg your pardon?"

"Three. Althea was pregnant."

"Yours?"

I nodded.

"A list doesn't always work. Why don't you just talk to your aunt and me about how you feel. And stay busy with your classes. That helps ease the pain."

But I made three lists anyway and framed them from three frames that Simon used in his Holocaust shrine in the basement. That shrine, being in the basement, was untouched. It was stupid of us not to go down there during the tornado. It was stupid of me not to call Althea. It was stupid of me not to use a rubber. It was stupid of me to ask if the baby was mine. I started making other lists, three and four and five a day, most of them filled with stupid things I'd stupidly done.

I went back to classes Friday. Professor Hart nodded when I walked in. A couple of students stared. By the end of the next week, no one was sitting near me. Professor Hart told me I didn't have to do the St. Francis spiel that he'd assigned me, since it was extra credit anyway. But a month ago in Bardstown Father McKenna had set my confessional penance as reading a book about St. Francis, and I had to do that if I was going to be clear of the mortal sin of sleeping with Althea out of wedlock. So I told Professor Hart that I wanted to do it still, if he didn't mind. Anyway, I'd already bought the stupid book.

That night I considered cutting my palms so that I could show the class what stigmata meant, but I didn't. Instead, I told them about St. Francis and the wolf of Gubbio that Francis talked into not killing any more people. I told them how St. Francis's father disinherited Francis. I told them how Francis of Assisi addressed every natural phenomenon as "brother" or "sister" in his preaching and in his *Canticle to Brother Sun*. "Sister Moon, Brother Worm, Sister Nightingale," he called them. I told the class about Simon's conjecture that if St. Francis and Spinoza had lived in the same century the two would have melded Christianity and Judaism into a New Age pantheism before New Age even became vogue. But I didn't really mention Simon because that would make the class and Professor Hart feel bad. I told them about Sister Clare, the patron saint of piano players. I told them how she and Francis held onto a Platonic relationship that went beyond men and women, sort of maybe like Jean Paul Sartre and Simone de Beauvoir, whom Althea admired so. But I didn't really mention Althea either, because that would make the class and Professor Hart feel bad.

So my penance was completed, but I didn't feel the giddy lightness I usually felt after confession. Instead I kept losing weight. At first I thought this was because I'd quit working at the greasy spoon where I could eat all the chili and hamburgers I wanted. My aunt thought it was because I was grieving over Althea and Simon. So did my mom. I never told them about little Simon or little Simone, whichever. My aunt dipped into her savings and drove me to Newport, Kentucky, where Althea was buried. The next weekend she flew with me to Newark, where Simon was buried. Althea's grave was flat and modern so that a tractor could pull a Bush Hog to mow over it. Simon's grave wasn't a grave but a walk-in mausoleum. I left a white votive candle burning at each.

By mid-August, fall semester began and my aunt's leave time ran out. She left me alone in the apartment, though she and my mom thought I should get a roommate. My eyes bugged at that. Since I had one last basic curriculum elective to take, I took physical anthropology with Dr. See-See Bones. Of course that wasn't her real name: everyone just called her that for some stupid student reason. Simon and Althea had loved her, so I took the class. My grief counselor agreed and thought it might help purge the guilt. I wasn't sure I felt guilty, just stupid. I should have, I realized, left two votive candles at Althea's grave. Stupid, see what I mean? I started another list, on purple paper to honor Simon.

Outside, someone on my block was cutting grass and I could smell it. I guess that's what reminded me of Althea's grave: a man was cutting grass in the cemetery when we visited, riding right over the graves just like nothing but old chicken bones were buried underneath.

Besides taking physical anthropology, I wound up in a probability class because of scheduling problems. My academic advisor thought it couldn't hurt things and might give me a different insight. But just like with the first philosophy class Simon and I took, this one was taught by a graduate student, and she was nearly as ignorant as the philosophy guy. One day she mentioned game theory and dismissed it as a childish concept originating with warmongers. She actually used that word, *warmongers*. America was already in Afghanistan and talking about going into Iraq. She also mentioned fuzzy logic, calling it nothing but probability dressed up with fancy jargon. This sent me to the computer that night. Two days later I burned all my lists except the first three that I'd made and framed.

A + Ω

My grief counselor told me that it would be normal to see Simon and Althea in other people. He was right on about that, but I didn't think it would keep happening in the fall. Stupid, again. Like eight weeks would be enough to forget. Just walking around campus I counted fourteen Simons and eighteen Altheas by October. I had no idea there were that many skinny students with hooked noses or freckles and red hair. So what I did instead of making lists of my stupidities was wait around where these people would show up. Benign stalking. And what I did instead of listing past stupidities, was to list probabilities. A book I was reading about fuzzy logic by a guy named Kosko claimed that some philosopher (Althea and Simon would have thrown a fit at the adjective "some"—"Can't you be more specific?" they'd surely snarl), some philosopher said all humans have a probability instinct. Oh yeah? Just what instinct would have ever said that your roommate would be killed by a tornado on the same afternoon that your lover put a revolver to her skull and pulled the trigger? Even good old Ms. Samantha Johns, the dork graduate student teaching probability, would have sense enough to balk at that likelihood.

I refined my lists by combining game theory and probability. I assigned the look-alike students science-fiction names to keep some type of distance. One of Simon's look-alikes, for instance, became Zorn:

Zorn sees that his roommate is being an asshole. He takes a spatula that he used previously to make roux for beef burgundy and thwacks his roommate into sense.	Zorn sees that his roommate is being an asshole. He emails his roomie's girlfriend and they concoct a plan to get roomie drunk over a Dracula movie and talk sense to him.
Zorn sees that his roommate is being an asshole. He walks out on the porch to talk with him, but this does no good. He sniffs the air with his fine-tuned nose, then goes inside to sulk and gets killed by an errant tornado.	Zorn sees that his roommate is being an asshole. He calls his mother, who wires him enough money to move out of the house that very hour. His roomie finally notices Zorn is gone when he walks into Zorn's empty bedroom. The stupid roomie gets killed by an errant tornado.

As I kept studying game theory, I realized that I was leaving the roommate—we've figured out who he is, correct?—out of the decision-making process. Very convenient for a Roman Catholic conscience, but very untrue to game theory, where each participant must make a choice. So I was being as stupid as my probability teacher, in whose class I was getting A-pluses with all the ridiculous extra points she kept tossing at each test. My first test grade was 117%. What's the probability of that? I realized that I hadn't worked fuzzy logic into the scenarios yet, either. All the choices came up one way or another. Death or Life; Love or Hate; Abortion or Birth; Tornado or Clear Summer Sky. Lovely whites and blacks.

Professor See-See Bones, meanwhile, was going hard at her infamous No One Touches Anyone theory. I guess she wasn't getting laid, though a rumor kept going around that she'd capped some guy who'd been raping her, capped him eleven times, blasting his brains all over a house. If that was true, it seemed to contradict her theory. She certainly touched him, right? But in spirit I knew exactly what she meant, so after Halloween I decided that I wanted her to look at one of my new, improved tables of what I came to think of as the lover's paradox.

This table concerned an Althea look-alike. It held six options and input from both actors, including the mystical roomie, so the game theory part was now pat, though the fuzzy logic component still evaded me. Nonetheless, I figured my table would vindicate Professor Circle's viewpoint, for in only one of the six scenarios do the couple, whom I'd named Altair and Franza, in only one scenario do they, ahem, *couple*. In this new table, keeping the original game theory spirit, I assigned numerical values to emotions: complete happiness got 10; 5 represented partial happiness at overcoming; and -10 represented complete pain at being thwarted in love. After brooding I decided that -5 would be appropriate partial pain for someone who was being teased with flirtation. Other small notes: Lover Altair's happiness value is listed first, Lover Franza's second, separated by a comma. "Respond" means that the actor receives romantic advances favorably. "Rebuff" means the opposite. "Flirt" indicates ambivalent teasing action. Lover Altair's (A) actions run horizontally; Lover Franza's (B), vertically. Simple, like life.

LOVER ALTAIR'S AFFAIRS

		Respond	***Rebuff***	***Flirt***
		HAPPINESS VALUE	HAPPINESS VALUE	HAPPINESS VALUE
LOVER	RESPOND	10, 10	10, 10	10, 10
FRANZAS	REBUFF	5, -5	-5,-5	-5,-5
ACTIONS	FLIRT	-5, 5	5, -5	-5, -5

Note again that chances are only one out of nine for happiness, the asymptotic opposite of Russian roulette, which offers one out of nine for a bullet to the brain from a nine-chambered .22. So: falling in love is like playing Russian roulette with a revolver loaded with eight bullets.

I anonymously placed the table along with a typed explanation in Professor Circle's faculty mailbox. The next day in class, she not only thanked the anonymous donor but displayed it on PowerPoint, adding only one refinement: in her mind, she said, it wouldn't be fair to say the chances were one out of nine, because in love you have to repeat the table every day, so it was really like waking up each morning and spinning a revolver's cylinder and pulling the trigger before going to work. Which significantly lowered long-term odds. My probability teacher, however, pointed out that the odds still came to one out of nine each day, regardless of the previous day's results.

Not if you were dead from a bullet to the brain from the previous day, I told her.

A + Ω

It wasn't until my second year of part-time graduate school when one Altair finally attracted Franza. (Again, we know who he is, don't we?) The middle stuff between consisted of books, a 4.0 average, the President's list, graduation with Mom and Aunt slobbering all over me, a job at Lextronics, and my continual benign stalking.

I suppose it was good that this Altair didn't look like Althea. She looked like Liza Minnelli. When I first saw her sitting on some concrete steps outside a building I nodded. The reason that I know what Liza Minnelli looks like is because my aunt and mom went through a decadent stage before I turned teenager and they played and replayed *Cabaret* on a VCR. The reason that I noticed the girl on the steps was that she was still there when I came out, because the algorithm class let out early. And guess what she was reading? Bart Kosko's *Fuzzy Thinking*.

"What's a nice girl like you doing reading that?" I asked. My TV upbringing through thousands of daddy actors was coming through in typically clever manner.

She reached into a small purse and pulled out a pack of cigarettes, lighting one and blowing the smoke in my direction.

"I'm serious," I said. "It's a good book. I'm trying to work out a computer program incorporating fuzzy thinking and Van Neumann's game theory into a social decision making process."

"Professor Circle warned me about people like you."

"See-See Bones?"

She grinned. She had the most magnificent smile that showed her pink upper gums. She had the type of eyes that dance when they look at you, sort of clippety-clopping a street tap. At that moment they looked like the emerald green current along the Gulf of Mexico.

"So you're in physical anthropology? Forensic?" I asked.

She put the book on her lap and scooted against the brick wall lining the steps. "No, cultural, but Professor Bones keeps trying to recruit me."

I grimaced. "All those bloated or dried corpses . . . I couldn't do it." I wondered if Professor Circle had been called in for Althea. But no, she only was consulted for cases when the body had gone undiscovered and had begun to decompose.

"That's what I think, too. At least some of the time. But Professor Circle keeps pointing out that what I'll probably be doing in cultural is just what you were talking about: a modern version of game theory where I'd be professionally advising the military how to best conquer some poor third world country we think has violated our democratic rights."

"A warmonger's assistant," I said.

"Exactly. That's how a lot of cultural anthropologists wind up, professional consultants for the CIA or FBI or . . . you know, some other alphabet. Like Professor Circle points out, I'd be helping to make corpses and cause suffering, instead of helping to identify them and ease suffering. She's about got me convinced."

She put out her cigarette and said she had to go to class.

"I take a computer class here every Monday, Wednesday, and Friday at this time," I said. "We got out a bit early today . . . just in case you want to stalk me," I added.

That grin and those eyes again.

A + Ω

My grief counselor and my aunt remained vigilant during that summer and fall after Althea and Simon died. They looked for signs of suicide, which I never showed. Now here it was, three-and-a-half years later, with me making great money at Lex-Mart and attending graduate school courtesy of that same company. I met a Liza Minnelli look-alike who was as bright as the energy beam Scottie used to transport people up to the starship Enterprise.

Three-and-a-half years. Here it all was coming together. Yet and still, I bought a Charter Arms revolver from a guy at work. It didn't have nine chambers, but it would do. I wanted to blame that purchase on paranoia: Professor John Hart had been killed by a religious kook living near Professor Bones. Professor Hart had taught me, Althea, and Simon. He had recommended my presentation on St. Francis of Assisi. Yet and still . . . so. So, did that increase three to four? And why not one more number? Yet and still . . .

Leigh Lathan. That was the Liza Minnelli look-alike's name, and she was sitting on the steps again, not before the next Wednesday class, but before Friday's class. She was again reading Kosko and had made progress. She smiled, I smiled. Yet and still . . .

We went out for pizza, a studently enough occupation.

"Garlic and green peppers?" the waiter asked, raising an eyebrow.

It was more kismet, since both of us had read that garlic cleansed the bloodstream, even at ages 23 and 20.

The pizza place was painted in purple and yellow and green—some fruitcake's idea of what would please the 18- to 23-year-old crowd.

"I wonder if a psychologist picked these colors," Leigh said.

"The kismet keeps mounting," I replied.

"You were thinking that, too?"

"Yeah, but I bet it was a cultural anthropologist who picked the colors."

She glared at me until I had to say I was just kidding.

"You might be right. That's what I'm really worried about. I've made an appointment with Professor Circle next week."

I proceeded to tell her about my anonymous donation to Dr. See-See, and how she'd used it as a joke in a PowerPoint presentation for the next class. I even drew the tables on a napkin.

"Do you really think love's like that?"

"I . . ." I was on the verge of telling her about Althea and Simon, but she'd think I was a freak, losing two people I was so close to in one day. I mean, it seems as if a great patch of uncouth must attach to anyone that happened to. Then I remembered it was really three people who I'd lost. Uncouth wouldn't even touch the matter. And now was it four?

"Wake up, Francis," she sang. "Do you think love's like that?"

"I guess I used to." Her Liza Minnelli eyes—except hers were prettier than Liza Minnelli's because hers were green—stared me down again, and I looked to the table I'd drawn.

"It doesn't have any fuzzy logic," she commented, popping a fingernail on the table that lay on the table. She wore French nails, the type with white tips. Althea always wore a deep red nail polish—when she wore any at all. Would that nail polish factoid represent a bit of fuzzy logic?

On Saturday I went to Wal-Mart and bought a box of .38 bullets. I told myself I was going to take the gun out to the river and shoot it. Listening to the bullets rattle in the box while I drove home I concocted another table trying to fit fuzzy logic and its accompanying chaos theory with misfired bullets. I finished the table on my back porch then put it on my computer to print on appropriately blue paper. In this table I called the two lovers Frank Sinatra and Liza Minnelli:

THE LOVER'S PARADOX, REVISED

Scene: Frank Sinatra loves Liza Minnelli. But she has rebuffed him after their third date because she found out his girlfriend of three years before had killed herself because of his Mafia connections. F. takes his pearl-handled Colt .38 to a prestigious Las Vegas diner, sits in his sun-baked emerald green Jaguar convertible and awaits L. When F. sees L. getting out of her sky-blue Ferrari in the parking lot he spins the revolver's cylinder and pulls the trigger . . .

The pistol fires, sending a soft-nose .38 expanding into his brain.	The pistol misfires because the bullet had been mis-manufactured without any gunpowder.
The pistol fires, but F's hand jerks at the last moment, so the bullet only grazes his flesh. L sees him bleeding and runs to him.	The pistol fires at the same time a fan knocks on the window asking for his autograph, so the bullet grazes the fan.

The pistol fires, but the barrel has corroded from the time F and L went skinny-dipping so that it explodes, blinding F. L runs to him and nurses him, thereafter toting him to recording sessions and concerts.

F removes the pistol from his head, aims toward L and pulls the trigger. She falls onto the hot parking lot and dies, F's latest recording playing in her Walkman.

It was lame, it was stupid. But it kept me from taking the .38 down by the river. I unloaded the .38 and stuck the blue paper in my algorithms text. Was this chaos theory working? I mean, did I surmise that Leigh would find it sooner or later?

A + Ω

"This is funny," Leigh comments, holding up the blue paper she's found sticking out from my algorithm text.

"Funny?"

"Yes, funny. You know, instead of putting your lips together and whistling, you part them and chortle. You do know how to chortle, don't you?"

"Did you have an aunt who made you watch Humphrey Bogart and Liza Minnelli?"

"An uncle. Just Humphrey Bogart and John Wayne. That's what attracted me to you. You walked like you'd memorized all their movies."

She's sitting on the steps again. We've been chatting about Professor Circle, who's convinced Leigh to enter UK's forensic anthropology program.

"Then you're not moving back to Ohio?"

She grins and her pink gums make me shiver. *It's spring*, I think. *Dogwoods are blooming.*

"Can we go get a beer?" I ask.

"It's four o'clock on Wednesday."

"But it's hot."

"The Kentucky Derby hasn't even run. It can't be hot yet."

"I want to tell you something." I nod toward the sky. "While Brother Sun's still shining and traveling overhead."

"A mystic *and* a computer scientist," she says.

We go to the same pizza joint we've been going to, since they accept Leigh's fake I.D. Two more months and she won't need it. Her birthday's in June, like mine. Strange attractors. The walls in the pizza place are still purple and yellow and green—no chaos has intervened to import a streaking schizoid spray painter.

"We're drawn to this place," I moan, sitting in a wobbly booth that skews me out of balance like a wild four-polynomial graph.

"It's a well. That's what's wrong with your Lover's Paradox, by the way. It doesn't allow for any energy wells."

"But I've—"

The waiter walks up and we order garlic and mushroom pizza.

"What happened to the weird guy who cooked here, the one with the tiny fuzz beard that never made it to beard-dom?"

"He got fired for preaching to the customers."

"He must have thought he lived in Alabama."

"Yeah," the waiter agrees. "Good riddance to him."

We order beers and the waiter walks off. Someone Leigh knows walks in and waves.

"Strange attractors," I say, tapping the blue paper stuck back in the textbook. "They're in there, aren't they? I mean, I've got the Sinatra fan who knocks on the window and sends the bullet flying."

"That's chance. Which isn't wrong, but it's different than the equation skewing *itself*, don't you think? It's more like inserting another polynomial."

The colors on the wall meet in an odd rainbow over the waiter's drink stand, to birth a galaxy that spirals purple and yellow and green in a rush toward the door. Watching the waiter draw our beers from a tap I point out the tri-colored galaxy, and Leigh says that's exactly what she means: all three colors are already swirling and colliding in the pattern, no other color needs to intrude for a re-creation.

"What is it that you want to tell me?" she asks when the waiter brings two Heinekens. I put the beer to my lips and remember my nineteenth birthday when Simon, Althea and I were celebrating with pizza, Heineken, Old Forester, and Francis Ford Coppola's *Dracula*.

"We never did make it through all the Dracula movies," I stutter-start. And then I explain about Althea and Simon. And I explain. And I explain.

"Why did she kill herself? Do you know?"

"She found out she was pregnant."

"Yours?"

I tap the table hard enough to hurt my finger. "Yeah. One time. Otherwise we were both virgins."

Leigh's big green eyes are staring at the spawning purple-green-yellow galaxy.

"Maybe you and this woman were energy wells to one another. Negative ones. Is this why you work out all those weird game theory tables? Is this what your Lover's Paradox is about?"

I nod. My aunt, my mom, my grief counselor—none of them ever put it so simply.

"Did you know that Professor Circle dates a cop?" Leigh asks. I blink and shrug. "She does. A black homicide detective. I caught them pawing one another in the parking lot, so she introduced us. He wore a gun under his armpit . . ."

I listen, waiting to see where her sentence is going.

"They moved nice together. Easy, you know?"

"Like Fred Astaire and Ginger Rogers?"

"Your aunt and her movies?"

I nod.

"Yeah, like them, I guess. They moved easy together. So nice that I imagined them in bed."

"Leigh!" My voice breaks in a whine.

"Guys don't have a corner on sex, you know. The chthonic runs deeper than the phallic runs high."

"Tonic?"

"Chthonic, with a C-H and a T-H. Womb symbol. Mother Earth and her countless caverns. My point is that even though the detective wore a gun he wasn't spinning the cylinder and putting his finger on the trigger like your Frank Sinatra. Point is, there are positive energy wells and negative ones."

"You just need to stay out of the event horizons of the negative ones, right?"

"Event—yeah. You sure do, or the ol' black hole will suck you in for a grand finale. Thought you'd trip me up on that *event horizon* to make up for *chthonic*, didn't you?"

I recover miraculously and point out that Professor Circle is right in directing her to forensic anthropology where she'll be able to use all her logic and inference. "If only Dr. Circle were as good directing her own life," I add.

"What do you mean?"

"I mean this black cop who's so perfect for her. If she could let go of her No One Touches Anyone Theory long enough . . ."

Leigh sighs and rubs a French nail over my algorithm book. A corner of blue paper, the one with The Lover's Paradox table on it, sticks out, and she pinches a scrap off and tosses it at me. I look into her green eyes. Verdant. Mother earth. Chthonic. Curative, like a mineral water well. I touch her nail, and I take a sip.

I don't hear Althea and Simon stepping out the pizzeria's front door.

I don't see them wave good-bye.

I grab Leigh's hand and squeeze to bring forth a lovely smile. I'm not falling into her positive attractor energy well. No I'm not. I'm diving headfirst, from the high board.